CALLER UNKNOWN

CALLER UNKNOWN

OLIVER JOHNSON

POINT
BLANK

A POINT BLANK BOOK

First published in the United Kingdom, Republic of Ireland and Australia
by Point Blank, an imprint of Oneworld Publications Ltd, 2026

ISBN 978-1-83643-022-3
eISBN 978-1-83643-023-0

Typeset by Geethik Technologies
Printed and bound in Great Britain by Clays Ltd, Elcograf S.p.A.

The authorised representative in the EEA is eucomply OÜ,
Pärnu mnt 139b–14, 11317 Tallinn, Estonia
(email: hello@eucompliancepartner.com / phone: +33757690241)

Oneworld Publications Ltd
10 Bloomsbury Street
London WC1B 3SR
England

Stay up to date with the latest books,
special offers, and exclusive content from
Oneworld with our newsletter

Sign up on our website
oneworld-publications.com

MIX
Paper | Supporting
responsible forestry
FSC® C018072

To Caroline

PROLOGUE

THE LETTER

The note on the envelope was addressed to a man who had been declared officially dead three years earlier. It read: "To Ed Constance. If you've come this far, that is your name."

He had had another name only yesterday: Martin Cruz. He had a wallet with credit cards, a driver's license, and a social security card to prove it. He had a photograph of a woman who, only last night, he could not remember. But now he did: Sarah, his wife. His pregnant wife. They had taken her. How long ago? Two, three days?

So, here he was. Yesterday's man was gone. The contents of the wallet were a lie. All he were the photograph, this letter, and the slowly returning memories.

Memories of all the events of ten years before, when he'd last had his true name: Ed Constance. It had been the same then: he'd been alone and desperate; the killers had been close; his time was nearly up.

The only thing that could save him now was the letter. He opened the envelope and read.

PART ONE
THE MAINE WOODS
SUMMER 1970

CHAPTER ONE

That last evening at Eriksson's Lot it was warm, and the late June sun was still falling westwards at 7.30 p.m. Outside the cabin nothing stirred. All that existed was the falling light and the endless trees of the forest.

The seven children waited in their cots, four on one side and three on the other, under the sloping roof of the loft. At the far end, away from the solitary, sealed window, two of the cast-iron beds had been pulled close to one another in the shadows. In one lay a boy, in the other a girl. He was called Ed, she Shannon. Like the other five children, both were nine years old and skeletally thin.

Ed and Shannon held hands across the space. In their free hands they clutched the single personal possession they had been permitted in all their years at this place: his was a one-eyed teddy bear; hers a black nylon jacket with a yellow cartoon of a dog on the back dressed in a pilot's outfit. They had decided this creature must be called Snoopy because of the scrawled, loopy signature below the cartoon. The jacket was much creased by age and overhandling.

For the last two hours there'd been loud noises in the cabin's concrete basement two floors down. The children knew what this meant: Mr. Frome was positioning the seven wooden chairs with their leather restraints, the trays of drugs, the cine equipment, and the loudspeakers ready for the evening lesson.

As if in confirmation, the wooden stairs creaked. "The witch's coming," Shannon whispered, and instantly closed her eyes. It was forbidden to look on Mrs. Frome until she permitted it. Three times now in the years they had been reading the Bible they'd come to the place in the Commandments where it said: "Thou shalt not suffer a witch to live." Ed and Shannon had wished their captor's end with the fervent devotion only nine-year-olds possess, but their wishing hadn't been enough, for here she was again, ready to take them to the basement.

Unlike the others, Ed kept looking through batted eyelids long enough to see the woman's head rise up the stairwell. Her auburn hair flared in the shaft of evening sun from the window. As usual her face was fixed and expressionless. She placed a large shopping bag on the floor.

"Get up," she said.

The kids, all of whom had only been pretending to be asleep, sat up uncertainly, then, as she clapped her hands, got out of bed. They stood on the bare boards, hair and pajamas disheveled, staring at their feet. One or two of them shivered, though it wasn't cold. One of the shiverers began to sob. She was a thin, waif-like girl with a kidney-shaped birthmark on her right cheek.

"Stop sniveling, Catrine," Mrs. Frome snapped, and Catrine's sobbing ended in a strange, strangled hiccup.

Mrs. Frome bent and took some things from the bag and placed them on the table under the window.

"Come here," she said. The kids shuffled forward obediently.

Mrs. Frome had placed seven bags on the table: they were square and blue with white shoulder straps. The sides had a globe decal in the same colors: a white line of longitude through the poles, and curved lines of latitude radiating out from the central logo text, all against the background blue. The logo text "Pan Am" was stenciled across the globe.

All the kids could read. They had been through the Bible many times, from infanthood. But "Pan Am" was unfamiliar. Unfamiliar, too, was the globe: they, from their limited observations from this mountaintop, which they had never left, believed the Earth was flat. Neither did they know what an airline or airliner was, though they had seen the contrails of planes high above in the blue summer sky: they had thought them to be God's chalk marks on the blue board of heaven.

There were price stickers on the bags. The children looked at the dollar symbols as uncomprehendingly as at the Pan Am logo. They had never seen a dollar or the symbol that represented it.

Next to each bag were cardboard placards, a length of butcher's twine looped through the holes in their tops, and crayons.

Mrs. Frome gestured to the bags. "Pack one extra set of clothes and toilet items. Nothing else. When you're done, write your names and the scripture I taught you this morning on the cardboard." The children stared uncomprehendingly. Was there to be no lesson this evening? She clapped her hands again. "Go on now."

That started them. There was an old chest of drawers in the dormitory containing a spare set of summer clothes: blue Airtex shirts, khaki short trousers, white socks, washed and ironed by the kids themselves, as they had been taught when very young. "Cleanliness is next to godliness" was one of Mrs. Frome's favorite axioms.

When they came to put the clothes in the bags they found that each already had a copy of the Bible in it, taking up half the space. Then they wrote their names and the passage that they had learned that morning on the placards:

"For I think that God hath set forth us the apostles last, as it were appointed to death: for we are made a spectacle unto the world, and to angels, and to men."

The words were meaningless to them. Their hands shook as they wrote; there were quite a few mistakes.

When they were done, Mrs. Frome looked upon their misspellings and smudges with a frown. Ed expected her to tell them to do them again. Such was the way of the Lot, endless repetition of verses, chapters, even entire books of the Bible.

But instead she said, "Now get dressed. We're leaving in an hour."

The second surprise. The kids couldn't help glancing at each other. One of them tentatively raised a hand.

"Yes, David?" Mrs. Frome said.

"Leaving, ma'am? What do you mean?"

He was a tall, dark-eyed boy, and, despite the Lot's meagre diet, bigger than any of the other kids. He was normally cocksure and had a cruel streak, which he took out on the wings and limbs of captured insects and fledglings and, also, on his slighter, less muscular companions. Mrs. Frome had done nothing to correct this behavior.

She had named him well: David. A king and, one day, a giant-slayer.

But this evening David didn't look tough, only scared.

She smiled thinly. "It's time for you to go out into the world." She gestured at the forest through the window as if willing it to disappear and reveal this mysterious "world" behind.

David looked in that direction. All that could be seen were trees, which, naturally, looked no different to how they always looked. His eyes welled. He swallowed but didn't let the tears flow.

As Mrs. Frome had taught them: for hadn't the Lord in his short life wept only twice: once for dead Lazarus and once for sinful Jerusalem? Why should they, mere children, have the luxury of tears?

"Now get dressed," she said.

The children discarded their pajamas and pulled on the underpants, pants, shirts, socks, and sneakers they had worn earlier.

When she saw they were all dressed, Mrs. Frome nodded and said, "Wait here," then went back down the stairs. The kids looked at each other again. What was about to happen?

CHAPTER TWO

An hour later the children heard the engines of the two vehicles start outside. Some of the kids had lain back on their cots and begun to doze; it was way past their normal bedtime. But they woke immediately at the noise.

Mrs. Frome appeared moments later. She was dressed as if for one of her fortnightly supply trips: sunglasses, a flower-patterned scarf that complemented her yellow and red house dress, and a pair of black leather gloves. She had applied her makeup with some care: plenty of foundation, the red lipstick matching the red in the dress pattern. She was carrying a small blue handbag on her shoulder. It was not so unlike the blue airline bags she had issued to the kids earlier.

She told them to pick up their bags and the signs and follow her down the stairs.

As she disappeared, some of the kids tried to save their personal items. Shannon stuffed her Snoopy jacket in her bag. Ed looked at his large, languidly limbed teddy bear. The bear's name was simply Bear. Bear had only one remaining goggling eye rotating in its white plastic socket. To Ed, it made Bear seem both vulnerable and heroic at the same time. He had made up a little rhyme about the eye, which he recited to Bear every night before sleep: "As long as I can see your eye, I cannot die."

But Bear wouldn't fit into Ed's bag; he was just too big. He was not coming with him, wherever they were going.

Ed looked at him sadly. "Bye, Bear," he said. He hugged him, then tucked him under the threadbare blanket on his cot. The toy's remaining goggling eye stared up at the ceiling beams. Maybe after he was gone Bear would go on sleeping here, forever and ever?

Ed followed the others downstairs to the kitchen. There was no bread or orange juice on the checkered tablecloth as there would have been at breakfast time. Mrs. Frome stood at the open door. "Into the bus," she ordered.

The yellow school bus, which had never been out of the outbuilding next to the cabin in all the preceding years, was idling outside in a haze of blue diesel exhaust. The red Chevy pickup was parked behind it, engine also running.

By now the sun was casting a slanting blaze over the house and the vehicles. All appeared to be on fire in its last light.

Mr. Frome grinned down at the kids from the driver's seat of the bus, his red lips showing through the black bush of his beard. His eyes were recessed, shrike-like. For some reason he was wearing thick workmen's gloves.

Ed went up the three steps and past Frome. A sour body odor came off the man's stained mackinaw.

There were six rows of seats and a wide bench in the rear. Ed went right to the back and sat down on the hot buttoned cushions. He stared, unseeing, out the window at the side of the log house. For a moment he thought about Bear. A cold shiver went through him. He played the mantra in his head: "As long as I can see your eye, I cannot die." But in that moment he was sure he would never see Bear again.

There came a slight pressure on the seat next to him and then the press of a warm side and he turned from the window, and there was Shannon. He reached out and squeezed one of her hands.

David climbed into the bus and swaggered toward the back. He was grinning now, though earlier, when Mrs. Frome had told them they were leaving, he had been terrified.

"Just look at you two," he said, flopping down in the seat in front of them. He leaned over into their space.

"You gonna kiss her, Ed?" he asked.

Ed knew how these situations ended. He let go of Shannon's hand and balled his fists, ready for a fight.

"Why don't you sit somewhere else?" he said, hating the sound of his voice, which, to his ears, was small and whispery.

"What, and miss you two making out?"

The other kids were now all on the bus.

"Hey, you, knock it off back there," Frome yelled from the driver's seat. He yanked the lever by his side and the bus door shut with a hydraulic whoosh and thunk.

David sneered. "See you later, lovebirds." He stood and made his way back down the aisle just as Frome rammed the stick into gear and the bus lurched forward, nearly throwing David onto the floor. He grabbed a seat back, then sat next to his buddy, Carl. They were behind Hope, the timid blond girl. David leaned over to her, said something inaudible that made her flinch away. He laughed and back-slapped Carl.

The sudden, surging movement of the bus made Ed feel sick. He swallowed bile.

Shannon didn't seem to have the same problem. "Where're they taking us?" she asked, wide-eyed.

"I dunno." He swallowed again.

"Maybe it's like the witch said," she said, "we're goin' to see the world. Maybe there'll be no more movies, or readings or 'noculations, no under the stairs..."

The bus was rolling down the unmade road in a huge cloud of dust. Ed looked back through the fly-specked rear window. The sight of the rapidly receding log cabin where he had slept every night of his conscious life made him light-headed.

The Chevy was following. He wondered how Mrs. Frome could see to drive through the dust.

Ahead was the gate in the fence. It had always been padlocked, the limit of their world until now, but this evening it was open. The bus swept through it. Ed was surprised that in the instant they passed it the world didn't change completely, revealing some remarkable new vista. But all there was beyond were more of the endless trees.

The bus plunged down a steep track in the forest, juddering and shaking with the sudden gear changes and braking required to negotiate the switchbacks. Ed retched slightly, shut his eyes and clutched the back of the seat in front in a death grip.

After twenty minutes the gradient eased. Ed tentatively squinted forward. They were on the flat; the bus rolled up to a junction with the Chevy right behind. Frome brought the bus to a stop. There was another gate in a fence ahead and a gravel road beyond it. Frome opened the door, got down and pulled aside some heavy limbs of brushwood obscuring the inside of the drive entrance, then used a key on the padlock on the gate and pulled it open.

He returned sweating, swearing and swatting at a cloud of black-flies that had materialized around his head. He climbed back into the driver's seat, engaged the door mechanism, jammed forward the gearstick, gunned the engine, and, with a roar, swung left onto the gravel road.

Behind them Ed saw Mrs. Frome drive the Chevy through the gate, then get out to pull the branches back over the track. Maybe they were leaving her behind—maybe that was the end of the witch? He felt a faint tick of hope in his chest. He stared out the rear window, hoping it would be so, but five minutes later the Chevy reappeared, hurtling around a corner behind the bus like a furious red hornet. The bile rose in his throat again.

The new world was the same, yet terrifying. The bus was full of the noise of tires, the slanting orange light, the roar of the wind through the window vents, the flapping of the faded curtains. A lake flashed past, large boulders stood hunched by the roadside, a large

Prussian-blue river rushed by, then the bus labored up an avenue of pines to a pass between two mountaintops. Frome pulled down the visor against the dropping sun.

Ed shut his eyes against the light and held tight to Shannon's hand.

CHAPTER THREE

They drove for over an hour. Shannon was asleep on Ed's shoulder. His own eyes opened and closed as he dozed then woke abruptly. Suddenly the tire noise went from a gravelly roar to a hum. He looked out and saw they were now on a black-road surface. The bus braked. There was a boarded-up building on the side of the road with a shot-scarred red and green star sign on a high pole. Four rusty, red metal boxes sat under a sagging canopy on the weedgrown asphalt.

The bus pulled in, circled the boarded office and parked on the back lot, and the Chevy came to a stop behind. Frome turned off the engine and opened the door.

"OK," Frome said. "Out of the bus. Leave the bags and signs."

Silently, the seven children stepped down to the hot, cracked asphalt, blinking at the last rays over the trees and staring at the alien vision of the gas station. The cicadas sang in the long grass, a pulsing chorus, loud then subsiding, loud then subsiding—the pulse of a summer evening. There were birds singing the evening chorus. The curious whistling song of the white-throated sparrow sounded: *Ah, te,e,e,te,e,e,te*.

Mrs. Frome was out of the Chevy. "Follow me," she said. She walked toward the woods at the back of the lot, around a mound covered with Johnson grass and white and yellow flowers. The children followed unhesitatingly. They plunged into the semi-dark canopy of trees and after fifty yards came to a rusted chain-link fence. There was a gate set into it with a padlock; both were rusted and apparently disused.

Beyond, Ed could make out the faintest of paths disappearing into the trees.

Frome, who had been at the back of the group, pushed through and went to the gate and shook it with his fists. Flecks of rust fell from the fence but the lock held. He took hold of the padlock and rolled the tumblers. Despite the rust they moved freely, as if the mechanism had been oiled recently.

"All good," he said to Mrs. Frome.

"Alright, come here," she said. The kids dutifully arranged themselves in a semicircle around her. Mr. Frome positioned himself behind them and Ed felt his sour breath on his neck. Mrs. Frome reached into her handbag and drew out a crucifix on a silver chain and held it up in her gloved hand. It flashed in the light through the tree canopy.

Ed closed his eyes. Bad things happened when the crucifix was out.

"Look at the cross," Mrs. Frome said.

On more than one occasion he had refused to look, but each refusal had brought pain and humiliation—beatings, or the closet under the stairs. He reluctantly opened his eyes. All the other kids were staring at the shining metal as Mrs. Frome began to swing it from side to side. It flashed in the dim light of the forest canopy and he found his eyes matched its oscillations, rocking his mind... His eyes began to get heavy.

And then there was black and he went down to the silence.

Mrs. Frome saw that the children had fallen under the spell of the cross: to a one, their pupils were dilated, their faces slack.

She slowly stopped the motion of the cross.

"What's the first number?" she asked the children quietly.

Like a choir of ghosts they whispered, "Sixty-six."

"Louder now," she said, and they repeated "Sixty-six," but this time the number burst from them, sharper, higher; shocking in the otherwise growing stillness. The birdsong died. It was as if nature heard.

The children were a little out of time, but a cold thrill went up Mrs. Frome's spine.

She composed herself. "Louder," she ordered.

Again, they weren't quite together. The drugs and sessions of group chanting in the basement had instilled in them a perfect synchronicity, but the strangeness of the day had apparently thrown them out of it again. Did it matter that they were off cadence a bit?

"Sixty-six. Sixteen. Sixteen. Fourteen." Their voices sounded stronger.

They were on the path. "Where do these numbers lead?" she asked.

"To Armageddon," they answered.

"Where is Armageddon?"

Their voices went down several octaves, to an unearthly growl that thrilled her even more. It was as if the Devil spoke. "We are here," they chanted.

"And what is Armageddon?"

"The final battle."

Mrs. Frome shivered again. She whispered, *"Consummatum est."*

With that, she turned and walked back toward the gas station. The kids turned and shambled after her, their faces slack, like the undead.

Frome shepherded them from the rear. They circled the mound and walked across the back lot to the bus. Mrs. Frome stopped at its door and the kids bumped into each other like zombies, then shuffled into their semicircle again.

"OK," she said. "Now it's time to forget—forget the numbers of Armageddon and all that you have learned here in the woods. Your past is nothing, your future blank, until you are awoken to do the Lord's work. What must you wait to hear?"

And she led them in the verse: "How long wilt thou forget me, O Lord? Forever? How long wilt thou hide thy face from me?" The kids followed, their voices high once more, almost innocent—it was like a prayer in church when the congregation lags just a tiny beat behind the celebrant.

"When will you wake again?" Mrs. Frome asked when the last of the voices had trailed off.

"When the Beast calls." The voices fell down those octaves again.

"What are the Beast's numbers?"

"Sixty-six. Six. Six."

"And what are these numbers called?"

"The Beast and One," they intoned.

"And what are the words of the Beast and One?"

"And I heard a voice in the midst of the four beasts say, A measure of wheat for a penny, and three measures of barley for a penny; and see thou hurt not the oil and wine."

This time the chorus was perfect.

She clapped her gloved hands and said abruptly, "Wake!" and they did, like those suddenly woken from a deep sleep. They looked bewildered when they saw her, Frome, the bus, the gas station, and the Texaco sign now almost invisible in the twilight, as if seeing them for the first time.

Mrs. Frome nodded at Frome. He opened the door of the bus and the interior lights came on, flooding the scene with a wan yellow light. He went up the steps and pulled out a J.C. Penney bag from under the driver's seat.

"Get onto the bus," Mrs. Frome ordered.

As they started to file up, she frowned. She had been distracted earlier and so, too, it seemed, had Frome. One of the kids, Hope, had brought her personal item with her despite her instructions. It was only a pink plastic ring that she was wearing, oddly on her engagement finger. Mrs. Frome took hold of Hope's tiny hand, yanked the ring off and threw it across the lot.

"What did I say to you?" she growled as the girl's face scrunched. "Mr. Frome, inspect the bags."

Frome lumbered back down the steps and roughly took each of the bags from the kids' shoulders and unzipped them. He got to Shannon's and found the hidden Snoopy jacket, unballed it and showed it to Mrs. Frome.

Before she could take it, Shannon took a step forward and ripped it from his giant paw. She hugged the jacket defiantly to her chest.

"Why, you—" Mr. Frome growled but Mrs. Frome held up her hand, stilling him.

"Give me that," she commanded. Shannon stared back, unyielding.

"Give me it," she repeated. When Shannon didn't comply, she lunged forward, seized the girl's braids with one gloved hand and the hand with the jacket in the other and twisted savagely. Shannon yelped in pain and the bundle fell to the ground.

Ed jumped forward but Mrs. Frome released her hand from Shannon's hair and back-slapped him; he collapsed, his eyes glazed, his nose trickling blood.

Oh well, nine years of no slapping and now this, Mrs. Frome thought. The instructions had been clear: no corporal punishment, no injuries, no hospitals, no records. The slap was satisfying, though, she had to admit that. And only a slap. She reached down, picked up the jacket and hurled it after Hope's ring into the weeds.

"Now, on the bus," she said.

Shannon helped Ed get back to his feet. He wiped the snot and blood from his nose.

"You OK?" she asked. Her brown eyes were full.

He didn't answer.

Mrs. Frome turned and went to the Chevy, yanked open the door and got in behind the wheel.

"Come on," Shannon said and took Ed's hand. They went up the steps of the bus.

CHAPTER FOUR

Frome ordered the kids to sit facing him on the benches at the front of the bus, then took a two-gallon plastic container out of the J.C. Penney bag along with some of those tiny paper cups found by watercoolers in doctors' offices.

"Thirsty work, eh?" he asked with fake solicitude. He ignored the sniffs of Ed, Shannon, and Hope. "I have some OJ here for you." He sloshed the liquid inside the container invitingly, though, given the heat of the evening, the juice must be blood-warm by now. He took one of the cups and poured a measure, then approached Kevin on the first bench. Frome told him to open his mouth and tilt his head back. Kevin complied. Frome forced the cup between the boy's lips. Kevin gagged but swallowed.

He went from Kevin to Hope and repeated the procedure. Hope also gagged and Frome wondered if, in fact, he should have checked in with Mrs. Frome before he added that extra dose; he had tried a little by way of experimentation a week or so before. The stuff tasted a little chemical even in beer. And, boy, talk about lights out. He'd woken in the depths of the night, disorientated, without any idea where he was or what time it was.

Well, it was too late to start second-guessing now. He would give the others a little less. He went from one seat to another until he reached the last two. Ed and Shannon. There was a smear of blood on Ed's lip from Mrs. Frome's blow. The two kids held each other close.

Frome held up the by now soggy cup to Shannon. Some of the liquid splattered on the floor. "Drink," he said.

"No," she said.

She was giving him the look again. He eyed her braids—they were a weakness, as Mrs. Frome had already proved. He reached out his free hand, seized a handful and yanked back, then applied the cup to her lips and tilted it. She gagged, then spat the stuff out on his shirt front. He cursed, released her hair and, forgetting all restraint, cuffed her heavily. Ed's arm shot out but Frome back-slapped him too and the boy's head cracked against the dusty window behind him and for a moment the kid's eyes rolled up into their sockets. Oh well, three slaps in one night. In for a dime, in for a dollar.

Frome reached behind for the container and chugged some more OJ into the paper cup, not minding that it overflowed and splashed on the buttoned cushions. The boy was still groggy and Frome grasped him firmly by the lower jaw so his mouth opened, tipped his head back and forced the OJ between his teeth, then clamped the mouth shut again, the way you give a cat a pill.

He let the kid go and Ed's head flopped back against the headrest; the whites of his eyes were still showing. He was out, whether through the blow or the drugs, he couldn't tell.

He turned to Shannon. A purple welt showed through her brown skin by her left eye. She was staring at him.

"So, little lady, what's it going to be? Wanna fight? It makes it more fun." He gave her the smile.

She swallowed, then held out a hand. It trembled. She took the cup. Frome wondered if he was going to get it on his shirt again. She dry-swallowed, then tipped the paper cup back and the drugged juice was gone. Like a Greek philosopher taking hemlock.

Shannon stared at him for a moment longer, then the light seemed to ebb out of her eyes, just like when Mrs. Frome had been swinging the crucifix, and she leaned back against the headrest, her eyes rolled up and she was gone. Christ, maybe he *had* overdone that dose.

Frome checked on the other kids. All out. He glanced at Mrs. Frome waiting in the Chevy. She had the vanity light on, doing her makeup. Cool as ever. He waved to her. She closed the compact, nodded at him, then the vanity went off, the headlights came on and the engine of the Chevy roared into life. She put it into gear, drove out to the road and turned in the direction of the Lot and the Canadian border.

Nine years of the ice maiden and, poof, just like that, he was finally out from under her feet: "Now, Mr. Frome, do you think it's nice to leer at the children so much?" or "There's an odor in the cabin, Mr. Frome. I do hope you have been washing?" and so on.

The taillights vanished and she was gone.

He still didn't know her real name; he guessed he would never know it. She had ordered, he had complied. Occasionally the loneliness of the cabin had gotten the better of him and he'd thought of making a play for her, then, invariably, thought better of it—he was pretty sure how such an overture would be met. But a man had to dream better than the whores he met on Highway 1 during his resupply trips. Skinny heroin addicts for the most part. Nine years of not much satisfaction.

Anyway, there was one big attraction remaining before he dumped the kids. He had timed the explosion for just after she had passed the turnoff to the cabin. By then it would be nearly full dark and the smoke would likely not be noticed until the next day, but no point taking any chances.

There was going to be nothing left as evidence of what had happened at Eriksson's Lot. He had placed the dynamite, blasting caps, det cord, the 55-gallon drums of gasoline, and several unused propane canisters strategically at the house's core, beneath the wooden hall floor and the wood staircase.

The house had a nice wooden heart, Frome thought. The scent of pine sap, rich with fast-burning pitch, had been heady as he'd worked.

His real name was Eugene Macdonald Dubois. He had missed college, but had caught up when serving time in Stillwater for arson and then the nine years here in the woods. He had learned, for one, that all nature yearned to return to ash. After all, that was the Earth's ultimate fate: it would be swallowed by the sun in seven and a half billion years. But not all Creation had to wait that long. Yes, if the Lord pleased, when the Lot went it would be that friggin' hot, as hot as the sun at its core.

After Stillwater he'd left Minnesota for Maine, intent on turning his back on his fire-starting past. He began hauling loads over the border into Canada. Tough years in which the temptation raged in him, like a burning imp stirring the embers of his heart. Yet he kept the desire in check—at first. There were nights when the gas can and rags and Zippo under the driver's seat called out to him with such intent that they drowned out the chatter on the CB.

It was his nature. He had to succumb, and did so eventually—three times, in short order.

One night soon after the third of the incidents he was in a truck stop outside Waterville. A man sat down on the banquette opposite him in the diner. There were plenty of spare seats elsewhere in the joint. After prison, Eugene didn't like being crowded. Keeping people at arm's length—that's how he liked it. So he was irritated when the stranger didn't yield to the "don't fuck with me" look he'd worked on in Stillwater.

The man looked back at Eugene placidly: a gray square jaw, gray buzz cut, steely eyes, taut muscled body that suggested military veteran; a man who might now be an agent of some sort. Alarm bells began going off.

"Don't think I invited you," Eugene said, but with less assurance than he would have liked.

The man didn't blink. "So I noticed," he answered.

Eugene stopped chewing. "So why don't you git?" he asked.

"Strikes me you might like some company," the man said. "Bad for the digestion eating alone. Besides, I like shooting the breeze, you know? Especially talking about my travels, places I've visited. Maybe you're the same? You're a trucker, ain't you? Bet you've visited some.

How about Godley's Farm, Dark Ridge, and Jesmond's Country Store—bet you been to them places."

Eugene's blood ran cold; the stranger had named the sites of the three burnings.

He stood abruptly, ready to punch the guy in the face or maybe run—in the split second he wasn't sure which—but the man's hand was suddenly gripping his forearm like a vise. He stared at Eugene with those impassive gray eyes.

At Eugene's sudden movement the diner had gone quiet and heads were turned. One of those looking over in his direction was wearing a sheriff's uniform.

The man's voice didn't lift despite the effort of restraining Eugene. "Just sit the fuck down and don't make a scene, Dubois. If you do, Sheriff Watson over there is likely to come over and ask what's goin' on. He happens to be a particular friend of mine."

"I ain't done nothin' wrong," Eugene said. Nevertheless, he sat.

"I didn't ask you to talk," the man said. The man held on to his arm. To an onlooker it must have looked like they were in an arm-wrestling match.

"As I was saying," the man continued, as evenly as before, "if you continue to attract the attention of the sheriff, you may be arrested. Then Watson'll start making inquiries about you and I think we both know where that will lead. With your record and the unsolved arson attacks in the area, he'll have probable cause to search your truck. And, if he does, he's going to find some interesting stuff under your driving bench, ain't he? There's enough to tie you to those three burnings right there. In addition to mean ol' juries up here we have some mean ol' judges on the circuit too. Why, I wouldn't be surprised if you'd be looking at the full thirty years, without parole."

As well as never blinking, the man seemed not to draw breath.

Eugene shrank back into the banquette. "If you want money, I ain't got much," he said weakly.

OLIVER JOHNSON

The man smiled and relinquished his grip. Eugene rubbed his fore-arm. There were five distinct red marks on it as if it'd been squeezed by a five-fingered vise.

The stranger's lips formed into what might have been a slight smile but the expression didn't reach his eyes.

"Eugene—you mind if I call you Eugene?" he said. "I'm Henry. Relax—I don't want your money. Fact is, I may want to pay you some. Quite a bit. A lot more than you'll ever earn hauling loads on the 95."

Then Henry laid things out. It was a harsh deal. In fact, it was, in quality, not much different to doing time. It differed in two crucial aspects: the duration and a very large cash payment at the end. A million bucks. As Henry described it, nine years in the wilderness, "just looking after a bunch of kids. It'll be like falling off a log."

The reality had been far different. When Mrs. Frome laid out the program he thought it was a joke: a twisted joke, but a joke nonetheless. He'd heard the rumors about the CIA and its brainwashing programs but hadn't really believed them. Now he did.

The nine years in the cabin were nothing like falling off a log. They had sure "looked after" those kids: after all the sessions in the basement, some of them were now no better than the walking dead.

There was one cherry on the dung heap. Back in Waterville, Henry had told him he would get to burn the place down when the nine years was up. He would get to burn bodies too. It would have to be done real good, because in the end these corpses, or the very little that remained of them, would have to pass for him and Mrs. Frome.

The corpses were now waiting at the Lot for their moment. Last night, after he'd set the charges, he'd applied Vaseline under his nose, put on a face covering and gone back out to the truck, dropped the tail and dragged out the two human-sized packages wrapped in plastic and duct tape that were concealed there. Though he had chosen new ones from his contact at the Paris Town Crematorium in New Hampshire, the long journey and the summer heat had had the obvious consequences, hence the Vaseline. The relatives of the two

24

corpses had already been given some ashes in an urn, but the remains were from animals cremated at the veterinarian's. Eugene smiled: the actual cremations of their loved ones had been deferred, but only for a little while.

He'd pushed the bodies through the coal hatch and they thudded onto the basement floor below. He went through the cabin and down the cellar steps, took a breath and dragged the corpses over to the gasoline drum, the propane tanks, and explosives. Then he pushed the trolleys with the drugs and hypodermics, the tape machine, home-movie equipment and the reels of film, and the chairs with their leather restraints over to join them.

Nothing could save this house and its secrets. When the Feds came, as they surely would, all they would find would be a vast smoking crater and traces of his and her bones. Unidentifiable; known only to God.

And even if the Feds somehow worked out that he and Mrs. Frome were still alive, there would be no retribution. The kids would never speak of what had happened to them here: the seal of the Lord, or, properly speaking, Henry's people would be on their lips.

So, he should have been happy this last evening, but the thought that things could go wrong had begun to weigh on his mind over these last few days. He had spent a lot of time in the garage tinkering with the engine of the school bus. The vehicle had been decommissioned ten years ago and there was no knowing what state its carburetor was in. A breakdown would be a disaster. And, if the state troopers arrived before he could fix the problem, a yellow school bus out at night with seven unconscious kids in the back would take some explaining.

He'd become obsessed with the risk of one of the kids regaining consciousness as he was transporting them; they might signal a car through a window. That was when he'd first begun to doubt the dose of sedative prescribed by Mrs. Frome would knock them out for long enough. They still had to be unconscious when he got to the dumping ground. A couple of the boys, David and Edward, were quite big for their age. Hence his decision to double the dose. Mrs. Frome always thought she knew best. Well, not in this case—it wasn't her ass on the line.

He stared toward the Lot. It was now what is known as nautical twilight. The sun was gone but the forest horizon showed like a black saw edge over to the northwest. The first planets were glittering like jewels against the indigo. On the furthest black ridge he saw a sudden eruption of smoke, like a distant volcano blowing. What looked like tiny meteors fell from the cloud. A couple of minutes later he heard a low rumble. The smoke thinned and aligned itself into a narrow column rising straight up to the starry sky.

As he stared at the smoke, the battery-operated clock above the driver's seat clicked around: one, two, three—and he realized he had been drifting. Each tick had been a minute.

At the Lot, after the engine noise died in the distance, the only sounds were the timbers of the house creaking in the lessening heat, and the song of the white-throated sparrow off in the woods. Then it began to grow dark.

Below, in the basement, the timer on a cheap plastic clock ticked down and down for two hours until there came the tinny shrill of its alarm.

Before any more sound could be heard, the world simply turned into sheet white. There came a roar like a Saturn rocket at launch, and the house lifted itself off its basement, up into the skies.

Bear did not flinch even as a wave of white heat reached upward through the wooden heart of the house into the dormitory. A heat so intense it was very much like the heat of the eye of the sun.

And Bear and the bed rose up on this wave of superheated air through where the shingles of the cabin had once been (they were now far above him, tumbling upward like playing cards in the pewter-colored sky), into the orange cloud, his incurious single eye taking in the tops of the pine trees that stood around the lonely mountainside now starkly illuminated in the hellish glare and the birds departing

26

the treetops like clays from a catapult at this unexpected orange sun rising when the other had set.

But then there came a secondary ignition as the propane tanks blew and all below became a red and black furnace reaching up to Bear with fiery fingers. He fell back into the inferno and, within a second, his beige fabric and his straw stuffing were first black then gray ash. His eye, which had once seen all the evil that had passed at Mrs. Frome's establishment, but which, alas, was only attached to Bear's face by the flimsiest of threads, separated during his descent and fell to one side of the furnace. The tiny jewel looked back at the sky and the eye of the moon looked back on it.

And there it waited. A goggling toy eye knows no time.

CHAPTER FIVE

In the bus the sky was fading to utter black. Soon it would be time to move.

Frome stirred himself. He needed to check the kids. First was Hope. He felt for a pulse, found there wasn't one. Her skin was cold. His heart lurched uncomfortably. He tried another pressure point on her wrist but still felt nothing. He thumbed open one of her eyelids and her pupil contracted; a reaction to the interior light. Good—she was still alive then.

But then he remembered something from a mystery he'd read in Stillwater. The exact same thing occurred when a doctor examined a dead person's eye. The pupil contracting was just some weird post-mortem reaction to light like a corpse's leg twitching. Was that some writer bullshit? These guys just made stuff up, right? The pupil had reacted. Hope was alive. End of.

Despite the evening's warmth, he felt cold, cold as Hope's skin. Henry's people regarded everyone but the children as expendable. He really should have checked before doubling the dose. But why was that on him? Do this, do that—nine years of crap. They weren't taking the risk here. Fuck 'em. He would just lie, tell them the kids were fine when he dumped them. Must have been hypothermia; after all, the country got damned cold at night despite it being June. Should have given the kids more than Airtex shirts to wear. It was down to them, not him.

There was a groan. Another dagger stabbed at his heart and his sphincter opened and he pissed himself slightly. Was the noise from Hope? No, the girl's face was still like marble. He steeled himself and forced himself to turn his head. David lolled on the floor behind him, muttering and stirring. Frome reached for the OJ, lifted the boy's head, prised open his mouth and gave him another dose. The kid subsided again.

Frome went back to his seat. He mopped at the wetness around his groin with a Kleenex. He'd brought one of his magazines along to kill time, but the pink flesh didn't excite him as it normally would. The cold in his pants lingered. He threw the magazine aside. He felt Hope's sightless pupils fixed on his back. He got up. Though it was getting chilly, he took off his mackinaw and dropped it over her head.

Gradually total night closed in until all was utterly black outside the globe of the interior light. The clock now read 10.51. He stared at it, scarcely crediting that the time had come. With a shaking hand he twisted the key in the ignition. The engine fired. He switched off the interior light, turned on the headlights, shifted into first gear, drove around the back lot and onto the abandoned spur of highway toward Ashland.

When he reached the town there was not a light showing. He turned north onto the 11. Every sense was on alert for the Highway Patrol. The schools had finished up for summer over a week before: the sight of an empty bus heading toward the depot at Presque Isle shouldn't arouse too many suspicions. But bad luck had a habit of following Eugene Macdonald Dubois around. He knew he was not just transporting seven abducted children.

At least one of them, he was sure, was dead.

CHAPTER SIX

A young mechanic, Brent McAllister, discovered the kids. He had been coming home late; late enough that he was almost in danger of coming home at dawn. But for now, as far as he could establish, for he was very drunk, it was full dark, no hint of brightness in the east, and he had his lights on full beam. Though Highway 11 was a major artery leading up to the border, after midnight there was no traffic.

His problem had been the blond waitress at the honky-tonk on Highway 1 outside Presque Isle. Though the place was a good thirty miles from his marital home, once he had set eyes on Charlayne two months previously he'd been returning there on a regular basis. Working overtime was what he told his wife, Patrice. But he'd never been "working" so late as this and wondered if tonight, or today as it might well be, things were going to explode back home.

Charlayne had a pretty, lived-in smile. Her lipstick was always slightly smeared, and the kohl around her eyes was not perfectly applied. There were gummy little balls of it in her eyelashes. Before each visit he'd slipped off his wedding band. After each beer Charlayne became more beautiful to him. He decided her eyes were kind, and so was her smile… Tonight finally, their fingers touched as he slid over some dough. They talked. He spilled his whole life plan. Well, almost everything except the existence of Patrice. Charlayne went to serve at the other end of the bar.

He found he was in a state of some excitement and couldn't wait for her to come back. But she didn't return for a few minutes. He found he was drifting… Gotta get it together. Gotta be around when her shift ended. Where was she? He saw she was talking to a couple of guys. They were wearing cowboy hats and denim jackets with Confederate flag badges sewn on the back. What was that about in rural Maine? Damned if she wasn't patting one of them on the hand in the exact same way she had patted his hand a few minutes before. And batting those lashes at the dude just as she had at him. She said something and the two tilted their heads back and showed their teeth. Like mules. One of the cowboys glanced his way. Were they laughing at him? His fist clenched and his face burned. He felt like punching them, stopping their laughter, knocking those stupid hats off and stuffing them past their mule teeth and down their throats.

Yes, that's what he was going to do. He got off the stool. But then the world started spinning. Charlayne and the cowboys seemed a long way away. Too far to get to in his current state. He needed some air. He zigzagged to the open door, guided by the breeze. He stood unsteadily on the saloon porch and breathed deep of the cool, loamy air of the night. He took a couple of unsteady steps, unzipped and relieved himself off the porch. His aim was unsteady. Some of it splashed his boots. He thought of going back inside. After all the country tunes on the juke, a new type of song had come on: "The Long and Winding Road." He had never been much of a fan of the Beatles, but this song, which was at that moment number one on Billboard, struck him with a wave of sentiment. He thought of Patrice back in Portage, waiting for him. He forgot the likely harsh words that would greet his return; thought only of her sitting there, fretting, lonely—pretty, dammit. He found his ardor for Charlayne had vanished. He also realized he was very tired.

The next thing he knew he was driving in the pickup. The brights slid over the center line as the truck swayed into the oncoming lane. How had he gotten in his truck, started it and driven away? Where was he? He pulled back onto the right side of the road and braked down to the speed limit. You never knew when the sheriff or one of his deputies would be out. He looked for a passing landmark, recognized a barn as it flashed past. Highway 11. He had somehow gotten past the regional airport, transited the state road and was now on 11 heading north.

He drifted again and woke with a start. He found he was, once more, over the center line. He braked violently again, gripping the wheel with both hands. Gotta stay awake. Gotta hold it together… Just ten miles to Portage; halfway there already.

At first he didn't register what he saw on the verge just after the next bend. He went another fifty yards or so before braking sharply again so the road behind lit up red. He sat there a moment, breathing heavily, wondering if what he had just seen was some alcohol-induced hallucination. No doubt of it, he decided: he should just go on home.

Then a better angel prevailed—it would only take seconds. Just go back, have another look. If it was just a hallucination, no harm done…

He turned the truck in a slow circle across the highway, drove back in first gear, craning forward over the wheel, trying to see beyond the cone of headlights.

There. It had been no illusion. In the high beams he saw it again, but starker now as he suddenly sobered, his mind jolted by the strangeness of the scene. He rolled to a stop.

Seven children were lined up on their backs in the dew-wet grass on the verge of the northbound highway, each in a uniform of blue Airtex shirt, khaki short, white socks, and sneakers. So neatly laid out they looked like corpses on mortuary blocks. And they were so still they might, indeed, be dead because who could lie unmoving in that wet grass? Even on a June night the temperature was down in the mid-fifties.

His second thought was this must be the aftermath of an alien abduction. The Betty and Barney Hill episode had happened on a night not unlike this nine years ago across the border in New Hampshire. He looked up into the sky, half expecting to see a rotating, illuminated saucer, but there was nothing but the stars.

His eyes went back to the roadside. The kids were laid out so neatly. There were little Pan Am bags arranged precisely next to each of them. There were placards hung around their necks with butcher's twine.

He noticed that on the roadward side of the kids there were the deep tire tracks of a large vehicle showing on the verge.

McAllister stared, paralyzed. What should he do? Drive off and find help? Or just carry on as if he had seen nothing? He would sleep off the booze and it would be just a bad memory when he woke up.

The better angel spoke to him again and he pushed open the door and got down from the cab. His work boots crunched on the standing between the asphalt and the verge, seemed to carry him forward absent his conscious will. He looked down at the first kid. A black child, maybe about nine, pretty braids, her eyes closed. He could see the message on the placard hung around her neck: "I am Shannon. For I think that God hath set forth us the apostles last, as it were appointed to death: for we are made a spectacle unto the world, and to angels, and to men."

Her chest heaved.

Shannon was alive.

Another light showed over the trees to the south. The beams filled the sky and caught on the tops of the pines before the curve. He snapped out of his mind freeze, staggered out into the middle of the road, his hands waving. It was a lumber truck bound for Canada, an eighteen-wheeler—the sort that doesn't stop for anything. McAllister was blinded as it thundered around the curve and headed straight toward him. He dropped his hands to his eyes. There was the deafening sound of air brakes. The truck grille halted a bare twenty feet in front of him. The Canadian driver jumped down, was about to curse him out when he, too, saw what McAllister had discovered.

The truck had a CB radio. Within the hour that lonely section of Highway 11 was swarming with vehicles. There were ambulances from Caribou and Presque Isle, the cruisers of the state troopers from Houlton, and reporters' cars from as far away as Bangor.

CHAPTER SEVEN

Ed came back from a blackness as deep as the one before birth, and maybe the one that awaits in death. There were lights playing before his closed eyes.

He opened them. It was night. Emergency stutter lights flashed: blue, red, blue, red... Flashlight beams cut here and there through the dark. Black figures moved through the glares of light, like aliens.

His back felt wet. His hands reached out and felt to either side: he lay in soaking, dew-dampened grass.

A shadow fell over him. Then a voice belonging to the shadow shouted: "This one's alive!"

Other shadows came quickly, blocked out the light. He felt breath on his face. It smelled like meat: raw meat.

"Son, can you hear me?" Meatmouth asked.

Ed blinked.

The voice again: "How many fingers are there?"

Something blurry and white passed across his vision. A hand? He found he couldn't speak.

Three floating faces now. A new voice: "What're his signs?"

"He's unresponsive; looks like a barbiturate overdose, same as the others."

The newest, commanding voice said, "Take him to the ambulance, stat."

There came a rattling of wheels and a contraption was parked next to his body. He was lifted up and laid down again; canvas now not wet grass at his back. His shirt was soaked through.

He stared at the bright silver blanket they had laid over his middle. It was bright *and* warm, so warm after the cold of the grass, like something from God.

Above, the night sky spun with brilliant diamond stars.

The man pushing him wore a green smock and was upside down. He had fearful, rolling eyes and a sweaty, stubbly face.

Ed was lifted up into a brightly lit vehicle. There were two beds, and the interior was filled with canisters and tubes and racks of bottles. He was sure he had never seen anything more strange or beautiful. He was laid out on one of the beds. Hands were placed on him.

"This may hurt," a new voice said. Something was inserted into his arm: a needle. But he felt nothing. He looked at the needle through half-closed eyes. It was as if the needle and arm belonged to someone else. The blanket was taken off his trunk, his shirt unbuttoned and a cold disk was put on his chest, and the man said, "Breathe in." This he knew how to do and he sucked in a breath and the man said, "Good—good chest sounds. Pulse steady but slow." Then fingers lifted up an eyelid… A probing light stabbed in.

The light snapped off. He began slipping into the black.

"Stay with me," the voice said, but from far away.

He was drifting. Whatever had been in the needle was working on him. A warm bullet raced through his veins, waking his dead blood. It was aimed at his heart. It exploded there and he felt his whole body spasm. His eyes shot open. The world tilted, then whirled, then stilled again.

They propped up his head. Suddenly his vision cleared. He saw the lights and bustle outside. But there, amidst the chaos, was the dead stillness of six other bodies lined up by a road. They each wore the same blue shirt as him.

But he did not know who they were.

CHAPTER EIGHT

Aroostook County had never seen a crime like this: seven abducted kids, two of them dead. Its resources were slim and stretched. The county was bigger than some states and the second largest east of the Mississippi, but the sheriff's office in Houlton was manned by only thirteen law enforcement officers. So the incident on Highway 11 had been swiftly escalated.

It was around ten in the morning when the FBI arrived. The Boston Field Office had been called in to "provide additional resources" and by mid-morning several government sedans carrying Supervising Special Agent Greg Hennessey and a dozen field agents were on the scene. They set up a command post at Houlton and the media descended upon it like flies on a corpse.

In response to the media furor Hennessey's SAC in Boston demanded quick results. The Child Abduction Response Plan was upended. The Bureau's job was usually to find missing children and return them to their families, but in this case they had found the children but there were no families to return them to. With the agreement of the Houlton sheriff, Hennessey took the decision in the first hour to issue police pictures of the seven children to encourage people to come forward. Five were taken in hospital wards, two in morgues. The pictures went onto the front pages of local and national newspapers. Five of the children stared out of the front pages, glassy-eyed and confused, but two others were shown with eyes closed and with an unmistakable pallor. The images shocked the nation. The signs with their names and the biblical passage were also published, in case they jogged anyone's memory. A hotline was set up in Houlton.

Neither the mugshots nor the signs elicited any worthwhile leads, though there was a call from someone who had seen a suspicious flying object in the night sky over the dump site and another from a person who claimed to have contacted one of the dead children on the astral plane.

One of the dozen field agents was called Gloria Gonzalez. She was fresh out of Quantico and this was her first major case. She was paired with a veteran of the Bureau, Chris Madden. The two were chalk and cheese. He was thirty-seven, a Korean war veteran with a buzz cut and stern frown but otherwise no visible emotion, and on the older end of the spectrum for a field agent. Despite the regulation gray pantsuit she was wearing, Gloria knew how to have fun and accessorize. She was big in voice, on hair, perfume, and jewelry—the new face of the FBI just emerging in these last days of Hoover.

Hennessey called the first case meeting early the next day. Present were his own agents and assembled police officers from Aroostook and the two neighboring counties of Piscataquis and Penobscot. He said that the medics had forbidden any questioning of the trau-matized kids for now, since the doctors reported that each of the five survivors was suffering from acute memory loss, to the degree that they were unaware of the names on their placards. The only clues thus far were the tire tracks on the roadside verge at the dump site and the Pan Am bags. The bags were widely available at every airport gift shop and identifying a point of origin and a purchaser would be near impossible. The Bibles in the bags were the Douay version, used by Catholics, so there was a slight clue. However, these had been printed back in 1941 and so again their origin was difficult to discover. The children's clothing was so commonplace as to be untraceable. They puzzled over the biblical quotation written in childish hands on the placards.

Molds of the tire tracks had been made by the Evidence Response Team and sent for analysis at Quantico. Yesterday's canvasing had yielded nothing, but had only taken in the couple of dozen farms, cabins, and trailers in a four-mile radius of the dump site. Apart from the alleged unidentified flying object in the sky, nothing unusual had been noted until McAllister came across the kids at 3 a.m. the day before.

The sheriff ordered the search to be expanded and, short of any other clues, all other officers and agents were sent to man roadblocks and canvas Presque Isle to the east, Ashland to the south and as far north as Fort Kent on the border. A handful of officers were left to man the newly opened public information line.

Madden and Gonzalez were assigned to Ashland and here, at the combined convenience store and gas station, got the first lead.

They showed their badges to the owner, Louis Grandfleur, a garrulous, rotund, thickly bearded French Canadian.

Madden took the lead. "You heard about the abduction case?"

"Who hasn't?" Grandfleur answered, nodding toward the newsstand, where the pictures of the Seven Apostles, as they were now being called, stared out in life and death.

"We want to question anyone who might have seen the children."

Grandfleur shook his head. "Believe me, we'd notice seven strange kids around here. This place ain't exactly teeming."

Madden tried a long shot. "So, anything else unusual been going on around here?"

Grandfleur shrugged and stroked his beard. "Folk here keep themselves to themselves and that's fine, but we have some outsiders come through."

"Such as?" Gloria asked.

"Well, we get our share of out-of-state hunters, folk on a back-to-nature Thoreau trip, a few anti-draft kids heading north to Quebec, but they're all here today, gone tomorrow. Strangest permanent folk around here would be that couple living out in the woods. Name of Frome, place called Eriksson's Lot. About the only piece of the North

Woods not owned by the big logging companies. He's some kind of survivalist I guess, but she don't look like that at all. She's more housewifely, you know? They drive through in a beat-up Chevy pickup every now and again. But never together. Just one or the other. Never stopped here neither, which is weird, given there ain't another gas station within ten miles of this place. Only reason I know their name is one of the guys at the forestry checkpoint told me it."

"So, you never saw them with kids?" Gloria asked.

Grandfleur quirked an eyebrow. "Like I said, in this town you'd have noticed something like that. But if you want to know more, go out to the forestry checkpoint. It's on the abandoned highway west of here. There's a story there—shoulda gone all the way to Canada but construction got pulled in the Fifties. Land slips and environmentalists, you know? Checkpoint's manned eight to four this time of year. Those guys are meant to log everything. Must have processed that Chevy a bunch of times. And they may be able to tell you where this Eriksson's Lot is. Me? I ain't got a clue. Back of beyond is all I know. Watch you don't get a flat—no tows out there."

Madden and Gonzalez exchanged glances. They had been assigned to assist in canvasing the town. But, as it was, the place was already crawling with police teams. There was something in Grandfleur's story. Loners were behind most non-family child abductions and these Fromes fit that bill exactly. They thanked him, called Special Agent Hennessey and told him they were investigating a lead and set off down the highway. A sign gave it a name, Realty Road, but after a few potato farms and a sawmill on the edge of the forest there was no other property.

The officer at the checkpoint was new to the job but showed the agents the logbook. Sure enough there was a record of the Chevy's journeys back and forth, its registration and two barely legible signatures, always on different dates. He, too, had heard that the Fromes were some kind of survivalist couple, maybe even cultists of some nature. The one time he'd seen the Chevy, its bed had been piled with dry goods, good enough for a month-long siege, but, hell, survivalists were hoarders, weren't they? With the Missile Crisis not that long ago he guessed these folk were just stockpiling against a nuclear winter. He gave the two agents directions to the turnoff to the Lot.

Madden aimed the sedan down Realty Road. It was strange to be following a blacktop into the middle of an uninhabited wilderness. They drove down this dull, undulating arboreal tunnel, the monotony broken only by glimpses of distant blue-gray mountains, streams rushing under the road in culverts, and the hint of blue lakes glimpsed through the lattice of trees.

Then an aberration appeared. They came around a wide bend and saw that the firs and spruce had been cleared back some twenty yards from the road and there sat a ruined Texaco station. The place had apparently been dropped from the heavens to serve the abandoned highway, then forgotten. The Texaco sign with its red star and green T on its post was rusty and pitted with buckshot. Rusted pumps stood under a sagging canopy on the overgrown asphalt. Beyond, the office front was boarded with rotten panels. At some time the entrance had been broken into and the hole looked like a dark, sinister mouth. A few yards further on, the blacktop abruptly ended and the road became shale and gravel.

They didn't stop. The agents' attention had already been drawn to a plume of smoke rising from a mountain ridge some twenty miles to the northwest, roughly where the forestry officer had told them the Lot was. Madden pressed down on the gas, heedless of Grandfleur's warning about flats.

They could hardly miss the turning when it came. There had been no other side road, just firebreaks, in the last hour. A chain-link fence appeared by the side of the road and ran alongside it for a half-mile to a padlocked swing gate. There was a metal sign with "Eriksson's Lot: Private Property. Trespassers will be Prosecuted," stenciled in faded red paint on the fence next to it. Rusted buckshot holes decorated the sign in several places. A passing wit had scored through "Prosecuted" and scratched the word "Shot" above it. The unpaved track behind rose steeply into the forest.

Seeing the locked gates, Madden went to the sedan's trunk and took out a pair of bolt cutters.

"Let's call it probable cause," he said. He swiftly dispatched the padlock. They cleared the scattered deadfall on the track beyond. There were two vehicle tracks in the mud underneath: one heavy, possibly correlating to the heavy tracks found on 11, the other lighter and perhaps those of the pickup.

Madden looked at Gloria. "Looks like a match, but we need a warrant and the ERT before we go further and we're out of radio range. I'm going to have to go back while you hold the fort. No one in, no one out."

"No one's coming, Chris," Gloria said.

"I won't be long," Madden said. But, of course, he was. It took four hours before he was back with the warrant and the ERT. The four hours were the loneliest Gloria had ever spent. She sat on a tree stump, fished out a packet of Salems and lit up. There was utter, total silence. You would have to believe in some crazy stuff to live out here in this nowhere. A millennial cult who drank the blood of living children perhaps. She shivered. There was a sudden rustling in the trees across the way. She dropped her cigarette and pulled her service .38, thinking it was a bear. She was ready to fire a warning shot but the rustling moved off. Her heartbeat stilled. She sat back on the stump, let the sun beat down on her, hoping it would drive the unease from her. But she couldn't rid herself of it, or the sense of being watched. She looked around but there was only the rusted gate and the track leading up to God knows what on the top of the mountain. Not a single vehicle passed.

By the time Madden was back with the ERT in the midafternoon, there were a half-dozen lipstick-ringed Salem butts around the tree stump.

The ERT confirmed the heavy tracks looked a match with the ones on the 11. They took molds and photos for analysis. Then Madden,

Gonzalez, and two others drove up the track. Gonzalez clutched the gold crucifix around her neck. She decided she hated these woods.

The second gate lay open at the top. A little beyond, smoke rose from a blackened crater some forty feet across and twenty feet deep. No trace of a dwelling remained, just charred wood scattered for 100 yards around. The surrounding trees were scorched but had not caught aflame. Even in June the Maine woods had a pervading dampness about them.

The neighboring lean-to had partially collapsed but otherwise survived the explosion. The ERT went into it first. They found tools and empty fuel containers, which they dusted, but these had been wiped of fingerprints.

More agents arrived and an incident site was established. A mechanical digger was brought in from a logging camp and a six-foot radio mast was erected with the range to reach Ashland. Tents were set up and a latrine dug. The summer bugs descended on the sweating agents. Gloria spent three nights in that godforsaken place without a change of clothes or anywhere to wash. The ERT sifted the pulverized concrete, melted metal, and charcoal at the bottom of the explosion crater. On the third day they found fragments of carbonized bone, possibly lumbar vertebrae. There was not much left for the pathologist. All he could determine was that they didn't belong to a child; the fragments seemed to belong to a mature adult, or adults.

It could be the Fromes, but two vehicles had been driven away from the Lot. Did the Fromes have accomplices? Other members of the same cult who had disposed of the kids while the Fromes killed themselves?

On July 1, the abandoned school bus was discovered in some woods near Fort Kent. The tire treads of the bus were an exact match with those gathered at the Lot and on Highway 11. The bus had been purchased for cash in a sale of state assets ten years previously. The purchaser's ID was discovered to be fake. The bus contained the fingerprints of the seven children, but not its driver. A J.C. Penney bag with a jug of OJ and barbiturate mix, a *Penthouse* magazine, and some used Kleenex were found under the bus driver's seat. The driver had presumably skipped across the border into Canada from Fort Kent.

Identikit pictures of the Fromes were produced and warrants for their arrest issued, just in case they were still alive.

CHAPTER NINE

The children were transferred to hospitals in Massachusetts. Who were they? All the authorities had were the names on the placards. The Missing? The Trafficked? The Abducted? Survivors of Homicide? The doctors determined that their ages were probably within six months of one another, from nine to nine and a half years old. Young for runaways, but still possible. In that year there were over a half-million missing person cases in the US. But after a solid month of exhaustive cross-checking it was established that the kids could not be linked to a single one of them.

The FBI's Kidnapping and Missing Persons department had a list of the rare cases of babies being snatched from childcare situations, but nearly every one had been solved and the child returned to its parents. There were only unsolved cases every five years or so. Seven concurrent cases had never happened.

Homicide: what if both parents had been murdered and the child taken by the perpetrators? Despite some 16,000 homicides in the US in 1970, there were no reported cases of double homicides *and* child abduction that year, or, for that matter, in the preceding decade.

The only remaining theory, bar the alien abduction one, was one that actually approached the truth. The children had been born off the grid and their parents had simply vanished.

Gonzalez was given the task of examining the land registry for the Lot. The public record office in Houlton had all she needed. The place got its name from a Swede, Matthias Lars Eriksson, who bought it shortly after the creation of Aroostook County in 1839. Eriksson logged the valuable white pine out of it, then departed the woods leaving only his name behind.

Afterwards the Lot changed hands twice and was then sold just after the Second World War to what her investigations would eventually reveal was a shell company registered in the Caymans. As the islands were a British Overseas Territory, further information about the directors of the company would have to be sought from the UK. Companies House in London did eventually supply some names, but these, unsurprisingly, also turned out to be entirely fictitious.

It was time to begin questioning the children. The Massachusetts psychiatrists and the FBI established a protocol: the five survivors were to be kept under observation in separate institutions. The separation was intentional: if their memories did return, and the case ever came to trial, the Feds didn't want any cross-contaminating false memories. Child witnesses were tricky enough at the best of times.

An agent was designated to each child. On his return to the Boston Field Office, Hennessey, who was pleased with his new agent's performance in the backwoods, got Gloria assigned to one of the boys, Edward. Gloria was to feed information back to the investigative coordinator. How much could be obtained from the kid was doubtful. The psychologists were certain that the children had been subjected to some kind of deep brainwashing regime. They used the word "zombie" in private to describe them, but never in public.

CHAPTER TEN

Dr. Roger Gant, the child psychologist at the Boston Children's Hospital in Brookline, looked like an eccentric scientist in a TV show: he was bearded and wore a stained lab coat and half-moon glasses. He liked to keep things informal and decided he'd address the kid as Ed. He wasn't happy to learn that an agent had been assigned to shadow Ed's treatment.

He met Gloria in the corridor outside his office before the first session.

Gloria had ditched the serious pantsuit. She wore coral lipstick and a sangria-colored blazer and skirt combo. The skirt had quite a high hemline. She smiled warmly, and Gant couldn't help but smile back. Whoever had chosen her for this assignment had chosen well: this could work.

"Good to meet you, Agent Gonzalez—"

She held up a hand. Her rings flashed in the corridor light. "Please, call me Gloria."

"OK, Gloria. Before we go in, I just wanted to review the case." He gestured to a bench in the corridor.

"Fine by me." She sat, pulling down her skirt, but not before Gant had admired her knees.

He cleared his throat and sat too. "The kid's suffering amnesia brought on, we think, by some sort of traumatic mind control. Are you familiar with the topic?"

"You mean, have I seen *The Manchurian Candidate*? Yes, as a matter of fact."

Her smile was really quite infectious. He smiled back. "Well, I guess the movies and books have a lot to answer for. Fact and fiction kind of blur. I hear that some of the defendants in the Tate–LaBianca trial are pleading coercive persuasion."

The trial of Charles Manson had just begun and had quickly replaced the Apostles' story in the national headlines.

"Do you believe they were forced to commit those murders?" Gloria asked.

"As a matter of fact, I do. I think given the right circumstances—drugs, sleep deprivation, torture—quite normal people could be driven to murder on command. They're called robot agents. I'm sure you've heard the term."

Gloria's smile faded a little. She wasn't going to admit it to Gant, but at Quantico the trainees had heard all about MKUltra, the CIA's program of research into behavioral modification. Prisoners, psychiatric patients, and women suffering postpartum depression had been subjected to electroshock and LSD treatments by their secret service colleagues disguised as innocent medical research students, all with the intention of wiping their subjects' memories.

"You think the kids have been programmed in some way, like Manson's followers?" she asked.

"Too early to say. First up you have to ask yourself to what purpose? We don't know what the kidnappers' motives were: whether they were cultists or pedophiles, or something else. Secondly, what sort of threat is a nine-year-old kid going to pose to society? They're not adults like Manson's people. But there must have been some purpose for what happened to them. We have to take this step by step. The kid is very withdrawn. Monosyllabic at best. He has no recollection of anything before the discovery."

"So where do we start?" Gloria asked.

"First, I'm going to repeat a post-traumatic amnesia test I did when he was first admitted. We'll take it from there. Ready?"

She nodded and they both got up, then Gant ushered her into his office. It was unlike a typical doctor's office: no diplomas, no banker's desk or medical paraphernalia. Instead, the couch and floor were littered with children's books and soft toys. Soft furnishings in bright colors, framed cartoons, a cheerful summer sun beaming onto the hand-woven Navajo-style rug—all gave a decidedly non-antiseptic warmth.

Ed was sitting on a plastic stool reading a book. He was an extremely gaunt, dark-haired child, pallid despite an olive complexion. His only clothing was blue-striped pajamas. His pitifully thin wrists and ankles protruded from them. His entire body language was hunched and introverted; the getup and appearance reminded Gloria uncomfortably of a concentration camp survivor.

Gloria saw he was reading Judy Blume's *Are You There God? It's Me, Margaret*. She wondered at Gant's choice: the book was a super-realist coming-of-age story; but the shrink must know what he was doing. He probably wanted Edward exposed to the "real world." If so, he would have been pleased with the degree of absorption the child was exhibiting. He seemed utterly lost in the book, to the extent that he hadn't noticed Gant and Gloria come in.

"Ed, I have a visitor," Gant said. The boy looked up very slowly and blinked when he saw Gloria.

"Hello, I'm Gloria," she said, not sure if she should offer to shake the kid's hand, but neither Gant nor Ed seemed to expect this. The boy continued staring; there was a worrying blankness in his eyes.

"OK, Ed, I'm going to ask you some questions today. Would that be OK?" Gant asked.

Ed slowly turned his attention from Gloria to Gant and nodded. Gant took a seat on a low stool, indicating that Gloria should sit on the couch. He took a clipboard and pen from the desktop and peered at the boy over the top of his half-moons, pen poised.

"OK, you ready?"

Ed nodded again.

"What's your name?"

"Edward."

"Do you have a last name?"

"What?"

"What are your parents' names?"

He merely stared.

"OK. What is the name of this place?"

"A hospital."

"Good. Do you know its name?"

"No."

"Do you know why you're here?"

"No. I just woke up, then…" His voice died and his face crumpled.

Gant held up a hand. "It's OK, Ed. Let's move on. How old are you?"

Ed shrugged. "I don't know."

"Alright, do you know what year this is?"

The boy's face creased. "The year?" he whispered. He repeated the word. Then his voice deepened suddenly from a treble to a basso profundo and he said, "Twenty-nine. Two. Twenty-five. And I will restore to you the years that the locust hath eaten." Then his eyes glazed and his face went slack. He suddenly seemed far away. Gloria shivered despite the warmth of the room. She looked nervously at Gant: had they lost him?

"Ed," Gant said. "Ed, are you still there?"

Slowly the boy's eyes came back into focus. His posture straightened slightly.

"You OK, kid?" Gant asked.

Ed nodded slowly.

"Let's stop there. We'll try something else," Gant said.

He picked up some picture cards from the desk and showed them to Ed. The kid did better with these: he recognized a cup, keys; he called the seagull picture "a bird," which was good enough.

When the nurse had taken him back to the ward Gant confirmed to Gloria that it was PTA alright. They were in it for the long haul.

"What was that with the years and the locusts?" Gloria asked.

Gant said, "Had to look it up the first time. The Book of Joel. The numbers are the number of the book, the chapter, and the verse. It's the same with the other kids. They all quote numbers and random passages from the Bible, like that's their entire memory."

"Why the Bible?"

"I'm guessing it's something to do with their conditioning. It could be that particular passages trigger something in them. I suppose we could go through the entire scripture with them and see what happens, but that has risks. We don't want them regressing. Besides, it would take a while: there are eight hundred thousand words, give or take. I checked that too."

"Hopefully you'll make progress without having to do that."

"I wouldn't bet on it—this is the worst case of PTA I've come across. I wouldn't rule out any approach."

"What are the other options?"

Gant smiled grimly. "Regressive hypnosis, drugs. I'm not a fan of either. As I said, God knows what kind of traumatic memories could be dredged up. It might aid your investigation but I don't know if it'll help Ed."

"I've heard of cases where hypnosis has been used on witnesses to aid their recall, but always adults, never kids."

"No, never kids," Gant agreed.

That was the end of the first day. There were many more like it. In the months to come, Gant had recourse to hypnosis, therapy, stress-inhibiting drugs: every measure known to alleviate memory loss; but still nothing came.

Only the eye remembered. All the people had gone around and around the eye and then into the deep hole, searching. Now the people had gone and the Lot was silent again. The eye lay there in the mud and rock by the crater of the House of Horrors, observing the sky, passing clouds and birds. If an eye could speak it could have told the Feds all they needed to know, but an eye only observes. And waits.

It was not impatient. Which was good, for nine years is a long time to wait and stare when you have no body and are just an eye. The winds of autumn came, then the snow and the melt, when it had thawed in late spring, they carried the eye a little further from its first resting place, and now it stared at another corner of sky. But all sky was the same to the eye. As was the sun and the moon and stars. Nine years the eye drifted slowly downhill from where the new sun had placed it, waiting for the hand that had last put it down to pick it up—and remember.

Ed and the others couldn't stay in hospital forever. The state authorities posed the same question to all the psychiatrists: did the kids have a chance at "normal" life? The psychiatrists as one frowned at the word "normal;" in their canon there was no "normal" for anyone, let alone kidnapped and possibly abused nine-year-olds. Each one patiently explained all this to the police, press, and prospective adoptive parents. Prospective homes would have to be scrupulously vetted.

Some concerned couples had already put themselves forward as potential adopters. Stuart and Bettie Constance were a childless pair in their forties from Boston. They owned a house on Winthrop Road in Brookline, close to the Children's Hospital. It was a handsome nineteenth-century edifice with a large backyard, three stories high. They claimed an extra interest in the Apostles through a cabin they owned up on Lake Tranquility, a vacation spot in Baxter Park. They happened to be there on Saturday, June 27, and professed to know every detail of the case even though Tranquility was a good 200 miles from the dump site.

The Monday after the kids' discovery, the Constances contacted the police station at Presque Isle. Their names were passed on to the adoption agency and they were vetted, as thoroughly as these things were ever vetted in those days. The Constances explained that they had left it late in life to have a child—now, after countless procedures and tests, they had to accept they would never have their own biological offspring. They claimed the story of the kids pulled at their heartstrings and it was their dearest wish to adopt one of them.

Summer by now had turned to fall—a decision had to be made. The proximity of the hospital to their home in Brookline was in the Constances' favor. In addition, they had led apparently blameless lives. He was a real estate developer, she an elementary school teacher. They were church people: First Episcopalian, regular every Sunday. Grace before meals, prayers at bedtime; vouched for by Woodson Bates, their pastor.

The adoptions of the five were anonymous; the files were sealed and could only be opened in the future by order of the presiding judge. The media adhered to a voluntary gagging order: after all, the news was by now monopolized by the Manson trial.

It was just before Christmas 1970 when Ed left the hospital. Gant and Gloria waited with him in the consulting room. Ed had one piece of luggage, a battered second-hand leather suitcase given to him by Gant. He had only a few clothes, charity donations to the hospital, but no toys. The Bible from the Pan Am bag had been taken for analysis. Gant had given him some classics to continue his reading, all fantasy, as was right for a boy who had never lived in the real world: *The Hobbit*; *The Lion, the Witch and the Wardrobe*; *The Little Prince*.

Stuart and Bettie were dressed in their church clothes when they arrived. Stu, as he was known to all, was short, only some five six, sporting a tweed suit and horn-rimmed spectacles. He had a beaky nose and a broad mouth that beamed the kind of big, toothy smile needed when persuading customers that some dilapidated brownfield site was a once-in-a-lifetime real estate opportunity. Bettie was also in tweed, a two-piece dress suit, horn-rims like her husband, crocodile purse, and white gloves like a Jackie O. knockoff.

Stuart took off his fedora and fired up his 100-watt smile. All the boy saw were his teeth, big for a small man, almost predatory, stained yellow by pipe smoke. Stuart vigorously shook Gant's and Gloria's hands, then turned almost shyly to the boy. He was only a foot taller than the kid.

"Well, Edward, here we are then." (Ed found out later Stu was very fond of the "here we are" phrase.) "You ready to come home?"

Ed swallowed hard and turned to Gant and Gloria.

"OK, kid," Gant said, "you're back here every Wednesday, remember? And Gloria is going to visit you every week."

Gloria crouched and hugged Ed. The Constances exchanged glances as if this was not what they expected from a federal agent.

"Next week, OK, kid?" she whispered in Ed's ear. He bit back a tear and nodded.

The Constances had been briefed by Gant not to expect much in the way of conversation and that day they didn't get it. Not in the walk down to the parking lot, where sat Stuart's Volvo P220 eggshell-blue station wagon, acquired a year before and his pride and joy.

"What do you think, kid?" Stu asked, pointing at it. "Four cylinders, ninety horsepower. Comes all the way from Sweden." His enthusiasm elicited nothing from Ed, who just looked blankly upon this Nordic engineering marvel.

Nor did he utter a word during the brief ride to Winthrop Road or when being shown the house. Not even when he realized he was to have his own room up in the attic. Stu had decorated the walls in a primrose yellow and put up a world map and some outdoorsy pictures involving men with shotguns and rods. Bettie had supplied a brightly colored throw from her women's group. There was even a sink in the corner of the room.

By now Stu was somewhat fazed by Ed's utter silence. "Well, here we are then. Why don't you wash up, then we'll have dinner?" he said, and with that he and Bettie left and, amazingly, shut the door and Ed found himself, it seemed for the first time in his life, utterly alone. He stood there, paralyzed, and was still staring at the wall when Bettie came back to tell him dinner was ready.

The Constances decided that Ed's captive name was at least familiar to the kid, so they kept it. Stu claimed there was Scottish blood somewhere in the family. There was a stag at bay on the wall in the Winthrop living room and Bettie had upholstered the furniture in Stu's supposed family tartan. Ed got a middle name, "Burns," to honor the dubious Scottish connection.

The problems began at the first elementary school, Pierce. Ed arrived in January, a couple of weeks after the winter break. Given the uncertainty of his true age and that he was a recluse, with socialization skills way below those of the first graders, he was assigned to the fourth grade. He had reading aptitude and a remarkable memory, particularly of the Bible, but he knew nothing of math, history, or geography.

On the first day Principal Farmer brought Ed to Mr. Preston's fourth-grade class. He was the only newcomer that spring term and all the kids turned and stared at him as he stood, shuffling from foot to foot, in front of them.

"Children, please welcome Edward Constance to your class today," Farmer said primly, then nodded to Preston to take over. There was a whispered buzz of conversation as Farmer departed and Preston brought Ed over to a spare desk: Ed caught words and phrases: "found by the side of the road"… "two of them killed"… "aliens"… "freak."

"That will be all, children," Preston said and the buzzing died down. "Please sit, Edward." He returned to his desk. There was a projector pointed at the wall. Preston pulled down a screen. "First lesson is history. Edward, you'll have to catch up with the other children. We've been studying the twentieth century and the Second World War. We didn't quite finish the subject last week. Open your textbooks at the chapter entitled 'The Atomic Bomb' and those of you sitting next to the windows, please pull the shades."

There was a rustle of books being opened as two of the kids did as Preston bade and the room was cast into semidarkness. Ed felt the first stirring of uneasiness. There was a textbook on the desk in front of him. He was not sure where he was meant to find the chapter Preston had referred to, but the book fell open as if of its own accord on a page showing a black column rearing up from the earth into the sky, a halo of vapor, then a mushroom-shaped cloud above it.

He had seen that image before. He had seen it back then. Some delicate shell fractured in him: blackness began seeping in. The blackness was filling in his vision. He tore his eyes away from the picture and looked up, but there, now in color, on the projector screen was the same image amplified ten times. He heard Preston's voice droning on as the slideshow cycled: President Truman, the *Enola Gay*, Colonel Tibbets and his crew, "Little Boy," the egg-shaped bomb, Hiroshima, then Nagasaki... but the world and the classroom were slipping away—all was fading to that all-conquering black...

Out of the darkness another scene materialized. He was in another room, a classroom of sorts but not the one at Pierce with its twenty boys and girls. There were only seven children here. The other kids' names came to him for the first time since Highway 11: David, Carl, Hope, Kevin, Catrine... and Shannon. Most importantly, Shannon... There were no windows in this room. A cine projector cast a shaft of white, flickering light onto a blank wall. And, yes, he and the others were singing as the mushroom cloud rose and rose and the sky turned blood red; a ruined city lay beneath; there were shadows on the sidewalk where people had been when the flash had turned the heavens white; the images of hideously burned victims began to shutter across...

He heard a scream, then arms grabbing him, shaking him, and urgent voices calling for the nurse to come quickly. "One of the boys is having a seizure."

After consultation with Principal Farmer, it was agreed that Ed should be excused certain lessons, particularly Preston's twentieth-century history ones. He was allowed to sit with Farmer's secretary in his outer office during them. By now the story of the screaming kid and the rumors surrounding his past were all around Pierce. School is a jungle with predators and prey. Ed was now prey. Not long after the incident, the ringleader of the fifth graders, Todd Reilly, stood over Ed in recess.

"Hey, freak, look at me." Reilly had a way of addressing everybody bar adults with hands on his hips and legs planted apart like some union enforcer.

By now Ed was making good progress with *The Little Prince* and was wishing he was far away in the Sahara with its hero rather than in this freezing playground. But one thing his books had taught him: you had to stand up to aggression or continually be a victim. The moment he had been anticipating since he arrived at Pierce had come. There was only one option. Mustering all the feeble courage he felt inside, he lowered the book and stood. He gave up a good six inches to Reilly.

"Do me a favor, leave me alone, will you?" he said, but even to his own ears it carried no conviction.

Reilly broke his posture and took a step nearer, bunching his fists.

"Say again," he spat.

"I said, leave me alone," Ed repeated. It was maybe a little stronger this time, but not by much.

"You know who I am, kid?" Reilly asked.

"I'm getting a fair idea," Ed answered.

"What's that?" Reilly's face flushed and spittle speckled Ed's face. He took another step forward and pushed Ed with both hands, hoping no doubt to land him on his ass, but Ed had braced himself and didn't fall. He pushed back and Reilly tottered. The older boy snarled and this time he came in with his fists swinging. Ed tried to duck but a fist deflected off his cheekbone and crunched his nose. He tasted blood.

Reilly was a bit unbalanced, his sweaty face bowed just inches from Ed's.

There was a roaring in Ed's ears. Then, like a monstrous dark snake, it came swarming up from the depths: a long-buried rage. The roar became a scream. His mind went blank.

When he came back to himself—it could have been hours but was surely only seconds later—Reilly was lying on the asphalt holding his face. His nose was shattered, flattened against one cheek, and his mouth was a bloody hole. He gurgled something through the blood. Ed's knuckles were skinned so they bled. He was being restrained from behind by a male teacher, who was pinning his arms.

"Easy, boy," the man said. Though he was wrestling with a supposed nine-year-old, the guy sounded out of breath as if barely able to cope with the boy's sudden, frenzied strength.

The meeting in Principal Farmer's office was attended by Stu and Bettie. The principal appeared unnerved. The teacher who had restrained Ed had reported how Ed had suddenly exhibited a berserk, homicidal rage. Reilly could have been killed.

"OK, Edward, perhaps you could explain to your parents and me exactly what happened in the playground this morning," Farmer said.

Ed had been staring at the floor. His nose had a Band-Aid over the bridge, his knuckles were scabbing over. He shrugged without making eye contact.

Stu said, "Ed, the principal's trying to give you a chance. Tell him what happened."

Ed shrugged again. "I dunno. The kid hit me and then it all went blank."

"That it?" Stu asked.

Now Ed did look up. "Like I said, I don't remember." There was something dark behind his eyes that none of the adults felt comfortable with.

"Alright, Edward, you can go now. I'll have a separate word with your parents," the principal said.

When he was gone, Farmer lowered his voice as if frightened Ed might overhear what he had to say next.

"Mr. and Mrs. Constance, I know there are mitigating circumstances here. Post-traumatic stress and all—we've read the papers—but I have to tell you the teacher who witnessed the assault was quite shocked at what he saw. It seems Edward literally went berserk. He said his face was transformed; monstrous, if you don't mind me using that word. He could have killed the other kid."

Stu glanced at Bettie, then back at the principal. "Listen, Mr. Farmer, I hope you can cut Ed some slack. As you say, you know his background. As far as we can establish, he was kept in some cabin in the woods all his life up to now. God knows what happened to him. Everything's new to him. There're problems, but he'll get over them. You know, I'd be happy to settle the other kid's medical bills if that helps." He tried to fire up his winning smile, but for once it failed him.

Farmer eyed him dispassionately. "OK," he said. "I'll put that to Reilly's parents. Meanwhile Ed is confined to the classroom during breaks until further notice. And if this incident is ever repeated, that's it—he's out."

As it was, Reilly was hospitalized for the reconstructive surgery required for his nose and some dental prosthetics for his shattered mouth. His parents, however, refused to take Stu's money for treatment. They seemed abashed that their son had been so badly beaten by a wimpy nine-year-old. As for Ed, being confined to the classroom during breaks suited him just fine. He got on with his reading.

But after a few weeks Farmer decided he had served his time and he had to go out to the playground again. He could have milked the adulation of the other fourth and fifth grader; after all, he had vanquished the fifth's most notorious bully. But he didn't encourage the popularity and shunned the other kids' advances.

His fellow pupils decided this was not the way of heroes. After a while they forgot what had happened to Reilly. Every recess was now the same: the questions, the hectoring, the insults when he didn't answer. Popularity turned to hostility: "Here comes the Freak from Outer Space," he'd hear as he approached a knot of kids, or, "What happened to your brain in the Space Lab, weirdo?" Because of his olive skin some called him "spic" to his face.

The second fight was not long in coming. The same welling-up from the depths, the same red mist, the same blackout. Luckily the second kid wasn't as badly injured as Reilly. Nevertheless, the principal delivered on his promise and Ed was removed from Pierce. The Constances arranged a place at a school a little further from Winthrop Road. But by now Ed's reputation preceded him: it was inevitable that a kid at Pierce knew another kid at the school a few blocks over. And at the new school there was, of course, another Reilly intent on proving his superiority over this strange newcomer. So it happened again, and again. A succession of schools followed with another broken nose, broken fingers, some more scattered teeth...

Stu's "and here we are thens" at each successive school gate became more and more tired. Neither he nor Bettie could bond with the strange, awkward, angry boy they had taken in. Each time he regressed, each time he and his parents were brought into a principal's office, each time he cleared his locker, he clung to his failure as the only real thing. But despite the turnover of schools, his learning never suffered. He was always top, or nearly top, of his class. The other kids added the sin of "trick memory" to his other transgressions.

Gant ordered a police-certified hypnotist to be brought in. It was unclear whether the man had ever had a child patient before: usually his role was to coax evidence from forgetful or unwilling adult witnesses. He got Ed to lie on Gant's couch and tried to get him into a state of deep relaxation. This proved impossible the first time and no easier over the next several sessions. On the one or two occasions Ed began to drift and regress, he would snap out of it with a sudden cry of terror. He claimed he remembered nothing of what he'd recalled in those moments. The sessions were eventually aborted.

Gant realized they were only scratching the surface of something big, dark, and evil. His colleagues were experiencing the same with the other four children: violent mood swings, black aggression.

In the end, some forgotten hostility in Ed transferred to Gant. When the shrink smiled, his red lips broke the fuzz of the beard in a way that reminded Ed of someone—someone he didn't quite remember but had disliked. Gant tried to work on this cue, but, since the distaste was half aimed at him, didn't make progress.

Gant confided to the Constances that Ed's PTA was concerning him, and he wondered aloud if the child needed to be institutionalized again. Though Stu and Bettie regretted their decision to adopt Ed, they were at least resolved on this one issue; they refused to let Ed be readmitted to an institution. They would tough it out, somehow.

Gloria's hospital visits had become house visits. As he grew distant from Gant the two of them became closer.

She visited Winthrop Road every week to begin with; less later on as other assignments took her away. She didn't seem set on information gathering; she called her visits pastoral. She would sit with Ed in the large living room, her manicured nails red against the bone-white tea service. The exotic scent of Youth Dew and menthol cigarettes supplanted the habitual odor of cake and Bettie's staid perfume. Ed got to admire her bright crimson lipstick and eyelash thickener close up. He guessed personal jewelry and heavy makeup were not encouraged by the Bureau. He liked that Gloria Gonzalez was a bit of a rule-breaker in that way. Perhaps this appreciation of her was a clue to the child he had once been but could no longer remember?

Either Stu or Bettie was always in attendance at these sessions. To keep an eye on things, they said, as was their right as parents. They sometimes intervened: the kid wasn't ready to drag all that stuff up yet, they'd say, or he was tired. Gloria would just flash her smile then. Ed could read that smile: it was insincere, not the smile that Gloria saved for him. He knew she felt his parents were interfering. And yet, she never complained, just said "Another time" and picked up her purse and thanked Stu and Bettie. To begin with she would chat about nearly everything, anything bar the investigation. Once or twice she elicited a smile from Ed. When she smiled back it was like the sun to him.

However initially casual Gonzalez appeared to be, over time Ed realized there seemed to be method behind her approach. Later he wondered if there wasn't some FBI handbook on the subject of interrogating traumatized minors. Questions and answers: never too forceful; wide-ranging but slowly funnelling down to specifics. Only when that moment was reached might she take from her purse some documents or pictures and lay them out on the coffee table and invite Ed to have a look. Her gold bracelet with a heart pendant trailed on the table between them as she gestured, making a pretty tinkling noise.

One day he summoned enough courage to ask her a question: "Gloria, will you tell me something?" he whispered.

"Sure, anything," she answered.

"What happened to the other kids?"

Gloria looked around uneasily, but Bettie, who had been overseeing this particular session, had disappeared into the kitchen to take a call.

"They found homes, Ed, just like you," she said.

"All of them?" he asked.

"Yeah, all of them," she answered, but she looked away again and he wondered, for once, if she was telling the truth.

"There was a girl called Shannon—is she OK?"

"Yes, Ed, she's fine. She was taken in by a family near here."

"A family like this one?"

"Sure."

"Did they give her a last name, like me?"

Again, Gloria didn't look entirely easy with this line of questioning. "Look, Ed, I'm not meant to tell you this, but, yes, her surname is now Quincy; she's named after her foster parents. They take in lots of kids without homes; give them a good life."

"Can I see her?"

"No, Ed, you know the courts wouldn't allow that."

Ed held her gaze for a moment, wondering whether, if he held it long enough, she would relent and somehow spirit him out of the house to where Shannon now lived, but just at that moment Bettie came back from the kitchen and any faint hope of Gloria accommodating him vanished.

Gloria's methods, whatever they were, were no more productive than Gant's. Apart from the names of the other kids, Ed's mind remained blank of any further details of what had taken place at Eriksson's Lot.

He was in middle school when she was reassigned from the Boston Field Office. Gloria was not smiling when Stu ushered her into the living room for the last time.

"You OK?" Ed asked. Gloria glanced at Stu, who had gone to his armchair and seemed immersed in the *Herald*.

"Ed, I have news," she said. "The Bureau are sending me to the El Paso office."

Ed's knowledge of geography was still short of what it should have been for a typical sixth grader. "Is that near?" he asked.

Gloria shook her head sadly. "No, Ed. It's down on the border. Texas."

"Texas?" She might as well have said the moon. Ed felt a big hole open in his chest and his eyes welled a bit. He was distracted for the rest of their half-hour. There was not much more to say anyway. There were no more questions, and no more answers.

At the end, Gloria rose and he did as well. His hands dangled helplessly by his sides. She took a step and embraced him in a wave of scent and softness. He felt the swell of her breasts against his thin chest, the press of her necklace crucifix in between them through his jumper. Her hand reached down to one of his and, with a little pressure, forced open his palm and placed there a scrap of paper. His hand closed on hers and then her fingers were gone, leaving the paper.

When the front door closed on her, he ignored Stu and went upstairs. In his room he looked at the message. It was a phone number. Area code 915. He pressed it to his face and breathed in the faint scent of Youth Dew.

No new agent replaced Gloria. The Apostles case, though open, was not being actively investigated anymore. Everyone involved was advised to get back to "normality." Final theory? The kids had been trafficked over the border and were victims of a mysterious rapture cult.

For the first five years the Constances decided that their Maine vacation cabin was off limits to Ed in case it acted as a trigger. The house on Tranquility was rented out. Vacations were taken far from the Apostles' discovery site, on the long strands of Cape Cod. These holiday trips didn't soothe Ed: the large Atlantic rollers on the beaches were terrifying to him and the continuous roar of the sea and the shriek of seagulls assaulted his troubled mind.

When he was fourteen the Constances made a decision to give up on Cape Cod. They had, after all, a perfectly good holiday cabin in Tranquility, fully paid for and going to waste. It was 200 miles from the Lot and the dump site. Surely there was no risk in taking the kid there?

Stu invited the boy into his study at Winthrop in the early summer of '75. There had been many conversations in here over the years, particularly after the successive incidents at the various schools. As usual the desk was littered with plans of shopping malls currently in development at Stu's company. To Ed, who had been taken to each of Stu's openings, the constructions were getting progressively uglier. Stu was tamping down his pipe. He gave Ed the fake grin. His teeth were yellowed by baccy.

"How you doin', kid?" he asked

"Good, sir," Ed mumbled.

Stu leaned forward and pointed his pipe. "Kid, I told you before. Call me Stu."

Ed merely nodded.

"Ed, this July, Bettie and I have decided to go back to our place in Maine."

There was a pause as Stu stared at him with the same benign but earnest owlishness as Dr. Gant. "So, what do you say?"

"Me?"

"Sure, you. What do you think, kid? Wanna go?"

Stu then launched into a lesson on why Tranquility would be good for Ed. Ed knew every detail of the speech already, having been subjected to it a half-dozen times before: there was everything they could ever want on the lake; as pretty a cabin as you ever saw, boats, fishing, swimming, why, you could even find knapped stone left over from the Native American tribe that once lived there—flints made into arrowheads and tomahawks. What could be better than that?

Ed merely nodded. It was finally happening—he was going back to where he had come from.

Stu broke into a broad smile. "Attaboy. You'll have a whale, you'll see."

But by now Ed was far away. As he stared sightlessly past Stu, he heard a tiny sound in his inner ear. At first it was the distant song of the white-throated sparrow: *Ah, te,e,e,te,e,e,te.* But the song slowly morphed into a whine, like a mosquito whine, and he heard the faint sing-song of children, just like in Preston's Hiroshima lesson. They were chanting:

"And I heard a voice in the midst of the four beasts say, A measure of wheat…"

And the room spun and everything went black.

He woke with Stu and Bettie leaning over him.

"What happened?" she asked.

"He fainted. Overexcited about Maine, I guess," Stu said.

CHAPTER ELEVEN

Jim Dove was now thirty-one years old and, bar his time in the Marines, had lived by the shore of Lake Tranquility for most of his life. It had been good in his youth. Easy summer days: crewing the steamer on the lake that serviced the hotel; working at his father's store; gassing pleasure craft at the dock; fishing; gardening for the vacationers; drinking beer and smoking reefer; flirting with and bedding some of the pretty girls who came to the cabins from away. It was a lotus-eating life, without ambition: he went through high school without any distinction.

Tranquility was faded now, the bait store he had inherited from his father less busy each passing summer. Some of the cabins around the lakeshore went whole seasons without visitors. The Sun Mountain Hotel ten miles away at the top of the lake, popular in the Fifties with presidents and gangsters, was derelict. Back in the day it had the finest suites of any hotel in Maine. The entrance featured a porte cochere, marble stairs, a belle epoque ballroom, and dining room on the lower floor, gilt fittings that would have done credit to the outfitters of the *Titanic,* and manicured gardens based on celebrated ones near Lake Como in Italy. The freshest seafood and produce were sent up from the coast to the railhead at Madison, along with the finest European wines. But the allure of foreign vacations and jet travel had slowly killed off the Sun Mountain in the Sixties.

Unlike the vanished vacationers, Jim Dove was content with Tranquility. He had gone to the West Indies once but the heat reminded him too much of the jungle in Nam. This cool green wilderness was his home. The Dawnland, the Wabanaki who had once lived here called it. The high mountain that caught the first rays from the east had a Native American name: Nakuset, Sun Mountain, after which the hotel was named.

There had once been a billboard on the access road to the hotel, advertising fireworks and a dinner dance with "Fred Geary's Swing Band—Featuring Glenn Miller Classics!" on July 4, 1966. But the hotel had never opened that season. The poster had faded and then been shredded by the elements. The billboard followed: rotted through, it collapsed into the grass by the verge. In a few short years the hotel had become a wreck; shingles poured from its roof, its forecourt cracked and was overgrown with weeds. It had become another sort of attraction: a haunted house that summer teenagers went to for a dare. The floor of the ballroom was littered with burst mattresses, used rubbers and crushed beer cans.

Jim's life had changed a year after the hotel closed, when he was twenty-one. The postman arrived with a buff government envelope. Inside was an Order to Report for Induction into the US Armed Services at the army recruitment office in Bangor. He had fallen foul of the draft pick. Of his age pool there was only a one-in-ten chance of being called up. He'd somehow drawn the short straw.

It was a two-year conscription. Among the raw conscripts, there was little chance of being drafted into the Marines, but that was what happened to Jim. The recruiting officer shrewdly assessed the lean, fit kid who reported that day in Bangor, asked him some searching questions about his outdoor skills and handiness with a rifle and assigned him for Marine training all the way to Pendleton: 1st Division, 1st Regiment. Even then he had only a one-in-three chance of actual deployment to Vietnam. But Jim's luck with numbers was out again.

He got to Nam just in time for the Tet Offensive. He had fought at the ancient imperial capital Hue, one of the bloodiest battles of the war, characterized by savage street fighting and booby-trapped buildings and atrocities against civilians. His right cheek had been laid open by shrapnel from a deflected AK-47 round, giving him a permanent scar, but since he had not had the time nor the inclination in the heat of the combat to seek treatment from a medical officer, he had not been awarded a Purple Heart.

After that close shave, his luck with the numbers improved. Bar the scratch in Hue, he was unscathed. Sixty thousand never made it back alive from the Suck. One in four deployed US Marines were designated KIA or wounded.

His father passed away during the first tour. Like his mom before, it was the big C. Cigarettes. People were beginning to make the connection by then, though America was still getting through half a million metric tons of them a year. Jim missed the funeral.

America was a different country from the one he had left when he returned to it from his first tour in '69. Though he had dreamed of the lake for two years, he didn't make it back to Tranquility. As he crossed the country, his uniform and buzz cut brought angry looks from people his own age. The narrative was anti-war and the pictures of napalmed children fleeing burning villages condemned returning servicemen as murderers of innocents. He'd gotten as far as Baltimore before turning back to San Diego to reenlist.

As the US began to pull out of Vietnam, the First Division hung on longer than any other outfit. They fought around Da Nang. More casualties in a hopeless cause. During Jim's second tour he retrained as an explosive ordnance disposal expert, considered one of the most dangerous jobs in the Corps. There was a sea of unexploded bombs, mines, and booby traps in Da Nang. His newfound luck with the odds held.

He returned to Tranquility after six years in the Marines, in November 1973. Though he was only twenty-seven, he already looked old beyond his years.

In his absence they'd buried George Dove in the family plot in the Hadsville Episcopalian Churchyard ten miles from the lake. Jim stopped at the cemetery after he got off the Trailways bus. It was a cold day. He turned to the church on the hill. The November sky matched the drab gray granite of its stones. The stone panels of the belfry were painted an anomalous blood-red, the only splash of color in the whole piece.

In the cemetery he stared at the polished granite inlaid with his father's names and dates in gilt lettering. His mother's grave lay next to it. Eighteen years strangers and now back in bed together in the earth's cold embrace. He didn't know where that notion came from but it was strong and sad enough to make his eyes tear.

He walked back toward the gate and the country road. Even then he had had second thoughts. Turn back, wait for the Trailways bus to Bangor. Leave forever. Go back to California. But for what? The chances of employment for returning servicemen were slim. Many of his fellows had already ended up on skid row. At least he had a living, of sorts, here.

He tried thumbing a ride toward the lake, but the traffic was thin, as it always was after Labor Day. As he walked north, only logging trucks passed, each at the maximum permitted fifty miles an hour. They didn't stop. Company policy was not to stop for anything. They were kings of the road and kings of the millions of acres of pine, spruce, and fir that lay all around.

After a half-hour Deputy Sheriff MacDonald pulled over in his cruiser and offered him a ride. In the six years Jim had been away MacDonald had acquired a paunch that pushed at the buttons of his uniform shirt, and some gray hair.

The deputy took him all the way out to the lake and left Jim in the weedgrown lot in front of the store. The hand-painted sign stood out front, with its faded stencilled lettering in a Wild West wanted poster style. It read "Dove's Tack and Bait." Beyond, the lake water was gunmetal blue, the mountains and conifers draped in sinuous wreaths of mist. The cold rain of late fall promised snow.

The place was as his father had left it the day he had been taken away to hospital in Bangor, never to return. There were two dozen graying unpaid bills crushed into the mailbox on the road. The store key was where he always left it—in a jar on the lintel ledge. Jim was surprised the place hadn't been broken into.

The interior of the store had the dead air of every long-unlived-in place. Spiders had festooned the windows, rafters, and chairs. The worktable was strewn with a tangle of fishing tackle that his dad must have been unraveling right to the end. A tin ashtray held two fossilized butts—he'd never been able to kick the habit that killed him. There were some thirty fishing rods in racks behind the sales counter. Orange price tags hung off each one of their reels, written in his dad's neat hand. Given inflation was running at about ten percent, they would no doubt be considered bargains now.

Under the thick coating of dust on the glass countertop were boxes of rifle ammo, elaborate flies and lures, specialist reels. There were still some outdoor slickers and hats for sale on the steel clothes racks and dusty shelves.

The guns were missing. He wondered if MacDonald had taken them for safe keeping or if some concerned person had sold them and was holding the money for him. He would have to ask about that.

It seemed the utility company had long abandoned its attempts to reclaim what was owed and had simply cut the place off. The old rotary phone was dead, and neither the lights nor the electric pump for the well worked.

Someone had taken bolt cutters to the padlock on the pump on the dock and the gas tank was, unsurprisingly, drained dry. He lit a hurricane lamp and found a propane stove to boil some water. He found a half-drunk bottle of Beam and some rust-speckled cans and made a rudimentary meal.

He contemplated his future over the whiskey. He had saved a little of his pay and now, with the stock in hand, there was just enough for when the place reopened in the summer.

That first winter Jim was back, the silence set and the banked snow lay about. Only the footprints of the house mice disturbed its virgin expanse, trails sometimes abruptly ended by the brush of a wing in the snow where a barn owl had swooped and taken them. Some nights wolves howled far away. These nights he stared into the bottom of a bourbon bottle or toked on the last shreds of his homegrown reefer and wished an AK-47 bullet or a mine had taken him in Nam. Or that whoever had removed the Remingtons and Winchesters from display had left one behind so he could eat its muzzle and pull the trigger.

The icicles by now were one- or two-feet needles hanging from the eaves. He spoke to no one, did not even have a TV for company.

Spring came slowly and indecisively, one step forward, two back, with snow flurries and nor'easters. But, finally, there was the raucous cry of crows and the drip of the eave icicles melting and falling like daggers. Then the lake ice broke with the sound of fracturing bones. The honking of the returning geese seeking clear water in the breaking ice sounded, and followed most gentle of all, by the soft hooting of the mourning dove; and, finally, the true sign of spring: the song of the white-throated sparrow.

In Maine this time of gray renewal lasted almost to the solstice and a man might wonder if he would ever see the yellow face of the sun again, but finally here it was, turning the lake blue and the forests a verdant green, shining on the retreating snowcaps of Nakuset and Katahdin. And with the sun came the summer people.

The store was busy from morning to dusk. The vacationers bought dry goods and cigarettes and gas for their boats, ammo and fishing equipment. Just as his Marine savings ran out, cash finally went into the register. The visitors might not have known what to make of the taciturn, scarred owner of the store. His answers were gnomic and in a language sometimes barely recognizable to them, like the obscure utterances of a minor character in an Elizabethan play. But all the outsiders knew this was the Maine way. Its people were fiercely independent, cautious in speech to strangers, slow to befriend, stoic and hardworking.

Over time, tentative conversations were struck up with Jim. There was roundabout talk about how difficult it was to find contractors to maintain the lake cabins since the passing of his father. Did Jim know of anyone? As the lake's only year-round resident, the answer was plain enough. If you didn't want to bring someone over from Hadsville, Jim was the only option. Negotiations on rates were indirect, oblique.

Jim first met Stuart and Bettie Constance during one of these round-about exchanges. They had a cabin on the west side of Tranquility named Brantwood. It was just visible from the bait store a couple of miles down the western shore of the lake. Bettie had begun an explanation of the name of a house once owned by an English artist in the English Lake District. She'd pointed at a photo of a Victorian house. Stu and she had visited it on vacation. The lake in the photo didn't look like much in comparison to Tranquility, that was for sure. The house and surroundings were a little polite and manicured compared to the wilderness here.

Jim didn't know what to make of the Constances. They were not much like the other summer people, not involved in the social life of the lake, rarely, if ever, attending drinks parties or barbecues. Bettie seemed mousey and bookish, Stu was more outward-going but, Jim thought, a little slippery. He, too, liked reading, but, unlike the literature that Bettie devoured, his taste ran to Mickey Spillane.

The Constances had an adopted child. A silent, morose, unprepossessing boy, he looked Hispanic with his mop of dark hair and olive skin. He was the subject of gossip in the store. The Constances had stopped visiting their cabin for five years straight and had now returned with this mystery kid whom they had adopted in the intervening years. It didn't take long for the rumors to crystallize into fact. He was one of the kids found out on Highway 11 back in '70. Though the case was now some time ago, the gossip on the lakeside sparked with the thrill of notoriety. Everyone remembered the TV news reports, the banner headlines, the shocking pictures of the seven kids; five alive, two dead. Whenever he was seen in public, Ed was the target of everyone's sideways glances and whispers.

Highway 11 had happened when Jim had been in the Suck. The media had called the kids the Apostles from the signs found hanging around their necks. From the Bible-studying of his youth, Jim thought of the Apostles filled with Pentecostal fire and speaking in tongues. There could be no greater contrast with this silent boy on the few occasions he braved the glances and whispering and appeared at the bait store. A gaumy, sulky-looking fellow with his hair falling over his acned face, hands always in the pockets of his jeans, never meeting Jim's eyes. At fourteen he was getting quite tall for his age but not growing into it very gracefully. His body was permanently on the hunch. On his rare solo appearances at the store the kid silently shoved a list of necessaries across the counter to Jim and then paid in cash without uttering a syllable.

During the years they had been absent from Tranquility, Stu had brought in help from Hadsville, but the arrangement hadn't gone well. That winter of '74 an overhanging branch had fallen in a winter gale and dislodged shingles; water had gotten into the house. Despite repeated calls, the Hadsville guy had not been for weeks. Now Stu had water damage *and* mold. He needed a new handyman. He made the same roundabout overtures that all the summer people made to Jim, said he needed some "advice" on a job. Maybe Jim knew someone who would be good for it? Jim said, sure, he would have a think and be along about Monday when the store was closed.

He arrived at 7 a.m., not actually waking Stu, whose office hours fortunately extended into vacations. Jim eyed the damage to the roof and declared it to be a day or two of work for the right man, not in any way suggesting he was that man or was willing to do it.

"So how much would you expect a job like that to cost?" Stu asked.

"Depends," Jim answered. "A hundred dollars might do it."

"That seems a fair price," Stu answered.

"Well, there're shingles and nails in the truck. Could fix things up for now until a contractor comes," Jim answered.

"That would be mighty good of you, Mr. Dove. I'll make it right with you," Stu said.

Jim gave him a look that suggested nothing was, in fact, likely to make it right with him. Nevertheless, he fetched a ladder from the pickup, leaned it against the cabin wall and went up with his toolbox. Not sure what else to do, Constance retreated into the cabin and conferred quietly with Bettie as the hammering and banging commenced over their heads. Whatever a quick fix was, this work of Dove's was not quick. The work continued apace all morning. Mrs. Constance timidly came out and offered coffee but Dove politely declined and, as far as the couple could make out, he didn't descend once, even for a call of nature.

Sometime in the late afternoon the hammering ceased, and they heard footsteps on the ladder and Jim's blue coveralls descended past the window.

When Stu went out Jim was wiping his hands with a rag. "Reckon that will hold for a while," he said.

Stu stepped out on to the gravel and craned up at the place where the damage had been. The repair was perfect and seamless. It appeared to be the work of a craftsman. As Jim fetched his ladder and toolbox Stu hurried back into the cabin, went to the tin where he kept his cash, quickly counted out a hundred in notes and got out just in time to catch Jim as he got in the truck. Jim rolled down the fly-stained window and looked at Constance without expression.

"For your time," Stu panted, offering the fan of notes.

Jim glanced down at it. "It looks like there's 'bout a hundred dollars there."

"Well, you fixed up the roof, didn't you?"

"Ayuh."

"Well then, take the money. I don't need a contractor anymore, do I?"

Jim took the proffered cash, folded it up and stuffed it into his bib pocket. "Obliged to ye," he said, then rolled up the window, stuck the shift in reverse, and Stu had to step back smartly as Dove went back, turned and disappeared in a cloud of dust up the driveway.

A roundabout arrangement followed by which Dove would be invited to give more "advice" on repairs and improvements to the property, until, that was, the "real contractor" could come, and these fixes, never suggested to be permanent ones but in actuality permanent, Constance would readily agree to, and Jim somehow had always brought the very materials required to carry out whatever needed doing. When the Hadsville man finally did show a month or so later, he took one look at Jim's work, silently disappeared and was not heard from again.

So Jim began working for Stu, but without either of them actually acknowledging it.

Jim didn't need much company but got his first dog, Laramie, that spring, a Border collie who was biddable, quick, and loyal, riding in the back of his Chevrolet truck where he stored the mower and his tools. On the Sabbath, after the bait store closed early in respect of church hours, Jim's religion was mainly the liquor bottle or the joint. But sometimes he was out walking Laramie when the Sunday exodus to church in Hadsville occurred. There was a regular convoy of vehicles heading to the Baptist, Methodist, Episcopalian, and Catholic churches in town, and the Constances' foreign station wagon was no exception, joining the cavalcade up the Three Mile Road. The silent kid would be in the back, brushed up, in a suit and tie, looking grim. They said his captors had been some religious nuts, and Jim could well believe that the kid hated church.

In the summer Jim was up from dawn to dusk. Running the store and, when that closed, off mowing a stranger's lawn or up on a ladder fixing their shingles or a gutter. The folk from away didn't encourage their children to play outside when he was about these chores. Generally, the neighbor kids were happy to avoid the man with the teak face and savage scar and the Winston permanently clamped between his lips, who mumbled in the strange patois of Maine.

Sometimes clients wanted him to take them out on the lake fishing for smallmouth bass, lake trout, and pike. The excursions were not as frequent or as popular as they might have been if conducted by anyone but Jim; he was at best a taciturn skipper. Though they were paying clients, the vacationers were not exempt from criticism: a sharp rebuke from Jim for a tangled line, lost fly or clumsy unbalancing of the boat was common. Most didn't come back for a second trip.

Stu had never asked for one of these excursions. In all the time he had been maintaining the Constance cabin, Jim had never seen a single item of hunting or fishing equipment around the place. There was a perfectly good boat in the lakeside shed that had never made it out onto the slipway.

The second season of their return to Tranquility, Stu turned up at the bait store one late-June afternoon and asked a favor.

"Say, Mr. Dove, you out in your boat much this summer?"

"Depends."

Stu quirked an eyebrow. "On what?"

"Depends on the fish."

Stu smiled. "But if they were biting, you'd go out?"

"I guess."

"You wouldn't be interested in a charter, would you?"

"A charter, Mr. Constance? I ain't a tunny boat."

"Well, maybe charter isn't the word in these parts. Leastways, a trip, you know. I'd make it worth your while."

"You the fishin' type then?" Jim inquired.

"I was thinking more of the kid. He's kind of moping about, needs to get out a bit. His birthday's on July Fourth. If you could take him out the Sunday after, it'd be a belated treat for him."

"Look, Mr. Constance, I ain't got time for nannying a kid. Fishin' is fishin'. You do it right or stay ashore."

Stu held up his hands. "Hey, Jim—I can call you Jim, can't I?" Jim gave no encouragement to being thus named but Stu went on: "Don't get me wrong. The kid likes the outdoors. It's just me and Bettie... I guess we just never got used to it—can't teach him like you could.

And on a Sunday… Well, all I can say is he doesn't take to the church too well. You know his story, right?"

"Yeah, I heard," Jim answered.

"So, what do you say?"

Jim looked at him evenly for a few moments. The Constances were not bad people. Soft and city-like, but they had showed they had good hearts by adopting a troubled kid, however weird he'd turned out. They didn't harm no one by reading their books and leading the quiet life, unlike some of the jacked-up summer residents who were ignorant know-it-alls.

Against his better judgment he said, "OK. Just wouldn't want to take your money if the kid ain't interested."

"He'll be here the Sunday after the holiday then."

"Alright."

CHAPTER TWELVE

At 7 a.m. on the Sunday after July Fourth, Jim was sitting in a camp chair out on his dock staring at the lake mist burning off. If the kid didn't turn up he decided he'd just slob around all day drinking whiskey. He'd been busy enough recently. The week before there had been boats racing all over, fireworks in the night sky, stoned teenagers driving trucks at breakneck speed around the road. No human fatalities, thank the Lord. One of their dogs got run down. Glad they hadn't called on him to put it out of its misery. One of the city folk had the brass to shoot it. Maybe they weren't all soft.

Today all was quiet. Some of the summer people had already started packing up and heading to the cities. He could hear the distant drone of their trucks on the Three Mile Road.

Yup, today there was a feeling of entropy, of falling away, even the hint of fall in the mist burning off on the lake. Laramie pricked up his ears and now Jim heard it too, the squeaking of unoiled pedals on a bike. He turned and there down the unpaved road to the store came the Constance kid, wearing some blue denim overalls and a check shirt underneath. Perhaps Bettie had thought this was a kind of standard fishing garb. But even on a bike the kid had to be different. Not riding like a normal boy with somewhere fast to get to, legs pumping like fury, ass up in the air, but pedaling slow and reluctantly, like a Victorian gent out on a penny-farthing. He squeaked up to the store sidings and deposited the bike against the wooden wall.

Jim rose slowly. "Mornin'," he said.

The kid didn't answer but was patting down his pockets as if looking for something.

"You lost somethin'?" Jim asked.

Finally, the kid found what he was looking for in the bib pocket of his overalls and pulled out a small roll of cash held by an elastic band. He barely looked up through the mop of his hair as he thrust the roll toward Jim. "Here, my pa told me to give you this." His voice was a hoarse whisper.

Jim stared at him for a beat. "Keep the cash, kid," he said. "You pay after. If you don't take to fishin' we'll be back in an hour."

The kid's shoulders were slumped as if he already knew he was going to be a failure at it. Jim wanted to shout at him to brace up and stand straight but a better angel prevailed.

"OK, help me get fixed up," he said, pointing at the rods and bait pail and the cooler for the catch on the dock. The kid stuffed the money back into his dungarees without making eye contact as Jim climbed down the short ladder to the boat and took the equipment off the kid. He still didn't utter a word, nor did he show any inclination to follow Jim.

"OK, kid, you comin'?" Jim asked.

"What about the dog?"

Jim stared, surprised the kid had volunteered a question. "The dog minds the store."

"Can't he come?" Somehow knowing he was the subject of discussion, Laramie looked between Jim and the boy, ears pricked, tail working, pink tongue hanging out.

"Well, OK, then, he ain't no bother," Jim said.

Ed picked up Laramie somewhat awkwardly and handed him down to Jim and the collie circled his tail once or twice before going to the prow and taking up position as lookout. The kid climbed down quickly as Jim yanked the starter cord. The outboard cover of the engine might be rusty but the Yamaha fired first time and

Jim threw off the painter, twisted the tiller around and gunned the throttle. The boat described a wide arc away from the pier.

The kid had taken up position next to Laramie at the prow thwart and was rubbing his ears. "You fond of dogs, kid?" Jim asked, raising his voice over the outboard.

"Never had one." The kid was mumbling, but Jim could just make out his reply.

"Oh?" Jim said.

"Asked for one on my birthday, never got one."

"Your birthday was on the fourth?"

Ed didn't answer straightaway. "It's not my real birthday. No one knows when that is. The judge just chose it because it's a holiday near the date I was found." He glanced at Jim. "You know about that, I guess?"

"Sure. In '70." Jim left it at that. There was silence between them. Jim opened up the throttle and they crossed the lake to a lonely cove with a sandy banked area, lake reeds waving in the gentle ripples, the last of the mist hanging on the water but the July sun rising higher and already beginning to burn their necks.

Jim threw down the anchor with a dull plop and it caught on the bottom.

The kid was looking at him when he turned around. "Were you here in '70?" he asked.

"No, I was in Vietnam," Jim said.

This seemed to get Ed's attention. "You were in the army?"

"Marines. Part of the navy."

"You volunteered?"

Jim fixed him with a stare. The kid had sure opened up and he wasn't certain he liked it as much as the silent version. "They got me in the draft."

"You fought?"

"Some."

"Shot people?"

"Some."

"Dead?"

Time to change the subject. "This is a good place," Jim declared. "See the bottom?" The kid dutifully looked over the side.

"Sand. The bass love that, change their scale color to match it so they're well camouflaged. Plenty of critters flying around in the air and minnows in the shallows too." And, indeed, the boy could see the cranes and dragonflies flitting between the reed heads and below, in the golden, rippling light, the pulsing forms of small fish.

"Two ways of catching bass," Jim continued. "One on the fly, but that's for streams and running water, and then there's this. OK, let's set up. We'll have a rod either side. If you get a bite I'll come and show you what to do."

Jim opened the bait bucket and shooed Laramie away as he put his snout into it. He pulled out a wriggling pink worm and held it up so Ed could see it. "First things first—this is how we bait the line." He took the worm between one calloused thumb and finger and assertively thrust the wriggling body through the barbs on the end of the hook.

Ed was suddenly very pale. A tremor went through him.

"You OK, kid?" Jim asked.

"Y-you have to do that?"

"Sure. Can't have the worm slipping off. Got to get it well through the hook lest the fish just takes the worm and not the hook." He took another hook from his fishing vest and picked out another worm. "Here, you try."

But Ed didn't reach for the worm and hook. "It's still alive."

"Has to wriggle to attract the fish."

The kid still didn't make a move. "Here, this time I'll do it for you," Jim said. "Bit squeamish, ain't ya?"

Ed swallowed hard, his hands clenched, then his eyes rolled up and showed their whites.

Jim dropped the bait and hook and grabbed Ed by the wrists.

"Kid, what's wrong?"

Gradually the kid's pupils came back into view and his eyes came into focus.

"Jeez, sorry, Mr. Dove. Just got a bit lost there." He was panting.

"It's OK, kid, just take some breaths." Ed did so. His eyes still looked blank. The thousand-yard stare. Jim had seen it enough in Nam.

"Maybe we should get back," he said.

Ed shook himself, as if trying to slough something off. "I'm OK, really. It's just the worms…" He paused.

"What about them?" Jim asked.

"Just reminds me of something, is all."

Jim paused. "What, kid?"

Ed swallowed again and looked away over the lake. "I dunno. Just stuff from dreams I have."

"What sort of stuff?"

"Bad stuff. I guess like you and the army."

"Marines, kid."

"OK…" Ed swallowed before he went on. "Anyway, what happened when I was a kid… Sometimes it comes up, like with the worm."

"You don't have to talk about it, kid," Jim said, hoping to kill the conversation there and then.

Ed looked over the lake again. "Hits me sometimes. A picture, some words—when you're least expecting it…" He paused again.

Jim guessed this was more than Ed had said for months, if not years.

The kid took a deep breath. "Like now, I see that worm. It's hooked right through, wriggling in agony. Then the worm turns and looks at me, and it has my face."

Jim had packed some sandwiches and Cokes for the trip, not that he was expecting to be out there on the water for lunch, but just in case they got peckish, particularly if the kid skipped breakfast as customers sometimes did. He opened up the pail, took out one of the Coke bottles, banged the cap off on a thwart and thrust it at Ed. "Here, drink this—you'll feel better."

Ed stared at the Coke, then tilted his head back and chugged it, his Adam's apple working. He let out a sigh, whether because of the sugar rush or the release of tension Jim could not tell. Whatever, he had no intention of provoking another trip down the kid's memory lane. He detached the hooked worm and threw it back in the pail, shut the lid and pulled out one of the sandwiches instead.

"See, kid, no need to use worms. We can bait with bread and some of this corned beef. We'll use these hooks with lures. They flip about in the current. Attract the bass." He broke off some bread and meat, took another hook from his fishing vest and showed Ed how to bait the line. The kid seemed to calm a little now the worms were out of sight.

They settled with their rods, one on each side of the boat. Silence fell. The kid was staring north.

"What're you lookin' at?" Jim asked eventually.

"Just thinking, Mr. Dove, about Highway 11. My pa says it's more than two hundred miles away. But it feels like it's just over that mountain."

Jim followed his gaze. "Heard you were found over to Presque Isle. Far enough not to dwell on."

The conversation lapsed there. There was a tug on Jim's line and he reeled it in. In an hour each of them caught a medium-sized bass. Unusually, Jim let the two go, declaring them to be marginal-sized for eating. He certainly would have taken them home if he'd been alone, but there was something that made him think the kid wouldn't take well to witnessing him killing and gutting the fish.

They headed back when the sun was high and the fish would be at the bottom of the lake. Laramie and the kid sat together, the collie with his tongue hanging out, Ed staring north across the lake's expanse to where the distant white outline of the Sun Mountain Hotel sat under the lowering brow of Nakuset. He had fallen silent again and Jim couldn't read his thoughts about his morning out.

When they had moored by the dock, Ed shyly handed over the money. He shook his head and refused to take some back when Jim offered a rebate because of their lack of success. His brow furrowed. "We caught a couple. My pa said you should take it all, Mr. Dove—no refusal."

Jim eyed him for a moment. Good, the kid had an assertive streak after all. "OK, obliged then," he said.

Ed turned. "You know, you're kind of an odd kid," Jim said despite himself.

And then Ed looked back and smiled for the first time that day and said: "No odder than you, Mr. Dove." And with that he took the bike from where it leaned against the side of the bait store and, without a glance back, went his slow, squeaky way down the track toward Brantwood.

Assertive and lippy, Jim thought. The bike needed some oil; best to lay some aside for when the kid next came in for groceries. He wasn't really expecting to see him again for fishing.

But on Tuesday Stu was back in the store. "Say, Jim, Ed really enjoyed Sunday."

"He did?" Jim answered.

Stu smiled. "I guess he didn't say much. That's his way. But when he got back he was quite excited—well, excited for him. Bettie and I were wondering if you'd take him again."

"Didn't catch much."

"No matter, it's just the experience. My money's good, ain't it?"

It couldn't be denied the money was good.

"OK then,' Jim said. "Next Sunday. And here you go, some 3-in-One. That kid's bike needs some oilin'."

There was no more church for Ed. For the rest of that summer and the few summers after, he went out on the lake with Jim. And after the lake, it was the woods or helping out around the store. The Constances barely saw their adopted son for the two months they spent each year at the cabin. Perhaps both were relieved at the kid's long absences.

Unknown to them, he changed—changed beyond recognition in practical terms. The bookish introvert was still there, but now there was a connection to the outdoors, and, with it, a self-reliance. The kid proved himself an able backwoodsman. In time he could shoot the whiskers off a rabbit at 100 yards, was a better shot than Jim. The worm incident was forgotten for now. Dying and death were not triggers, yet… His first kill. He saw with equanimity the light ebbing in the buck's eyes as it bled out from his shot. The skinned and quartered carcass hung from a tree in a clearing held no terror for him. At Jim's instruction he painted the creature's blood on his forehead.

CHAPTER THIRTEEN

In the summer of 1979, after graduating from high school, Ed came up to Tranquility alone. Bettie had fallen ill and started chemo. Her illness had driven his father into a perpetual gloom. Stu was glad to wave his adopted son away. Ed was delighted to be free of the funereal air of Brookline. He spent the summer working at the store, gassing boats, serving in the shop.

By now, in addition to the fishing and shooting, he could bait and trap, use a knife and an axe, start a fire with a bowline, process an animal from head to toe, build a shelter, use bark and berries as natural remedies.

In time, he shunned even Jim's company. He trekked into the wilderness and camped out alone. He did it almost as a dare. There was no hiding in the forest. Everything was stripped bare, elemental. If the past should come, it would come to him here, he was sure.

The last trip had begun innocently enough. He headed to the northwest of the lake, down game trails untrod by man for years, if not decades. Occasionally there would be signs of vanished humanity: a spent shell casing, orange with age; a blackened ring where a campfire had been set; a brick standing on a rock in the middle of a stream. Otherwise, his kind had been erased from the green canvas through which he went. The only sounds were his hiking boots on the bed of pine needles.

In an unnamed clearing in an unnamed part of the forest he set up his pup tent and watched as the sun set at half past ten. The light held for another hour or so and the stars came out. It was the time of year when he thought of the Lot. Nine years had gone and none of its questions had ever been answered.

He looked to the north. Two hundred miles and change, but it felt so close. What was he? What was he doing out here? What waited for him here that he could find nowhere else? He sensed he was both far from and near danger. The darkness was in him—indelible. He had come here alone because *he* was the danger.

Sometime in the night he must have slept.

The cold woke him. It was yellow dawn. He was naked and shivering. He was not in his tent but lying on some long grass. The grass was damp, just like in that awakening on Highway 11 all those years before. But the light was that of the sun, not the stutter lights of emergency vehicles.

He was shivering. He sat up. He was in a forest clearing and the dawn chorus was loud in the trees. Sparrows, warblers, robins, and phoebes: a mazing cross-meshing of songs and calls sounded all around, warning of an intruder. The sound was all directed at him. He was the intruder. He did not know where he was, but wherever it was, it was far from his tent. He looked down at himself, bewildered. How had he come here?

His hunting knife was in one hand and something soft and sticky in his other. He opened his fist and saw that it was a heart: he stared at it, fascinated and disgusted. He tasted the iron of dried blood on his mouth. He forced himself to look at the object again: it looked like a deer heart. He felt a strange relief. Did it touch him then, like a cold finger to his own heart, the conviction that he was a killer?

He rose, stiff and white, like a corpse reborn. There was a spotting of blood on the grass of the clearing. The crimson on the emerald burned into his eyes. He looked up: the blood trail vanished into the pines. He followed it. After a quarter-mile he reached another clearing. There was no birdsong here. Nothing stirred.

A brown and white dappled mound lay in the middle of the open space. He approached and saw it was a ravaged doe carcass, its chest savagely cut open. He knelt in the tacky pool of blood by the deer. An impulse rose in him and he dropped his knife and with two hands placed the heart back into the gaping chest cavity, as if life might then return. A Bible story came to him: Solomon's lion. If bees could nest in a lion carcass and bring forth honey, could not the same come from this dead doe? But the doe's staring pupils spoke otherwise. Death was death.

After another hour he found his tent. His clothes were shucked off by his sleeping roll as if whatever had arisen in him in the night had unpeeled itself from the cocoon of Edward Burns Constance and left his shadow-self behind. A killer was what he was: naked, primal, deadly.

Not until the very end did he trek into the wilderness alone. Not until that day when all that was left to him was this killer inside. He had learned: nature held no darkness, only him.

On July 4, he used the phone at the bait store to call Stu to receive the obligatory birthday wishes, but his father didn't answer and he wondered if Bettie's condition had worsened. Jim had no use for him that day—the store was closed for the holiday. His boss was no doubt spending the day with a bottle of Beam.

Birthdays had always been uncomfortable days. He thought of the four stranger kids who, like him, would be celebrating this state-appointed anniversary. David, Carl, Catrine, and Shannon. All he knew of them was their names. He knew he had some special connection to Shannon; but what she had been, what any of them had been, was unknown.

A distance away there was the drone of vacationers' outboards on the lake. Later, as it got dark, there would be fireworks, but this arm of Tranquility was otherwise quiet. The only neighbors, the Sproules, were abroad. He spent the day fishing off the dock, then reading. But in the late afternoon, Jim's pickup nosed down the long gravel drive through the shadows of the pines and came to a stop in front of the porch.

Ed stood up and placed the book on the deck as his boss got out of the cab. He was carrying an object wrapped in oily rags. "Hey, kid," he said.

"Hey," Ed answered, eyeing the package in Jim's hands.

Jim looked at it too. "Brought you somethin'," he said, and handed it up to the porch. Whatever was inside the cloth package was weighty and metallic. Ed unwrapped the bundle and gawped. The gray mass of a pistol lay on the oilcloth.

By now Ed had studied guns and recognized it as a military-issue Colt. Its government serial number could be clearly seen, stamped into the metal above the right grip. "For me?"

Jim nodded. "Couldn't think of a better person to have it."

Ed looked from it to Jim. "This your Marine sidearm?" he asked.

Jim shook his head. "Not mine. Belonged to a friend: Sergeant Lenny Piazzola from Little Italy, NYC." His face wrinkled. It might have been sadness or just the last afternoon sun in his eyes. "Cong ambush in '71. Lenny went down first." He hesitated for a beat, as if remembering. "Anyway, sometime during the shootin' my rifle and sidearm were out of ammo, so I took Lenny's sidearm. He didn't need it anymore. Then the jets came over with the napalm. The treeline where the Cong were exploded. One of the finest sights I ever saw. When we got back to base no one worried about Lenny's sidearm. The US military bought millions of M1911s in its time. What was one lost in a paddy? It's nigh-on untraceable, that gun."

"I don't know what to say," Ed said.

"Nuthin' you need to say, kid. Just keep it to yourself. Stu and Bettie don't need to know about it."

Jim searched in the pocket of his parka and brought out a box of ammo and handed that over too. "Just wanted you to feel safe, you know?"

They exchanged looks, then Jim said, "Happy birthday, kid," and got back in the pickup, turned it around and headed back to the bait store.

When the call came into the store a month later, Stu told Ed that Bettie had only days to live. Ed had the Colt concealed in his backpack when he went back to Boston.

It was eight years since Jim had taken it from his dead friend's hand. It would be used once again. But not by Ed.

CHAPTER FOURTEEN

He was too old for the Children's Hospital now. He had a new shrink, Cowdray, who practiced out of a tree-lined street near Winthrop. Where Gant had all the genial eccentricity of a Doc Brown, Cowdray looked like a German scientist from an old war movie. Lean, thin face, aquiline nose, widow's peak. He always wore a starched, white lab coat. His appearance was reflected in his manner: precise, somewhat formal, and cold. And very knowledgeable about the very issue that had baffled every expert in the Apostles case: their memory loss. Unlike Gant, he was happy to discuss the science with Ed, whom he deemed old enough to at least hear the facts, even if he was, for the moment, beyond a cure.

So it was that Cowdray laid out the history of amnesia and coercive persuasion, from Nazi experiments to the American POWs tortured by the communists in the Korean War, right down to the adoption of these same techniques by the CIA's Project MKUltra, the mind control program that had run for twenty years between '53 and '73.

"What purpose was there behind this stuff?" Ed asked. He was both disturbed and pleased how Cowdray was so unguarded, almost empathically so, compared to the babying Gant, who had never touched on difficult subjects but skirted around the issues.

Cowdray quirked an eyebrow. "Why, to make the subjects of these experiments more... quiescent, shall I say. To control and subdue them. The hope was to perfect interrogation techniques. But some say it went further."

"Further? In what way?" Ed asked.

Now Cowdray did hesitate, as if he realized he was perhaps straying into forbidden territory. He cleared his throat. "Shall I just say that some of those experimented upon became susceptible to what I would call triggers?"

Cowdray's uneasiness only encouraged Ed. After hundreds of hours of one-way therapy sessions, it was now the psychologist who was on the hook. "What sort of triggers?" he asked.

Cowdray looked even more uncomfortable. "Well, in certain situations, prompted by actions, images, or even just plain words, something in their psyche takes over. They lose consciousness... act blindly, under the stimulus of those controlling them."

Ed stared at the shrink. He was thinking of all the playground incidents—then, more lately, the dead deer. The violence and hostility of the other kids had triggered the blackouts in the former incidents. But the deer? He'd brought his own brand of darkness to that party.

"Is there any way of guarding against these... impulses?" he asked.

Cowdray frowned. "Impossible to say. These blackouts you have experienced and the, ahem, unfortunate consequences, I think are your psyche overloading and responding to some unremembered trauma. The brain shuts down as it purges itself through violence. It's unusual but not unheard of. Look at the Viking berserkers, for instance: uncontrollable rage in a trance-like state."

"So what can I do about it?" Ed asked.

Cowdray turned to the window and the sun reflected off his eyeglasses. Now he did look like the epitome of one of those Nazi scientists. "We'll try some anger management techniques, of course. But ultimately the only way to overcome trauma is by confronting and defeating it," he said.

Ed smiled back grimly. Catch-22: the only way to solve the problem was to invoke it. He didn't think much of his chances if that was the only solution.

Cowdray held up a hand. It was near the end of their three-quarter-hour. Did he look relieved? "Anyway, this is just guesswork on my part. As I said, these experiments were just that—experiments. There is no actual proof that there are what might be called robot agents out there right now. There may be a simpler explanation for what happened to you, Ed. So let's concentrate on that, shall we? Accentuate the positive."

Ed tried the various therapies that Cowdray suggested but there was nothing the shrink could do about death. Bettie passed that early August. Cowdray told him to isolate his grief and put it to one side. But he found there was no need: he had detached from his adoptive parents long before.

Afterwards, Stu's bubble burst. What little remained of his bonhomie and 100-watt smile vanished. He became dour and silent. He spent longer and longer hours downtown at his offices, and the little time he was at home he hid in his study, curtains half drawn even in the bright late summer, hunched forward on his wood swivel chair, the Tiffany lamp casting a kaleidoscope of color over his sunken, jaundiced, and unshaven face. The pipe was always clamped in his mouth, but never lit. He wore a gray cardigan even on the warmest of days. He was always looking at his plans, but there hadn't been a mall opening for a good two years now. Ed wondered if he was drinking. If so, he went to some pains to hide it. There was never an empty bottle in the trash.

Stu neglected to go to church. Letters and circulars piled up on the hall table. Well-wishers appeared, then quickly disappeared, put off by Stu's spiritless conversation. The rejected included hopeful divorcées and widows. Their casseroles went uneaten. Ed figured Stu could have done with one of those women around the house, putting things to rights, pulling him out of his study, sharpening up his dress, which now consisted only of shiny pants and moth-eaten cardigans.

CHAPTER FIFTEEN

College loomed. Ed's disciplinary record at Brookline High was an improvement on the many elementary and middle schools he'd attended in the town and adjacent neighborhoods. His grades were exemplary, good enough for Northeastern. He excelled in the humanities and, perhaps because of some mystery of his heritage, Spanish. People sometimes commented on his dark hair and olive complexion. He looked more Hispanic than Anglo-Saxon.

He'd hesitated over a major. Law school was the ultimate goal. He wondered if law would explain something about this strange world he had been dumped into. What he needed was an understanding of now. In the second year of Carter's presidency the world was in churn: the Soviets had invaded Afghanistan, President Bhutto had been executed, Idi Amin overthrown, the Shah had been deposed and civil war had broken out in El Salvador. Things fall apart; the center cannot hold… He chose political science.

The terms of his adoption precluded a faraway campus. The distance between Brookline and the Northeastern campus on Huntington Avenue was barely two miles.

Though it had not been an issue these last four years, Stu was mindful of Ed's socialization issues. A touch of his old, blustering stepfather came to the fore then. He arranged a single room for Ed and said, "Screw the expense." Ed wondered at his generosity—the development business was clearly sinking.

Welcome Week at Northeastern was after Labor Day. Stu didn't volunteer to get the Volvo out of the garage and drive him downtown. The car had sat idle since that last trip from the hospital carrying Bettie's belongings. Ed was going to have to take the bus.

Stu saw Ed to the door, no further, then stared at his slippered feet.

"Well, here we are then," he muttered, just as he had done so often before.

"Yeah, I guess so," Ed said. He shook Stu's limp hand, picked up his suitcase, walked up the front path and turned left toward the bus stop, vowing that he would not be back that semester.

His first stop was the dorm at Stetson East. It was a nondescript gray brick-and-glass block. A number of cars were double-parked on the street outside, disgorging eager-looking freshmen, half of whom seemed to sport beards, tie-dyed T-shirts, and bell-bottom jeans. The resident assistant, a kid not much older than the ones moving in, stood behind the desk in the hallway with a clipboard. He had a name tag that read "Garval" on his white Oxford shirt and the buttoned-up air of petty officials with clipboards the world over. A sign read, "All Visitors to Register at Front Desk. Please Present Valid ID." It seemed even when you left home, rules followed you. Ed pulled out his billfold with his driver's license and showed it to Garval.

Garval consulted his clipboard. "Constance, eh? One of our more favored guests. Single room. Sixth floor." He handed Ed a key and a handout.

"House rules," he explained. "No drugs, no alcohol, no visitors, especially broads, after ten p.m." He gestured at the register on the desk. "Before that, all visitors in the book. Have fun."

"How could I not?" Ed replied.

He took the elevator to the sixth floor. The single room's window looked over Hemenway Street and Back Bay to Fenway Park. Though reception had been bustling with freshmen, these upper floors were quiet. Only an occasional echo of a voice or a door shutting came from the marble corridors below. Was he the only one on this floor?

He sat on the unmade bed and contemplated this new life, trying to steel himself for Orientation.

There was a sudden rap on the door, startling him out of his reverie.

Maybe Garval had forgotten something. He went to the door and opened it.

It was not Garval but one of the other freshmen from the lobby. A small guy about five six; curly, gingery hair; alert, pale blue eyes popping out of a pale face; a shit-eating, slightly manic grin that made Ed instantly suspect he was on something. He wore an AC/DC T-shirt advertising the latest album, *Highway to Hell*; ragged jeans that looked like they'd been mauled by a wild animal; and sneakers that had once been white, but were now graying. Ed immediately felt stuffy in his polo shirt and chinos.

The small guy popped out a hand. "Moss," he said.

"Err, Ed… Ed Constance," Ed replied.

"Pleased to meet ya, Ed." Moss jerked his head to the right. "I'm down the corridor."

"Glad there's someone else up here," Ed said.

"Right? It's like my father chose this residence because it's totally dead."

"Or maybe because of the RA."

Moss laughed. "Garval? What a prick, eh?"

"Moss your first name?"

"My only name. Given names are given by the man, you know?"

If Moss knew how Ed had come about *his* first name, his view would have been doubly amplified, but Ed wasn't here for the past. The future was now.

"So, what's your major?" he asked.

"Whaddya think? Political science. Gotta understand the belly of the beast, you know? You?"

"Same."

"Cool," Moss said. "Say, how about some weed? I got some pretty good Acapulco Gold in my room."

Ed really didn't want to get strung out on his first day. "Maybe later," he said. "I was going down to Krentzman for Orientation."

"You doing all that 'Go Huskies' shit?"

"Well, in for a penny, in for a pound, you know?"

Moss laughed. "OK, come on then—I guess it might have unintentional entertainment value."

So they went out together. The weather was early-fall beautiful, in the mid-70s. For Ed it felt wonderful to be alive, to be away from Winthrop and Stu. And, after the years of struggle at school, of being called "spic" and "alien," it felt good not to be picked on in a new place; to make a friend instantly and apparently without effort. The world seemed to smile on him that late morning.

They walked the five minutes through Opera Place to the crossing that led over Huntington Avenue to Krentzman Quad. The green space ahead was enclosed by three of the main university buildings and awash with freshmen, some sporting Huskies T-shirts, others Northeastern baseball caps. There were dozens of tables manned by faculty members with information on the various courses, seniors advertising every society and campus magazine under the sun, banners announcing coming concerts, talks, and sporting events.

The pathway was blocked by a smiling young woman handing out freshman wristbands. Ed worried that Moss would bridle at the idea of being forced to wear such a thing, but instead he seemed instantly taken by the girl and fell into an animated conversation with her. Ed took his wristband and snapped it on without complaint and left them to it. He joined the line waiting to pick up information from the political science faculty table.

It was hot in the line and the students in front of him were taking their time grilling the teachers. Ed's mood was changing—he felt a prickle of anxiety, always present in crowded places. He regretted not bringing some shades. A faint trickle of sweat made its way down his back. He pulled the collar of his polo away from his neck.

He looked away toward the steps leading up to the monumental facade of Ell Hall some fifty feet away. His gaze fell on an individual standing in the shade of the entrance looking in Ed's direction, although, given the crowd, he could have been staring at anyone in the immediate vicinity. It was a tall, young man, his eyes hidden by shades, dressed in black jeans and a denim jacket. The hair was slicked back and it looked, despite the fact he seemed of student age, like he had a widow's peak.

There was something about the intensity of that stare that made Ed think he was the one being observed. And then there was something, too, in the man's posture that felt eerily familiar. Ed went cold. He had seen that person before. A long time before.

Déjà vu is just a trick—brain electricity delaying the transfer of a signal from one temporal lobe to another and making it seem that what you experience now you experienced also a long time ago. But something told Ed this feeling was no trick of the mind. He knew the person who was staring at him.

It was one of the seven. David.

His vision tunneled so he saw no one else and now he was sure that David was looking at him because a smile broke on the other young man's face, a devil's grin, and he nodded slowly at Ed.

Ed took a step away from the line. His vision was going dark. He was going down into silence. He reached out in front of him like a blind man. His hand was seized and he nearly screamed out but then he heard a voice come from the void. It was Moss.

"Hey man, you OK?"

Another voice cut in. Maybe the young woman Moss had been talking to. "Is he going to faint? He's gone awfully pale."

Ed felt Moss's grip tightening on his arm as he swayed blindly. "Too much sun, I guess. Better get him back to the residence. I'll see you at three, OK?"

The girl apparently retreated. "Hey, buddy, how're you doing?" Moss asked.

"I'm OK," Ed muttered. All he wanted was his sight back.

"You better be. I got a date with Madeline later."

"It's OK, leave me."

"No way. You're coming back to my room and getting straightened out. Screw these lame-ass meet and greets anyway."

He took Ed by the arm and they retraced their steps across Huntington and Opera Place. Ed's vision started seeping back, but he still felt faint.

Garval was still in the lobby of Stetson East.

"What's the matter with your friend?" he asked Moss immediately on seeing them.

"Too much sun is all," Moss replied.

"Yeah, like hell. Looks like he's taken something."

"Jesus, do you have to be so hard-ass?" Moss answered. "Can't you see the guy's unwell?" He led Ed away to the elevator before Garval could reply.

The elevator whooshed up and Ed fought the sudden vertigo. The doors opened with a ping and Moss fairly dragged Ed down the corridor to his room and deposited him in an easy chair. It seemed he'd had time to fix things up a bit in here. There was a stereo and some posters up, a coffee table with rolling tobacco, rolling papers, and a small freezer pack of grass.

Moss filled a glass with water from the sink faucet and handed it to Ed. "Here, drink this," he said.

Ed took a sip and the cool liquid steadied his world a little as it slipped down.

Moss picked up one of the many albums littering the floor. Ed saw it was *Rust Never Sleeps*. Moss slid it onto his turntable and carelessly dropped the arm on record a couple of bars into the intro.

Then he got busy rolling a joint. "What happened back there?" he asked. He suddenly sounded sober and Ed found this more disturbing than the extroversion that had gone before.

Today was the day the past was meant to be over. But here it was again: it had been David on the steps of Ell, he was sure. But even as he thought this he began to doubt himself. Many times in the last nine years he had thought he had seen something, only to discover that his overheated mind had constructed a false connection. A remembered face that was not a remembered face; a place he had been before but could not have been before. Déjà vu. Gant and Cowdray had called it the same: PTSD. They avoided adding the word "psychosis," but Ed had done a bit of side research and discovered that hallucinations and delusions were common when both were present.

"I think I saw someone I knew. A long time ago," he answered.

Moss fired up the joint. "I'm guessing this person was bad news?"

"You could say that."

"You think they could be a student here?"

"Maybe. We're the same age." Ed didn't say the exact same age.

Moss passed over the spliff. "Like I said, Acapulco Gold. A vacation in smoke."

Ed hesitated. He wasn't sure if getting wasted was the best idea given his state of mind. He took a couple of exploratory puffs, coughed, then felt an almost contradictory sharpening of his senses and a mental drifting away. "Pretty good shit," he said.

Moss gave him one of those smiles. "Party time," he said.

An hour or so drifted. Another joint was passed. The sun angled across the room. Time appeared stationary. Moss rose once and flipped the album, then sat again.

The album ended where it had begun. Déjà vu. But now it was not the gentle acoustic "My My, Hey Hey (Out of the Blue)" of the first track but the thrashing, doom-treading three-chord rocker "Hey Hey, My My (Into the Black)." Neil Young admonished: "It's better to burn out than to fade away." The words went to Ed's very soul. The track seemed to go on forever and yet be over almost before it had begun. The album ended with the sound of slamming doors and screaming crowds.

Moss stood and took a denim jacket from the back of the door. Ed came back to himself, looked at his watch. It was a quarter to three. Where had the time gone?

"Got to split, man," Moss said. "You going to be OK?" The dope didn't seem to have made much impact on him. Ed, on the other hand, still felt buzzing, distant from himself.

"Sure. Got to unpack, you know?" he replied, standing up gingerly.

Moss gently fist-bumped his shoulder. "Attaboy. Say, maybe Madeline has a friend. We could go on a double date later?"

"That would be nice," Ed answered, but thinking he would like nothing less. It seemed very important to get back to his room and stay there until the next day.

They parted at Ed's door.

"See you later, then," Moss said and punched the call button on the elevator.

For years afterwards Moss was sometimes asked about the disappearance of his fellow political science student, Edward Burns Constance. A young man he had only known for a few brief hours and who, after that Orientation Day, vanished into thin air, much to the consternation of the university authorities, the police, and the missing persons unit of the FBI.

CHAPTER SIXTEEN

He didn't unpack. Just as before Moss's arrival that morning, he sat on the unmade bed and stared off through the window at Back Bay in the distance.

He didn't look at his watch again. An unspecified amount of time elapsed.

Then there came another knock on the door. Maybe Moss had returned. Maybe he had, indeed, brought Madeline and a friend and they were waiting outside. He got up stiffly, mentally trying out excuses to turn down a night out. He pulled open the door.

It was not Moss.

It was David.

He had not seen him before today for nine years—had not remembered him as anything more than a name. Yet he knew him as he had known him in that first glimpse at the Ell. Knew he was not a delusion. Knew what this young man had once been. Knew what he had been to him.

The boy had grown into a six-foot-plus man, towering a good three or four inches over Ed. He looked a lot older than his supposed eighteen years. As earlier, he was dressed in black jeans and a denim jacket, Ray-Bans now in the pocket of his check shirt. His upper body had filled out. Some stubble covered his sculpted cheekbones, marred by acne pockmarks. But the cold, furious eyes and nasty grin were the same.

David gave Ed a short, mock-playful jab. However innocent the gesture, it was not like Moss's playful punch earlier. He hit him hard in the shoulder, leading with a big signet ring on his middle finger.

"Do you remember me, Ed?" he asked.

Ed found he couldn't answer. The words stuck in his throat. He guessed his face registered shock. His hand was nursing his bruised arm. David took advantage of his momentary distraction and pushed Ed back into the room with one hand. Ed's feet skidded from under him; though he was strong, he seemed to have nothing on David.

"I guess you do remember." David smiled. His incisors were showing. He slammed the door to with his heel. He bunched a fist through Ed's collar. His fingers on Ed's neck felt like pincers.

He twisted the collar into a choke hold and got right in Ed's face. Ed could smell his aftershave: Old Spice.

"Guess you didn't think you'd see me again, eh? Well, guess again, kid. You can't lose the past."

Ed left off rubbing his shoulder, grabbed David's arms and tried to break his grip, but, though he had held his own in every playground in every school he'd attended these last nine years, it was like trying to detach steel vises. David's smile widened. There was a drip of saliva hanging from one of his incisors, like Dracula in the movies.

"I'm here to collect your debt."

"I don't know what you're talking about," Ed gasped. The pressure on his throat was unbearable. "Just let me go, will you?" His voice sounded high and strained.

It was coming back: the bullying boy, the helpless feeling he had when confronted by him back at the Lot...

"No can do," David answered. "You see, I have a job for you and refusal isn't an option. You and I have to move on. We got some exciting times ahead. Well, exciting for me. Less so for you."

"I'll call security," Ed managed.

David laughed. "Still lippy, eh? Well, there's a cure. 'See thou hurt not the oil and wine.'"

It was not the lack of oxygen from the choke hold that now edged Ed's vision with black. It was the eight words.

Only eight words.

Just like before when he'd seen him on the steps of the Ell, it was as if a lens aperture was closing in his mind. Where all had been bright, now the peripheries of his vision hurried into a pinprick. The darkness and silence were coming.

"You remember that at least," he heard David say from far away. The pinprick vanished. All was black.

He was no longer in the dorm room. It was night. He stood at the head of some stairs leading down to what looked like a basement. The sound of chanting children came up to him. *"A measure of wheat for a penny, and three measures of barley for a penny; and see thou hurt not the oil and wine."*

Then, just as he was about to go down forever to what awaited him, he was suddenly back from the blackness, rising to the surface, to the light…

He found David shaking his bruised shoulder. His head wobbled back and forth like a broken puppet's.

"Wake up!" It was David in a whisper. "There's someone at the door."

The room came back into focus. Ed found he was sitting on the edge of the bed. David loomed over him. He had let go of his collar.

"Tell whoever it is to go away," David ordered.

Like a zombie, Ed got to his feet and zigzagged to the door.

Garval was outside with his clipboard. He looked flushed; his brows were knitted. "OK, not a good start, Constance," he said, looking behind him at David. "First thing I said was all visitors to register, the next thing I see this guy walking past to the elevators. Spent the last ten minutes looking for him and there must be a dozen students waiting for their keys downstairs."

Ed just stared at him blankly, his brain hardly computing the words.

"Something the matter with you, kid?" Garval asked. He leaned in closer, waved his free hand in front of Ed's face. "You still on something? I told you about drugs. This guy your connection?"

When Ed didn't respond, he turned to David. "Let's see your ID."

"You gonna make me?" David asked.

"Those are the rules around here. The ID or I call campus security," Garval answered.

David grunted, reached for his billfold and showed Garval his driver's license, over Ed's shoulder. "We're just friends, you know. No drugs in here."

Garval ignored him. "David Krige, huh?" he said. "Well, Mr. Krige, if I see you around here again, you can be sure security will be here within minutes and then you'll have a few questions to answer. Maybe they'll call the cops, *capisce?*"

David stuffed the ID into his back pocket and glared at Garval. "OK, I get it. I'm going." He turned to Ed and gave him a look. Even in his spaced-out state, Ed could see the meaning: wait here, I'll be back. Then David brushed past him and was gone, leaving him with Garval.

"OK, Constance. I'm going to report this to the resident head," Garval said. "If I was you, I'd get myself straightened out before he summons you." He spun on his heels and followed David down the hall.

Ed slammed the door, stumbled into the bathroom and was violently sick in the toilet.

He cleaned himself up. His head was still spinning in two directions at once and he was cold all over. Half of him wanted to get out of the room immediately. Yet his deepest wish seemed to be to sit down on the bed again and wait for David to return.

He stared at himself in the mirror. The face of a madman stared back. But behind that mask he recognized someone—himself. With this self-recognition came a slow drift of returning awareness. What had just happened? What had David wanted from him? One conversation, one fragment from the Bible and he was like this? Nine years and five hundred hours of therapy and it took just eight words?

He thought of the police. But what had he got to report? David had simply visited; they'd talked. It was a breach of the dorm rules—hell, it was a breach of the adoption agreement, which forbade the kids from contacting each other. So what? The cops would laugh it off. Just a chance meeting. Even thinking of the police made him feel sick again.

He splashed more water on his face and shook his head. All he wanted to do was to return to the bed. But if he sat on it again, he was lost, he was sure. Some invisible hand would keep him there until David came back.

He had to fight that impulse at all costs. He had to move fast. No waiting, no luggage.

He opened the dorm door. The corridor was empty. He took his jacket from the hook, stumbled to the elevator and went down. There were a few kids waiting at the front desk. Garval was occupied with them and didn't notice him. No sign of David. He went outside.

The golden early fall sun on the leafy square was tarnished, a lustrous decay. He staggered out on to Huntington Street. The 39 bus was just pulling in and he boarded it, blindly handed over a dollar, was called back for his change and, unseeing, went down the aisle and collapsed on the back bench. As the bus headed west to Brookline, a new memory came. He was at the back of a yellow school bus, the evening light slanting through the windows, Shannon asleep on his shoulder... Shannon.

He remembered her.

CHAPTER SEVENTEEN

He had no recollection of the bus ride, or getting down at his stop, or the key in the lock, but suddenly he was back in the hall at Winthrop Road. He closed the door behind him. Stu would be at his office. It seemed a year ago since he'd left, but it had only been a few hours. The house gently creaked and settled in the September heat, enduring another lonely day in the sun. He went toward the stairs.

Then a voice came from the study. Ed froze.

"Who's there?" It was Stu.

"It's me—Ed." His voice sounded distant to his own ears, as if another person was talking in a far-off room.

Stu shuffled out into the hall in his carpet slippers. The gray stubble covering his chin matched the shabby cardigan, part of what he called his "den wear." His eyes were watering behind his glasses, whether from tears or the unaccustomed light of the sun shining through the transom, Ed couldn't tell. He had his pipe in one hand and a Ronson lighter in the other.

"Ed? Did you forget something?" he asked.

Ed shook his head.

"So what're you doing here?"

"I could ask the same."

"Just late getting off is all," Stu answered. Given his undress and the fact that it was by now late afternoon, this seemed unlikely.

"Something came up at Northeastern," Ed said.

Stu scrunched his eyes, reminding Ed of Mole in *The Wind in the Willows*. "Came up?"

"One of the kids was there," Ed mumbled.

"You mean *your* kids?"

"Sure, Stu, one of *my* kids. David."

"Oh—you remembered him?"

"Yeah, I remembered him alright," Ed answered.

Stu had inserted the stem of the pipe in his mouth and was trying to fire the Ronson up, but his hands were trembling and the lighter just sparked and didn't flame. He gave up and stuffed the pipe and the lighter into his cardigan pockets. He seemed as jumpy as a sack of frogs. He didn't meet Ed's eyes.

"What did he want?" he asked.

"I dunno," Ed answered. Now he was talking, another wave of dizziness threatened him. He braced himself against the doorframe of the study.

"Let's go into the study," Stu said, taking his arm. Ed wanted to refuse: he needed to get to his room and then get out of here. But he was weak as a kitten, and Stu led him unresisting into his lair.

As ever, the curtains were drawn, the air was stale and the lampshade cast its weird patterns over the desk and cabinets. A bottle of Smirnoff, half full, sat at the center of Stu's desk. An empty shot glass stood next to it.

Stu caught Ed looking at the bottle. "You guessed, didn't you?"

"Yeah" was all Ed could manage.

"Put the empties in the neighbor's trash. Not proud of that." He let go of Ed's arm, went behind the desk, and sat down abruptly on the swivel chair. He poured himself a stiff shot and chugged it back. "Maybe you could use some. There's a glass on the sideboard," he said.

Ed thought: spoken like a true drunk. Couldn't tolerate a sober person across the table. But Stu was right in a way: he needed something to settle his nerves. He went and picked up a glass, then sat in the chair facing Stu and poured himself two inches. He tipped half of it back, grimacing at the acrid taste and fire. The spinning world slowed a bit.

"So, what happened with David?" Stu asked.

Where to start? Ed wasn't going to tell Stu about the blackout.

"He talked about calling in a debt," he said.

"A debt?" Stu had been reaching for the bottle again, but now went very still.

"Yeah, a debt," Ed said.

Stu lowered his head. He picked up the bottle, but this time his hand trembled so much some of the vodka spilled on the desktop. "The debt," he sighed quietly. He stared past Ed at the window.

"You know something I don't?" Ed asked.

Stu swallowed. "I guess it's time I told you something."

Ed already felt cold fingers on his spine. "Like what?" he asked.

Stu still couldn't look at Ed. "About your adoption." His eyes had teared again and he removed his glasses and wiped at them with his cardigan sleeve. He swallowed and put the glasses back on. "It started innocently enough, I guess."

"What started?" Ed asked.

Stu didn't answer immediately but stared past him at a spot a few yards behind. "You know Bettie wanted a kid, wanted one bad," he said. "But it wasn't our idea to adopt you. We wanted a baby, for Chrissakes. You were already nine."

Ed felt himself sinking again. There had not been much love in Winthrop Road. Just a correctness, a ticking of the boxes. Christmas and birthdays delivered, but without joy. The discussions of grades. The lip service of encouragement. The lectures when the behavior was out of line. The "here we are thens" at each new school gate, each time with increasingly fixed smiles from Stu and Bettie.

"So if it wasn't your idea, whose was it?" he asked.

Stu picked up the Smirnoff bottle and stared at the label in the dim light before hitting himself with another shot. He grimaced. "Woodson Bates, the pastor at the church. Paid us a visit in '70.

Talked about your case. Well, everyone on the eastern seaboard was talking about it back then. Bates said that he knew some influential people who would be awful grateful if good Christian homes could be found for the kids… That these people would be generous in settling some money on whoever took them. Didn't of course specify who these people were. Well, Bettie and I just shrugged him off, said if we were to adopt we'd set our heart on a baby, maybe one from overseas.

"But it didn't end there. Turned out he knew my company was struggling and I had debts here, there and everywhere and there was a loan guaranteed on this house, and it was a big loan, believe me. That same evening when I was sitting here the phone rang and it was Bates again, and now Bettie was out back in the kitchen and wasn't around to listen, he laid out all that he knew about my problems, and in some detail—more like a banker than a pastor, truth be told. And he told me if I didn't want to be foreclosed I better reconsider his offer. There wasn't much sweet and reasonable in his tone, I can tell you. He told me, should I reconsider, not only would the debts go away but there would be enough extra to refloat my company.

"I guess I had a bottle in the desk even then. After he hung up I poured myself a good one and considered. I'd hidden my problems from Bettie, thinking something might come up to save my ass. All we had built, Bettie and I, was about to disappear and here was a magic solution. Long story short, I got up and went through to Bettie and you know how she was a little old-fashioned, how she went along with me on decisions? I said I'd been thinking, and it was selfish of us to want to have an infant when the children of that awful tragedy up in Maine were going without homes. How God would be displeased with our selfishness and that I had reconsidered Bates's proposal in that light. Well, she put up a bit of a fight, talking about the adoption agency we'd been involved with, the kids from Vietnam and Cambodia and all, but I wasn't for turning and in the end she gave up, as I knew she would, and… Well, things just unfolded as they unfolded…

"The money came in, a lot of it, and my debts went away. These payments were from some offshore clients I was supposedly about to build something for. Needless to say I never met them, no plans were ever drawn up, not a clod of earth was broken, but the money kept coming, enough to get me going again. I started thinking of new projects for myself. I began to dream again. Maybe dreamed too big. Took out new loans." He sighed. "Yeah, history repeats…

"Bates would ring every Sunday night asking after you and how you were doing. Always interested in your 'mental welfare' as he put it; always a big emphasis on that. Asked me if you had bad dreams and such—weird images. I guess I kept him and whoever was behind him happy for a few years till he had that stroke. Since then there's been another guy. Name of Vermeulen. Operates out of Pittsburgh. Says he owns a large part of my debt."

Stu poured and chugged another shot. He didn't invite Ed to partake and Ed felt dizzy enough from what Stu was telling him to not need any more.

Stu went on. "Vermeulen made it very clear: like Bates, he wanted to know how you were getting along. His questions got more and more specific. Down to what you had for breakfast, how you interacted with the other kids at school, what TV shows you liked… All of it. I asked him why he needed to know all this stuff, but he just laughed. Said one day it would come in useful. And I said, what day? And he said when it came to settle up. I told him I could handle my own affairs, but he just laughed again. By then I was half crazy anyway with Bettie in hospital and all those bills mounting up on top of the old ones. Then, after she passed, the bottle took over totally."

He stared at his shot glass. "This stuff makes you brave… foolishly brave. I told Vermeulen I wouldn't take his calls anymore, wouldn't do anything more for him; not a thing. The phone rang off the hook the next Sunday and the one after but I didn't pick up. Then the offshore clients stopped paying. There were no new deals. I was cut dead. My new partners scooted. Money dried up. Had to let my secretary go.

The firm went bust six months ago. The landlord repossessed the office. Thought I could fool you when you were home. Used to go out to bars all day."

Ed wasn't listening anymore. "You spied on me?" he said.

"I had no choice. Listen, Ed, I thought there was no harm in it. I needed the money. Then I thought I could cut Vermeulen off. I've never met him. He was just a voice on the phone. Cut him and hope he would just go away…"

"Do you know what David wants from me?" Ed asked.

Stu held up his hands. "No, I swear." But Ed knew he was lying. He guessed Stu knew a lot more; maybe everything. Maybe had an understanding with this Vermeulen despite what he claimed. Why had David approached him the very day he had left Winthrop? That seemed very convenient. So whatever happened didn't happen right in front of Stu? Don't shit in your own backyard and all that.

"What're you going to do?" Stu asked.

"Me?" Ed laughed. "You ask me that now? Well, I'm not going back to campus for a start, not with David around. Maybe I'll just hang around here until he shows and then the two of you can explain it all?"

Stu didn't answer. He looked shrunken. There was a drop or two of vodka left in his glass. He knocked it back, his knuckles so white on the glass that Ed thought it would shatter.

His silence was eloquent enough. Ed stood up. "I guess we're through," he said.

Stu didn't look up. "There's money in the safe," he said.

"I don't want your money," Ed spat.

He went out into the hall and upstairs to his primrose bedroom. He looked at it anew; it had never been a safe haven. Instead, it had been a cage for a laboratory rat.

There was a childhood trunk full of toys in the closet. He lifted it out and removed the battered Six Million Dollar Man toy, the Easy Money game, the Spirograph, the Magna Doodle, the pile of comic books. Yes, Stu and Bettie had not failed in generosity when it had come to spending Vermeulen's money.

He expected to find the oilcloth-wrapped Colt and the cardboard box of .45 ammo that Jim had given him at the bottom of the trunk.

They weren't there.

Below there was a cry from the study, like the howl of a cat, then a single, deafening shot.

Ed got to his feet. His vision was crowding in, just as when David had confronted him at Stetson East, leaving only a narrow black hole through which to see. He reached out for the wall, felt his way blindly out of the room and, holding the banister, went down the stairs slowly.

He hesitated at the study door. There was the smell of cordite in the air. His vision came back. He went in. Stu was still in the swivel chair, what was left of his head tipped back at an unnatural angle. His rheumy eyes stared at the ceiling, unblinking. He'd shot himself through the temple. There was a wide splash of blood and gray brain matter on the wall behind the desk and that end-of-firework smell in the air. The Colt lay under his hand on the table, his index finger still curled through the trigger guard.

A quote came unbidden into Ed's mind: "Nothing in his life became him like the leaving of it."

CHAPTER EIGHTEEN

Outside, he heard birdsong, the sound of a passing car, a child crying—no indication anyone had heard the shot. Life on Winthrop went on; no one cared that a man lay dead with his brains on the wall.

Should he call 911? Something told him summoning the authorities would be a big mistake.

His eyes fixed on the gun. He had come here to fetch it. Nothing had changed, apart from the fact that a dead man's finger was now in the trigger guard.

Stu's hand was still warm as he lifted it and the gun slipped the quarter-inch from the finger onto the desk blotter. The tiny movement disturbed Stu's body; it sank in the swivel chair and a little escape of gas came from the dead man's mouth like a sigh.

Ed pulled the gun toward him by the barrel. Some of the blowback from the shot had filmed it. He felt the warm damp and his fingers came away bloody. He wiped them on Stu's desk blotter. He noticed the papers scattered there for the first time: loan agreements, bank statements, default warnings, plans for malls that would never be made. There were doodles, ribbons of what looked like inverted tadpoles or musical notes drawn the wrong way around covering the tops of some of the plans.

He listened again. The silence was almost physical, touchable. He had a gun. He had a vehicle in the garage. But there were only nickels and dimes in his pocket. Stu's last words came to him. There was money in the safe. What was more, now Stu was dead, it was *his* money.

Once, through the door of the study, he'd seen his stepfather fiddling with the safe. It was set into the fake chimney breast behind the oil painting of the Highland scene. He went to the fireplace and took hold of the side frame of the painting and swung it out on its hinge. The safe was mounted in the flue underneath. Its dial winked at him in the sun falling through the half-open curtains and yellowing ivy outside. He knew there would be three numbers. Stu had never told him the combination. What could it be? Birthdays, birth months, birth years? Even if he could guess the numbers there had to be the correct movements: clockwise and counterclockwise. Clockwise, counterclockwise, clockwise? He was pretty sure that was right.

He took hold of the tumbler. He tried to calm himself. As far as he knew, there were unlimited chances, no lockout.

He started with the easiest: Stu's birth month, day, year. Nothing. Then Bettie's. Nothing. His: 07.04.61. A bust again. Then combinations of the house number, the phone number, the first six numbers of Stu's social security, same for his driver's license. Nothing again. Sweat beaded his forehead. He glanced at his Timex. He dropped his shaking hand from the tumbler and leaned against the mantel.

His eyes fell on the papers piled on Stu's desk. Maybe there was some clue there? He pushed himself off the mantel and went around the desk, careful to avoid catching Stu's dead eyes. He stared down at the papers, examining the scribbles he'd noticed earlier, but this time from what would have been Stu's perspective. The ribbons of inverted tadpoles were not as he'd first thought. Stu's handwriting had always been curiously upright, without curlicues. The doodles were sixes. Endless sixes. But now he looked closely in the mottled light and saw that there were points between the numbers so each number combo read: "66.6.6'"—endlessly.

It struck him like a mallet. He leaned hard on the desk, his arm brushing inadvertently against Stu's corpse. It was as if an invisible giant hand squeezed his heart. He gasped for breath. Blackness began creeping into the edge of his vision again. The floor gave way.

He was back in the place he had visited before: at Pierce, at Stetson... Six other upturned faces watched a flickering movie reel. Their heads were held in restraints at the backs of the chairs to which they were tied. So they must watch. The old-time film projector whirred quietly as it turned. There was no other sound. A funnel of light flickered on the gray wall. His head, too, was pinioned. He stared helplessly as violent images cascaded before him. A worm wriggling on a hook; Hiroshima and the burnt people; a public beheading; a razor cut across an eye; the furnace of a cremation oven; then an ocean of lapping blood... Then, point by black point, a shape was inching out of the sea, becoming whole, like the first lizard life on Earth. Details formed: the top half of the head was vaguely human: a mop of shaggy hair and deep-set human eyes; but from where his mouth and nose should have been burst a hundred snakes like an obscene beard. The rest of his body was human-shaped, but all of it was covered with more serpents, encasing his chest, arms and legs. Instead of fingers there were five more snakes, and both his feet were ganglions of serpent tails.

The name of the monster came to him: Typhon.

He was sovereign of all, the emperor of fear. All must obey their fear. He owned all who looked upon him.

He owned Ed.

Above the sanguinary sea something large and white began to form, and he saw it was a huge, horseshoe-shaped dam between two ocher cliffs. Water geysered from the sluices and tumbled into space and down to a river far below. He knew this place, every child knew it. It was one of America's greatest feats of engineering: the Hoover Dam.

The monster spoke and Ed knew they were the true names of the children: "The Angels of the Sores; of the Blood of Dead Men; of the Polluted Fountains; of the Sun's Burning Power; of Darkness itself; of the Death of the Euphrates; the Angel who will say, like Christ, *tetelestai*: 'It is finished.'"

The monster pointed at the vision of the dam, the serpents parted around its mouth and it opened its jaws agape like a python swallowing a cow and within was a ferment of more roiling serpent tongues, which spoke in the voice of the seven children: "And the sixth angel poured out his vial upon the great river Euphrates; and the water thereof was dried up, that the way of the kings of the east might be prepared."

The dam began to crumble like a sandcastle in the surf. A wall of water burst forth and fell toward him, crushing, atomizing...

Dark again and then the dream cycled back to a vignette, almost innocent compared to the others, but seemingly of great portent: a countertop in a domestic kitchen, a spreading pool of blood and what looked like a pink worm in the center—but, as the focus tightened, he saw it was a severed finger, cut above the middle joint.

There was a noise like thunder. Maybe the thunder of that wall of water going down the Colorado.

The thunder was rousing him.

CHAPTER NINETEEN

He woke up. The thunder was his heart. For a moment he panted, covered in sweat, utterly disorientated.

At first he had no idea where he was. An orange beam of light blinded him. Then he remembered. He was at Winthrop. The light was the late-afternoon sun through the crack in the curtains in Stu's study.

He was lying behind Stu's desk. There was a damp patch at his elbow: Stu's blood, not yet dry. He had only been out for an hour or so. But he had gone deep, very deep. First David, now these numbers, just as Cowdray had predicted.

He stood shakily and forced himself to look down at Stu's doodles again. The room spun and he braced himself on the desk. But knowing the attack was coming was power of sorts. The world stilled. He could resist. Good.

How had Stu known these numbers? He remembered David's words at Northeastern. Debts. Stu had owed these people everything. Owed and therefore been owned by them. As he'd reasoned before, why had David appeared the very first day, no, the very first *hour*, he was away from Winthrop? Was it a prearranged agreement with Stu? Ed's disappearance from his dorm would not be considered too strange; after all, many freshmen couldn't take the stress of the first day of college.

He was conscious of time slipping away. David would return to the dorm room the moment Garval was off duty, no doubt expecting to find Ed waiting like a zombie. And when he found Ed gone, his next stop would be Winthrop.

There came a creak of the floorboards outside the study and his heart jolted. Was he here already? The creak came again. He picked up the Colt, thumbed off the safety, pulled the slide back, chambering a round, and aimed it at the threshold. But now there was only silence. The house was just settling.

He went around the desk to the window, parted the curtains a little and peered out. The tree-lined street was empty.

He pulled the curtains firmly closed, then switched on the overhead. The safe combination was back at oo. He quickly spun it left, one full rotation past "66" and all the way back to it, turned the lock right to "o6", then left again through "o6" once, and back once more to the same number. The mechanism gave a click and the safe door opened fractionally.

He took a breath. He pulled the door fully open and looked inside. There was cash alright—a lot of it: three thick bundles of used dollar bills held together by elastic bands. Ed riffled through them: singles, fives, tens, twenties, and fifties, randomly intermingled. At a glance, thousands. A rainy day fund Stu'd kept from his creditors.

He set the money on the mantel. There was a thick, official-looking envelope at the bottom of the safe. He took it out. Inside were birth certificates, Bettie's death certificate, the deed to Brantwood—the cabin at Lake Tranquility. He saw that the deed was in his own name. Maybe that had been Stu's last attempt to protect an asset. The transfer had only been notarized two months before. Ed was now the proud owner of Brantwood and everything in it.

Pushed to the back of the safe was a small Woolworth's spiral notebook with a red cover. Ed opened it and flipped through it quickly. There were only a few entries: names and telephone numbers arranged alphabetically. Woodson Bates was there, but the number was not the one for the parish office that Ed had sometimes had occasion to ring. There were seven other numbers. One of them, Grant Fitzgerald, rang a bell. But why? At the back was Vermeulen. Area code 412. A Pittsburgh number.

He pocketed the notebook, the deed to Brantwood, and the cash.

He went back up to his room. There was a book of Auden's poetry on the night table. He picked it up. The bookmark was the scrap of paper that Gloria had given him nine years before with the El Paso number. It might have been an olfactory illusion, but did he still detect the faintest whiff of Youth Dew? He felt her vanished warmth, her softness as she'd hugged him and the furtive burrowing movement of her ringed fingers into his with this scrap. He pocketed the piece of paper.

Would she still be in El Paso? He had no idea how the FBI worked. She could have been reassigned several times since. Moreover, it would be midafternoon there. She would presumably be working? And, if she answered, would she even remember him?

He crammed some clothes in a bag, stuff he had rejected the day before but which was now his only choice, and added the Auden. Everything else was in his suitcase at Stetson East. He knew he would never see it again.

He carried the bag down, went to the rotary phone in the hall and dialed the El Paso number with numb fingers.

On the third ring a dusky voice answered: "Yes?" It was her. He heard a TV and a grumpy male voice in the background asking, "Who is it?"

Was this a terrible idea? "Gloria, it's me, Ed Constance."

"Ed?"

"Yes, do you remember me?"

There was a rustling and the sound of the TV diminished. The faint male grumbling continued.

"Wait a minute, Ed. I'll take this on the other line. My husband's watching something."

There was the sound of another receiver being picked up, footsteps, the original phone being placed back on its cradle. Then, after a few seconds, her voice again.

"Ed? How are you? What's happening?"

"Listen, Gloria, I've gotta make this quick."

"Why, what's the matter, Ed?"

So he told her. The conversation lasted some ten minutes. Even to his own ears his story sounded mad, though it was exactly as Cowdray had laid it out to him in his consulting rooms. When he finished he was half expecting Gloria to tell him to check himself back into the hospital.

"I know I sound kinda crazy," he said when he was through.

"No, Ed, you do not," Gloria said. "There was always something a bit off about Stu. And the adoption? The process was too slick. I didn't honestly think you were ready to go out into the world, but everyone in the chain just waved it through double-quick. Washing their hands of it, you know?"

"I don't know what to do, Gloria. Just a phrase or some numbers and I could go under again. My shrink warned me. What I can't figure is what's the purpose of this?"

There was silence for a beat and then the sound of Gloria drawing a deep breath. "Listen, Ed. Your shrink might be on to something— there have been rumors flying around in security service circles for years. They're mainly about the CIA. Operation CHAOS: targeting left-wing groups with brainwashing, making them commit atrocities, upping the ante against them. Some say the Tate murders were part of it." She paused. "It's just what I've heard, but you can't trust anyone, Ed. Not anyone."

"I found this notebook in Stu's safe. It has names and numbers."

"You got it on you?"

"It's right here."

"How many entries are there?"

"Just eight."

"OK, read them out."

Ed did so slowly, sensing that Gloria was writing them down.

When he got to Grant Fitzgerald, he heard an intake of breath.

"What's the matter?"

"Fitzgerald? That's my deputy director."

And now Ed did remember why he'd recognized the name: from newspaper reports. Fitzgerald cleaning up this or that, a big, heavyset man smiling wide for the camera as another crime syndicate boss was led off.

"Jesus," he said. "What're we gonna do?"

"First, guard that notebook with your life." She paused again, as if stiffening her resolve. "Remember Hennessey, my old boss?" she asked.

"Sure," Ed replied.

"He's the agent in charge down here. I can trust him. We've been in a few situations. He's gold. I'm going to talk to him and try to figure something out. Call here again at midnight EST tomorrow. OK?"

"Yes," Ed replied.

"Good, hang up now. We'll speak again tomorrow."

"Thanks for everything, Glor—" But Ed found himself speaking to dead air.

CHAPTER TWENTY

All was not well with the world this September 4 in a mock-baronial house on Hoodridge Drive in Mt. Lebanon. The seigneur of the house was Thomas Pieter Vermeulen, whose name had appeared in Stu's little red notebook and whose calls Stu had so imprudently ignored up until his demise.

Vermeulen didn't look like an archetypal criminal mastermind. He was no more than a slightly stooped, middle-aged man. His face, which hardly ever saw the sun, was unlined and exhibited not a follicle of hair on his skull, eyebrows, or chin; despite his babyish expression his gaze was a cold, icy blue behind the round spectacles he had favored since he was a young priest. He deployed the look often on the staff assembled in the control room of the mansion.

He had once been an innocent: a newly ordained, idealistic priest fired by zeal for the Mystical Body and a burning hatred of Jews and communists. There had been many like him then but the world of the ungodly had increased incrementally until the whole earth seemed overrun with unbelievers, lawless racial minorities, and left-wing beatniks. He had once dreamed of a new world order in which the Deicides and Ungodly alike were consigned to a living hell. He was not sure anymore if he would live to see that day.

His mission had begun on the evening of Monday, February 20, 1939. He had been in in the lobby of the Belvedere Hotel on West

48th Street waiting for the summons to meet one of America's most notorious fascist leaders.

Outside the hotel's front doors a massive crowd of protesters surged toward Madison Square Garden a block away. There were handheld placards that read "Stop the Fascists" and "No Nazis in New York." Zionist flags and the Stars and Stripes were carried side by side.

Inside the Garden were 20,000 members of the German American Bund. The thirty-foot-high portrait of George Washington at the back of the hall was flanked by the national flag and the swastika. A banner commanded: "Americans! Stop Jewish Domination of Christianity." It was the largest, and last, Nazi rally in American history.

Vermeulen was newly ordained at St. Joseph's seminary in Yonkers, where he had been considered one of the most brilliant minds of his generation. Nevertheless, the summons to attend the rally had come as a surprise: the inviter was no less than Father Charles Edward Coughlin of the National Shrine of the Little Flower in Royal Oak, Michigan. Coughlin was the biggest media celebrity of his day: his weekly radio broadcast attracted audiences of 10 million. He was also the inspiration for the fascist militia known as the Christian Front. In the last year the Front had boycotted Jewish businesses and openly assaulted Jewish-looking people.

Vermeulen had no idea how he had come to Coughlin's attention. He had been but one of many novices at St. Joseph's alarmed at the threat to the church by the Judeo-Bolsheviks who had, as the novices and their teachers saw it, come to dominate every aspect of American life. But to have been picked out by Coughlin was an unimaginable honor.

Vermeulen fairly squirmed in his seat in anticipation of the approaching meeting—pride was the deadliest sin but he could not shrug off the pleasurable glow that Coughlin's call had given him.

He was trying to distract himself from such thoughts by reading Coughlin's newspaper, *Social Justice*, which had been handed to him by one of Coughlin's lieutenants when he had announced himself.

In truth he had not gotten further than its headline: "Who Are the Enemies of Christianity in the US?"

Another of Coughlin's aides, a somber-looking man who would not have been out of place in a funeral parlor, approached.

The man leaned down and said quietly, "Father will see you now." He pointed across the art deco lobby. "Take the express elevator to the top." There were six elevators in the bank. Five served all the lower floors, but one of the central ones had an indicator only for the fourteenth floor. It was guarded by another somberly dressed henchman.

Vermeulen put down *Social Justice*, cleared his throat, ran a finger under his collar, then rose and went across the lobby, conscious that other Coughlin acolytes, less favored than he, were staring at him with envy. The aide at the elevator frisked him lightly, then gestured for him to enter.

He punched the button for the top floor. The doors closed and there was a moment of weightlessness as the elevator rushed upward. The bell in the car indicator pinged as he reached the fourteenth floor. The doors opened directly into the hall of a luxurious suite. The room beyond the hall was dimly lit by a couple of lamps and the flickering fires in the streets far below.

And there stood Coughlin. He was in front of one of the two floor-to-ceiling windows, looking down at the protest, the light reflecting off his round glasses. Like Vermeulen, he was dressed in a dark suit and dog collar. Vermeulen was surprised to discover his hero was short, only about five feet eight. From his voice on the radio and the telephone he had imagined him a giant.

Coughlin turned from the window and beckoned his visitor to come forward. The plush shag underfoot practically swallowed his brogues as Vermeulen approached. The Radio Priest had a round face and seemingly mild eyes behind the spectacles, but his eyebrows, which were spectacularly thick, were known to arrange themselves into thunderclouds when he was aroused, as he appeared to be now. In fact, his demeanor was not welcoming but stern, and Vermeulen swallowed nervously. Coughlin extended his hand. Vermeulen took it. It was surprisingly soft and plump, like a baby's.

"Ah, Vermeulen," Coughlin said. His eyes were cold and gray. "A terrible day for America when an innocent rally is attacked by Jews and communists."

Coughlin had a voice with that finely articulated, faintly anglicized diction so prized by radio stations in those days. The emphasis on "innocent" fell firmly on the second syllable.

Vermeulen bowed his head. "Nevertheless, it's an honor to be here, Father."

"There, there, no need to stand on ceremony," Coughlin said, now smiling a little. He went over to a sideboard, raised a decanter and quirked one of those famous eyebrows. "Drink?" he asked.

Vermeulen shook his head. "I don't, Father."

At this Coughlin outright smiled. "Well, maybe you will—in time." He poured himself a finger and lifted his glass. "To the Front," he said, then gestured to two armchairs either side of an ornamental fireplace. "Come, let's sit. Vermeulen is a Dutch name, isn't it?" he asked when they were settled.

"My family came over with Van den Broek in '48, sir. I'm from Appleton, Wisconsin."

"There are good Catholics in the heartland of this country," Coughlin said. He gestured at the window. "But here in the east? We know who reigns here. Who silences the voices of believers with their lies. The left-leaning Jewish newspapers and their communist friends." His brow furrowed even more. "I know I invited you to join our Bund allies at the rally tonight but this demonstration has led me to take a painful decision: I will not be attending." He saw Vermeulen's disappointment and held up a hand. "My bodyguards tell me it's too dangerous—they are habitually overcautious, but, given the high emotions and the chance of actual bodily harm, I, for once, have to agree."

He took a sip of his drink and stared into the middle distance for a beat or two.

"So, it comes to this," he said with a sigh. "Freedom of expression is dead. And if we cannot communicate what is actually going on in America, what hope is there? They speak of the persecution of the Jews, but what about the persecution of Christians? Silenced by the howling mob. Our cause is under threat." He paused. "Dire threat. Thomas—may I call you Thomas?—I have to confess I always thought this evening would end like this. I'm going to tell you a secret. I came to New York City not for the rally but for another purpose altogether." He fixed Vermeulen with those compelling gray eyes. "You are that purpose."

Vermeulen felt the same rush of pride he had felt at Coughlin's telephone call and when entering the elevator. He was sure he flushed.

Coughlin went on regardless. "We are of like mind. Our faith is under attack. Democracy is dead. We must choose another path.

"To that end I am about to tell you something that cannot be shared." He paused again to let that sink in, then went on, "A great movement, greater than the movement taking place tonight, is afoot. These American Germans think jackboots and swastikas are everything. But though Hitler began as a Catholic, he may very well now be an atheist. We will follow our own path to power." He paused dramatically. "God's sword is not only figurative. The Bund have no weapons, but we do. I'm talking 30-06 Springfields and Enfields, Browning automatic rifles, bombs. Loyal Fronters have gathered them. Many are National Guardsmen. When the time comes, and it is coming, Thomas, we'll take over the public utilities and the radio stations, round up the Jews and their cronies in Congress, take control of the Federal Reserve, and install a new government."

Vermeulen was both stunned and elated. He had never heard sedition uttered so baldly, or with such conviction.

A great roar as of a wounded beast came up from the street outside. A shadow passed over Coughlin's face at the noise.

"But there is a problem—a major one. I have influential friends: friends in Congress, in the armed forces, in the secret services. They tell me things. There's bad news—our movement is under scrutiny. The FBI is very interested in what we do. There are informants in our ranks. The weapons and explosives that have been taken from the armories have excited the agents. It could be, Thomas, that Roosevelt's lackeys will close in on us before we are ready."

"I hope not, Father," Vermeulen said.

"Hope may not be enough, Thomas." Coughlin paused again and once more smiled softly at the younger man. "I'm going to ask something very special of you, because you are a special soldier of Christ. Are you ready for an exceptional duty?"

Vermeulen swallowed. "Anything, Father."

"Good, but it will be a hard road, a very hard one. I have devised another plan should our current one fail. It must have no savor of the Front, bear no reference to the Mystical Body. In short, it will be untraceable to me. I have given the naming of this organization of which I want you to be a major part much thought." He paused again. "I hear the brothers were most impressed with you at the seminary. *Magna cum laude* in Greek."

"Thank you, Father," Vermeulen said.

"Then I hope you will recognize the name I have chosen: Typhon."

The Callicoon seminary syllabus had confined itself to the Greek New Testament, but Vermeulen had read his fill of myths and legends. Typhon was one of the deadliest creatures of mythology, with a hundred fire-spitting serpents wreathing his body. Only Zeus had been able to defeat him.

His expression must have given him away. "I see you approve," Coughlin said. "All those who look upon Typhon will fear and obey him. A new order will arise in America—the unjust will be cast out."

Then he laid out his plan.

It was nearly dawn when Vermeulen exited the Belvedere. Outside, the streets were littered with discarded placards, flags, and ripped items of clothing. Trash-can fires smoldered, filling the deserted street with acrid smoke. He stepped over a swastika banner and walked south toward Penn Station with a light step and, for the first time since leaving Wisconsin, joy in his heart.

Seven months later war had been declared in Europe. Anti-isolationist, anti-German sentiment swept the country. The Neutrality Act was repealed and on January 13, 1940, warrants were issued for the arrest of the Christian Front group known as the Nazis of Copley Square. A large quantity of arms and explosives was found in their possession. They were accused of planning an armed insurrection with the intent of setting up a dictatorship. Coughlin promptly disowned the group on the radio and in his newspaper.

The eventual trial of the seventeen Copley Square ringleaders descended into chaos, then collapsed as the defense attorneys filibustered, obfuscated, and dragged up obscure precedents under the Second Amendment. After several months the trial judge died, necessitating a retrial, but this never happened. The seventeen were exonerated and their arms returned. Coughlin performed a volte-face and trumpeted their release in *Social Justice*.

But on December 7, 1941, the Japanese attacked Pearl Harbor, and four days later Nazi Germany declared war on the US. A patriotic outpouring followed. The Christian Front were damned for their pro-Nazi sympathies and vanished.

Shortly after the declaration of war, Thomas Vermeulen had renounced holy orders and disappeared from the world. His last act was to steal seven Bibles from his sacristy.

Vermeulen was barely seen in public again, but the Bibles would resurface: they were found with seven children by a Maine highway on a June night in 1970.

Every year on October 25, Vermeulen had left the house, walked down the broad, tree-lined avenue to the public housing projects at Hoodridge Court and used the pay phone there to call a Royal Oak, Michigan number. The twenty-fifth was Coughlin's birthday. The Radio Priest continued to serve at the National Shrine of the Little Flower, but his days on the radio were long over: he had been drummed from the airwaves in the anti-Axis sentiment after Pearl Harbor.

The Christian Front was gone, but, as Coughlin had promised, another organization had taken its place. Typhon had been born out of the Front's collapse.

The twenty-fifth of October, then, was the day that Vermeulen imparted birthday greetings and received instruction from his leader. Typhon's aims were the same as the now proscribed right-wing organizations of the thirties: the downfall of Judeo-Communism, to be achieved through false-flag operations intended to incite troublesome minorities into an uprising; the destruction of the government by insurgents; the reestablishment of law and order under a right-wing, Christian dictatorship. The soldiers of this new militia were not adults, as they had been in the time of the Bund, the American Nazi Party, the Klan, the Silver Shirts, and the Front, but the children Vermeulen and others had assembled in hidden locations around the country.

It had taken decades to reach this point, far longer than Coughlin and Vermeulen had anticipated. Fundraising amidst extreme secrecy, the establishment of headquarters, the creation of the hidden camps in the wildernesses around America, the stockpiling of arms and munitions, waiting for the kids to be old enough... all had meant a delay of thirty-one years. Vermeulen's youth and part of his middle age had gone during it. Sometimes he had despaired. His faith had wavered, but not his hatred. That last, alone, had kept him going.

Now the day had finally come for the 1961 Maine intake. If he had qualms about using innocents to die doing God's will, he had subsumed these concerns to the pressing realpolitik: sacrifices had to be made to preserve the Mystical Body and ensure godly leadership.

But the operation that was to begin with Edward was not what it once would have been. Three decades ago Coughlin and he had shared a vision: seven acts of terror that would shake America. "The Angels of the Sores"—an anthrax attack on the New York subway; "of the Blood of Dead Men"—contaminated blood spread throughout the Boston public health system; "of the Polluted Fountains"—nuclear waste in the water system of Chicago; "of the Sun's Burning Power"—a truck bomb of agricultural fertilizer, diesel fuel, and other chemicals to be exploded outside a crowded federal building in Oklahoma City; "of Darkness itself"—a smart-bomb attack on the Oakland Air Route Traffic Center causing a radar blackout and the chance of a midair collision; "of the Death of the Euphrates"—the blowing of the Hoover Dam; "the Angel who will say, like Christ, *telestai*, 'It is finished'"—a nuclear warhead detonated in the Twin Cities...

Well, that had been the plan. Things had changed with the death of the first two children. Then Coughlin had insisted that David be taken out of the pool. Why had he done that? Had he begun to harbor doubts about Vermeulen? Was David's elevation so he might ultimately replace Vermeulen himself? A brainwashed child in place of the leading scholar of his generation at St. Joseph's? A man described as "quite brilliant" by the fathers there? No, however compromised the Maine mission, before that day came Vermeulen intended that some of the original plan would be carried out. It was no longer possible to imagine the world in flames. No more Kristallnachts, no more Nazi banners lining the streets, no jackboots. The scale of the operation had had to be curtailed.

Still, even as things stood, thousands might die thanks to Edward. That might be enough to show all those doubters he had not lost his touch. After Ed, there was still Shannon, Catrine, and Carl. It was a bonus that two of them, Edward and Shannon, were either entirely or partly from racial minority parents.

Reprisals, race riots, and an uprising against the government would follow. The National Guard and the army would restore order. Then *become* the order. Dictatorship established. The left wing and minorities subdued, then eradicated.

Edward would reach the dam in a week. The legend of Edward Constance, America's most notorious left-wing terrorist, was already established in notes left behind at Winthrop Road and, if all went to plan, in the luggage he would leave at Northeastern.

But David's call this midafternoon had brought yet another delay—he had fallen foul of some university functionary in mid-extraction. The guy had almost called security. David was going to have to wait until later that evening, when the said functionary went off duty, before going back into Stetson East. He was confident that Edward was zoned out enough to wait for him. An annoying but not terminal delay. Vermeulen withdrew to his quarters and awaited events.

Stu's number had been tapped by Typhon for nine years. The listener in the basement started recording the conversation between Ed Constance and Gloria Gonzalez a few seconds in. He knew Vermeulen would want to hear it right away, so he reached out for the special phone connected to his private rooms.

Vermeulen showed a couple of minutes later. The Operator stared fixedly ahead, trying to avoid Vermeulen's gaze as he listened to the tape.

After it finished, Vermeulen said, "So Edward has escaped. Where is David?"

"With Carl. They're parked in the Back Bay area waiting for the building manager to get off duty at five."

"Get them on the radio."

The Operator made the connection on the two-way and handed the transceiver to Vermeulen.

"It's me," he said without prelude. "The target is no longer at your location. He's gone back to Winthrop. Pick him up after dark and settle with his stepfather while you're at it. Over."

He cut the connection without waiting for an answer.

Vermeulen paced the room. "So, Constance kept a notebook, did he?" he said to himself. His expression was now something between sphinxlike and terrifying.

He took off his glasses and polished them on his tie. His ice-blue eyes stared away at the backlit map of the United States that stood against the wall in front of them. There were various colored markers winking on the display.

His mind made up, he went to a regular phone, lifted the receiver and dialed the dedicated number of Grant Fitzgerald at FBI headquarters.

There was a dull ringing tone for a few seconds before the phone was picked up and a gruff voice answered. "Who's this?"

"You know perfectly well who it is," Vermeulen answered.

There was a deep sigh at the other end. "How can I help?" Fitzgerald answered without enthusiasm.

"It seems we have a problem with one of your agents. The one we had assigned to Edward Constance before she got a little too nosy. You remember her?"

"Gonzalez? What about her?"

"It seems she shared her Texas number with our boy and, guess what, he called her just now. After nine years."

"Why?"

"Let's just say he's scared and on high alert. He slipped through our clutches just as we were beginning the operation."

"Ah," Fitzgerald answered. "That's bad."

"I have a couple of people who can sort it out. Edward is in... how should I put it? A suggestible state. He'll succumb again. But unfortunately there are other problems."

"Oh?"

"Number one is that Stuart Constance appears, contrary to instructions, to have kept a little notebook. There are significant names and numbers in it. Your name and my name, for example, and now Gonzalez is aware of that fact."

"That's very bad," Fitzgerald said. He sounded fully engaged now.

"Isn't it? Gonzalez is now a major risk. She's going to have a chat with her superior. I believe that would be Special Agent in Charge Hennessey, wouldn't it?"

"Yes, that's right; we assigned him down there at the same time as her."

"I seem to remember Hennessey was quite reliable up in Maine."

"He can be counted on. What do you suggest?"

"A little accident for Gonzalez. Tonight, please. After all, the border down there is pretty dangerous, what with all the narcos and people traffickers."

"I think I can arrange that."

"No, Fitzgerald, you *will* arrange it."

"And Constance?"

"After my boys take him, we'll assess him. He may no longer be any use to us."

"You seem to be losing agents rather quickly, Vermeulen."

"The program was sound. After all, it was devised by your cousins in the CIA. This part of Operation CHAOS can still go ahead, but with fewer participants. Edward just didn't take to the program as well as, say, a few of the other homicidal maniacs who were on it."

"Mind control is hardly the most reliable MO. We nearly got in trouble at the Manson trial."

"But no one believed those crazies, did they? Now they're all behind bars exhibiting the behavior everyone expects of them, thanks to the special oatmeal or whatever it is we provide for their daily sustenance. No, no one will ever believe them, just like the Weathermen and that poor heiress of yours, Patty Hearst. You see, Fitzgerald, the system works. All we need to do is sort out this little problem and we can be on our way again. Please don't stand on ceremony." And with that he hung up.

CHAPTER TWENTY-ONE

It was just after six. Ed slipped the Colt into a windbreaker and took the car keys from a hook inside the pantry door. He went to the garage. The Volvo station wagon, Stu's former pride and joy, was showing its age now, the odometer nearly around the clock. Given that Stu's profession was, basically, ripping down old buildings and replacing them with new, it seemed odd that he had kept an affection for the old jalopy. Ed unlocked it, turned the ignition and backed out slowly. He got out, then shut the garage door silently so as not to alert the neighbors. He left the house unlocked. He was not coming back and, as Stu had told him, he didn't own a stick of it anyway.

Ed drove cautiously down Winthrop to the intersection with the freeway. Traffic was light into the city. He went past Harvard, then, as the road became Huntington Avenue, the faculty buildings and dorms of Northeastern loomed up. They were still packing up things from the freshmen's fair on Krentzman when he passed. He watched that promise of a future he now would never have as it disappeared in the rearview.

CHAPTER TWENTY-TWO

It was a warm early evening in El Paso and the AC was running in the suburban ranch-style house Gloria Gonzalez, now Gloria Santiago, shared with her husband. They had decided to extend the holiday by a day. *Happy Days* was on the TV and Juan didn't like interruptions. The phone call that afternoon had been enough. As a sales executive, his whole life was phone calls, and on his day off he switched off from them, and even from his wife. He had failed to notice Gloria's preoccupation after the call, or how she had spent the rest of the afternoon.

He cursed when the phone rang again.

"If it's that kid, tell him to call back tomorrow like a normal human being," he said.

Gloria went out to the kitchen and picked up the receiver. She came back two minutes later. "Juan, it's the office," she said. "We got a tip-off. Child trafficking at Lejana. They're calling in extra agents. Don't wait up for me." She strapped on her gun belt, then picked up her purse.

Juan waved her off. It was just getting to a really funny part with the Fonz.

The abandoned farm was called Casa Lejana. It was far out in the desert, surrounded by arroyo and scrubland. The Feds had been watching it for weeks. It was thought to be a hub for child trafficking across the sparsely populated borderlands with Chihuahua.

There were three black sedans at an intersection of the dirt road ten miles south of I-10. It was dusk, getting full-on dark. SAC Hennessey was not present, but his deputy, Fuentes, was. He ordered the agents to put on FBI-labeled bulletproof vests and baseball caps and proceed cautiously the last half-mile to the isolated ranch. The agents went to the trunks of their cars and started strapping on their vests; a couple armed themselves with carbines. Gloria made to do the same but Fuentes held up his hand.

"Not you, Gloria. Stay here and monitor the radio."

Gloria put the vest back in the trunk with some relief. She wasn't too sorry not to be hiding out in the scrub with the other five. Lying prone in a possibly snake-infested arroyo was not her idea of fun. She leaned on the side of the sedan as the five other agents crept into the now-total darkness toward Casa Lejana.

A crescent moon beamed down and a coyote howled far off. The sudden call had prevented her thinking about tomorrow, when she was going to seek a private meeting with Hennessey and reveal what she had learned from Ed. Her pulse accelerated at the thought. Her career depended on whether Hennessey believed her or not.

She shook out a Salem and was about to light it when she heard a car approaching from the direction of I-10. It was coming with no headlights. The only building out here was Casa Lejana. She eased the clip off the holster of her sidearm as the vehicle crested a low rise and came into view in the moonlight. She let out her breath when she recognized the outline of another government-issue sedan. A Crown Vic, just like the others. It was approaching with only side-lights, rocking up and down on the undulations of the track. It was just more agents joining the operation. She wondered why they hadn't radioed ahead.

The sedan pulled up next to her. She was surprised to see that Special Agent Hennessey was the sole occupant. These days he was rarely seen on field operations. He got out as Gloria slipped her cigarette back into the pack.

"Hi, Gloria," he said.

"Good evening, sir."

"Have the others gone on?"

"Some twenty minutes ago."

"Child trafficking, just like the old days," he said.

Gloria thought he looked a little sad standing there in the moonlight. She cleared her throat. "Actually, sir, now you're here, there was something I wanted to discuss with you."

Hennessey looked down and pulled something out from inside his coat. She saw it was a Luger with a six-inch silencer on the barrel. He leveled it at her.

"I know," he said and, with something like regret, shot her through the forehead.

Later, when they had rounded up the people smugglers, who had not after all gone by Casa Lejana, but who had passed very near the Crown Vic parking site, one was found to have a weapon of the exact same caliber as the one that had shot Gloria. There was powder residue on the trafficker's fingers. He swore at trial that the gun had been planted on him by the arresting agent, but the jury was not convinced. He was just another profiteer of human misery who had turned his gun on a lone female agent when challenged. Though he was a foreign national he was sentenced to death under federal statute. Because of the then moratorium on federal executions, he was serving a life sentence at USP Terre Haute when he was fatally stabbed by another inmate in the showers.

The life of Gloria Gonzalez was honored on the Wall at Quantico and at the El Paso Field Office.

CHAPTER TWENTY-THREE

Vermeulen returned to his office in the ten-bedroom baronial in Mt. Lebanon. The medieval theme of the outside of the house—turrets, crenellations, and Gothic arches—was repeated inside in the monastic austerity of his personal quarters. The furniture was heavy oak and unforgiving—there was not a cushion, or throw, or even a mirror in sight. The diamond-paned casement windows were deep-set and narrow as if in expectation of a siege. The only embellishment to the suite was the stained-glass inlay of a monstrous creature, a being with a hundred serpents emerging from its head, feet, and talons, in one of the windows. Typhon. Father of Hydra and many other horrific creatures of mythology. And Vermeulen's current creation.

He wondered at his pride. The original sin. It had been his weakness, even at St. Joseph's. If he had been asked about his faith, he would have struggled to answer. Perhaps he had lost it many years ago. Christ would not have approved of what he had done in his name. But Coughlin had taught him well: the meek do *not* inherit the Earth.

The stained-glass window along with a number of unread sixteenth-century leatherbound Latin books on the occult were there as dressing should the place ever be raided—an unlikely event given the friendly relations between him and the local law enforcement agencies. He was aware that the British occultist Aleister Crowley had espoused what he called a Typhonian system of magic, and his works were also represented on the shelves, they too for misdirection if the worst

138

happened. Typhon? Half-crazed occultists, nothing more. The books he had once cherished in the seminary were long gone. Not a smidgeon of his Catholic past could be seen.

The only gesture to modernity was an internal rotary phone: the same device with which the Operator had summoned him an hour or so earlier.

He sat heavily and stared at the granite blocks of the wall. The conversation with Fitzgerald weighed on him. It was true, things had not gone well. The funding for Operation CHAOS, the CIA's plan to infiltrate and to discredit left-wing organizations in the USA under Johnson and Nixon had once been more than generous, but now the money had dried up. The operation was under congressional investigation and many old allies were running scared. Before he went, Director Helms had ordered all papers relating to MKUltra destroyed. So, at least the kids from the Lot and other sites would never be associated with it.

The deputy director's words earlier had stung him. Only Edward, Shannon, Carl, and Catrine were left to carry out the mission. On Coughlin's orders, David had been deprogramed years ago. But Vermeulen sometimes wondered if it was that easy to strip away the conditioning. David was a psychopath, through and through.

So four of the original seven were left operational—barely enough to stir the cataclysms that once would have changed the mindset of the entire country. The operations had all been scaled down from the original vision, bar Edward's mission to the Hoover Dam. The dam might be enough, but Edward, it seemed, had grown a mind of his own, was telling tales to federal agents; maybe, if he had recalled his past, he might have stashed evidence somewhere that could compromise everything. From now on it would be a binary decision: terminate him if he could not be brought in, continue with the mission if he could. There were no shades to it.

Vermeulen had never entirely trusted Stuart Constance, despite the latter's huge debt to Typhon. His refusal to take Vermeulen's calls had proved Vermeulen's instincts correct. It was good that he had doubled down on insurance: the phone tap on Winthrop Road had been in place for a long time and, in addition, in the last year a tracker had been fitted under the offside rear-wheel arch of Stu's Volvo. It was linked to Rockwell's Block-I GPS satellite, which had just been launched. Typhon had invested heavily in Rockwell and as a result benefited from privileged early access. Despite the downgrading of his operation, Vermeulen still got to play with all the new toys. The result was the pretty backlit map in the Mt. Lebanon headquarters, which would not have shamed NASA Mission Control in Houston.

Despite the high-tech setup right in front of him, or maybe because it was so new and therefore unfamiliar, the Operator was more focused on listening in for any further activity on the Winthrop line than viewing the tracker map. It was only an hour after Ed's departure that he finally stretched, yawned and noticed the marker had moved on the backlit display and was now approaching Seabrook, New Hampshire.

He hastily picked up the internal phone.

"Constance's vehicle is on the move, sir," he reported.

"Where are David and Carl?"

"Brookline, sir."

"Well, Constance has given them the slip. Tell them to follow him. Two cars. They're to wait for an opportunity. If there's any resistance, any whatsoever, they are to terminate him. Otherwise they're to bring him to the rendezvous. Understood?"

"Yes, sir."

"Also, get hold of Washington Street. Tell Smith to send an officer around to Winthrop Road. An anonymous tip-off. Possible gunfire noise from inside. See if he can arrange it to look like a homicide. That way if the worst comes to the worst the cops can pull Constance in and we can deal with him in custody."

"Right away."

The Operator was quickly on the radio to David.

"He's heading north on the interstate. You're to follow. Tracker's working. Over."

"Shit," David answered. "We're on our way."

The Operator frowned. Comms would be a problem. David and Carl would soon be out of radio range. Though *he* could see what was going on, David and Carl would have to stop and phone in for information. No matter, he was pretty certain that Ed was heading to the Constance cabin up on Lake Tranquility. Where else could he go?

Despite his goof with the tracker, which he was sure Vermeulen would not forget, his boss at least would be pleased with that information. Tranquility was pretty much a dead end. With their skills, David and Carl wouldn't have too much of a problem cornering Edward. Then it was up to Constance if he was going to cooperate or not.

CHAPTER TWENTY-FOUR

It was 300 miles and just over five hours to Tranquility. Traffic was mainly back to the city after Labor Day. His eyes were as often on the rearview as on the highway in front as dusk fell. The road rose up and down the undulating hills of New Hampshire. Headlights came on behind. On the crests it felt as if you could see miles forward and backward in the twilight.

The Colt sat heavily in his windbreaker pocket. He'd not found the box of ammunition, so, aside from the one that had taken care of Stu, there were seven rounds left in the magazine. He realized in hindsight that taking the gun had been an error. When the cops finally discovered Stu they might wonder where the suicide weapon had gone. In fact, when they discovered Ed's bloody fingerprints on Stu's blotter, they might start wondering where the *murder* weapon had gone. Every law enforcement agency up and down the east coast could be looking for the powder-blue Volvo.

He tuned in to WBZ. No news of a suicide or homicide in Brookline. Maybe one isolated incident didn't warrant a news story? The media fed on stuff like the dozen homicides in Roxbury in the early months of the year. If it had been discovered, the death on Winthrop Road was no doubt accounted small beer.

Such thoughts occupied the five long hours. It was around eleven when he approached Brantwood. With headlights on high beam, he drove down the old, familiar track from the logging road. The gate leading to the Constance and Sproule cabins was locked. He used his key on the padlock, then went down the track. It was a cloudless night, lit up by the stars and a crescent moon. At the bottom of the track the woods fell back. The lake stretched away. The silhouette of Nakuset rose like an arrowhead in the distance.

At midnight tomorrow he would make the call from the pay phone at Jim's store. There was a whole day to kill before then. If things didn't work out with Gloria, the border was not far, but his chances of getting across it and then staying across it without some fake ID were slim.

He found the key on the lintel over the front door, unlocked the cabin door and breathed in the slightly stale scent of the house. It had been only two months. There was a Coleman lamp hanging on a hook by the door. He lit it and looked around. A shrunken orange, blue with mold, sat on the dusty side table in the hall. He must have forgotten it when the message arrived that Bettie had only days to live and he had raced back to Boston. He placed the book he had brought from Winthrop next to it.

He'd decided he wasn't going to fire up the generator. For one, he wasn't going to be here long. Secondly, the noise would mask the approach of another car.

The door to the living room creaked as he pushed it. The lamplight cast wild shadows. He went to Bettie's desk by the front window overlooking the lakeside, opened a drawer and took out writing paper, an envelope and a ballpoint. He wrote quickly. It was a true account of everything that had happened that day: the encounter with David, the threat and his blackout, Stu's confession, how he had taken the gun from his stepfather's dead hand. It would not be enough to exonerate him should someone wish to pin Stu's death on him, but maybe someone, someday, would look at it and put two and two together and not blame him for what happened next.

He sealed the message in the envelope and then went back to the longcase clock in the hall. It was silent. It had not been attended to since the summer before last, Bettie and Stu's last at the cabin. He opened the case, slipped the envelope between the pendulum weights and relocked it. Then he hid the key. He bookmarked and replaced the collection of Auden on the side table.

Next, he went to his bedroom out the back. There was a bunk bed and sports pennants and film posters on the wall: Raquel Welch in a deerskin bikini in *One Million Years BC*, *Star Wars*, *A Clockwork Orange*. He levered up the loose board under the bunk bed and took out one of the books from his hidden cache. It was *The Anarchist Cookbook*.

He went through the kitchen and got the boathouse door key. He exited into the night and listened. A screech owl called. No sound of another car. Out here, you could hear them half a mile away. He crossed the gravel yard and unlocked the door of the boathouse. Everything he needed was on the workbench: dusty old bottles, rags, kerosene, and gas.

He had just finished making the Molotov cocktail when the night lit up with headlights approaching from the logging road. His heart leapt into his mouth. He killed the Coleman lamp, picked up the Colt, thumbed the safety and racked a round. He aimed the gun out the boathouse window at the gravel track leading down from the gate. He wasn't certain what he was expecting: an anonymous sedan or a police cruiser. There was the blaze of headlights straight into the boathouse, and then, as the vehicle swung around and came to a stop in front of the cabin, he saw it was Jim Dove's beat-up Chevy pickup. Jim was peering at the cabin and the Volvo suspiciously; Laramie was beside him on the bench. Ed let out a sigh of relief, uncocked the gun and tucked it away. His hand was trembling.

Jim said something to Laramie, picked up his rifle, then got out of the cab slowly. He went up to the Volvo, then looked around.

Ed called out softly, careful not to startle him. "Jim, it's me, Ed."

Jim lowered the gun as Ed came out of the boathouse.

"Hi, kid," he said. "Saw some lights over here as I was turning in. Thought it might be trouble." He gestured at the Volvo. "Stu with you?"

Ed took a breath. "Stu's dead, Jim," he said.

Jim stared. "Dead?"

"This afternoon," Ed said.

"What happened?"

"He shot himself."

"Shot himself?"

"Yeah, Jim. He used this." Ed drew the Colt from his windbreaker. "Remember it?"

Jim stared at it for a beat. "Yeah, I remember," he said quietly. "Won't the cops be looking for it?"

"The cops aren't involved—at least not that I'm aware. I didn't call the emergency services."

"Jesus, why not?"

Ed let out a sigh. "I'm not sure you're going to believe me."

"Try me."

"OK. Long story. Some weird shit happened today even before Stu capped himself." He held out his arm. The white wristband with "1979 N Welcome Week" printed on it was still on his wrist. "Today was my college orientation day. I was in a line waiting to pick up some information when I saw this guy staring at me. He looked really familiar. Like I knew him well. Then something clicked. It was David, one of the kids from... you know... back then. The shock did something to me. I came over faint. A friend took me back to the dorm, tried to calm me down. But later there's a knock on the door and it's David again.

"We faced off unnecessary, but then—this is the weirdest thing—he just said a few words and I was gone, Jim. It was like some spell—I was totally zoned out."

"Son, you feeling alright? You're sounding kinda crazy," Jim said.

"I said you wouldn't believe me. But I swear—this is the truth. I could be there still if the building manager hadn't come up and interrupted us. David split, but I knew he'd be back. And what he wanted me for was some really serious shit. I went home to fetch the gun."

"Why?" Jim asked.

"I figured I was going to shoot him—that's how I was feeling, Jim. But when I got home, Stu was there. Turned out he had only been pretending to go into the office all these weeks. The office didn't exist anymore. He told me he was bust.

"I told him about David, then he kinda broke down and confessed. He said he'd been in the pay of some people who'd been watching me. He acted as their spy: reported back on everything I did, like I was some kind of experiment. We argued, then I left to fetch the gun. But when I got to where I'd stashed it, it wasn't there. He must have found it. I'd never believe he had the guts to kill himself…"

"I guess he'd hit rock bottom," Jim said.

"You could say that."

"But why no cops?" Jim asked.

"Because of what Stu told me. The adoption was all rigged. Everyone was in on it. I have this notebook with Stu's contacts. One of them is the deputy director of the FBI, for fuck's sake. You tell me one reason why Stu would know a person like that."

Jim shook his head. "I don't get it. Why're they interested in you? And why is this David acting like some kind of enforcer—isn't he in the same boat as you?"

"One, I guess whoever is behind this, they picked David out. He's now one of them. Second, it seems we all had some deep conditioning when we were kids. It's buried deep, but when it's triggered we won't know what we're doing. We're just going to go out and do bad stuff."

"What kind of stuff?"

Ed fixed Jim with his gaze. "Like blow up things."

Jim shook his head. "That's not possible. You'd need explosives."

"These folks have them, Jim. With the deputy director on board I'm guessing they can start wars. A truckload of explosives is no big deal."

Jim took a deep breath. "I don't know what to say, kid."

"I just need someone to believe me."

"Oh, I believe you alright. There's nothing about the government that surprises me. We're just meat in their machine."

"Listen, Jim, there's one other person I can trust: that agent I told you about that looked after my case to begin with, Gloria Gonzalez."

"I remember. What about her?"

"I called her just before I left Boston. Told her everything. She said she might be able to figure something out. I have to call back at midnight tomorrow. I was going to use your pay phone."

"And you were going to stick around here until then?"

"Didn't have another option."

"You could have come over to the store and discussed things."

"Jim, you don't have to get involved in this."

"Seems to me that I already am, what with that gun."

"You told me it's untraceable."

"Maybe, maybe not. If these people really are as powerful as you say, they can do anything, frame anyone, buy a judge, buy a jury, buy an election, buy the whole friggin' country. There's no obstacle. You have a gun that killed a man. If they wanted to, they could pin you with murder."

"I guess they want to take care of things themselves rather than involve the police. Otherwise there would be an APB on the Volvo and I doubt I would have gotten here."

"They know about this place?"

"Jim, they *own* this place. At least they did, before Stu signed the deed over to me a few months ago."

Jim looked back up the dark driveway. "Well, they're not here now. As far as they know, you could have taken off in any direction." Then he frowned. "Unless…" He went to the pickup, laid down the rifle and picked up a flashlight. He went back across the gravel to the Volvo.

"What're you doing?" Ed asked, following him, but Jim ignored him and knelt at the near wheel arch of the station wagon and shone the light into the recess.

"You told me these people are connected," Jim said. He ran a hand under the arch. "An old navy buddy of mine is into spook shit—tells me the intelligence agencies and military have trackers linked to satellites nowadays."

Apparently, he found nothing under the first arch. He went to the offside front, then the rear, and repeated the process on the driver's rear arch. On his first pass there he did find something. He pulled hard and brought out a small black metal box, ends of tape flapping from it. He held up his discovery to the light. It was mud-spattered, insectoid, and menacing, with a winking green light and small antennae.

Jim contemplated it with some repugnance. "Well, look at this."

He took it to the dark lakeshore and, like a quarterback throwing a Hail Mary, bowled it high into the night sky over the lake. It disappeared with a plop some fifty feet away. Tiny waves rippled into the shore in the Chevy's headlights.

"OK, that's one problem solved," Jim said. He turned to Ed. "Listen, kid, they'll be on their way. We can't stay here. You'll have to make that call from somewhere else. They'll know you got a ride out of here if we leave the Volvo. Get up to Dickson Camp. I'll join you there after I've gotten some supplies, OK?"

"You know you don't have to do any of this?"

"I do, and we already discussed it, OK?"

"OK, and thanks, Jim."

"Don't thank me until we've figured a way out of this mess. Hang tight." With that, Jim got back in the pickup and hit the ignition, then turned back up the track.

Ed watched him go. Dickson was an abandoned logging camp with derelict Quonset huts some five miles north. Was there anything left that needed doing here? Suddenly it seemed his preparations might not have been necessary. Jim might have another way out for him.

Ed went back into Brantwood. He replaced the boathouse key, then, on a whim, he unclipped the freshman wristband and placed it on the side table in the hall next to the book he'd put there earlier. He locked the house and replaced the key on the lintel above the door.

It took a half-hour to reach Dickson. The Quonset huts, left over from the war, were brown with rust. He killed the engine and wound down the window. You could hear the silence.

After another half-hour he heard the whine of a transmission from the south and the Chevy appeared. Ed got out of the Volvo as Jim pulled up next to him. He could see the bed of the truck was now laden with a two-man canoe, rucksacks, two Winchester .30-30s, fishing tackle, camping gear, and what looked to be enough supplies for a week.

"OK, let's beat it," Jim said. They took off in convoy, the Chevy leading, the Volvo following. They went in the direction of the border at St. Zacharie fifty miles away. The road was another one given a strange name by the logging magnates: the Golden Road. But there were no pots of gold along it, only plenty of potholes. It looked like it hadn't been maintained since the previous winter. Culverts stood proud of the road surface and log fillers had been added to bridges where the grounding had been swept away. These obstacles required inching over. It took three hours to travel forty-five miles. The scenery in the headlights was the same: the forest, broken by moonlit waterways and lakes with occasional glimpses of the distant mountains, not a car ahead or behind.

Five miles short of the border they came to the first settlement: Dole Pond. Here there were a few cabins, a maple syrup manufactory, and a bait and tackle store not unlike Jim's.

It was now the small hours of the morning. They drove past the settlement toward St. Zacharie and onto a forestry track. After a mile, Jim signaled and stopped and Ed pulled up behind him. The two of them got out and looked around at the circle of dark trees. "We'll sleep in the vehicles. Go on in the morning," Jim said. "You look exhausted, kid. I'll keep first watch."

Ed didn't feel like arguing. His day had begun in his bedroom at Winthrop had taken in Stetson East, Krentzman Quad, the dorm again, and back to Winthrop and what had happened there, before this marathon journey north. He was dead on his feet. He lowered the Volvo front seat and was out like a light.

It was dawn when he woke. Jim had started a fire and was brewing coffee. He handed Ed a bag of biscuits. "Best to chow down; we have a long wait," he said.

After they'd eaten and shared some with Laramie, Jim got back into the pickup and slept for a few hours. Ed walked up and down the track a ways with the dog. There was nothing to see but the track and the trees. Meanwhile, his head was racing. His whole life appeared to pivot on the coming conversation with Gloria. The hours before midnight seemed very long.

Around midday, Jim woke up; they relit the fire and ate some pork and beans, then Jim scuffed out the fire. They killed a few more hours before Jim told Ed to reverse the Volvo into the treeline.

He was already picking up branches and throwing them over the Volvo as Ed got out. "We don't have to do this too good," he said. "When they find the car they'll think you dumped it and skipped across the border on foot." When the Volvo was pretty well buried in vegetation, they got in the pickup.

"Where we going?" Ed asked.

"Back south a ways—you'll see," Jim answered. He told Ed to slide down in his seat so he was hidden by the dash. He retraced their route. They saw only one logging truck and a couple of jeeps loaded with fishermen heading away from the lake after the holiday.

By now it was late afternoon. They turned south toward Seboomook, where there was another small settlement by a dam. There had once been a POW camp here in the Second World War, for Germans captured in North Africa. The internment area had long ago been bulldozed and redesignated the township's wilderness campground. Today there were no tents. There was a pay phone outside the campground store.

Jim drove the pickup down a rutted track to the east and parked by the lake. It was a muddy, reed-ringed shore. A black band of conifers ringed the lake. The peak of Katahdin, cloud-free for once, stood lit like a golden beacon to the northeast in the late light. The true wilderness began here.

"I reckon we're far enough ahead of them," Jim said. "We'll make camp and go back to the pay phone at twelve."

Ed wasn't sure. It seemed a long time to midnight. His unease was growing by the minute.

The two men pitched the tent on the lakeshore but didn't light a fire. Jim produced some MRE, which they ate cheerlessly. The night settled around them. The air chilled. At 11.30 they left Laramie behind at the camp and set off the mile back to the campground store. At Jim's insistence, they didn't use a flashlight but navigated the path by the light of the crescent moon and the stars.

The lights were off in the store, just one security light in the yard. It was silent. Ed waited by the Bell pay phone, watching the seconds as his Timex crawled to the hour. His heart was in his mouth as he picked up the receiver, quietly announced a long-distance call and then, on the operator's instruction, loaded the machine up with dimes and rang the El Paso number.

The phone rang about half a dozen times. Then it was not Gloria but a man who answered.

"Yes?" The man's tone was abrupt. Maybe it was that irritated partner of hers. It was late, after all.

"Hello," Ed said hesitantly. "I'd like to speak to Gloria Gonzalez."

"Who is this?"

Ed wondered if he should hang up, but Gloria was his only hope. "I called her yesterday," he replied. "We had an arrangement to talk now."

"Wait a minute," the man said. Ed could hear a muffled conversation. Was he fetching Gloria? Then the first voice came back.

"Am I speaking to Edward Constance?"

Ed went cold. He looked at Jim, who stood by in the dark. Ed covered the mouthpiece.

"What's wrong?" Jim whispered.

"It's a guy."

"Where's Gonzalez?"

Ed shrugged.

"Let me hear," Jim said and leaned in, then nodded for Ed to uncover the mouthpiece and go on.

"Yes, this is Constance," Ed said.

"Mr. Constance, this is Special Agent Gene Roscoe with the FBI. We were hoping you would call. We have some questions for you."

"I don't understand—where's Gloria?"

"She can't come to the phone right now," Roscoe replied.

"Why not? We had an arrangement."

It seemed Roscoe now covered the mouthpiece at his end. A muffled exchange, longer than the first one, was just audible.

Then Roscoe was back. "Mr. Constance, I have some bad news. Agent Gonzalez lost her life during an assignment yesterday."

Ed went cold. "What're you talking about? I spoke to her just that afternoon."

"I'm sorry, this must come as a—"

Jim snatched the receiver from Ed's hand and slammed it back onto its cradle. Unused dimes rattled into the coin return. Ed stared at them sightlessly.

Jim shook Ed's shoulder. "They're going to trace the call. We gotta get out of here."

Ed just continued staring at the Bell logo on the fascia of the booth. Gloria was dead. The phone at Winthrop Road must have been bugged. He had as good as killed her.

Jim pulled at Ed's parka sleeve. "Ed, we gotta go."

Ed came back to his senses. He wiped away the tears. There were still no lights on in the campground store. The call hadn't woken the proprietor. They went in a stumbling run through the darkness to the lakeshore. They arrived at the camp minutes later. Laramie barked excitedly at their approach.

"Shh, boy," Jim said, calming him. The dog was instantly silent. The two men listened. There was only the rush of the wind in the reeds and the call of a far-off loon. No sound of a car on the track.

"OK, let's get out of here," Jim said. "We'll leave the pickup here. They're only looking for the Volvo."

They broke the tent down and loaded their gear into the canoe, then launching it onto the still, dark waters of the northern reaches of Moosehead Lake. It was nearly one in the morning, but the crescent moon shone down. Tonight, though, it did not cast a silver path but only a sickly yellow light. It was the kind of moon that looked like Mr. Punch in the puppet show: cruel jutting chin and devil's forehead.

They struck out in the dark waters toward the black wilderness and North East Carry.

CHAPTER TWENTY-FIVE

David and Carl approached Brantwood an hour after Jim and Ed had left. They were in two government-style sedans. When they'd called Mt. Lebanon at five, the Operator told them that the tracker had not moved from the vicinity of Brantwood for a few hours. Ed was caught in a rathole. He might, however, be armed. The cops who had been to Winthrop Road had reported that Stu's suicide gun was missing.

But when they approached the cabin there was no powder-blue Volvo on the drive or in the carport. The cabin was empty, though there were signs that Ed had been there recently. They hurriedly drove over to the nearest pay phone: coincidentally, the one at Jim's bait store. The fact that the place was deserted didn't surprise them given that it was the end of the holiday.

Vermeulen was quickly on the line. The tracker, accurate to a few hundred yards, still pointed to the immediate area around the lake. Ed must have discovered it, discarded it somewhere nearby and taken off in the Volvo. In Mt. Lebanon, Vermeulen unfurled a large-scale map of Somerset County on a table. He saw the logging road leading to St. Zacharie.

"He must be heading for Canada on the Golden Road. Get after him." Given Edward's head start, he could be almost in Quebec by now. Vermeulen's jurisdiction was less established in Canada than it was in the United States. Things could be arranged over there but it was more complicated.

There was nothing more to do apart from wait. It took another twenty-four hours for more news to emerge.

It was just after midnight when the rotary phone he'd used for Fitzgerald rang. Vermeulen picked up the receiver instantly.

It was Hennessey from the FBI field office in El Paso. A call from Constance had been traced to a store a few miles short of the border, at a place called Seboomook.

Vermeulen hung up. "When David and Carl call again, tell them to get to Seboomook stat. And wake up our man in Quebec and get him over to the St. Zacharie gate. If they intercept Constance he's to be returned here alive."

CHAPTER TWENTY-SIX

Jim and Ed paddled into a small side creek near North East Carry. The moon provided a little light. They didn't bother setting camp, just threw down a groundsheet and a tarp over a branch.

They slept for four hours. In the gray light of dawn, they dressed in waterproofs and carried the canoe and the supplies over the track to the West Branch of the Penobscot. The river was thirty yards across at this juncture, still sluggish after the summer drought. They paddled northeast. In one or two places the canoe grounded on shingle and the two men got out and dragged it; in others, cascades forced them onto the porterage paths. Laramie paddled in the shallows and roamed to either side. The blackflies and mosquitoes of the height of summer were largely gone. If it weren't for the backward glances the men constantly made it would have seemed to an outsider as if they were on an early-fall hunting expedition.

By evening they had reached Chesuncook Reservoir. Like Seboomook, it was another reservoir dammed a century before for the spring log run. There was an unincorporated settlement with all of ten permanent residents, none of whom appeared actually to be in residence this evening. The boarding house, which went back to the days of Thoreau, was locked and unlit. There was a small, grassy graveyard in a spruce clearing and the headstones of some two dozen of the pioneers who had once made this wilderness their home.

Jim got out the fishing tackle and they cast until they got a couple of brown trout. Tonight they risked a campfire. They cleaned and gutted the fish, then skewered them on spruce twigs and cooked them.

"It's quiet," Ed said, only to fill the silence.

"Maybe they've lost us," Jim said, then stripped the white flesh of the trout from the wood with his teeth and chewed ruminatively.

Ed wasn't so sure. Roscoe was no doubt one of Fitzgerald's men. They would have traced the call to Seboomook. Their operatives would by now be heading to the area. But there was comfort in the thought that the North Maine Woods consisted of 3.5 million acres with nothing man-made but the unpaved roads and a few of these tiny settlements. Those who passed through the region in canoes or on foot were virtually untraceable.

The elation of having momentarily escaped whatever was coming after him was short-lived—he still had no future. Stu and Bettie were dead. Gloria too. All that was left was Jim, Laramie, and the canoe. A tiny bubble of safety in the vast, dangerous universe.

"Hey, kid, where you gone?" It was Jim's voice. Ed realized his eyes were closed and his fists clenched.

He came back with a start and looked around at the darkening lakeshore. The spruce twig and trout were quite forgotten in his hand. Laramie looked at him, his head cocked to one side in the way dogs have when unneeded food might be offered.

Jim was opening the top of a clear plastic gallon container full of a frothy brown liquid. "Looks like you could use a drink."

"What is it?" Ed asked numbly.

"Sap beer, kid. Made with birch. It'll put hair on your chest."

Ed took the container and tilted it to his lips. Bitter. Bitter as wormwood. But good. He swallowed. A thin film of peace settled on his mind.

The lake was calm. The rising, laughing treble of loons came from afar. The stars came out and then the crescent moon. Tonight it looked less sinister than the night before. But there was a black band in the northwest, another front coming out of Canada; it would get cold later. At least the night wouldn't be full of the last mosquitoes.

Jim pulled out a joint and fired it up with his Zippo. The odor of White Widow filled the air. A shooting star arced over. It reflected exactly in the mirror of the lake, so for a second up seemed down and down seemed up, and heaven and earth were indistinguishable. Laramie let out a little whine.

Jim offered Ed the joint and he took a toke and shivered. All was right but at the same time not right. He stared at the woods and thought of his last camping trip. The problem was not with nature—nature did not care one way or another for man. Man had enough evil on his own.

He realized the weed was too strong, was taking his mind away. The stars spun in reverse polarity for a moment, as if time was going backward.

"This feel right to you?" he asked, as much to break the silence as anything.

Jim didn't answer straightaway but stared at the face of the moon in the still lake. "For now. Not many know the place we're headed tomorrow."

"You haven't told me where we're going."

Jim's teak-like face split into a fractional grin. "Oh, if I told you now you wouldn't believe me."

Ed shrugged. His old friend occasionally put on this mystique.

"Yeah, it'll be as good a place as any to camp out, figure out the next move," Jim went on. "No one can find us there."

He paused, then continued. "You know, I love the woods but I fear 'em equal. It's mostly been forgot, but they're ghosts here. The Wabanaki that hunted and lived here. Just arrowheads and odd little clearings where the winter camps stood—all that's left. And once or twice, since you don't see 'em much anymore, wolves that look at you like they were half dog not so long ago and you wonder maybe a generation or two they *were* dogs around the Indian campfire, waiting for the bones from the hunt.

"No, sir, never far, the ghosts. Sometimes up here"—he tapped his forehead—"when I'm passing through in winter and it's colder than a witch's tit, it rises 'bout seventy degrees in my mind. Suddenly I'm sweating and I'm back in Nam." He paused. "I guess it's the trees telling me that's where we'll all go—they'll own me one day, when I'm bones."

He threw the roach into the fire and watched it turn to gray ash. "No, I don't guess, I know it." All was silent save the crackling of the fire. Laramie was asleep. No more shooting stars.

"Let's turn in," Jim said.

Two hours later the front came in, but there was no rain. The night was dark as pitch. Birch liquor can blind. Make you talk in tongues. All that manganese. Probably best not to combine it with White Widow.

Ed woke in the darkest night, heart racing. For a moment he was utterly disoriented, as he had been the morning of the dead doe. He had fallen far in his dreamless sleep, he was sure. What had happened when he was gone? He could hear his partner's breathing in the little bivouac tent. Inside it was like the darkest womb, muggy and black, no stars, no moon through the canvas opening. Jim had been muttering in his sleep. Then the pitch rose and, from nothing, he was screaming full bore. Laramie began barking and whining outside, trying to push in through the flap.

Jim was awake now.

"It's OK, boy," he said to the dog, a little out of breath, "it's OK. It's nuthin'." And then he must have fallen asleep again, because all Ed heard was heavy, stentorian breathing. At least he was not alone in this one thing—Jim also knew the darkness.

He lay awake, listening. The wind soughed around the tent and Laramie gave a whimper, asleep again. Minutes passed. Ed was in that stage between waking and sleep. He felt a tremor through the earth as if from a heavy footstep and then another, the vibration heavier and heavier, as if something large was approaching the tent. A bear? Then he heard a heavy breath, the sound of slithering, as if the ground had suddenly come alive and dozens of snakes were swarming around the tent. Were they coming through the tent flap? Why didn't Jim and Laramie wake up? He held his breath until he felt he was suffocating.

Then the slithering receded. Silence again.

His eyes snapped open. He had been asleep after all. Laramie had not stirred. The only sound was Jim's breathing.

He knew all was not right. That old darkness of the Lot was here, in the forest. The question was: was it already in him? It was a long time before he could get to sleep again.

CHAPTER TWENTY-SEVEN

No word was said as they packed up the next morning. Both men were tired and mute. Ed couldn't shrug off the dream. Jim silently pulled on a pair of aviator glasses. His eyes and it seemed his presence vanished behind them. Ed knew that when the black dog had him he would say very little for hours on end.

Only Laramie seemed enthusiastic for the day. They paddled up to the head of Chesuncook, past Gero Island. The hard work began at an inlet on the far shore. They unloaded their provisions, tent, guns, and tackle and carried the canoe a mile inland. The ground in front was swampy, the path wet and rocky, the rocks providing stepping stones through the wet, the evergreens leaning ever more closely overhead. There was no flow to the sitting water and the insects that so far had been largely absent rose and began swarming on them: mosquitoes, moose fly, and blackfly; all intent on blood. Huge rotting cedar deadfalls, some three or four feet high, lay across the path, but had at some stage in the past been chainsawed through to allow passage. Spongy moss often obscured the true way. Side trails went off in each direction, momentarily confusing Jim before he found the main path again. Fish hawks uttered their sharp, whistling cries nearby, fearful of these rare intruders.

They reached another lake, dumped the canoe and returned the mile for their gear. As they approached the Chesuncook shore, both men slowed, fearing they might be backtracking toward pursuers, but the early-morning lake remained empty, the only movement the fall mist burning off its surface in the sun. Only Laramie was unaffected by the tension, running back and forth unperturbed by the apparent waste of effort necessitated by retracing their steps. He disturbed wildfowl and startled an otter in a brackish waterway.

They passed over the second lake, which Jim named Mud Pond, an expanse of water no more inspiring than its name. On the far shore they repeated the porterage one more time. The path was a mirror image of the one before Mud Pond. They then came to another broad expanse of water, two or three miles across.

"Chamberlain," Jim stated. This and "Mud Pond" and some cursing at the insects was pretty much all he had said that day. They regained their canoe seats and, glad of the respite from the carrying, paddled northwest. It was now warm and Ed was sweating and, with the blood coursing, feeling more alive.

The vivid disturbance of the night began to recede, but still he couldn't shrug off the feeling of unease. This place was so primal and unformed that it was as if God had never expected or wanted man to step here. They passed a rock protruding from the lake surface into which a rusty mooring ring, just like in Thoreau's account a century before, had been screwed. It was the only man-made object, apart from those they carried, he had seen all day. Out here, any evidence of human existence felt like an artifact left not by history but by an alien race. The solitary mooring ring made the scenery around seem even more vast and lonely.

They paddled on steadily for two hours, covering ten miles. The lake narrowed as they reached its headwaters. They had started toward the right-hand shore, where Ed could make out what appeared to be a man-made clearing running down to the lake. At the same time another man-made object came into view around a headland to their left: a line of large wooden pillars protruding like teeth from the slate-colored waters at the top of the lake some half a mile away. The remains of a trestle bridge, lopsided and broken, stood atop it. What was it doing here in the middle of nowhere? Another anomaly.

But this wasn't what made Ed stop paddling. A tiny figure was standing on the westward end of the ruined trestle. It was too far away to make out distinctly. It had something long and rod-like in its hands, pointed toward them. Jim had seen the figure too and had also stopped paddling. Light flashed on glass from atop the rod. Ed suddenly thought: "telescopic sight." A high-pitched whine split the air between him and Jim. The sound of the shot caught up a second later. A flat retort. The reasoning part of his brain was still working.

Jim cursed violently. "Come on!" he shouted and set to again, thrashing at the water madly. Ed joined him. There was another rupturing of the air just where he had been a stroke or two before, and another retort. The adrenaline had not yet kicked in: his mind was still cold. He hunkered down and dug deep with his paddle. He risked a glance back at the trestle; the distant figure had shouldered its rifle and was now climbing spider-like over the jagged ruins of the bridge toward the eastern shore. The broken-down nature of the trestles and sleepers was making their progress relatively slow compared to the manic speed of the canoe.

They grounded on the north shore next to a muddy inlet. Jim jumped out and had already started hauling the canoe out of the water before Ed had stood up from his seat.

Jim pulled the gun bag from the canoe bottom, unzipped it and handed Ed one of the Winchesters and a box of ammo.

"Load up," he said and started doing the same with the other gun. He hushed Laramie as the dog began to bark. Laramie was instantly silent.

By now, Ed's heart was beating fit to burst with the violent exercise and the adrenaline that had finally caught up with him. He quickly loaded cartridges. Moving with an unlocked rifle was usually a no-no in Jim's world. He looked at Jim, who nodded. They each worked the lever and chambered a round. This was it, he realized: today he might have to shoot a man.

"OK, let's go," Jim said. He set off at a jog northward to the treeline. Ed looked to the left but the trestle was now hidden by the forest.

The end of the bridge had looked to reach the eastern shore about half a mile from their current position. He guessed it would take the shooter a few minutes to navigate the broken bridge, then a few more to intercept them through the dense undergrowth. But he wouldn't be far away.

Like with so much of the wilderness, the ground underfoot was spongy and wet; it never truly dried out from summer's beginning until its end. It sucked at their boots. Ed was careful to keep his finger out of the rifle guard but near enough to the trigger should the shooting start. Ahead, the woods that were now crowding around on either side appeared to have an avenue cut out of the middle of them, like an arrow-straight firebreak.

They passed around a stand of trees and there, again, as if randomly deposited from the skies, stood a cabin. Two stories: two up, two down; a corrugated iron roof, rusted red; a stone chimney stack and a radio mast. The front door and windows were boarded up and wild clematis and Virginia creeper choked the clapboard walls and gutters. The porch pillars and door and window frames had once been picked out in white paint, but this was peeling and gray now. A large Maine Forest Service sign hung under the gable over the two upstairs front windows, the paint peeling on the state's name. A flagstaff stood on their left in an area of knee-high grass that might once have been a lawn.

Beyond the hut was a wreckage of sheds but these were now sunk into the damp clay. The roofs sagged almost to the ground and the creepers covered nearly everything except a pair of massive cogged wheels and a rusted boiler that struggled up through the entanglement of fallen iron, wood, and weeds. Rails protruded like tongues from either mouth of the wreckage. One end ran down to the shore behind them but was quickly lost in the mud and rushes, the other went onward through a tangle of new-growth saplings and bushes along the cleared line Ed had noticed on their approach.

He guessed they would hole up in the cabin, but Jim shook his head. "We can't get trapped in there," he said. "There could be more than one of them." He nodded toward the avenue formed by the rails. "We'll follow the tramway north."

He set off northward up the avenue. Ed followed. A tramway? What on earth? The sleepers and ballast formed a half-buried path and the footing was better. But they were still out in the open. He glanced nervously to his left in the direction from which, presumably, the shooter was on an interception course with them.

He heard something crack in the treeline there, and he whirled and dropped to his knees, tracking the barrel of the gun in that direction. There was nothing but the impassive forest face to be seen, but the branches stirred, suggesting recent movement. He turned back to the track. Suddenly Jim and Laramie were gone.

"Shit," he whispered. He felt cold, betrayed. He thought of calling out. But that would only alert whoever, whatever, was in the forest.

He went forward at a crouching run, expecting the killing shot at any moment. The trees were opening up ahead. He came to a desolate lakeside, a wreckage of gantries, twisted rails, tree boles, and logs in the sucking mud of the shore, like a First World War picture of no-man's-land. Abandoned iron headworks lay in the weeds and new saplings poked through cog wheels and rusted boilers. Beyond, the gunmetal surface of the lake was miles wide.

He took cover behind a rust-red boiler and peered over it toward the forest line. Where in hell had Jim and Laramie gone? He heard a distant bark off to the west, swiftly silenced. Laramie. He left the tramway and edged into the treeline in that direction, treading carefully, conscious that he might be heading straight toward the shooter.

A solemn pall fell on him as he entered the choking undergrowth. It was wet and mossy underfoot, a tangle of fallen trees and new growth. His eyes tried to pick out detail in the undergrowth, but here was the pure wilderness, utterly unaccommodating to man: brown, gray, and green; interlaced branches; fallen, moss-covered logs; saplings and bushes; no defined path. The only sound his breath and the snapping twigs.

Ed stopped. Now it was utterly and terrifyingly silent. Not even birdsong. As if nature held its breath and waited for... what? Then he heard it, not far off to the left: another body moving through the undergrowth with the snap of twigs and rustle of undergrowth. Too big for Laramie. Jim or the shooter? Whoever, whatever it was, they might as well have been invisible. Nothing beyond ten yards could be discerned in the green twilight.

Ed felt a little faint, and the woods spun in the periphery of his vision. He took cover behind a tree. He felt the hairs at the nape of his neck rise. The rustling noise suddenly seemed to be coming from behind him. He was being stalked. He whirled, the barrel of the Winchester up, but all he saw was the same choking vista that had been in front of him. The rustle of undergrowth faded. He leaned back against a tree, got his breath. He pushed off again, following the direction of the footsteps.

There was light ahead; an emerald light unlike the dun of the deep forest. A clearing. He went toward it as silently as he could. The sunlight of the September day came filtering back again and in one step he went from the choking forest to the edge of a sun-speckled clearing covered with tiny white flowers.

And here, finally, in this clearing, was the strangest of all the sights that last day he was Edward Burns Constance.

In its center, as if dropped from heaven, stood two rust-red behemoths on short lengths of rails: two 100-ton steam locomotives, side by side. Their driving wheels were as tall as a man, their smokestacks some twenty-five feet high. Both engines were slightly tilted from the sinking of the rails into the clay. The smokebox door was gone from the front of one of them, leaving a dark, Cyclopean eye. The rails disappeared into the small clearing's sides. If the scant signs of humanity had hitherto seemed anomalous, the presence of these monsters in the virgin forest was like discovering uncovered dinosaur skeletons or Ozymandias' shattered statue in the trackless wastes. Ed shook his head. Maybe he would wake now in the little bivouac tent by Chesuncook and start this day again. His thundering heartbeat told him otherwise.

The shot was like a slap in the face. It came out of nowhere. Too swift for pain or even consciousness. A rifle bullet travels a thousand miles a second. He breathed and realized he wasn't dead. He hadn't been struck.

Jim stepped from the undergrowth twenty yards to his right, a small waft of powder smoke dissipating from the muzzle of his Winchester. Laramie came slinking behind, almost on his belly.

Jim levered the action of the rifle, ejected a spent cartridge and chambered another. He was staring at a point by one of the engine cabs. Ed turned to follow his gaze. There was something lying in the long grass by the steps. It was writhing faintly. Jim shouldered the rifle and fired again. The body twitched as the round impacted. The writhing all but stopped. Jim ejected the spent round and advanced.

Ed shrugged off his paralysis and followed. He went past Laramie, who had lain down halfway to the engines at some silent command from Jim. The dog was whining a little, his tongue hanging out.

Ed came into the shadow of the giant abandoned loco and looked at the body on the ground.

Nine years might have passed, but he knew him like he had known David. Carl. That pasty face and slick mop of black hair, the stocky build and legs. A scoped rifle lay at a safe distance from the body.

The kid was wearing a blood-soaked camo jacket. It looked like one of Jim's rounds had punched through his upper chest, just under his right clavicle; the other had gone through his left side. Blood was seeping out of his mouth and into the mud. Ed now remembered that the irises of Carl's recessed eyes had always seemed particularly black and tiny. They were fixed on him. They had the glassy look of impending death he had seen in dying game. Carl's lips moved as he stared at Ed, but only another trickle of blood, no words, came from his mouth.

"You know him?" Jim asked.

It took a beat for Ed to answer him. "One of the seven," he whispered. "Name's Carl." The words came into his mind unbidden: "And the third angel poured out his vial upon the rivers and fountains of waters; and they became blood."

Carl's breathing became ever more painful; there were bubbles of blood at his mouth and nose.

The dying kid was trying to say something. Another trickle of blood pulsed out of his mouth. Ed glimpsed bloodstained yellow teeth.

"Talk to him," Jim said to Ed. "You might learn something."

Ed laid his rifle down and knelt next to Carl. The dying kid let out a strangled gargling.

"I can't hear you," Ed said. Carl made the sound again and Ed leaned closer. With what seemed a last, superhuman effort, Carl lifted his head and sprayed a gout of blood into Ed's face. Ed tasted bitter iron in his mouth. Carl sank back with a strange sigh and Ed saw his eyes were now open and fixed.

Ed fell back on his haunches, staring at the dead face.

Jim said, "No idea how that kid found us."

"Maybe they have a sixth sense, you know?" Ed answered. "Any time, any place—they know where we are."

"Well, I sure as shit hope not, otherwise more of them will be turning up," Jim answered. "At least we don't have to worry about this one anymore."

The shock was wearing off Ed. Now came the anger. He stood up. "You went on without me."

"I saw him, Ed. Wanted to draw him off you. Kid, you can shoot all right, but have you ever shot a man?" Though he himself had done just that, there was not a flicker of emotion on Jim's face. Ed wondered: would he have hesitated when confronted by Carl?

He looked away. The huge, abandoned locomotives looming over them only added to the hypnotic unreality. "Where are we?" he asked.

"About the exact middle of the woods," Jim answered. "We're to the watershed of the Allagash and the Penobscot. All the Maine pulp mills were to the south and any lumber north of here had to be brought across this neck of land, so they built a railroad across it."

"A railroad, here?"

Jim nodded. "This is the Eagle Lake and West Branch Railroad. What's left of it. Ten miles of track in the middle of nowhere, going nowhere. First they had that tramway back there to carry lumber, then this railroad built in '27. It started here, carried around to the west over them trestles on Chamberlain and down to Umbazooksus, where they dumped the spruce for the log run to Millinocket. When the business fell away in the Crash, they decided the engines weren't worth taking out for scrap. These two locos have just sat here ever since."

There were large inscriptions in white paint on the boilers of the two great engines. Names and dates, protestations of love or just notifications that a person had been here, in the back of beyond, for no more reason than to graffiti.

"Yep, and soon I guess these old ladies'll just keel over in the mud and lay down and be covered until Judgment itself," Jim went on.

He snapped out of his reverie. "Come on, boy, we got a body to bury. See if there's a coal shovel in one of them cabs, will you?"

Jim took Carl's corpse by the feet and started dragging him toward the treeline. As if in a dream, Ed climbed up the rusted cab steps of the larger of the two engines. He stared at the labyrinthine control panel: shattered dials and gauges, yellow with age, needles gone. Rusty levers reached up and out, in no apparent order, in the same positions they had been left in forty-six years ago at the end of the engine's final journey. The firebox stood open. A total and utter darkness lay beyond. The name of the engine works, Schenectady Locomotive Workshop, and the year 1897 were inscribed on a plate above the firebox hatch.

There were two rusted shovels at the back of the cab by the coal tender. Ed took these and followed the slick of blood that showed Jim's route into the treeline.

Jim was standing over the corpse about twenty feet in. He took one of the shovels. "Could just leave him for the animals, but they scatter bones. Might be found. We better start digging."

It was hard work in the tangle of roots. Almost straightaway, Ed's shovel hit metal. He pulled the object out of the mud. It was a rectangular plaque a foot or so across, six inches high, two rivet holes at each side, and some stamped capital letters driven into it:

"ENG NO.8 SHOP NUMBER 4553 ALLOWABLE PRESSURE 190LBS HYDROSTATIC PRES 239LBS."

The "3" of the shop number was printed the wrong way around. Carl's number. Reversed. Ed stared at it for a few beats, then laid it to one side.

It took two hours for them to dig down to where the sucking clay became mainly liquid. They dropped the corpse into this; it sank halfway. Carl's pin eyes were now filming over. Insects were crawling over the white pupils. It was as if he was taking a final bath in the mud. The engine plate lay on the ground next to the mound of earth. Best if it were returned to the ground, to be forgotten, just like Carl. Ed dropped it onto Carl's chest. An exhalation came from Carl's mouth. His last breath, forced out by the plate. Ed leaned to one side and threw up.

"Go and sit by the engines," Jim said. "I'll finish up here."

Ed went back to the clearing and sat on one of the engine steps with Laramie.

It was late afternoon by the time Jim emerged from the woods, by now in shirtsleeves, sweaty, and covered with mud. The light was beginning to fade in the west.

"Let's take a moment," Jim said. He sat on one of the loco's cab steps and pulled out some hardtack and a canteen. Ed did the same, but his eyes fell on the blood-slicked ground and he couldn't eat.

"What happens now?" he asked.

Jim threw Laramie some of the dried meat. The dog wolfed it quickly and looked up for more.

"Been thinking," Jim said. "This ain't the fellow that spooked you back in Boston?"

"No, that was David."

"So, David could still be out there, maybe with others. Could be close."

"I guess."

They were silent for a moment, listening. There was the wind through the foliage and birdsong, nothing else.

Jim turned and fixed Ed with a look. Ed detected something in Jim's eyes he had not seen before: sadness. He knew what would come next. Something slipped away inside of him. Maybe it was hope.

"They ever going to stop chasin' you?" Jim asked.

Ed shook his head. "I guess not. And I guess they've decided I'm better off dead. When I called Gonzalez they realized I'm a liability. The worst sort. If they're prepared to kill a federal agent and then send Carl after me, they're not going to let up. They've plenty more where he came from. Half the federal agents in America for a start." He stared up at the sun falling through the foliage. The future looked like an enormous, hopeless blank.

Jim said, "My thought too. Don't know how that kid did it, but he must have been well trained to catch our trail." He looked at the rifle lying on the ground. "M40. A1 model—remember it from Nam. Them weapons don't grow on trees."

There was silence for a moment, then Jim asked, "You got any money?"

"Some. It was in Stu's safe."

"How much?"

"'Bout ten grand."

Jim whistled. "Guess Stu held it back for a rainy day." He thought for a beat or two. "You remember I mentioned that guy I was in the Marines with?"

"Sure."

"George Dumfries. Good man. Like me, never really adjusted to civvie life. Lives off the grid in upstate New York near Wheelerville. Does a little PI work. But his real money comes from documents.

Forged documents. Reckon he's the man you want for a passport, driver's license, social security, high school certificate—that kinda thing."

"You're saying he could fix me up?" Ed asked.

"He wouldn't do it for nuthin'."

Ed looked at him sharply. "How much?"

"For a friend, maybe a grand."

"And his work is watertight?"

"Tight as a drum."

Ed was silent. He was about to let go of the last fragment of what he had been. The past was fading into black. There would be no more Maine, no Boston, no Northeastern, no Winthrop Road now. Stu and Bettie were dead. Gloria was dead. Jim was about gone.

Jim broke the silence. "Listen, kid, we got to move. I expect this guy was meant to report in about now."

"So, what're we going to do?"

Jim set out his plan. Dusk, then night came as he did so.

"One last thing," Jim said when he was finished.

"What?" Ed answered.

Jim looked down at his boots. The moon had risen and now appeared high overhead. Ed saw that it was back in Punch mode, casting a leering yellow light into the clearing and over the engines, which appeared to shift in the mottled shadows of the clearing. He'd listened to that line just two days before in Moss's room: rust never sleeps.

Jim said, "We been lucky so far. Nothing to tie us together. But after today, we got to go our separate ways. You know that, don't you, kid?" Ed merely nodded. "Don't contact me again, unless it's life or death. You understand? For both our sakes. You promise me?"

That was it. The last fragment had gone. "Yeah, I promise—only life or death," Ed heard himself say.

"Attaboy," Jim said sadly. He got to his feet. "OK, let's haul. We got some work to do."

The two rose from the engine steps. Ed cast one look back at the two hulking shapes of the engines. Dinosaurs lost in time in the depths of the Maine Woods.

They made their way back to the shore of Eagle Lake. The ruins of the conveyors that had once lifted the logs out of the lake onto the railcars stood out like iron teeth from the water. Jim had brought the M40. He picked it up by its barrel, assumed a hammer-throwing pose and flung it into the lake. The splash disturbed a pair of loons, which went hooting off into the night. His beloved Winchester followed, as did Ed's.

"You got the Colt?" he asked Ed.

Ed nodded and brought it out.

"Throw it," Jim ordered and Ed did so. There was another splash.

"Enough iron sunk in that lake from the workings. A metal detector's not going to be able to pick out those guns," Jim said.

They went back down the tramway. As they neared the forestry hut, they paused and listened, but all was silent. They went onto the Chamberlain lakeshore, got out their headlamps, unpacked the canoe and left everything but Ed's backpack by the shore.

They began the carry back to the north. The mile and three-quarters to Eagle Lake took about an hour. They set the canoe down in the water and loaded Ed's backpack in it.

Then Jim bound the two paddles together with duct tape to make them one.

"Should hold," he said. "Not going to be so easy just the one of you."

"I guess I'm gonna have to manage."

Jim pulled out a dog-eared map and handed it over. It looked like a forestry department issue from about 1950. "You'll need this, kid. Remember, just keep going north as far as you can go. This lake and the one beyond will lead you to the river. After that the first carry is at Churchill Dam. You're gonna have to junk the canoe there. Hide it good. There's an old logging trail by the river. Follow it, then cut out to the east and back south."

"What about you?"

"Like I said, kid. They don't know a thing about me. Never will. I'll get out on that trestle and follow the track south. Should get to the pickup without attracting attention."

Ed was sure if anyone could avoid a posse of agents it was Jim.

"OK, so long, Jim," he said, and bent to muss Laramie's head. He stepped into the canoe, sat and took up the makeshift paddle.

"So long, kid. Hope things work out for you," Jim said.

Ed swallowed. "Thanks for everything."

"Just keep safe. That's enough."

Ed nodded and pushed the canoe away from the shore, turned it around and, with one last backward glance, struck out to the north across the two-mile expanse of gray water.

CHAPTER TWENTY-EIGHT

David and Carl had arrived at the Seboomook Camping Ground in the depths of the night, but found no evidence of the Volvo or Ed. David told Carl to hang back: he could pass himself off as being in his early twenties, the minimum age requirement for the FBI, but Carl could not. He rousted out the camp store owner, a Canadian by the name of Hervey Leflaive, and showed his fake FBI ID. Leflaive had been roused from a deep slumber and had had quite enough, over the years, of federal agents and sheriffs pitching up inquiring about people moving back and forth over the remote and largely unpoliced border five miles up the road. He said he was unaware of anyone showing up at around midnight to use the phone. He'd been asleep for a good three hours by then. And no, no one had arrived any time earlier to buy supplies or rent a canoe, though there were plenty of the former in the store and plenty of the latter tied up waiting for anyone braving the post-holiday weather down at the lake. David asked if he would check none of the canoes had been stolen?

"I guess I'm awake anyway," Leflaive said. He put on a coat over his nightwear and grabbed a flashlight. But when they got to the lakeshore all twelve canoes were tied to the dock.

There was a slim chance that Ed was still around Seboomook. If so, he was lying low. There was literally no traffic on the logging roads. Headlights would be visible for miles around. The area was quiet as a tomb.

Two men dressed in suits and in two black Crown Vics would attract unwanted attention in the wilderness. And calling more fake agents into the area would make things worse. If they could find Ed without calling for reinforcements, so much the better.

David and Carl opened the trunks of their cars, donned the outdoor gear stowed there, grabbed flashlights and began exploring the lakeshore. A mile or so away from the campground they came across a beat-up Chevy pickup and an area of disturbed ground that looked like someone had recently pitched a tent. But the tent and the owner of the pickup were nowhere to be seen. There was the faintest impression of a canoe keel in the lakeshore mud. It looked like whoever had been here had taken off across the lake.

They returned to the campground. One thing was sure. Ed would not have gone back east. The two choices were to the border or the rough, dead-end road that led north, to Caucomgomoc Lake twenty miles away. There was only a slim possibility Ed had gone that way in an attempt to escape through the wilderness, but David had to anticipate all possibilities. Carl's summer camps had involved wilderness survival and tracking and the former special forces operative who had taught him considered him one of the best. He could go in that direction.

Carl silently slid a scoped M40 sniper rifle into his gun case. He was smiling to himself, then his dead eyes caught David's.

"You reckon on using that?" David asked.

"Shoot first, you know," Carl said.

"Not in this state," David answered.

"This a state?" Carl asked, looking around at the dark woods. "You want him dead, he's dead."

David didn't answer. Vermeulen wanted Ed alive but David had good reason to wish otherwise.

"OK," Carl said. "Guess I'm up to Caucomgomoc. I'll radio in."

He threw the rifle case on the passenger seat of the Crown Vic and got behind the wheel. The last David saw of him, Carl gave him another of those dead-eyed stares through the glass, then he threw the lights on, gunned the gas and roared away up the dirt track to the north.

David drove back west to Dole Pond and pulled into a side turn just shy of the border crossing by a sign that read: "All Loaded Trucks Must Stop At US Customs." This was repeated underneath in French. David was aware that there wasn't a customs post anywhere close, the nearest manned one being on Highway 201 crossing twenty miles to the south. The frontier was protected by a gate, left open and largely unpoliced. Customs arrangements in this remote corner were largely a matter of honesty (or dishonesty in the case of smugglers) and were only subject to random spot checks when the sheriff or the customs officers were in the area, which was rarely.

The two men's transceivers were operating at their maximum limit. Carl called in. He was at Caucomgomoc. It was about four in the morning. There was no sign of the station wagon but the track went northward from the lake. He was going to take it as far as it went.

It was the last David heard from Carl. David waited all the next day for him to radio in again. In the evening he tried him on the hour, every hour. The transceiver remained obstinately dead. Meanwhile, there was still no traffic on the logging road. His clothes by now were beginning to get pretty ripe. He thought of calling Vermeulen again but hesitated. He clenched his fists on the wheel of the stationary car, willing the Volvo to appear.

It didn't. He had a long time to think as he waited. He had not been given his life back to fail. He had been absolved from the tasks of the others; chosen as a leader by Mrs. Frome and then Vermeulen and then by whoever controlled Vermeulen. He was headed for the top. At nine he had been adopted by former Bund members—fervent but clandestine members of the American Nazi Party. His childhood had been carefully shaped with the help of the fascists and their friends. It had taken him years of deprogramming to become what he now was. The best doctor in the organization had administered the drugs that had slowly brought him to his current state. They had called the physician Doctor Death; he was a miracle man with phials and syringes administered in the death chambers of half a dozen penitentiaries. In David's case the drugs had brought him back from death.

His memory had returned and what he remembered about the basement at the Lot was not pleasant—enough to break a weaker man's mind. But not his. He was David, Mrs. Frome's king. He had in time confronted the monster seeded inside of him. Learned finally not to obey but only fear Typhon. He had stared into the abyss and the abyss had stared back into him. Now he could contemplate the serpent-headed nightmare, if not with equanimity, at least not in blind obedience. No trigger would work on him.

David was free to remember. But, somehow, Ed was too. David remembered Ed back at the Lot, and what he remembered he hated. No matter how much punishment the kid took, he would never go down. *Never.* Cracked lips, bloody nose, black eye. Nothing would stop Ed. And when David was blown and had dished out everything he had? David had hated the humiliation the two times Ed had laid him on his ass, sucker punched, and how the others, all but Carl, had laughed at him.

Entire and full and red and bloody was his hatred when he thought of Ed. David wished him dead. He hadn't contradicted Carl's suggestion that the M40 was more than window dressing. Shoot first. The end of Ed. End of a problem too. If casuistry was permitted in Typhon, maybe Vermeulen should wish Ed dead too. Had not Ed broken free of the mental block in Stetson East? The same could easily happen on his mission. What would happen to Typhon then?

So, David silently argued, was it not better if Ed died now? There would be another kid raised in the Typhon compound in the Gila Desert who could do the dam. A kid with no memory, no regrets, no resistance.

On the second evening he cracked. He used the pay phone at the campground. Leflaive was watching him from inside the shop. He turned his back on him in case the guy could lip-read. The conversation went as badly as he'd feared. Vermeulen told David he was relieved. Four more Typhon agents would be sent north. They could use the upcoming wild turkey season as cover while they searched the backwoods for Carl and Ed. Meanwhile, he was to get the hell out of there.

It was after he had hung up the phone and was looking blankly over the lake that he saw the beat-up Chevy they'd discovered two nights before coming up the track from the shore in the dusk. It had its headlights on, so David didn't get a clear view of the occupant, but he got the impression of a good old boy in front with a collie dog on the bench beside him. No Ed. The old guy looked like the kind of outdoorsman who would sneer at paying Leflaive for a spot on the campground. More out of reflex than suspicion, David memorized the number above the "Vacationland" sigil on the bottom of the plate. There was something off about the pickup. It settled uneasily at the back of his mind.

Only much later did he realize what it was.

CHAPTER TWENTY-NINE

Ed reached the dam at the north end of Churchill Lake at about five in the morning. There was already the faintest hint of gray in the east. The porterage was well used here; a path rose up to the dam and the road that ran across it. Had he had a single canoe he would have been able to carry it and his backpack over to the other side by first light, but the double canoe was heavy and the likelihood of him still hauling its deadweight up the slope when the traffic started moving on the road above was too much of a risk. He pulled the canoe into the reeds, moved his backpack out and then tilted the canoe sideways so it took on water. He finished its sinking by dropping a large boulder into the flooded hull. The canoe disappeared below the surface. He broke the jury-rigged paddle back into its constituent halves and threw them deep into the undergrowth.

He crossed the road as the first tips of sun caught the top of the forest to the east. He found the beginning of the faint, centuries-old native trail that wound through the evergreens. Spiderwebs and low-growth foliage blocked his path, showing no one had been down it for a while.

After two hours he heard a faint roar. It intensified as he went forward. The slate face of the Allagash appeared through the trees to his left, its surface here and there flecked with foam. He passed a small, shingled cove with a grassy area. Hunters had been here: there were a couple of stone rings for campfires and spruce frames for drying hides. The path opened up and looked to be in more regular use than the old Native American trail behind. Rapids now appeared to his left, a maelstrom of sharp rocks and white water. They ended in a small waterfall, and, below that, in the tranquil receiving pool, Ed glimpsed brown trout gliding at the bottom, every pebble magnified by the purity of the water. Dragonflies and water skaters darted on the surface. Here was another campground similar to the one above. It was here he threw down his groundsheet in a patch of sun and lay on it. He drew the knife from his belt and held it loosely on his chest, propped his head with his backpack and lowered his hat over his eyes. Despite the danger, he fell into a deep sleep.

He dreamed of the basement again. The dream was as vivid as the one he'd had in the blackout back at Stetson East.

He went down the stairs. There was a single bulb lighting up the concrete walls of the dungeon. It was swinging slightly, casting lurid shadows. There was only one child today. They were sitting on a fold-out chair with their back turned to Ed. He approached. Then the figure turned abruptly. It was Carl—though he was not the child he had once been, but the eighteen-year-old whom Jim had shot the day before: a shock of dark hair, pin-like eyes, pasty face. He held up his bloodied hands from his blood-spattered camo jacket and reached for Ed's throat.

Ed woke with a start, swinging the knife, but there was no Carl.

The clearing was as empty as when he had arrived. Cabbage white butterflies flew erratic courses over the last wildflowers. The distant roar of the fall was as it had been before. His heartbeat steadied.

He filled his canteen from the pool, drank deep, and then ate some crackers. He looked at Jim's map. It was greasy and thumbed almost to extinction, the folds split and frayed. The falls were named as Chase Rapids. The small outpost at Clayton Lake was to the west. There was a United States Post Office there for some reason, maybe serving the logging camps; beyond it only miles of logging road and the distant border. The border called to him. Surely there was safety there? But what could he do in Canada? Typhon no doubt was as strong there as it was here. He needed a new identity. Dumfries in Wheelerville was his only chance.

He had to go east, not west. But the route there would take him past the very place that had haunted him all his life: Realty Road was five miles ahead. It was as if all roads led back to the Lot.

He squeezed the old map in a death grip. After a minute his breathing settled. If he was to get out quickly and alive, he needed Realty Road, then Highway 11. There were no alternatives. After Ashland he could risk hitching a ride south.

He set off again, the rushing and occasionally roaring waters of the Allagash to his left, the deep woods dark and shaded to his right. Now he was away from the canoe landings, the path was virtually unbroken as if, again, unused from one season to the next. He was conscious he was leaving a trail of broken twigs and disturbed vegetation. So be it. Speed was his only friend. The fall day began to wane. Broad orange shafts of light swept across the river's course and lanced over the path, then were swallowed by the trees on the opposite bank until only the tops of them were alight, and then they, too, were gone and the stars could be seen emerging like lonely beacons in the purple sky overhead. He kept his eyes fixed on the polestar, around which the night sky began slowly to rotate. The path was hazardous in the darkness, but he opted against using his flashlight: by now he was near the road. Soon the natural shapes of the forest abruptly ended and there was space ahead. The black horizontal of a road bridge crossed the river. He had reached Realty Road.

He turned east, toward the Lot.

Evergreens leaned over the road to either side. The Milky Way arced overhead. Winking stars and the jumble of the constellations punched the blackness of space. Now and again an invisible stream rushed underneath in a culvert, and there was the distant gleam of a lake through trees. Not a human light in this black universe.

But the light of the leering moon was still there. It was waning and closer to the western horizon than it had been the first three nights in the woods. It threw a huge shadow of himself on the gravel road in front as if a vast, unformed giant strode before him.

He continued thus for five hours, walking in a trance, as quickly as he could, conscious of the gathering darkness of the waning moon and his ever-lengthening shadow as it sank further.

At an undistinguished curve of the road, no different to the hundreds he had passed before, he knew he had arrived. There was a rock buttress and, beyond it, the first man-made object he had seen for all that time: a chain-link fence that stretched away into the darkness on the left-hand side of the road.

He stopped. The steady crunch of his boots, the sole accompaniment to his thoughts these last five hours, ceased. The silence that followed was pregnant and terrifying. Not a night bird, not a rustle of undergrowth. Dead, dead silence.

But something was waiting ahead. The monster. Typhon.

He slid the knife from his belt. His hand was cold but took shape on the finger grooves. Nine inches of steel glinted. There is courage in such a weapon. Courage enough for a few steps toward a monster. His feet took him forward again. Around that curve.

The road ahead was empty. The rusted double gate stood in the chain-link fence in the shadows, wreathed in dead vines. A yellow nylon police rope sagged down in front of the gate. A leftover from '70. The gates had been pushed haphazardly back together. Whatever lock had been there had long ago vanished and, as if by way of invitation, there was enough of a gap to pass through.

It had not been his plan; would never have been his plan. But now he found there was no alternative.

If you do not confront demons, they will devour you.

He took a deep breath, drawing into himself all of this night, the moon, his eighteen years, the dark path ahead. He was in the Lot and the Lot was in him.

He went between the rusted gates and up the old, rutted track through the woods.

This was, after all, the last place anyone would come looking for him.

CHAPTER THIRTY

Under the trees, Ed was almost blind. Nine years' new growth of saplings, ferns and fallen branches blocked his way. No one had been this way since the FBI had abandoned their investigation. He still feared to use his flashlight. The monster must have no warning of his coming. The moonlight reached through the branches and trunks in spectral fingers.

He paused at each switchback and first looked back at the silhouettes of the undulating mountains of northern Maine and the moon now falling chin first into them, then up the dark way, trying to see the top of the mountain. But there were just the trees leaning over the barely discernible track, nothing more. Had the way been this long that day in June '70 when the school bus had come down it? He couldn't recall the journey. The way seemed as long as the night, as time.

He stopped looking up for the end of the track. The walk was endless; he might scale the height of a hundred Everests and not reach the summit of the cursed mountain. This was Typhon's punishment for those who refused the sacrifice: this endless track...

Exhaustion by now had numbed him so much that when he was next conscious of thought he found, without realizing it, he had stopped walking and stood upon an open space of weed-choked gravel. In front was the second fence. Rusted and fallen in parts, the "Danger Unexploded Munitions" sign hanging upside down, the gates lurched drunkenly open.

There was only 400 yards left, no more. He went forward as a zombie.

His dying shadow walked before him. His feet crunched down on something. It felt like brittle bone, but he saw it was a charred piece of timber, scattered by the long-ago explosion. The ground was littered with other such blackened debris. He was very close now.

He turned the final corner of the track and saw the mouth of hell, the black hole where the cabin once stood.

Dead silence still. Not a breath of wind. Not the call of an animal. All of creation feared to be heard in this place.

Just then the light went from behind him and he knew the moon had set: suddenly all was dark. An ice-cold spear fell from his mind and down his spine. The constellations faded as the darkness edged in, the lens contracting, and he only saw with an inner eye.

In the darkness the ghosts came. First the children, silent, as always—Mrs. Frome could not abide a raised voice. The dead ones came up slowly from the dark pit: blond-haired Hope and saturnine Kevin; Carl, the blood still running from his mouth. They drifted off like thistle seeds into the night, without a sound. Then came others, many others. One drew his attention. He drifted to the north and, unlike the others, looked behind him at Ed: dark hair, dark eyes, darker complexion. He smiled sadly. Then his wraith dissipated into smoke-like wreaths and was gone.

Ed fell to his knees. He may have fainted in that kneeling position. When he came to, the night sounds had returned. The wind soughed in the top of the spruce and birch, crickets chirped in the Johnson grass, the night was suddenly busy with noises. The light of the stars had returned. The contrail of an airplane bisected the sky high overhead. He remembered how the children had called the vapor trails the chalk marks of God.

He looked across the yard. Memories cascaded. The past seemed only yesterday. Before tonight the Fromes had been only names: names of dead people burned to nothing in this very place. But here they were again in his mind's eye as they had been: she of the cold face and cold blue eyes, and that accent, which only now Ed, reaching back through time, recognized as Irish; he, the hulking, malodorous bully with his full beard and shrike eyes and meaty fingers like blood sausages. The memory of them had gone with the crucifix swinging in the June evening of nine years ago. He remembered that now, the drugged juice afterward...

All those hours of therapy and all he had needed was to return here and see this place for it to all come back again.

His mind was suddenly too full to process thought. He had to sleep.

The shed where Frome had kept the school bus still stood, one side blown in and charred by the explosion. But there was a V-shaped crawl space where the wall had fallen against the opposite one. He stumbled over to it and found a dry spot under Frome's old workbench, pulled his parka tight around him. He was asleep in five seconds.

The basement came again, just as at the waterfall. The heavy oak chairs; leather restraints on the arms and legs; leather and metal helmet fastenings at the back like the restraints in the execution room on death row; bodies in spasm; backs arched; silver neon skulls lit up from within. The children singing, always singing, eager to obey Typhon, the greatest overbearing, indomitable force in the universe.

And he woke and saw that it was the first crack of dawn. He had survived the night. He crawled out from under the workbench. Frome's tools were still laid out on it, but the wrenches and oilcans were now brown with rust.

He looked to the east. It was going to be a fine day.

Wheelerville was nearly 800 miles away. He had to get going. But though his whole being screamed for him to leave this place, there was something tying him here—something he must find.

He walked to the edge of the pit where the cabin had stood and stared down into it. It was a mess of mud, charred wood, and metal fragments. The Feds no doubt had fine-sieved it after they found the bones down there.

He turned to the east and, as he did so, the sun peered over the shoulder of Round Mountain five miles away and a faint gleam came off an object lying on the rubble edge of the pit.

Ed walked over to it and picked it up. It was a plastic toy eye with a rolling black pupil under a plastic dome: he knew it, somehow, to be Bear.

He closed his fist over the eye and slipped it into a pocket. "I cannot die," he whispered.

And then he walked toward the eye of the sun, now free of Round Mountain. There was a rock to the east of the cabin from which, as kids, he and Shannon had gotten their only glimpse of the outside world.

The massive lump of granite reared from the mountainside like a bald, frowning head. Though the spruces grew a foot or two every year, their growth rate died off after they reached around sixty feet and this area had not been logged since Eriksson's time. A small stretch of Realty Road showed like a brown slash through the ever-stretching forest in the distance. Just beyond it, the blue eye of Carr Pond sat in the undulating green.

There was a large crack in the rock on the eastern side. He looked into the cleft. It was only some four feet high. Even so, the space seemed to have shrunk. There, scratched on the rock, were their initials. E and S. This was as close as they had ever gotten to freedom.

The inner perimeter fence stood a little way down the boulder-strewn slope. It, too, had turned to rust, but looked as unbreachable now as it had twenty years before.

Even though he was some 100 yards from the site of the log house, there was still fragmentary evidence of the explosion down here: charred wood beams and shingles and bits of random metal and plastic twisted by the heat. A little way down from the hiding place he noticed an anomaly: a gray object was stuck in a tight gap between two rocks just short of the fence. It took him five minutes to pick his way down to it.

It was a gray binder. Somehow the FBI had missed it. The boards were scorched brown by fire and peeled by exposure to the elements. He pulled it out of the gap and opened it. The inside pages were protected by plastic document sleeves. Nevertheless some damp had found its way into the outer pages, rotting them. But some of the pages toward the middle were intact. There was a list. He recognized Mrs. Frome's hand. The ink had run but the writing was in part legible:

David VIAL
Kevin VIAL
Edward VIAL
Shannon VESSEL
Hope VESSEL
Catrine VIAL
Carl VIAL

He started teasing apart other pages but could read only fragments. Formulas for the inoculations, Bible quotes, brainwashing techniques… He had seen enough. He unclipped the page with the children's names from the binder and stuffed it into his pocket.

The insects began to chirp in the grass. The day was warming. The long road lay ahead. A journey of a thousand miles and a first step to start it…

He breathed in the depth of the air. He was free: he had returned to Typhon's lair, but the monster had not taken him.

He went down the track to Realty Road. In daylight its menace was gone. When he reached the logging road he began walking east.

There were no trucks on the road that September day. There was a mysterious calm in the woods. He reached the Texaco station at midday.

So much was as it had been in June 1970. The calls of the white-throated sparrow and the cicadas, the white flowers swaying in the wind, the cast-iron red star on its pole, scarred by shot and rust.

The station office was boarded up, but one of the boards over the entrance had been ripped out. Darkness within. He could just discern in the thin beams of light that made their way through the cracks in the boards a counter with an old metal cash register on it. The cracked glass display showed a pop-up "No Sale" sign. The store display shelves had been toppled on their sides.

He circled out to the back lot. Here were the restrooms, an air pump, a pile of moldering tires, and a rusted dumpster. The woods crowded in. Small saplings had begun to grow in the cracks in the asphalt. Random bits of trash left over by visitors were caught in the sapling branches and against the walls of the office. One piece caught his eye. The glimpse of a cartoon dog: white face, long pointy snout, and black button nose. Cracked by long exposure to the weather, but the plastic, though degrading and gray, was still intact. He knelt. His breath caught. Shannon's coat. He looked up, almost expecting to see her nine-year-old self standing there by the yellow bus.

He draped the coat over the air pump. The next blizzard would carry it far into the woods.

A jarring new sound came over the noise of the forest. A helicopter. Far in the distance. His heart started to beat hard; he was suddenly in hunted mode.

He set off quickly toward Ashland, keeping to the part of the road shaded by the trees. For now, he only heard the chopper at a distance, coming in and out of earshot as if it was following a search pattern; further, then nearer. Toward ten he saw the forestry checkpoint ahead. He took a detour through the woods and rejoined the road at a lumber mill a few hundred yards past it. A mile or two further on, the first farm clearings appeared, and a little later some clapboard farmhouses. For the first time since leaving Seboomook he felt there were sufficient witnesses around to risk going openly. He got out on the side of the road and stuck out a thumb. Fifteen minutes later an old farmer on the way to Highway 11 stopped and offered him a lift in his battered pickup.

The old man seemed satisfied with Ed's explanation that he was a hiker coming back from a Labor Day expedition, though even to Ed's ears it was unconvincing. He had no tent or other equipment, just a medium backpack. But the old guy seemed distracted by something up in the sky. He pointed up with a gnarled finger.

"Well, look there," he said. "That chopper's been up since dawn. Some poor sap lost over to Eagle Lake or Chamberlain, I'd be guessing." With that he wound down his window and ejected the wad of baccy he had been chewing.

A half-hour later, Ed was hitching south on Highway 11 on the first leg of a journey that would see him become another person.

PART TWO
MIAMI
1979–1989

CHAPTER THIRTY-ONE

Thanks to Jim's Marine buddy, George Dumfries, he became Martin José Cruz. It was the name of a two-year-old child who had died in an automobile accident in Minnesota in January 1963. At least that was what Dumfries had told him. He hadn't sought any more information. As it was, being Cruz was like living with someone else's transplanted heart—that name never sat right with him.

Dumfries had been all that Jim had promised. Maybe more. He had taken pity on the poor, bedraggled kid who had turned up in the rain in the Adirondacks that September of '79; fed and housed him for a month while he worked on the papers that would turn Edward Burns Constance into Martin José Cruz. And in the end Dumfries had only taken $200 for his trouble, much less than Jim had told Ed to expect.

Ed was now a ghost person, with a fake passport, social security card and driver's license. The remaining money from Stu's safe would give him time, wherever he ended up.

As the leaves changed, he'd headed south on the Greyhound. He'd read the newspapers every day. This far south, news of the month-old disappearance of a freshman on the first day at Northeastern didn't make the pages. Nor did the investigation into the suspicious death of Stuart Constance, prominent Brookline developer, though the disappearance of the fatal weapon and the deceased's adopted son on the same day must surely have excited the interest of the police and, by now, the FBI.

As he traveled from New York City he shed everything that tied him to his previous life: his old clothes, the Timex watch, every last bit of paper... it went into trash cans and dumpsters on stops on the route: all that remained were the Constance Bible, the Woolworth's notebook, and the page he had rescued from the gray binder at the Lot. And the precious dollars, all 9,800 of them. He kept the last three items wrapped in some taped sheets of newspaper under his shirt. He kept the Bible open on his lap the entire journey. Fellow passengers avoided conversation with him, suspecting him to be some religious nut.

When he reached Miami he hid in plain sight. His unknown parentage helped him. From April to October 1980, 125,000 Cubans arrived at Key West in the Mariel boatlift. Miami was swamped. A new outreach center of Miami Dade College was built in Hialeah. Soon 70 percent of the students of the college were Hispanic. His faked high school diploma was perfect. The college authorities did not seek any further testimonials; they were too busy with the flood of immigrants. He was swiftly admitted.

Over the next four years he changed physically. He was barely recognizable as the gawky young man who had arrived at Stetson East in the fall of '79. His hair had grown out, he had a moustache, his olive skin was further darkened by the years of Florida sun. His dress went from preppy to beach chic. He was, in the eyes of God and man (but not himself), Martin Jose Cruz.

Stu's money had only gone so far. Other work was required to maintain his one-room apartment in a former social housing block in Overtown. He ended up doing bar work at the Over and Under in the DuPont Building on East Flagler Street. He kept his interaction with the clientele on a strictly professional level. There was only a million-to-one chance someone from his past would stumble on him, but it was still a chance.

His fellow students said he had a trick memory. But his memory had been trained in the basement of the Lot by means they could never imagine. Like a Mormon missionary, he could quote whole chapters of the Bible. Learning by rote was as easy for him as it was impossible for the average student. He took the LSAT in August three years on. The results arrived three weeks later. Martin Jose Cruz had ended up in the top ten percentile of all students in the country that year, way above the median for acceptance at Miami School of Law, not quite enough for the one-in-a-thousand shot at Harvard Law—a shot he would never have taken even if his scores had been good enough. A return to Massachusetts would have been insane. Miami was all he wanted, and with good grades he would certainly find an associate position at a Florida law firm afterward.

But even though he tried to stay beneath the radar, he attained notoriety of sorts: his score earned him a dean's merit scholarship, further easing the pressure on his vanishing dollars, but now the new face of Ed Constance was there in the university yearbook, grinning out at all who cared to look. Would anyone recognize the young man who had disappeared from Northeastern four years before?

By December '84 all was settled. One more semester and then law school. He could dump the bar job and concentrate on his law degree.

Then everything changed. The Over and Under was not busy that December day. The counter was fifty feet long, with four bartenders. His was the last workstation. A young woman entered from the sunlit exterior, and the three other bartenders who had been chatting to one another paused and looked as she walked past them toward Ed. He felt a frisson of uneasiness as she approached.

Not having much money of his own, Ed had nevertheless begun to appreciate the finer things in life, many of them worn by the better-off clientele of the Over and Under. The new arrival looked to be in her early twenties but her getup wasn't studenty, more like someone on an expensive date. She came to a stop in front of Ed and laid down her purse on the bartop. It was a Chanel clutch with the two interlocked gold Cs on its flap. She seemed to levitate without apparent effort onto a bar stool, then smiled at him. He began to notice things then: principally what she looked like but also that he had been holding his breath, and that his three fellow barkeeps were observing both of them from down the bar.

"Nice bag," he heard himself say. He had no idea why.

She didn't seem to mind. "It's not mine," she answered. "I borrowed it from a friend."

"Special occasion?" he asked. Curiously, he found he was hoping it wasn't.

"Maybe," she said. "Why don't you fix me a drink while I find out?"

"Sure." He felt his face flush. He never blushed. He hoped it wasn't noticeable in the dim interior light. "What'll you have?"

"White wine spritzer."

"Coming up."

While he fixed the drink, details about her that he had noticed earlier but had immediately repressed began to reregister. Her hair was in a bob. She had a delicate chin and high cheekbones. Like him, she had an olive complexion; hers was like a luminous dust. Her brown eyes appeared fathomless. Before she sat down, he had taken in her willowy figure, accentuated by a black swing dress; a small choker showed off the delicate pillar of her neck. Despite her borrowed bag she looked expensive. Or maybe the entire getup was borrowed?

She broke in on his reverie. "You look familiar," she said. "You a student?"

"Miami Dade, prelaw," he said. "You?"

"I'm a Romance language major. French... and Spanish." She laughed at that—more than two-thirds of the student cohort were fluent in Spanish.

"*Suena interesante*," he said. She shrugged. He pressed on blindly. "Don't you get to study abroad?"

"Sure. I spent some time in France."

"Oh?"

"It was OK," she said, but her eyes dropped to the counter, as if perhaps she didn't want to talk about it.

He plunked some ice into the spritzer. It was odd that she had said she'd spent "some time in France" rather than a year as would be customary for an exchange student. Why? "Anywhere interesting?" he asked. There was a strange relentlessness to him suddenly—he had to know.

"Paris," she answered, not looking up, sighing and quirking her mouth a bit. He set the drink on a coaster in front of her. "Paris" contained a host of exotic, and, with that sigh, mysterious possibilities.

She extracted a pack of More from her purse and drew one out. "Got a light?" she asked.

He took a Bic lighter from his shirt pocket and fired it up. She steadied his hand with her fingers for a beat as she drew in and then exhaled an elegant stream of smoke through her nose. He watched it drift away, a beautiful wraith.

"What's your name?" she asked.

"Martin... Martin Cruz."

"Nice to meet you, Martin. I'm Sarah, Sarah Cuervo."

She presented her hand. It fairly disappeared into his as they shook. "You travel much?" she asked.

"Never left these shores," he answered.

"Where're you from?" she asked.

"Minnesota, St. Paul," he said.

"Cold," she said.

"I don't go back anymore."

"Oh?"

"Both my parents died in a car wreck when I was a kid." For some reason these lies seemed particularly clangorous when spoken to her. He watched to see if her face registered suspicion.

"That must have been tough," she said, as if she meant it, her eyes never leaving his.

Something was thawing inside him. He went with the flow; let go a bit. The conversation was nothing special: campus, living arrangements, professors, friends—of these last, none shared. Her fashionista friend Emma who had lent her the finery for today was mentioned more than once. In the past he had found these conversations with other customers pointless and they had died a natural death. But he felt something alive beneath their banal exchange. The conversation was just a game. The pointlessness seemed to have a point. Why? Where was her date? If it was a date?

By now other customers were trickling in. Some got as far as his end of the bar. He served them unconsciously. Each time he returned for a bit of glass-polishing in front of her. The pleasantries, if that was what they were, continued. After some twenty minutes she looked at her watch. She took one last sip of spritzer and placed a five-dollar bill on the counter. "Keep the change," she said.

He couldn't read her expression. "Not waiting anymore?" he asked.

She shrugged again. "I guess some people aren't worth waiting for."

"I'm sorry," he said.

She smiled. "Don't be. Anyway, who knows, maybe I came in just to flirt with a bartender?"

She slid down from the bar stool. The words left his mouth before he could stop them. "Would you like to go out sometime?"

She had begun to walk away but she turned, her eyes fixed on his for a beat. He had a heart-yawning moment when he thought she was going to make an excuse, but then she took out a scrap of paper from her purse, took a ballpoint from a holder on the bar and wrote a number on it.

"Call me on that," she said matter-of-factly and was gone.

Apart from Gloria's and Jim's, it was the only number he never forgot.

He left it well into the next day before he called, asking himself if he really wanted to do this. He found he did. At about noon he swallowed, picked up the telephone and dialed.

Maybe his choice of first date was not a good one. It was Tom's party. He didn't know Tom that well. Just played racquetball with him occasionally. In fact, probably all Tom knew about Ed was that Ed was a lot better racquetball player than him, which was hardly a basis for a close friendship.

Why had he chosen to meet her in the most public arena he could think of? Loud music, loud conversation, a crush of bodies, a fug of beer and Hirondelle wine. After years of hiding was he trying to prove that he could meet someone openly, like a normal person? He remembered the shrinks: there was no normal—particularly for an Apostle.

He had been there an hour and he was sure she was a no-show. The telephone conversation had been fleeting, and nervous on his part. Maybe his gaucheness had put her off? He nursed a beer, leaning against the kitchen sink, apart from the others in the living room. He thought of leaving. This had been a mistake.

She came to him out of the cloud of cigarette smoke and strobe lighting like an apparition. Lovelier for it, even more beautiful than she had been in the bar. She planted herself squarely in front of him, so close he could feel the heat coming from the buttoned front of her printed jersey midi-dress.

"So you're Martin, the friend of Tom's I've heard about?" she playacted slyly and smiled. He had the impression of her dark hair and body, lipstick red but not too red, a few imperfections on her skin beneath the foundation, but really it was only her brown eyes, her dark-brown eyes, he saw.

"Want another beer?" she said. And on inspection, he seemed to have chugged the last of his beer some time ago.

He gathered himself and said, "Sure, why not?" He had to repeat this as he found he was whispering and the music outside the kitchen was deafening. Afterward, when they went into the living room, the music proved welcome. No conversation possible. You could only shout, cup your ear, not hear, shrug, and smile. It suited him. He had no idea what he wanted to say.

They had ended up just dancing and then, when a slower number came on and everyone else started getting in clinches, they did too.

When they left she said, "Come on, my apartment's not far and my roommate's away." So he had ended up at her place without him knowing how he got there, and they were on her bed, necking furiously now, hands wandering, buttons, zips, and clasps being undone, and then he was in her and the bed was rocking and creaking loud enough, he was sure, to wake every single one of her neighbors.

After that he had seen her nearly every day. As if she had absorbed him into her bubble; a happy bubble, the outside world muffled, distant. For once the loneliness was gone and it seemed to Ed that it would only come back if he ever questioned his luck.

He never did ask her who she had been waiting for in the bar that day.

Ed didn't have many friends on campus. His life was self-contained, compartmentalized. He didn't socialize with Sarah's friends. They met at strictly arranged times. He only met Emma, the friend who shared their small, off-campus apartment, a few times.

One day he arrived at what he thought was the prearranged time to find only Emma there.

She suggested coffee and a chat while he waited for Sarah to get back from class. Evidently there had been a mix-up with the times. She would not be long, she insisted. In fact, Sarah didn't appear for over an hour. It was quite an hour. Emma was surprisingly keen to talk about Sarah. Perhaps overeager, he thought later. Perhaps Emma had an agenda. Perhaps she didn't like her roommate. Or maybe the few times they'd met she'd taken a shine to Ed.

She began by saying her roommate was so lucky to have found him, given what had happened to her in Paris. There was a pregnant pause. Ed must have looked blank. He realized that Emma wanted him to follow up. He knew he was in a dangerous position if he did; he would ask those unasked questions that he had neglected for so long.

"Sure," he said, noncommittally.

"You know, you're kinda cool not letting something like that get in the way of things."

Emma was raising the stakes.

"I guess," he replied, still neutral. But his interest was nevertheless piqued.

"I mean, Sarah was really destroyed by that guy, you know?"

Ed had a sinking, cold feeling in his gut.

"But, now you're around, she's living again—you know what I mean?"

However much he didn't want to hear the story, Emma seemed intent on laying it out in small increments, like a death by a thousand cuts. And in an hour there was plenty of time for Ed to hear it not once but twice, if Emma had cared to repeat herself.

She told the story with qualifiers like "as you know," "as Sarah no doubt told you…" when it must have been clear from Ed's expression that this was the first time he had heard any of it.

Sarah had elected to study in Paris, at the Sorbonne, in her third year. Being bright, attractive, only twenty, and away from home, she might have decided to just have a good time. But for the first month or two in the French capital she had diligently applied herself to polishing her language skills, going to lectures on French literature and writing papers.

As the semester ended, one of the tutors, a reader in literature called Alex Leroy, kept her talking after a lecture and invited her to a colleague's party. Emma laid on the description at this point: Alex was a soulful-looking man, with dark spaniel eyes half covered by a flop of dark hair, dashing Gallic charm, both bohemian and urbane. He was eight years older than Sarah, had the air of a man of the world, a man who knew a lot of women, but maybe had been a little hurt by them too. Before she knew it, they were in a relationship.

It was not too long before Sarah was due to return to the States for the vacation. That evening there was the dash to Charles de Gaulle in his deux chevaux, the tearful parting, the scrap of paper with her home phone number pressed into his hand. Ed thought of the scrap she had given him at the Over and Under, which he still kept in his wallet.

Back home she waited for his call. Each day making excuses to herself why he didn't.

She took an early flight back. That cold January morning when she called from her apartment, he seemed surprised to hear from her. He couldn't see her immediately. He had something important to do.

At the university Sarah asked around. The story came out gradually: it appeared Alex was well known for dating female pupils. At least three others, she discovered. He had been with one of the other girls over Christmas: that was why he hadn't called, why he had delayed seeing her on her return.

Sarah went to her apartment, where the Gauloise-smoking old concierge gave her the same world-weary look of condolence with which she greeted all the girls with mascara-smeared eyes ending their tragic love affairs.

Sarah had returned to the States without finishing her year in France. When the fall came she was certainly not looking for any more romance, just concentrating on her studies. But toward the end of that semester she had met Ed…

They both jumped when Sarah came in. She halted at the threshold and stared at them, as if guessing what had been going on. Guiltily and slowly Ed rose from the couch, where he'd been sitting next to Emma.

"Hi," he said. He suddenly didn't know what to do with his hands, so wiped them on his jeans as if they were dirty and thrust them into his pockets.

Sarah silently placed her study books on the coffee table.

"Shoot, is that the time? I'm late for class," Emma exclaimed. She was suddenly all bustle, pushing herself off the couch and grabbing a satchel of books. She paused for a mere second or two to apply lipstick in a mirror and was gone with a cheery "Goodbye."

Ed stood awkwardly as Sarah went into the kitchenette. "You want coffee?" she asked coldly.

"That would be good," he answered.

She busied herself with the ground coffee and the French press. "What were you talking to Emma about?"

"You know, this and that."

Sarah slammed the measurer on the counter and coffee flew everywhere. "Don't give me that shit, Martin! You were talking about me, weren't you?"

Ed looked down, unable to reply.

Sarah took a stride or two toward him until she was so in his face he couldn't avoid her stare. "I thought so. Well, Martin, number one—if you have something to say, say it to me. I don't like being discussed behind my back. Number two—I don't belong to anyone, least of all you. You know, life's too short to suffer dicks, so maybe you should just leave now."

"Listen, Sarah, we were just chatting, OK?" he finally managed to say.

"Just chatting? Right. You know she has a thing for you?"

"Emma?"

She flushed, angry again. "Don't give me that crap. She's always giving you the eye. She almost had her hand on your zipper when I came in."

"We were just sitting, nothing was going on."

"Yeah? Well, tell me one thing. Emma is a Class A fantasist. I bet she was spinning you some pretty wild stuff about me, wasn't she?"

Ed blushed slightly. "It wasn't like that. We were just talking student stuff, you know?"

Sarah harrumphed, but he could see her mood was gradually subsiding.

"Let me fix you some lunch," Ed volunteered quickly. He had become a pretty dab hand at cooking. He wiped up the spilt coffee, then rummaged through the contents of the refrigerator. There were the makings of quesadilla and red salsa. He busied himself with a frying pan and a bowl. Thankfully there were a couple of cans of Pabst in the refrigerator too, and they drank those with the meal.

The storm had passed but Ed was disturbed by the glimpse of the hidden Sarah he'd just seen. They went into the bedroom, almost as a reflex: Emma was out so they had to have sex. They went through the familiar moves but, even when she arched her back and came, Ed's mind was far away. He was not in the moment and found he could not climax. That was a first. A big struggle was going on inside his mind. Sarah had withheld the truth from him. Perhaps he was just some kind of rebound from this Leroy guy. There was enough in Emma's story to have convinced him of that.

On the other hand, who was he to judge? His whole life in Miami was a giant lie, one he dare not confess to anyone, even, for the moment, to Sarah. That glimpse of her volcanic temper was certainly no encouragement to probe further into *her* past. It was clear she wasn't going to volunteer any more information to him than he was going to volunteer to her.

CHAPTER THIRTY-TWO

The relationship survived more moments like the one after Emma's revelation. And in time, of course, he had to tell her the truth about himself.

Sarah's mother died shortly after they met. He had attended the funeral with her. She was an only child, her father long gone. The New Jersey graveside was not crowded; the Cuervos were apparently not a numerous clan, or a social one—even at the wake the few uncles, aunts and cousins barely engaged with one another. A nodded acknowledgement and couple of sentences were the sum total of most conversations. Most of the mourners sat silently sipping coffee. Maybe the whole family held secrets? An uncle explained to Ed that there was a little money for Sarah, the sole heir. Enough for an apartment.

Her newfound, modest wealth bought a pretty, small walk-up in Matilda Street in Coconut Grove. Outside, the walls were made of light-blue clapboard. Spanish oaks and palms shaded the streets. The nightlife was open and easy. Ed abandoned Overtown without regret. Even with the relentless study, life was good, mainly spent outdoors, in palm-shaded cabanas or on sun-kissed beaches without winter.

Three years passed. In that time he got his JD, then passed the Florida bar exam. Ed had achieved everything he had set out to do in the seven years since he'd arrived at the Greyhound station in the fall of '79.

But success brought danger. His photograph was in various yearbooks and magazines again. Half of him was pleased, half paranoid at the attention. In his last year he had interviewed at law firms specializing in international tax law. This specialization had been chosen carefully: unflashy, not public-facing. He was a reserved young man who gave little of himself but had an air of quiet determination about him that fitted the profile of some of the more staid firms. Offers came in. One firm, Merriweather's, had an opening in Miami as a junior associate in the tax law department.

He was interviewed by a panel of senior partners. Three gray men in gray suits, studious, humorless. In contrast, the head of HR, Maria Benzema, who sat in, was dressed in fashion more suited to the Over and Under than Merriweather's: an Emilio Pucci kaleidoscope print that was like a psychedelic trip for the eyes, with pretty much all the hues of a tropical island. She had her hair up in a topknot and wore bright red lipstick and some exotic eyeshadow. Despite being at least twenty years older than him, she appraised Ed with a look that he took to be a little more than professional. Anyway, his looks wouldn't get him this job if the partners had anything to do with it. It was probably out of his league. The interview was just good practice.

The gray partners droned on: tax planning, or, if you wanted, "avoidance, never evasion," was the name of the game. Some travel would be required, mainly to Caribbean tax havens like the Caymans, Panama, the Bahamas, and others. His Spanish would be useful. They asked some technical questions about US tax regulations and the IRS. He barely remembered his answers.

The interview concluded. He stood, as did Benzema. "Mr. Cruz, would you mind waiting outside the door for a minute?" she asked with a smile.

As he sat outside there were murmured voices behind the door. Then Benzema opened it and ushered him back in.

The senior partner stood and said, "Mr. Cruz, we have concluded unanimously that you are the right person for this associate position. Are you interested?"

Ed said something, which again he could hardly remember afterward. He was led to Benzema's office: it had tropical plants and jazzy wall paintings and a view over the harbor. She laid out the terms and conditions: $20,000 plus bonuses. She asked him to think over the offer for twenty-four hours, then let her have his answer. The glint in her eyes was still there and she gave no indication that she thought he would decline. Despite his unease, how could he? He was down to the last few cents of his savings.

Nevertheless, he fretted overnight. Dumfries's passport would be tested by these overseas visits. The driver's license and other papers had held up, but would the passport survive the greater scrutiny involved in crossing borders?

Were the authorities still looking for Ed Constance? There were some 13,000 open missing persons cases in the US. Surely they would have given up on him by now?

It was only the documents that could betray him. Long ago he had surrendered his entire life to Dumfries's work. Without the trust he had in the papers he simply could not live from one day to the next.

He was seven years gone from Boston now. Seven years was the statutory period before a missing person was presumed dead. He wondered what had happened to Winthrop Road and the Tranquility cabin. No doubt Winthrop had been sold to settle Stu's debts. But the cabin had been put in his name. Was there a statute of limitations? Had a creditor petitioned the state for Ed to be declared dead so the equity could be released? Or were the executors even now trying to find some distant Constance relative to bequeath it to? Stu and Bettie had both been single children. It might take years before a blood relative was traced and probate on Tranquility could be settled.

But even after seven years, he was sure of one thing: the people in Stu's red book had not forgotten him, were searching for him. Even so, he could not live his life under that shadow. A life he had not expected had begun—a girlfriend, a home, and the offer of a steady job. If Sarah was going to be part of it, he would have to tell her the truth. It was just a question of when.

The next morning he rang Benzema and accepted the offer. And that night he told Sarah everything.

He prepared tamales and a key lime pie. Bought candles and a bottle of Newton Chardonnay. He told her that he had been offered a job as an associate in a prestigious law firm. The salary was good: enough to put down a deposit on a house maybe, buy a new car. He was honest: his work would involve advising overseas clients on tax affairs, shell companies, and property deals. Travel to the obvious tax havens would take up some of his time.

He realized he sounded nervous. The candlelight and the warm night air through the windows lent her an ineffable beauty that made his heart ache. He realized he could well lose her forever in the next few minutes.

"Sarah," he said, "there's something else I need to tell you."

Was this the feeling you had before your first skydive?

"That you think I'm beautiful?" she quipped, but she looked suddenly nervous.

"I always think you're beautiful," he answered seriously.

"Beauty's in the eye of the beholder," she said.

However light she was trying to be, however lovely the evening, he couldn't keep the earnestness out of his voice. "Sarah, whatever I say next—whatever becomes of us—I swear I never meant to deceive you."

She frowned. "You seem awfully serious tonight, Martin."

"That's because I have something very serious to tell you."

She didn't break off eye contact. "I guessed," she said quietly.

"You did?"

"Martin, we've been together for three years—you think I hadn't realized something?"

"Then why didn't you ask me?" he said.

She smiled, almost sadly. "I didn't want to risk this," she said.

"Risk what?" he asked.

She looked around the apartment. "This." She nodded to the candles and the table and the gently waving curtains. "Happiness."

"OK," he said.

She looked up. "So, what is it, Martin? Someone else? You know, I promised myself I wasn't going to be hurt again, not by anyone. But then I ran into this cute bartender in the Over and Under—"

He held up a hand. "It's not that," he said.

"Then what is it?"

He looked down. Where to start?

"You know what I told you when we first met—Minnesota, being an orphan…?"

"Yes."

"Not true. I may be an orphan, but as far as I know my parents weren't killed in a car wreck, and I've never been to Minnesota."

She just looked at him, waiting for him to continue.

"Second, Martin Cruz is not my real name."

"Second?" she said. "Wouldn't that be the first thing you mentioned, Martin, or whatever your real name is?"

"It's Ed… Edward Burns Constance. If you care to look, you'll find my name on the FBI's missing persons list."

She stared at him for a beat. "You changed your identity? Why?"

"This may take a while."

"I'm not going anywhere," she said and poured each of them another glass of Chardonnay.

So he told her the whole story. From the Lot to Matilda Street. He didn't leave out the deaths: Stu, Gloria, Carl. She had to know the risks. The candles had guttered by the time he'd finished, and the Chardonnay was all gone.

There was silence then, just the noise of the warm breeze and a faint car horn from outside. But she was still looking at him. That was good, he decided.

"OK… Ed," she said eventually. "Ed—I think I can get used to it." She paused. "So, Ed, tell me one thing. We gonna be OK? Are these people still after you?"

He took comfort in that "we." He said, "It's been seven years. Nothing has happened since. It's gone quiet. Maybe we all escaped. Maybe the bad guys gave up, or died."

Sarah took his hand. "I like that 'maybe,'" she said. "Let's just enjoy this, Ed—what we have. Can you do that? Because I can."

He put his spare hand on hers. "Yes, Sarah, I can—but we've got to be careful."

"Always careful," she replied.

They were married at St. Patrick's Church on South Beach. The ceremony was only sparsely attended. Barely two pews at the front of the large Romanesque-style church were occupied. Voices and footsteps echoed. The wedding march sounded tinny in the huge space. They didn't mind. Their eyes locked the instant she drew abreast of him at the altar and pulled back her veil. Their gaze didn't break away as they walked back down the aisle, man and wife. Beyond the porch steps, the drop-off zone was packed with a much larger wedding party about to enter. The guests politely parted and applauded as Ed and Sarah made their way through them out to the sidewalk. Their one solitary limo was now double-parked with a dozen others from the second wedding party. The driver eased out of the chaos.

The reception was a seven-minute ride away in a small suite at the Fontainebleau on South Beach. Outside was a balcony and awning overlooking palms, the boardwalk, and beach. The Atlantic stretched away, the view interrupted only by a distant freighter.

Two tables easily accommodated the two dozen guests. Her side of the family was barely represented: only four of the Cuervos from Sarah's mother's funeral made it down to Miami. The rest of the guests were friends and work associates of both of them.

The toast and speeches were given by Ed's best man, a very recent acquaintance from Merriweather's called Gordon Robertson, and by Emma, Sarah's maid of honor.

A lot of champagne was drunk and there was much laughter as dusk fell quickly. Ed felt light for the first time, maybe ever; light as a feather, free to drift, as if he could rise up, look down on the Fontainebleau and South Beach and all of Miami Harbor and the city beyond as the lights came on. Yes, maybe the bubbles made him high.

He looked at Sarah and he knew that with her he was at last complete. He had been one person for so long. No family, no friends; only unseen, unknown enemies with unknowable agendas… He had been a permanent stranger to the world, and to himself.

But she completed him. And she knew his secret. That lonely secret that had sat there, waiting, all his years. She knew, yet the other guests did not know. It was theirs alone. How well she played that role to the uncle who in New Jersey had told Ed about the inheritance—she spoke brightly of Ed by his false name, as nothing more than the associate attorney with a great future he pretended to be: not a missing person; not the wanted man of his reality. He was safe with her: this was theirs; according to the priest's injunction, until death.

She turned to him then and smiled and he saw in her smile that promise. And there was the spark of something else too, a spark of mischief. Like when she said maybe she had only gone to the Over and Under to meet him. Now she looked at him knowingly. And then outside at the darkening beach. What was she hinting at?

It was toward midnight when the bride and groom rose. The friend who had been manning the portable sound system in the absence of a paid DJ stuck in a cassette and Cyndi Lauper's "Girls Just Want to Have Fun" came on. Sarah turned and threw her bouquet over her shoulder and, whether through luck or judgment, Emma caught it and screamed with joy. The two women hugged, then Sarah grabbed Ed's arm, and the couple waved to the assembled guests and backed out of the suite to applause. But in the corridor outside she didn't head toward the elevator and the honeymoon suite they'd reserved for the night, but toward the back entrance of the hotel leading to the beach.

"Where're we going?" he asked.

"Let's have some fun," she said and pulled him after her. She lost the white bridal shoes in the corridor, then, with Sarah dragging him, they burst through the revolving doors and, whooping, ran across the boardwalk and across the white sand beach to where the waves were crashing in the darkness. The strand in either direction appeared deserted.

"Unzip me, Ed," she said and he did and the white satin dress cascaded to the white sand and then her stockings, bra, and panties dropped and she stood, unabashed, naked as the day she was born. He followed suit. The tux and dress shirt and striped pants were discarded, then the briefs and socks.

"Last one in is a wimp," she shouted and took off. He had been staring at her, taking her all in in the dim light from the hotel, so she got a head start. He ran after her. As he ran he briefly worried about sharks and jellyfish, but that was the old Ed, not this new version. He plunged into the warm rollers and waded out to where she was hollering in the surf zone and there they kissed, entwining and then thrust apart by the waves, until, at last, she said, "Let's go in."

They swam back to shore. The current had taken them north. They were 100 yards from the buildings of the Fontainebleau. They crouch-walked by the surf line back in that direction, hoping that no late-night stroller would be on the beach. They saw no one, but when they came to the place where they'd discarded their clothes, they were gone. They both burst out laughing at the same moment.

She punched him lightly on the arm. "Now look what you've gotten us into," she said.

"Me?" he answered.

"So, clever, what are we going to do?"

"In for a penny, in for a pound, I guess," he said. "Come on," and he took her arm and they ran back over the beach. There were some palm trees fringing the boardwalk. "I've an idea," he said and broke off three fronds from the nearest of them. "This will cover us up a little."

She giggled. "We can say we're going to a fancy dress party as Adam and Eve."

They held the fronds strategically and advanced toward the rear door of the hotel.

A couple of frat boys whistled at them as they went up the path, but luckily there were no police. Her shoes were still in the corridor and she slipped them on. There were a few people in the lobby. Some laughed, some tutted at the dripping naked couple.

One blue-rinsed matron, up way beyond her bedtime, accosted Sarah: "Young lady, what do you think you're wearing?"

"Two palms and Manolo Blahnik," she said back.

The night manager at the desk was unperturbed. Perhaps he'd seen it all before during spring break. "Ah, Mr. and Mrs. Cruz. We've been expecting you," he said, handing over their key. "But for future reference, it's usual for our guests to take their clothes off after they've gotten to their rooms, not before."

They were still laughing when they hit the elevator to the top floor.

Matilda Street was sold. An interest-free loan from Merriweather's had secured them a terracotta-colored, hacienda-style fixer-upper in Miami Beach at 1330 Lenox Avenue between 13th and 14th. The yard was large and green, overlooked by a generous deck: there were the obligatory bougainvilleas, hibiscus, palms, gerberas, blue salvia, Mexican heather, and purslane.

He kept the Bible, the Woolworth's notebook, and the papers from the Lot hidden in a Sunshine Biscuits tin. Soon after their arrival at Lenox, when Sarah was out, he buried it out in the garden under a palm: he didn't want her to know that, despite his promises, he was hanging on to these last vestiges of the past. He had left a sealed letter along with his will with a friendly attorney at the downtown law firm where he had interned. The letter told his whole story and directed interested parties to the buried box "in the event of my death."

There were not many ground rules in Ed and Sarah's marriage. But there was one that was non-negotiable: no children. He had explained that evening in Matilda Street: he could not imagine any other version of childhood than the one he had endured at the Lot.

So, they began in truth—but, as things do, the next two years changed them. His job took him away and became more demanding. He was on the ladder to partner—he had to climb it, like all associates, and work all hours. His home energy levels were low. He slept a lot. Reserved to begin with, he was now often silent.

Her mischievousness vanished. There were times when he found her in gloomy introspection. He wondered if it was the children she would never have or that mysterious past obsessing her. Or whether it was *his* past she was brooding about—whether it was about to catch them up.

Sometimes he didn't recognize the Sarah he had known since the Over and Under. Maybe that moment on the beach was the last time they were ever truly happy.

CHAPTER THIRTY-THREE

In the first year at Merriweather's he was invited to accompany some partners and senior associates abroad to meet with expat clients. Benzema made it clear that this favor was one not dispensed to many associates; Robertson and his other colleagues were left slaving at their desks in the office building in the financial district when he flew out. "Just do what the partners ask, and have fun," she said before he went. She looked like she regretted not coming with him.

The first day at border control was nerve-wracking. He landed at the tiny airport on Tortola in the British Virgin Islands sweating more profusely than even the 80-degree heat outside merited. But the border officer didn't note his unease, just gave him a wide smile, stamped his fake Cruz passport and wished him a happy trip.

He stared at the visa stamp. The first in his pristine, fake passport. The happy-go-lucky border officer had stamped it upside down.

Afterward, the three days were lazy, with only one or two late-morning meetings. Golf, scuba diving, lounging around the pools… it seemed these trips were unofficial vacations from the firm and families. The partners, single and married, chased the young tourists. Just as he had in the Over and Under, Ed stuck to the rules of self-preservation and stayed separate and sober.

Back at the office the unrelenting work was offset by Benzema's attentions. Of all the juniors, Ed was singled out for special attention.

Benzema had made sure his desk was near her door. She favored his workstation with visits, her pencil skirt often riding up to reveal an expanse of thigh as she sat on the corner of his desk. She tapped him lightly on the arm and told him to lighten up: he was doing well. His work was noted. Clients were satisfied. Large sums of money had been saved from the IRS. Promotion beckoned, if he could keep things tight, keep putting in the brutal hours.

If he worked late, it was certain Benzema would work late too. She would beckon him in for drinks in her office. By then all the other senior partners would have gone home. They would have two or three stiff drinks. More touching, more flirtation before she would suddenly say, "You'd better get home to that little wife of yours, Martin, before I do something foolish," and, abashed, he would scuttle out, grab his briefcase and leave. He found his heart was racing, he felt buzzed, whether from the booze or the company he had no idea. He found he desired Maria Benzema. A lot. After these sessions he was too wired to go to bed until late.

Benzema announced he was Employee of the Month. Normally this award was conferred in the form of vouchers for Bloomingdale's or Neiman's, but, when the staff assembled on the floor to congratulate him, Benzema handed over a box with a Motorola DynaTAC cell phone inside. Only the senior partners had these. There were intakes of breath and some backslapping from the other associates, but he sensed that they had begun to resent him. The cell phone represented a whole month's salary to most of them.

He felt unease about his prize. And not just because of the resentment from his coworkers. There was something alien and rather threatening about the brutalist piece of plastic. When he got back to Lenox he didn't even turn it on. He put it back in its box and placed it in a bedside drawer.

Sleep was becoming a problem. He felt permanently wired. The hours, the trips, the booze, Benzema, Sarah's silence—they all added up. When he did manage to sleep, flashbacks came thick and fast.

The second time he flew to Tortola he was alone, just there to certify some client's papers before filing them. A quick trip in and out. The border guard was less friendly than the first he'd encountered. He scrutinized the passport and then looked sternly at Ed and pressed a buzzer under the counter. The guard announced to those behind Ed that the line was closing and they should move over to the other booth. His fellow passengers grumbled and stared at Ed like he was a criminal as they tried to argue their way to the front of the other line. A senior officer arrived to join the one in the booth and a whispered conversation followed, interrupted only by frequent glances at Ed.

Eventually the senior officer said, "Mr. Cruz, there's an irregularity with your visa. Please come this way."

Now his heart was ice and a cold sweat broke on his brow. He barely registered his footsteps as he was ushered through a side door into a featureless side room with only a table and chair, an empty watercooler and a yellowing miniature banana tree in a pot.

The senior officer told him to sit and went away with his passport. A clock ticked loudly on the wall. Five minutes passed, five minutes that seemed an eternity, then the officer was back. Now he was all smiles and apologized: it seemed his visa was in order after all and he was sorry for the inconvenience. He handed back the passport and wished Mr. Cruz a pleasant visit.

Ed was led back into the arrivals hall. He walked out into the blazing tropical sun and got in a cab to take him to the main settlement, Road Town. He stared at the unfamiliar position of the driver on the right-hand side. His heart was beating fast, his hands were shaking and his lightweight suit was soaked with sweat. There was no air-conditioning in the cab, just the hot wind blustering through the open windows. They drove along the coast road: asphalt around the airport, then suddenly unpaved stretches, potholes rattling the suspension, then asphalt again. The road, such as it was, was flanked by green hills on one side and pristine white beaches and blue ocean on the other.

He pulled the passport out of his jacket pocket and rifled through it. There was the visa stamp from the first visit. He stared at it. Something was off about it. He couldn't put his finger on it. What was it that had made the border guard suspicious? What had he seen that the officer on his first trip had missed? Everything seemed the same as before. The passport had satisfied over a half-dozen immigration officers since.

He leafed back to the visa. A plain stamp with "Visitor, the British Virgin Islands" and the date of entry and a remain date with the first officer's signature. In all respects it was, as far as he could recall, exactly the same. Except now he saw one thing: instead of being upside down, the stamp was now the right way up. It had been changed. He flipped through the other visa pages. At first glance the other entry stamps looked exactly as they had been. But was there something minutely off about them too? The book looked very much like Dumfries's original work, with later accidental additions like the crease on the cover, the rubbed foil of the US eagle and ink blot on one of the pages. If it had been copied, someone would have had to have access to it for some time to reproduce it so faithfully. Yet the version in his hands just didn't feel right. He was confident it had been swapped as he waited in the immigration hall.

The taxi entered Road Town. It was a ramshackle place, not gussied up like many of the Caribbean tourist traps, despite its cruise ship pier for what the locals called the "pirate tourists." There were quite a few yachts sporting American, Canadian, or European flags.

His taxi suddenly swerved and pulled up abruptly in front of the hotel. There was a blare of horns and some colorful expletives from the vehicles behind.

He paid and walked into the lobby with its parquet floor and mahogany desk. There was a notable restraint about the colonial-era hotel after the riot of brightly painted houses and aquamarine sea outside. The foyer was cooled by overhead fans, and sparsely populated. Nevertheless, he had the feeling of being watched.

The meeting with the client was at lunch and only lasted a few minutes. The flight out was not until the next morning. The rest of the day was his.

When he got back to his room he took out the passport again and stared at it. Was he imagining things? With the long hours and the after-hours boozing sessions with Benzema, he hadn't been feeling himself these last months. He put the passport away. The walls of the well-appointed room seemed to be closing in on him. He decided to get out. He put on a Hawaiian shirt with a muted pattern, some jeans and sunglasses, and headed down to the harbor area. He sat at an outside table in a bar on the quay and ordered Red Stripe. It was served straight from the bottle. The other clientele were predominantly white yachties in Bermuda shorts and T-shirts. Beer and conch fritters were being consumed at a fair lick. He chugged his beer and the cold, sweet amber soothed him. Nothing to worry about: a couple more beers, sample some of the local cuisine and head back to the hotel for an early night—

Then there was a shadow over the table and someone sat abruptly in the seat next to him.

"So, dead men still drink," a voice said. Another Red Stripe was pushed in front of him.

He looked around. A short man in a loud Hawaiian shirt with Ray-Bans propped on his forehead was sitting there holding his own bottle of Red Stripe.

It had been nearly a decade, but Ed recognized him. The gingery hair had receded now and the pale face was freckled with exposure to the tropical sun. The grin was still there, though the teeth looked yellow from smoke. It was Moss, the student at Northeastern who had befriended him for that one short day so long ago.

"You gonna pretend you don't recognize me?" Moss asked.

Ed said nothing. Any words were stoppered in his throat. He felt cold despite the equatorial afternoon sun.

Moss leaned forward. "It's OK, man, I get it. We all read the papers back then: 'Northeastern student missing. Adoptive father's suspicious death.' Let me guess. You flipped out—another abusive patriarch bites the dust…" He laughed. "Wish I'd had the cojones to do the same." He took a hit of beer. "But, man, if I could have had a dollar every time I was questioned about you—by the police, then the Feds, then some super-secret anonymous government 'official'… Made me think you must be some Russian spy or something. They all had a massive hard-on for you, Ed—that is, if you still call yourself Ed."

Words finally came back to him. "What do you want, Moss?"

"What do I want? Jeez, that's gratitude. I just bought you a beer."

"I didn't ask for it."

Moss sighed. "Listen, Ed, I don't know what happened to you. I'm just glad things seem to have worked out. There you are: nice duds, hanging out in a nice spot. So what if you gave the finger to the man? Like me." He gestured at the blue ocean. "I'm just drifting where the weed's good and no one hassles me. Got a nice little boat out there. It's called the *Shona*. Successor to the *Madeline*. Remember her from Northeastern? She was cute but turned out temperamental. Same story with Shona. She split too. So now I need another yacht. Bad karma to keep the one with the old name, you know? So, tell me, what really happened to you?"

Ed stood abruptly. "Look, Moss," he said, "we didn't know each other back then. We just hung out for one day. But, contrary to what you're thinking, I didn't kill anyone. Sure, I disappeared. There was a reason. I did what I had to do, though it meant abandoning college even before I'd begun. That's all I'm going to say. So, now, please just forget you ever saw me, OK?" He threw down a ten. "That should cover the drink."

Moss's face closed—gone was the bonhomie. The pale eyes looked suddenly resentful, balked of a juicy story. "Have it your way; to be honest, you were a bit of an asshole even back then, Ed," he said.

Ed turned on his heels and headed off in the opposite direction to the hotel. He didn't want Moss to know where he was going. He glanced back. Moss was still staring after him, the same hostile look on his face. Ed ducked into a side alley, then looped back through the side streets. He was sweating heavily. He wiped his forehead and then his hands and entered the hotel lobby quickly. He went up to the receptionist, the same beaming West Indian lady who had greeted him that morning, with "Dolores" on her name badge. "I need to check out, please," he said.

"But, Mr. Cruz, you only just arrived."

"Something came up at the office. I need to fly back to Miami today."

"No flight until tomorrow, sir," Dolores said.

"Where's the nearest airport with flights today?" he asked.

"Puerto Rico."

"Is there a charter that could get me there?"

"Sure, Island Wings. But it will cost you."

"Price is not an issue. Ring them, please. Tell them to be ready in a half-hour. And here's some money for your trouble." He slid a twenty over the counter. He didn't wait for thanks, but hurried up to his unused room, picked up his overnight bag and hustled back down to the lobby.

"All arranged, sir," Dolores said. "There's a cab outside."

He was unaware of his response as he hustled out. He looked left and right up the street. No sign of Moss, no sign of the police. Would Moss even go to the police? The little he knew of him suggested not. Moss, though he was probably some kind of trust-fund millionaire, figured he was a rebel. Maybe he actually admired Ed for what he had done, just as he'd said. Maybe Ed shouldn't have been short with him? But sitting shooting the breeze with the guy would have revealed more and more of what Ed wanted forgotten. He'd brushed him off, and people did things against their nature when they felt insulted, and that might include going to the authorities.

The cab dropped him at the Island Wings hangar a quarter of an hour later. There was a pilot wearing overalls checking the engine on a Cessna. He wiped his hands on a rag and shook hands. "Mr. Cruz?"

"The same. Grateful for taking me at short notice."

"No problem. I'm Sam Saint. If you give me your passport, I'll get it stamped, then we'll stow your bag and we can go."

The passport. Was there going to be another problem? But it seemed Saint had a shortcut when dealing with customs and immigration. He returned in five minutes and handed the passport back. Then he ran Ed's proffered visa through the credit card imprinter: $600 he would have to explain to Sarah. In fact, there was going to be a lot of explaining to do. Why he was arriving back a day early for one.

Only moments later they were airborne and heading toward San Juan.

He just made the last flight to Miami.

He had plenty of time to think during the three-hour flight over the Caribbean. He began second-guessing himself. It was possible that Moss, instead of going to the local police on Tortola, would ring one of those old contacts he'd mentioned at the Boston police or the FBI. If so, there could be a reception committee waiting for Ed at Miami International. His life might be coming to an abrupt end: suspected murder and an assumed identity would be enough to put him behind bars.

Then a second thought came. Moss had mentioned the "super-secret" government official who had questioned him. Who had he been? Why had he been anonymous? Was he one of them, Typhon? And if they had now been told about Ed's reappearance on Tortola, with their resources, might they not already have questioned Moss, Dolores, Saint, and the American Airlines ticket seller in San Juan? Might they now know his assumed name and where he lived? And might they, rather than cause a scene arresting him at security at Miami International, be waiting quietly to snatch him from his home?

Since he was arriving from a US territory, there was no customs and immigration check at Miami. He passed security: no police reception. He got the shuttle to the parking lot, where he looked around cautiously before approaching his car. Maybe his brand loyalty had been inherited from Stu: his new Merriweather car was a Volvo station wagon. In this case, it was black rather than the powder blue of Stu's old jalopy, abandoned so long ago in the Maine Woods.

It was now eight o'clock in the evening. He drove across the waterway by the MacArthur Causeway and hung a left on Lenox. It was a long avenue, a mile and a third, interrupted between 11th and 12th Streets by Flamingo Park and its sporting amenities; 1330 was just north of the first of these, the Abel Holtz Tennis Stadium. He pulled in and parked in its lee, got out and took the path bordering the park. There was no one out. At the baseball stadium he turned left back toward his house. He inched his way around the wall surrounding the villa at the intersection of Lenox and 14th Street and peered back south toward 1330, fifty yards away. Nothing stirred.

He crept toward the house, keeping to the shadows of the shrubs overhanging the neighboring property's walls. There was the front path and a paved double-parking area currently only occupied by Sarah's Cavalier. Lights could be seen through the drapes in the front living room. All seemed normal. But he couldn't shake the feeling that something was waiting for him.

There were paths either side of the house leading to the back garden. He took the left-hand one and eased around the corner. As always, the back door was unlocked when he tested it. This was a virtually crime-free area. He quietly opened it and stepped into the unlit kitchen. The temperature was still in the high seventies and he could hear the muted roar of the AC from within the house. He felt his way around the kitchen promontory. The door to the unlit hall and the front rooms was open. He could now hear a voice over the AC. It was coming from the living room. It was Sarah. Who was she talking to? He crept down the hall past their bedroom. Now he was nearer, he could hear her better; he realized she was on the phone.

But there was something off about her voice. She sounded… afraid?

"No, he hasn't complained, but he seems very tired…" It was as if she were picking her words very carefully. The person at the other end of the line evidently cut in, as there was silence for a few seconds.

"In a month. Maybe two months," she replied. There was another pause.

"Yes, I better hang up now. I'm expecting him to call me." Then there was the sound of the receiver being replaced. He heard her intake deep, juddering breath.

Half of him had decided to silently back away, exit the house, retrieve his car and drive up as if nothing had happened. But the other half was on the threshold of a very dark place. That half demanded answers, now.

He stepped into the room. She screamed. Her face was a mask of unrecognizable, primal terror. He felt as a murderer must feel just before they pull the trigger, plunge the knife… do what they are about to do and it's too late to stop it.

She took a step back and nearly knocked over the lamp on the side table behind her. "Ed, what are you doing here?" she managed.

"Who was that on the phone?" he asked.

Did she hesitate? "It—it was just Emma."

He didn't reply straightaway. For reasons he couldn't explain, given they were talking about a phone conversation, he went around the room, looking for signs that someone else had been there. He even twitched aside the drapes to check there was no one hiding behind them.

He turned to her. "What's going to happen in a month or two?" he asked.

Again, was there a hesitation? "She was talking about coming to see us."

"And what's me being so tired got to do with it?"

"Ju-just if this was a good time for a visit, nothing more. For God's sake, Ed. You scared the hell out of me. What are you doing here? You're meant to be in the Caribbean."

"Yeah? Well, something came up."

"What do you mean?"

He tried to control his breath and lower his racing heart rate. "I ran into someone… someone from the past."

"Who?"

"A guy called Moss. We met that first day at Northeastern. Now he appears out of nowhere in the same bar as me on Tortola."

She was silent as she digested this.

"Could it have been coincidental?" she said eventually.

"I don't believe in coincidences anymore," he replied. "Has anyone been here?"

"No one. I haven't spoken to anyone but Emma all evening."

"No one outside? No cop cars?"

"Nothing." She was crying now. A reaction to the shock. "You're scaring me, you know? Really scaring me."

He heard his pulse pounding in his ears. He had a bunched expanse of the drapes in his hand. His knuckles were white. Something in her look was so beseeching that he felt his pulse calm, the buzzing in his ears clear. He felt the wave of darkness begin to recede. She was Sarah, just Sarah. But the imp whispered then: why had he never heard that scared voice before, the one he had heard on the telephone? That had not been Sarah.

If it had not been Emma on the other end of the line, then who? He could call the operator and ask for the number, but not in front of Sarah. And the chances of tracing a call were slim: it could have been routed through any number of exchanges.

He let go of the drape and stepped toward her. She flinched back into the side table and this time the lamp wobbled and fell with a crash. The light went out.

He held up his hands. "I'm not going to hurt you, Sarah," he said. "Listen, I'm going to get my car now. Why don't you fix us both a drink and we can discuss this, OK?"

She nodded but there was no trust in that look.

He backed away and went to the front door. "I'll be five minutes," he said.

She didn't answer.

CHAPTER THIRTY-FOUR

The week after Tortola he called into the office sick. He spent a lot of time looking out onto Lenox Avenue. But there were no cops, no suspicious people casing the house. Life outside appeared normal.

Something was gnawing at him. A hunger he could not assuage. Something was missing, something physical; his time away from the office only seemed to make it worse.

And he couldn't shake the strange sound of Sarah's voice on the phone. After his unexpected return, relations were strained. She seemed afraid of him. She slept in the spare room. They went without speaking for hours. In the emotional absence he began looking coldly on their relationship. He began to wonder: had things been too pat with them? Some questions he had never asked now seemed to demand answers.

One morning he told her he was going for a drive to clear his head. Instead, he went to the Civic Center Public Library. He spent an hour or so leafing through the phone books, picking those states he knew the Cuervos at the funeral and the wedding lived in. There were Cuervos, sure; it wasn't that uncommon a name, but did the initials and addresses match those of the people he'd met on those two occasions?

Next, he put in a request for the Miami Dade syllabus on microfiche. When it arrived, he rolled the film through the reader until he came to the Romance languages section. The course prospectus made much of the exchange program with the Sorbonne in Paris. So that, at least, stacked up.

Someone had helpfully microfiched information on the Sorbonne course and the participating professors and tutors. There were even photographs. As he scrolled through the list, there, suddenly, was the picture of Alex Leroy: he was just as Ed had imagined him. A guy in his early thirties: a suavely handsome Gallic face with fashionable stubble and piercing eyes stared back at him. The accompanying description of Leroy's credentials was, of course, in French and Ed knew little of that language. But right at the end of the bio there was a personal faculty phone number. Some imp of the perverse made Ed jot it down. His eyes went to the bank of phones across the library foyer. It was not yet eleven; still working hours in France. He felt in his jacket pocket for change. There was not much, and international calls were charged at $3.60 a minute. But he had enough for a short call; he decided he just wanted to hear Leroy's voice.

He rose stiffly and went across the hall to a booth. He lifted the receiver and slotted every last bit of change he had into the machine. Then he dialled 011, then 33 and the number on the prospectus. There was a pause, then the curious, short double burst of the French ringtone, followed by a pause, then a repeat. Half of him wanted no one to pick up.

The ringtone was abruptly cut short. "*Oui?*" a male voice said at the other end of the line. The coins dropped abruptly into the body of the machine.

"Is this Alex Leroy?" he heard himself say, without asking whether Leroy could speak English.

"Yes, this is Alex Leroy. Who is speaking?"

Ed thought quickly. The name of his friend from Merriweather's came to mind: "My name is Gordon Robertson. I am an American attorney in Miami."

"Yes, Mr. Robertson, how can I help you?"

"I'm trying to trace a former exchange student who was with you in Paris—Sarah Cuervo." He paused, then added, "I gather you knew her well."

There was silence for a beat at the other end of the line, then Leroy said, "Why are you interested in Sarah? Has something happened to her?"

"As I said, I'm trying to trace her—she's gone missing. Has she been in touch with you?"

There was another pause, maybe an intake of breath, then Leroy said, "Listen, Mr. Robertson, I don't know why you think she'd be in touch with me after all this time. I barely knew her; she was very unhappy in Paris. After the incident she dropped out of the course and, as far as I know, went back to America."

Ed went cold. "What incident?" he asked.

"Surely you know, Mr. Robertson? Sarah tried to take her own life. An overdose. The doctors got to her just in time. I assumed that's why you're calling. She has disappeared and you're worried she may have made another attempt?"

"Do you know why she tried to commit suicide?" Ed asked.

"As I said, she was unhappy: depressed, introverted; not the sort of student I would have recommended for an exchange in a city like Paris. Now, I think I've given you as much information as I can properly give. If you have any further questions, I suggest you contact the dean."

Was he being edgy? Defensive? And had Leroy described the Sarah he, Ed, had first met in the Over and Under?

Just at that moment a series of warning beeps sounded, telling him his credit was running out. When they cleared, there was just the continuous, ready-to-dial tone on the American side. Leroy had hung up. Ed cradled the receiver. A single 10-cent piece tinkled into the coin return.

The sickness he was faking to keep away from work was becoming a reality. Suspicion, or maybe something else, was reducing him, bit by bit. Sleep was difficult. He was prone to sudden flares of rage; the same rages as in his childhood.

He decided to seek medical help. Merriweather's had excellent medical insurance and there was a battery of experts at his disposal.

He needed Benzema to sign off on the insurance and he wasn't sure how she would react when she saw it was for a shrink. For this, too, he would have to go back to the office. Would his colleagues see through the feigned illness? But when the day came she was all sympathy, laid a carefully manicured hand on his sleeve. She confided that many of the junior associates were the same. Needed a little help with the hours. Maybe a little prescription to ease things along, she said with a wink. She knew a good doctor. No questions asked. The senior partners didn't need to know.

"Look after yourself, Martin," she said, exerting a little more pressure on his sleeve.

The doctor gave him drugs to help him sleep, but the drugs didn't ease the problem. He found himself still pacing his study into the small hours, Sarah long since in bed.

He was burned out. He got back to work, but his hours suffered, he filed less. His career was on the rocks; no more trips to the Caribbean. Making partner looked an impossible prospect.

A week later the bombshell fell. The doctor had referred Ed for some "Routine tests: just to see if there is any underlying cause for the insomnia." It began with a head X-ray. Whatever the doctor found, he didn't like it; Ed was referred to a specialist called Godin. However cold the atmosphere in Lenox had been in the last few weeks, the ice broke with the referral. Sarah's fear of him was replaced with concern. She returned to the bedroom.

There was a lot of hugging the day of the appointment at Baptist on North Kendall. The name of the clinic was enough to freeze the blood: the Department of Neuro-oncology. Godin's was an impressive office: tasteful leather furniture, cherrywood desk, family pictures in silver frames, and several diplomas on the wall. Through the plate-glass window was a palm-fringed reflecting lake. Godin resembled a kindly monk: about sixty, a bald, wrinkled, unassuming man with a gentle smile, expressive hands with long fingers, like a concert pianist, and caring gray eyes that seemed to carry all of human wisdom inside them.

At a hidden switch, the surgeon's expression morphed from polite and welcoming to empathic and concerned. He showed them the X-ray of the cranium, a small mass pressing down on the frontal lobe that, amongst other things, he said, was affecting Ed's sleep patterns. The growth was possibly malignant. A biopsy would be required. If Godin's suspicions were proven, an operation and then radiotherapy must follow.

Godin explained that Ed would need a general anesthetic for the biopsy as a trepanation would be required to remove the sample tissue. Results would be available in two days. He urged Ed to schedule the procedure as soon as possible. He insisted it take place before Christmas; with the uncertainty of the diagnosis, time was of the essence. If it was cancer, as he suspected, it was not necessarily fatal, yet. If the biopsy confirmed what he suspected, the trepanation hole would be used again in the ensuing operation. The operation itself was safe, the prognosis was good, the scarring would be light and invisible, soon to be covered with hair. He expected a complete recovery but he warned that Ed might exhibit headaches, nausea, impaired speech, behavioral issues, mood swings, and memory problems, but these symptoms would gradually ease in time. He suggested that Ed not have any visitors for a couple of weeks after the operation; the quiet would aid his recovery. Ed would be back to his old self within the month, he assured Sarah. All that remained was to schedule the trepanation.

Ed squeezed Sarah's hand and smiled as best he could and said, "Sure, Doc. Sarah and I'll discuss the schedule and get back to you."

Perhaps Godin's forehead creased a little, as if he were a tiny bit displeased that a mere patient should be dictating his schedule, but his kindly smile re-formed a moment later.

"Of course," he said. "Take your time. But not too much time, young man. It's a serious but curable issue." He stood and gave Ed a handshake, Sarah too.

"Why didn't you want to schedule right away? Is it about the money?" Sarah asked Ed as they walked out into the lot.

He stopped and glanced back at the facade of the oncology building. "We have Merriweather's insurance," he answered.

"So, what's the matter?" she asked.

"I want a second opinion," he said.

"But the doctors at Baptist are the best in Miami," she said.

Something raw began to burn in him, as raw as the sun beating down on the parking lot. "Just humor me, will you?" he said brusquely and strode off across the baking asphalt to the car.

As if in sympathy with Ed's medical troubles, Sarah had begun to suffer severe stomach cramps. She elected to visit Baptist as well. They recommended X-rays. Ed agreed to pick her up in the car after the exam. By now the corridors of the hospital were familiar to him and he made his way without even looking at the overhead signs, his face moody, his eyes downcast. He was surprised when he reached the familiar radiology waiting area to find Sarah not seated with the dozen or so people sitting inside on the waiting room chairs but standing just outside the doors. She was clutching in one hand a white and blue plastic object shaped like a pen.

"Did you already have the exam?" Ed asked.

"No," she answered.

"Why not?"

She looked away. "Ed, there's a certain class of person they don't allow into X-ray suites, unless there's an emergency. I'm one of them," she said.

"What're you talking about?"

She held up the stick. He saw it had a little panel set into the side. In it there was a heavy blue line to the right and a faint purple one on the left.

"What is it?" he asked, though he had a good idea.

"The radiologist asked me if I could be pregnant and—well, I guess the penny suddenly dropped. I excused myself and went to the pharmacy and bought one of these home pregnancy kits. This is what showed up."

"You're pregnant?"

She nodded.

"How?"

"I think you can guess how, Ed."

He was silent for a beat. "We discussed this, Sarah."

"Yes, Ed, we discussed it, but talking isn't everything. Sometimes accidents happen, and you know what?" Heads were turning in the waiting room and she lowered her voice a little bit. "Of all the crappy things that have happened these last few months, this could be a good thing. The only good thing, Ed."

He stared at her, and then at the people back in the waiting room, who, under his gaze, went back to looking at magazines or staring at the wall.

"Let's discuss this elsewhere," he said.

"Good idea," she replied.

They were silent on the way home. Ed felt afraid, yet lifted out of himself too. He surprised himself by getting out of the car quickly, hurrying around and opening the car door for her. She gave him a sideways look as they went up the steps.

"You OK with this?" she said.

"Let's get inside," he said. And that was the last they spoke about it that day. In fact, the last they spoke about it for a week.

He took another medical leave. Benzema seemed to know all about Godin's diagnosis, despite doctor–patient confidentiality. Merriweather's, after all, were paying for the opinion. She told him to be back the Monday after Thanksgiving.

He told Sarah he would go alone to Dr. Cusemano's surgery for the second opinion. He also told her it wouldn't be covered by the Merriweather insurance. The checking balance was going to take a hit. Just as it had done with his impromptu plane charter.

It seemed a very long wait for the results of the new blood work and X-rays.

Cusemano called the home phone the day before Thanksgiving. Ed had told Sarah he would prefer to receive the news alone. She had gone off in her Cavalier.

"There's good news and bad news," Cusemano said. "The big one is the X-rays show no occlusion to the frontal lobe—in other words, there's no brain tumor."

Ed, who had been standing upright with the phone clenched in his fist, sat down abruptly on his study chair. "What? No tumor?"

"Correct," Cusemano answered.

"How could the Baptist people be wrong?" he asked.

Cusemano was silent for moment. "Mistakes happen, Mr. Cruz."

"Not like this, they don't," Ed answered.

"It's not for me to comment on another physician's work," Cusemano answered primly. "My job is to give you the best advice possible. If you are unhappy with the previous advice, I suggest you file a complaint with Baptist."

Ed didn't really hear. His head was spinning. He had stared at death. Now the reprieve. He felt like laughing and weeping all at once. The emotions stuck there as cold fact took over. He had seen Godin's X-rays—still had them in his briefcase. It seemed they must have been switched with another patient's. How? As he had said to Cusemano, mistakes that big didn't just happen.

He realized Cusemano was waiting for him to respond. "Sorry. You said there were two things."

Cusemano took a deep breath at the other end of the line. "Just as it's not my job to criticize another practitioner, it's not my part to discuss patients' private choices either..." He paused.

"But?" Ed prompted.

"But what I see in the toxicology report, Mr. Cruz, may suggest the origins of your recent state of mind."

"Tox report? What about it?"

"Mr. Cruz, there are high levels of methamphetamines in your blood. Enough to suggest serious use."

"That's impossible," Ed answered.

"As I said, I don't pass judgment on my patients. But, on exam, I noticed a certain dilation of your eyes, weight loss, gum retraction... You had an elevated heart rate and what I can only describe as signs of hyperactivity. You wouldn't be the first. I see many patients who take substances to help them through their day. But methamphetamines take their toll: not just physically, but when the system doesn't react to the stimulation any more you enter what we call a tweaking phase. I would suggest you have reached that stage, Mr. Cruz. The psychological symptoms of tweaking present just as yours: anxiety, insomnia, mood swings, paranoia, and hallucinations."

"I have never taken speed," Ed answered, but with a hitch in his voice. He had never knowingly taken the drug—but had he been given it? How? When? Cusemano was suggesting use over a long period. Had he been systematically doped?

Cusemano said, "The first stage of addiction is denial, Mr. Cruz. I can recommend you a clinic if you wish. And, of course, this report is confidential and will not be referred to any other parties. I'll mail it along with my bill. Please let me know if you have any further questions." And with that the good doctor abruptly hung up. It was the day before the holiday, after all. No doubt he had an urgent appointment on the golf course.

He was going to live. The shadow that had hung over him since the first meeting with Godin was gone. It was like dazzling sunlight poured into a dark cell. The momentary happiness was total. Then came a switch. He reached down into his briefcase and pulled out Godin's report. There it was in black and white. His mood abruptly switched. Suddenly he found he doubted Cusemano.

His mood swung back and forth, then settled back on his original thought. Cusemano was right. Godin had lied. Why? He wanted to operate. Wanted to mess with Ed's brain, like one of those mild-aspected Nazi doctors in the Second World War with their human vivisections. When brain function was tampered with, behavior was altered. Was that what this was about?

Why would a doctor want to manipulate him? There was only one explanation: Typhon had found him.

In a country of 250 million, they had found him.

Realization settled on him like a lead sheet. It all added up. The fake diagnosis, the drugs, the passport issue, even the ease with which he had gotten the position at Merriweather's...

Why was it so cold in the study? The air con was only cranked halfway, but he was shivering.

He looked around the room. Maybe the phone was bugged—maybe the *house* was bugged.

If they had found him, what were they waiting for? The code of conduct was clear: should Cusemano's report ever find its way into the hands of an oversight committee, Ed would be disbarred immediately. That would be the end of Merriweather's, his career, Lenox Avenue, possibly even his secret identity. Prison beckoned. And what of the baby, this unplanned kid?

Maybe Typhon was waiting because they wanted him alive, biddable, trapped.

The periphery of his vision crowded in. He was as helpless as the nine-year-old boy he had once been. He stared sightlessly over the green lawn toward where he had buried his memento box. Maybe his little insurance wasn't as clever as he thought. If they knew everything else, they might very well know about that as well. The attorney he'd interned with had had a Merriweather connection. Perhaps he'd opened the letter already? And even if he was on the level, Ed was sure that after he was gone the box would disappear before his attorney could arrive to retrieve it.

On impulse he stood and went out the back, took a spade and dug up the mud-spattered tin. He cracked it open. All was as he had left it.

He'd had a sprinkler system set up a week or two back. It suddenly burst into life, sending arms of spray around the garden, spraying him and the contents of the tin. The morning light caught the spray and a rainbow showed. He hurried into the house, discarded the tin and put the Bible, notebook, and papers in his bedside drawer next to the abandoned cell phone.

He went back into his den and brooded. He needed somewhere else to hide his insurance. Hell, he needed to plan an escape.

CHAPTER THIRTY-FIVE

Sarah came back with Thanksgiving groceries. He didn't hear the Cavalier pull up on the driveway. Moments later a shadow fell across the entrance to his study and he turned. She stood there in the frame of the door.

"Did Cusemano ring?" she asked.

"Yeah," Ed answered.

She took a couple of quick steps forward and laid a hand on his shoulder.

"What did he say?" she said.

"There's no tumor."

"Oh my God—" She clapped her hands to her mouth.

She noted Ed's grim expression. "What's the matter? Aren't you pleased?"

Ed held up Godin's report. "If I'm clear, what's this about?" he said.

"It must have been a mistake, Ed."

He stood up abruptly. She took a step back, frightened, just like she'd been when he came back from Tortola. There was a stereo unit on the bookshelf. He switched on the amp, cranked the volume and swung the turntable arm mid-point over the record. His hand shook a little and there was a loud scrunch of needle on vinyl, then the first chords of Simply Red's "If You Don't Know Me by Now" blasted out of the mini speakers. It was a song he had been listening to a lot recently. Only when Mick Hucknall's voice was exhorting his listeners to sing the song along with him did Ed turn from the turntable and look directly at her.

She was staring at him. He put a forefinger to his lips and gestured around the room. Now she looked both anxious and bewildered. He guessed she thought he was going mad. He gestured for her to sit on the couch and, when she did, sat next to her.

He took her hand. "They may be listening," he said quietly as the backing singers chorused Hucknall's lyrics.

"Who?" she asked, her voice slightly raised.

"Whoever's behind this," he said, waving Godin's report. "The room might be bugged."

"You're scaring me again, Ed," she said.

He stared at her intently. "Listen to me, Sarah. I didn't want any of this for you."

"What do you mean?"

"Like I told you before we got married. Them. The organization. Typhon. Now this fake diagnosis. They found me."

"You were careful. How could they find you?"

"I dunno. Maybe the guy who forged my papers got busted and they got him to talk. We know the Feds are in on it. The deputy director, for Chrissakes."

She squeezed his hand. "Aren't you overreacting? Godin's X-rays could just have been a mix-up."

He stood up abruptly again. The Simply Red album he'd put on halfway through now ended on another chorus and he flipped it, crunching the needle mid-song, careless of the playing surface. Once the noise was deafening again, he went back to his briefcase, pulled out his passport and showed it to Sarah. "Exhibit B."

"What about it?" she asked.

"I didn't tell you, but the immigration people shook me down the second time I went to the British Virgin Islands."

"What of it?"

"The BVI officers took my passport away. Came back a few minutes later and returned it. But something was off. The visa looked like it was in a different place, some of the other stamps too."

"That sounds a bit paranoid. Why would they mess with your passport like that?"

"I dunno, maybe someone out there didn't like Dumfries's work. Saw some minor flaw in it that would get me busted at immigration one day, so they 'improved' it. Made it more like a legit one. You know, with the watermarks and all that. Then they got the BVI guys to swap it for them."

"Why would someone help you like that?"

"Maybe I made a wrong assumption. Back then, when they sent Carl after me, they wanted me dead. But it could be they've changed their minds. Maybe they think nine years' indoctrination at the Lot can't be thrown away. So they created this sham: this job, which no doubt they set up specially for me, this house… upped the stakes. When push comes to shove, I'll have no options. Just have to go along with their plan, whatever it is. And now I have two doctors who could ruin me."

"How?"

"They have evidence I have a meth addiction."

"Meth? You?" she said.

"I've been kind of hyper. Just thought it was the pressure of work, but it's something more. It's in Cusemano's report."

"This is unbelievable," she said.

"I swear, I've never knowingly taken drugs. For all I know it's the goddam coffee at work, laced with ground-up Desoxyn. Anyway, it's enough to get me disbarred. Another hook they've gotten in me."

Her voice nearly broke. "We'll figure it out," she said hoarsely. "Go back to Godin, confront him, make him explain."

"Explain what? They wanted to drill a hole in my head for no reason. They wanted to effectively lobotomize me when all the time the X-ray's showing some other sap's brain."

He saw the terror in Sarah's face.

He lowered his voice. "Godin's operation was a front. The operation wouldn't have been at Baptist's. The private ambulance would probably have taken me off somewhere else. I'd have woken up some kind of zombie, picked up a bomb, driven out west and—lights out. Everyone who knows me would just say I was acting strange, freaked out, paranoid, under the influence. It was because of my past, you know?"

She was staring at him, lips pursed, saying nothing. He couldn't work out whether she was on board or not. He went on nevertheless. "I bet my blood is sitting in a lab cooler right now, chock-full of those drugs, just waiting for the FBI to find it after I'm gone. Yeah, they have me by the balls, Sarah. I guess I'm just stupid. All those after-work cocktails no doubt laced with the stuff. At first I thought I was just coming home buzzed. Then I thought I had a drink problem. For all I know the drugs are in the watercooler outside my office at Merriweather's and no one else drinks from it except me."

Now she did speak. "Listen, Ed, I know you're trying to explain things, but you're still not making a lot of sense."

His fists clenched and he felt spots of red glow in his cheeks. "No? I guess it wouldn't, since you've just had your privileged existence and your tragic affairs and stuff, while I've been living this"—he waved his hands—"whatever this is, as long as I can remember."

Sarah flushed. "Ed, I'm on your side, remember?"

He took a deep breath. "You're right. Sorry." He sat again at the end of the couch, staring forward, his hands twisted together.

"Look, Ed. I don't understand any of this, but surely we have to go to the police. This physician is an impostor."

Ed laughed bitterly. "Yeah, an impostor, like me. Let's get Godin arrested: medical malpractice. 'Cept it'll be me who ends up arrested, lickety-split."

By now Hucknall had moved on to a song titled "Enough." It seemed the right soundtrack to end the conversation.

A silence fell between them. He felt a tearing inside himself. He made a decision. This life had to end—end in a few days. He was going to run. But there was no way Sarah was going to go with him; the baby had seen to that.

"What're you going to do, Ed?" she asked.

"Just thinking," he answered grimly. But the time for thinking was over.

Then the record came to an end, and the stereo arm lifted and recovered itself to its stand with a self-satisfied click.

CHAPTER THIRTY-SIX

He had nowhere to go that Wednesday. He was too hyped to leave the house. After hours of pacing his study, he switched on the evening news. There was talk of heavy snowstorms blanketing the eastern seaboard, then a newsflash: there had been a bombing at a mall in Pensacola.

Eighteen dead. Early information was sketchy, but the scale of the incident was apparent from the TV pictures. The network showed fires burning in a shattered entrance lobby and thick black smoke roiling up into the sky. Cut to a helicopter shot: the mall roof blown off and the center ablaze, the firefighters' hoses arcing up but barely reaching the angry red eye of the fire.

An eyewitness reported with some consternation that it had been a woman who had committed the outrage. She had seen her enter the mall, the bomb apparently hidden inside a baby sling. Cut to a policeman: the woman's picture was on a driver's license in a car that had been driven onto the forecourt of the mall and abandoned seconds before the explosion.

A photo of the perp flashed up.

It hit him like a sledgehammer.

He had last known her as a girl, but, even so, recognized the grown woman. The kidney-shaped birthmark on her cheek was a giveaway. Sniveling Catrine had turned into stone-faced Catrine in the driver's license photo. She had a thousand-yard stare and pinprick pupils. Her face, other than that telltale birthmark, was sheet white, bisected by a line of red lipstick. Her gaze looked all the way back to the darkness of the Lot. She had become what they had ordained her to become back then, the fourth angel, pouring out her vial upon the sun: "and power was given unto her to scorch men with fire."

He felt numb all over. The newscaster was asking for information from anyone who knew her. A number was displayed on the ticker tape at the bottom of the screen.

Ed got up stiffly. This, then, was the beginning of the end. Typhon had begun their work. There was a call he had to make. But not to the authorities. He braced, tried to still the shaking of his hands, exited the house and walked down to the local bodega, where there was a pay phone.

He rang a number he had promised to never call again.

It was picked up after a dozen rings. "Yes?" a voice he'd not heard for almost a decade said.

"Jim?"

"Ed?"

"Yeah."

"Jesus. It's been a long time. You OK?"

Ed paused. "I'm in a jam," he said finally.

"What kind of jam?" Jim asked.

Ed said, "You see the news tonight?"

"Sure. It's all over; the bombing in Florida."

"Did you see the name of the person who did it?"

"Yeah, Catrine Connelly."

Ed took another deep breath. "She was one of the five, Jim. One of those on Highway 11. Connelly was her adoptive name."

"Christ," Jim said.

"An eyewitness on TV said she looked like some kind of zombie when she went into that mall. Like she was hypnotized."

"I heard that too," Jim answered.

"She was programmed, Jim. I'm sure of it. The organization got to her. Just like they tried to get to me back at Northeastern and on Eagle Lake."

"Listen, kid, I don't know where you're calling from and don't tell me either, but you're OK, ain't you?"

"They've found me, Jim. I'm next."

"Next for what?"

"Same as Catrine. Another Pensacola. Something bigger."

"I don't buy it. To what purpose, kid?" Jim said. "Why you?"

"I've been asking that question since I was nine, Jim."

There was a pause on the other end of the line. "What're you going to do?" Jim asked eventually.

Now it was Ed's turn to pause before he spoke again. "Jim, I got a wife, and a kid on the way." He heard himself make a sound that might have been choked laughter; he hoped no one in the bodega was overhearing this. "I guess I was living the dream. You know, I used that money well: studied hard, became an attorney, got married, bought a house—the whole nine yards. But it's all over."

"Don't say that," Jim said.

"Listen, Jim, I just want you to do one thing for me. Can you do that?"

"Name it."

So Ed told him the favor. He spoke for about ten minutes. The details he gave Jim were accurate to a T.

There was silence again on the other end of the line. Ed wondered if Jim had hung up, but there was a buzz of static telling him the line was still live.

"You're asking me to kill you, kid," Jim said finally.

"It's a last resort. It may not come to it. I might get away."

"But if you don't, you want this?"

"Better this than thousands of others die. You have to see that."

There was another silence, then Jim spoke again. "Kid, you're resourceful. I taught you that. You'll find a way out of this, I know. But…"

"But you'll do what I ask?"

"Yes," Jim said eventually. "God forgive me, I will."

"Soon?"

"I'll go tomorrow."

Ed hung up suddenly, before Jim had the chance to reconsider.

The next day, as pleasing aromas wafted from the kitchen, smells he was barely aware of, he was still watching the newsfeed obsessively; more information was revealed. They had dug up the children's pasts: Catrine Connelly was one of the Apostles, the lost children of Highway 11. There were historic pictures of the dump site, yet another of the smoking crater where the house on Eriksson's Lot had stood, and a piece recounting the children's tragic mystery.

The report told how Catrine's adoption had proven disastrous: truancy and delinquency at school; the adoption dissolved; many runaways from the series of foster homes she was sent to afterward; an unplanned pregnancy; a spell in a juvenile detention center; no high school or college; records for drug possession and solicitation. She had become a drifter. Subversive literature relating to left-wing terrorist organizations such as the Panthers, the Weather Underground, and the Symbionese Liberation Army had been found by the police at her last-known address, a halfway house in Tallahassee.

She had somehow escaped the system that had let her down as a child. Now, it seemed, she had returned to punish it for its failures. As an aside, it was reported that the records of the other four survivors of Highway 11 had been sealed by a juvenile court nineteen years earlier and their whereabouts and current identities were unknown. An "expert" opined that perhaps they should be tracked down in case they, too, began exhibiting the same homicidal traits as Catrine.

Sarah came in during a break in the cooking, wiping her hands on a towel. Catrine's picture was up on the screen again. She looked from the picture to Ed.

"Don't you want to turn that off?" she said.

He didn't look up. "I knew her," he said.

"The bomber?"

He nodded. "She was one of us."

"My God, what happened to her?"

"I guess she went crazy. Just like me."

"You're not crazy," she said.

He turned from the TV and stared at her. "Are you sure?"

"Maybe you need a drink," she said.

He didn't need any booze. His mind was spinning already. She uncorked the red wine anyway and poured him a glass. The cabernet tasted too oaky, and when he tried to eat the turkey it was like cardboard. He picked at the food, but obediently chugged the three glasses of wine that Sarah poured him. She watched him with slightly narrowed eyes, sipping juice—"for the baby." He would have preferred the juice.

The Fourth Vial. Why had Typhon waited so long? Had they really wanted Ed to be the first ten years before? His vial would be poured in the Euphrates, so the water would be dried. Read "Colorado River" for the Euphrates, and blowing the dam would lead to the predicted drying of the river. He was their flagbearer. His act would prepare "the way of the kings of the east," whoever they might be… The shadowy kings behind Typhon. The grand statement of the Hoover Dam: better than a mere mall in Pensacola. There were going to be more than eighteen dead in his scenario. Thousands, in fact…

It was as if the wine was tranquilizing him; he could barely keep his eyes open. He went to the couch and lay down. In the background there was the sound of plates and cutlery being loaded into the dishwasher. He was too tired to help. All he wanted was sleep, but he was afraid of his dreams. He dozed, then woke twice with a start. He settled again and slipped into REM sleep…

…then he was back with Shannon on the school bus: the sunlight slanting through the trees; the roar of the gravel on the logging road. She leaned into him and she, too, slept, the weight of her head on his shoulder, and his own head leaned down too and rested upon her braided hair. It smelled of a plastic meadow from the scented shampoo that Mrs. Frome bought in gallon bottles on her monthly shopping trips. A meadow of flowers, of psychedelic pansies and marigolds breathing an almost visible cloud of scent over a meadow so green it was blinding…

…and he heard her whisper: "The blood of dead men is on my hands…"

Ed and Shannon: the last two Apostles.

CHAPTER THIRTY-SEVEN

Godin had insisted the procedure be performed before Christmas. Ed now guessed why. There were only two robot agents left: Shannon and himself. Maybe the Hoover Dam was going to be the *coup de grâce*, the cherry on the cake, the angel of destruction on top of the Christmas tree.

The five Apostles' papers had been sealed by order of the Boston juvenile court. But he remembered how, back at Winthrop, Gloria had let slip that Shannon had been put in the foster system in Boston and had taken the name of her first foster family, Quincy.

Black Friday. It was not a public holiday but was universally treated as such. No one except security and janitors would be at Merriweather's. But public offices were open. He told Sarah he was going for a drive. He headed to the Civic Center Public Library again. As before, the place was virtually deserted. A few down-and-outs leafing through the papers in the vestibule, one or two students earnestly hunched over papers, that was all. He went back to where the entire collection of US telephone directories was racked in a massive oak bookshelf. There were dozens of volumes.

He got down the phone directory for Central Boston. No Shannon Quincy listed. He moved on to the directories of nearby cities in Massachusetts: Roxbury, South Boston, East Cambridge, Dorchester, Brookline... Again, nothing. Of course, her name might have changed; she could be married, or, like him, be living under an assumed identity. Nearly two decades had passed. It was a wild goose chase, but, given the sealed files, it was his only way of getting information on her.

Anyway, it seemed his rudimentary approach had failed. He was about to leave the library, but something took him down the line of directories to where the local ones were housed. He picked out the one nearest the end. It was thumbed and battered from continuous use: Miami (Greater): Coral Gables, Country Club Estates, Fort Lauderdale, Hialeah, Hollywood, Homestead, Kelsey Beach, Lake Worth, Miami Beach, Miami Shores, Palm Beach, South Miami, West Palm Beach. There were not many listings under Q.

And then, there it was: Shannon T. Quincy, Apartment 2C, 1465 NW 15th Avenue, Allapattah. Just three miles from here. A ten-minute drive.

He stared at the line sightlessly. It couldn't be anyone else. She was here. Why would Shannon have ended up in the same city as him nineteen years after Highway 11?

He had a sudden urge to rip the page from the directory and stuff it into his jacket pocket. Having the page would somehow make this moment real. But when he glanced up, the grim-faced receptionist at the nearby desk was looking at him suspiciously over her horn-rimmed spectacles. He realized he had been staring fixedly at the entry for a good minute and sweat had popped on his brow.

He got out his pocket notebook. His hand shook a little as he wrote down the address and number. He shut the directory, avoided the receptionist's eye and exited into the blinding sunlight of West Flagler Street.

On the day of his cancer reprieve and the bombing, he had decided that bugout day would be Monday the twenty-seventh. It was the day of major office announcements: promotions, firings, and bonuses. Even the half dead, as Ed supposedly was with his diagnosis, turned up to what the Merriweather staff grimly called Black Monday. He would show, reassure any watchers of his presence, and then vanish without a trace. He might get a day or two's start on Typhon—no more.

There was a cold, empty place in his heart. That night he moved extra supplies from the house to the Volvo in the garage. Cash, spare clothes, canned goods, an extra gas can, a knife.

He wrote a note to Sarah, then scrunched it up and threw it away. She might show a note to the cops, and Typhon owned them. There must not be any clues to where he was going: better Sarah and the future child lived not knowing what had happened to him. She would have the house and the money in their checking account. She would know why he had gone. Hate him for it, sure. But by now, surely she knew it was their only chance? Sometime in the future, when it was safe, if it was safe, he would find her and the child. Even if it was years…

When it was really late, he took out the Bible that Stu and Bettie had given him. The trigger could come at any time, through any medium. He needed to send his future self a message: a note from his free self to his Typhon self. It might save him. He would turn their weapon against them. He remembered: "The sword devoureth one as well as another."

He smiled grimly as he wrote. One day, soon, or a long time in the future, should he live, what was written here might lead him back to himself. He inserted the note into the first pages of the Bible and placed it on the passenger seat of the station wagon. He took the Woolworth's notebook and the papers from the Lot in their taped newspaper wrapping. He decided he would carry them on his person from now on. Better they were on his corpse than waiting here in a drawer for Typhon to find them.

He would need a weapon. To protect himself against whoever came after him—or, if they cornered him, to be used on himself.

On the Saturday he went to a favela in Little Haiti. He dressed down as much as he could but his laundered chinos, polo shirt and Ray-Bans marked him. He parked a couple of blocks away from the address he'd memorized, then plunged into the carnival streets: a riot of color; a torrent of abusive Spanish in which every living thing was cursed or propositioned, sometimes in the same breath; streets thronged with vendors' carts selling fresh produce, tacos, rack on rack of knock-off clothes, and tables of fake accessories. No need to pay top dollar for Gucci or Prada here.

The man he was looking for had been in trouble with the IRS, amongst other things—Gustavo Esteban had metal teeth, gang tats, and a certain reputation that had given even the unscrupulous partners of Merriweather's pause before they intuited the balance of his checking account. They assigned Ed to the case. Ed had been nervous going through Esteban's affairs; the man had, as well as the metal teeth, a face like granite. But at the end, when the IRS had accepted a few thousand dollars as opposed to the half million in unpaid taxes they had initially claimed and the affair was settled, Esteban's face had cracked into a metallic smile and he had told Ed that if he ever needed a little favor, he only had to ask. Even then, Ed had known Esteban's little favors were unlikely to be legal ones.

He had never been to the man's place of work—their meetings had been exclusively at the Merriweather offices—and had difficulty finding the address. He asked his way. The instructions were brusque. His Spanish was fluent but his clothes marked him as a stranger. Esteban's office turned out to be a bodywork repair shop. Each of the expensive late-model automobiles on the lifts, though apparently almost factory new, were being stripped ready for new paint jobs and, no doubt, plates.

Esteban sat upstairs in a box office, counting cash. He smiled when Ed appeared, called him *mi amigo*, sat him down for a café cubano. Ed was frank about his needs and the amount of cash available to him. Esteban didn't seem fazed by his one-time attorney's request. He had, apparently, seen it all. A snub-nose Smith & Wesson was produced from a safe. Esteban told Ed the gun was less accurate than the longer-barrelled .44 Magnum but easier to conceal. The chamber was loaded with .38 ammo. Good for close work. One well-aimed shot was enough. The registration of the gun had been filed off and it was untraceable. His teeth glinted as he spoke. He patted Ed on the back and wished him good luck, as if he knew a man who needed a gun that bad was going to need it.

CHAPTER THIRTY-EIGHT

Sunday. Sunset. The stereo in the Volvo on loud, the windows down. The Black Crowes. He was smoking. A new habit that got him through the sleepless hours. A habit that had, in fact, become a crutch. There was only one left in the soft pack in his shirt pocket. He pulled off the Dolphin Expressway, crossed the Miami River and drove north into Allapattah, a flat, featureless area of low-rent apartment blocks, auto shops, bodegas, and cut-price outlets. There was a convenience store at the junction of NW 17th Avenue and NW 20th Street. He pulled in and bought more smokes.

Then he stood in the lot and lit up. Shannon's address was only two blocks over to the east. Latino music pumped out of the bodega across the street. There were a few tables out the front where men were drinking beer and smoking. He realized that one or two of them were watching him standing in the deserted lot. It was time to move.

He got back in the car and drove east, the stereo now silent, the windows up. NW 15th Avenue was flanked by low-rent high rises and a few duplexes behind spiked-fence-enclosures. Shannon's was one of these last. The rendered walls of the apartments around the courtyard were painted sandstone. Number 1465 had two dusty live oaks shading a concrete lot where half a dozen rusty cars stood under the sodium lights. Bugs swarmed.

He parked across the street and turned the ignition off. The Volvo's fan gave its signature death rattle and subsided. He opened the door and warm air poured inside. A dog barked nearby, worrying at a chain. He crossed the road and went through the gates and, after a moment's hesitation, up the steps to the second-floor balcony.

Outside the door to apartment 2C there was a clothesline hung with two onesies, plus a rocker, a glass-topped table with a couple of crumpled beer cans, and an ashtray filled with burnt-out roaches. He considered the baby clothes, beer cans, and roaches. Shannon may very well have a partner, and she definitely had a child, or children. He wondered, if there was a partner, what they might think of a strange man turning up after dark. It was, after all, a rough neighborhood.

He took a deep breath and rapped on the door. The silence that followed was absolute. He rapped again. Nothing. He wondered what to do. Leave a note? Was that a good idea? He mustered his courage. "Shannon, you there?" His voice sounded strange even to his own ears. Distant, hollow, ghostlike. He tried again. "Shannon, it's Ed. Open up if you're there."

Still silence.

If he was going to write a note, he'd left his briefcase with pen and paper in the car. He was about halfway back down the steps when the front door of the bottom apartment creaked open. He looked down. An old guy stood there in the sodium light, looking up. He was dressed in black dress pants, flip-flops, and a shirt as white as his thinning hair and parchment-pale face. His eyes, which were fixed on Ed, were pale too, like ice, bisected by an aquiline nose. He inspected Ed with a hawklike gaze. Given the deserted neighborhood and its reputation, the old guy seemed curiously unafraid of him.

He said, "OK, mister, I don't know your business, but you better scat before I call the police." He had a faint accent; perhaps Eastern European.

Ed held up his hands. "I'm sorry—didn't mean to disturb you. I'm looking for Shannon Quincy."

The old geezer said, "What's she to you?"

"I'm an old friend," Ed answered.

"Well, I ain't seen you around here before, mister."

"It's been a while since I saw her."

"So you decided to come and visit at night? That's what a bailiff or bond bailsmen would say. Get going before I report you." His voice was quite loud. A light went on in an adjacent apartment and Ed could see someone looking out.

"OK," he said. "I'll go. Look, that's my car across the road. I was just going to get pen and paper to leave a note. Is that alright?"

"It's your funeral. If her fella Nate catches you writing her, you better watch out. He has a real mean temper on him and don't care for strangers."

Just then Ed heard the chain being pulled on the door above him. He looked up as it was opened. A black woman, about five six, came out. She was wearing a yellow checked dress and a purple bandana above which a dome of Afro protruded. Her face was still youthful and perfect, a perfect adult projection of the child he had once known. Shannon.

She cradled a baby. The child had a pacifier in her mouth and was swaddled in a pink blanket.

Nearly twenty years. It was strange that eyes could look just the same after all that time, even in the sodium-lit dark. Shannon's eyes, just the same as when she'd been a kid. Fearful, wary—as they had been back then.

Ed and she stared at each other for a moment, a moment that seemed minutes.

The old guy piped up, "Hey, Shannon, should I call the cops?"

Ed barely heard him. In that moment the Thanksgiving dream returned: that last day in June '70; the feel of her head on his shoulder; the fake meadow scent of that bulk-bought shampoo; the dusty smell of the bus upholstery...

Then he noticed something else about Shannon. There was an upraised area on her left cheek just under the eye. Bruising from a blow.

Shannon broke the silence. "It's OK, Mr. Zielinski. I know him," she said. Her voice was huskier than he remembered it.

"You sure?" Zielinski answered.

The baby began to fret and she shushed it. "It's OK, really. He's a friend. Come on up," she said to Ed.

Zielinski tsked, repeated his mantra about funerals and disappeared, banging his door behind him.

CHAPTER THIRTY-NINE

Ed followed Shannon into the apartment. The moment he was inside, she pushed the door to with a foot.

Inside, it was dark, only lit by one lamp, but as his eyes adjusted he could see he was in a combined living room and kitchen area. An array of baby clothes lay tangled on a couch. A baby bottle lay on its side on a coffee table, next to scattered picture books and a stained comforter. The air-conditioning was not on and the cloying smell of formula and dirty diapers filled the muggy air. There was a travel cot by the couch and Shannon leaned over and lowered her child into it. The baby keened and thrashed a little, then was quiet.

"She should be OK for a while," she said, almost to herself, then straightened and looked at him. "I never thought I'd see you again."

"Same," he answered.

"You know, I wondered how you'd turn out."

He found he couldn't answer.

"How did you find me?" she asked.

"Long story," he mumbled.

"Oh?"

"Very long."

"You know I didn't open up at first because, whatever you're doing here, Ed, I know it's not going to be good news."

They held each other's gaze for a beat. "No, it's not good news," he said. "But it's urgent."

She sighed. "It's the Lot, isn't it? You can take the kid from the darkness, but not the darkness from the kid. You know, my shrink, my actual shrink, told me that? Before he gave up on me."

Ed didn't answer. "Well, why don't you tell me it?" she went on. "My fella's on shift till midnight. However urgent, we got a little time. I'll make some coffee."

He was tired from another sleepless night and now a wave of emotion hit him and he felt weak. He sat in the one easy chair as she busied herself in the kitchen. Eventually she came back into the lounge area and handed him a steaming cup. She moved the baby clothes and perched on the edge of the couch opposite him as he sipped.

"This is strange," she said.

"Yeah," he said. "After all this time, and here you are in Miami. You know, Shannon, there's not been a day recently that I haven't thought about the Lot, Highway 11, you..." He tailed off.

She looked away. "Me too," she said quietly.

He didn't answer. "Look at you," she said, turning again. Her eyes looked moist. She took in his jacket, expensive loafers, neat haircut. "You did OK for yourself, Ed."

"I'm an attorney."

She gave a low whistle. "You know, even back then you were sharper than the rest of us."

"How did it turn out for you?" he asked.

She shrugged and looked around the dilapidated apartment. "Isn't it obvious? Not so well. And what Zielinski said about my guy, Nate, is true." She pointed at her bruised face. "He has a temper."

"Jesus, Shannon, I'm sorry."

"Don't be." She gestured again. "It was my choice. But it's true he doesn't like strangers, so let's not make this too long, OK?"

Suddenly Ed didn't know where to start. "What's her name?" he asked, nodding at the crib.

"Alice Mae," she said. "Apple of my eye. Yes, in case you're wondering, she's Nate's. I had a baby with an abusive man, go figure. I got to think of her these days, otherwise I'd split."

"How did you end up in Miami?" he asked.

"Like you, long story. But I guess it was a different one for me. The father in my first foster home turned out to be abusive. Maybe there's a pattern here. They nailed his ass, but that was me done with that place. My foster mother hated me for exposing her husband. After that it was one home after another. No chance of high school. Minimum wage jobs. Lotta time spent in bad bars, lotta time spent with bad men. Men starting out promising, all turning out the same."

She touched her bruised cheek. "Nate's just the last in a long line of them. Shoulda seen him coming."

She caught Ed's look. "You know, he was kind of sweet to begin with. I was living in Dorchester then. Met him at the local bar. He was there alone. He looked kinda lonely, not at all aggressive. He was nice, given that every other man in there was some kind of redneck jerk. Bought me a drink, asked me about my life. Well, I didn't give him the whole story, as you can imagine. He seemed interested, though I was just talking about shit.

"He said he was a contractor, just moved to the area. So neither of us was in the jet set. He didn't come on strong when it was closing time. You know guys expect to get in the sack just for a couple of drinks? He asked for my number and I gave it him, and that's how it began. Afterward, he called. More drinks, dinner, little gifts: flowers, a necklace... None of the others done that. He dropped quite a bit of money on me—but then I got suspicious. The cash was too good for contracting, if you know what I mean. When I asked, he just said, 'Best not ask, sugar. Just got a good friend who loans me some dough when it's important, and this is important.' And so I was flattered, you know, that he's borrowing money to show me a good time, but worried, too, that he's in hock to this fella, whoever he might be, and so I told Nate not to do stuff on my account, and then he gets mad for the first time—you know, just for a moment, and I see that streak in him, but then he calms down and says, 'Sure, babe, whatever you want. Won't borrow no more. What we got is sweet enough.'

"And then he's back to being nice, and the little gifts, thoughtful stuff, and the phone calls, any time of day, just checking in from his work to see how I was doing. Never had anything like that before.

"Yeah, long story short: he moves in and it's good for a while, but one day he says we're moving south, a job's come up. And that's it. We just pack up the car and head down 95 and here we are in Florida. At first I kinda liked it. It's warm. Not freezing your tits off like Boston in January. But I don't know anyone. Not that I had many friends up north, but enough, you know? Call someone, see them for a drink, shopping, movie. Here, no one. Just me and Nate.

"And now we're alone, he's, like, pressurizing me all the time. Kids, always kids. And, you know, it's weird. Like it's normally the woman who wants the kids and the man saying no. So I say: 'Far as I know—cos I have this birthday given me by the authorities—I'm only twenty-six. Got plenty of time to be having them.' But no, he says, and he gets riled for the first time since that dinner and, as we're alone, he slaps me around some.

"Next day, he's super remorseful. Comes home with some flowers, says sorry. Tries to explain. He's an only child, was always lonely. He wants a big family… can't wait. Pleads with me: we got to get down to it. Well, I dunno, maybe I was lonely too. Maybe I thought a child would help with that. Wrong reason, I know. Well, we get on to it. Yeah, boy, we did. He's on me like a randy teenager all times of day till I'm sore and crying off and he's beating me again.

"And sure as eggs, a few weeks later the stick tells me I got one on the way. Nate looked mighty glad when I told him, said I did well, like I had just produced a magic rabbit or something.

"And you know what? He never touched me again after that. Apart from with his fists. Don't know where he's getting it now. Guess he hangs with the women at the bar, if he ain't paying for it. Wouldn't care what he does, 'cept when he's back here checking on Alice Mae he kicks up hell. If there's anything he don't like, like Alice Mae's diaper needs changing or there's a sock on the floor, he'll let me have it. And I got no way out. No relative to watch the kid, no money to have someone look after her so I can make my own dough. Just totally dependent on him."

"Jesus," Ed said.

"It gets worse. I had Alice Mae by cesarean. I was in pain after. The doctors prescribed some pretty strong painkillers. Opioid analgesics. I guess I just liked the feeling of being bombed, you know? So when the doc checked on me I told him the pain got worse and the dope didn't work so he gave me a higher dose. I guess I got dependent on it. When the doc told me I'd had enough and I had to go cold turkey, I had to get Nate to score me some. It's been like that for months now. I guess you would say I can't live without the stuff. Now Zielinski's pretty much the only person I give the time of day to. Nate don't allow no TV or radio. The phone's cut off because he didn't pay the bill. It's just Alice Mae and me and the pills, all day."

Shannon didn't know about Pensacola, Ed realized.

"Anyway, that's me," she said. "I guess things turned out different for you, Ed."

He took a deep breath. He was conscious of the time passing and the threat of Nate coming back. The last thing he needed was a confrontation with a controlling asshole. But he couldn't just lead in with the real reason he was here. Or the fact that he wasn't even called Ed anymore.

"I got lucky," he said. "A good adoption—a childless couple in Brookline took me in. A good house, good high school, vacation place. You know, the whole nine yards. But I couldn't leave the Lot behind."

"Same," she said sadly.

"Then it caught up. Ten years ago. My first day at college. A new life. Then David showed up."

"David?"

Ed nodded. "He hadn't changed much: big, loud, aggressive."

"What did he want?"

Ed paused. He had no idea what sort of regressive experiences Shannon had had over the years. "Do you remember much about what happened to us, Shannon? You know, when they took us down to the basement?"

She dropped her head. "Not much. I have nightmares sometimes. Dark stuff."

"It's come back to me over time. A pretty graphic recall: strapped into chairs, drugs, chanting, movies, brainwashing. Manson had nothing on the Fromes."

"Yeah, I get some of that," she said.

"Did you ever ask yourself what was the point of it all?"

"The point? Just to torture young kids, I guess."

"But they weren't pedos. Plenty enough of those around."

"Tell me," she said. "My first foster father, for one."

"So you never felt that you've been prepped for something? That you're just waiting for something to, you know, trigger you."

She was silent for a beat. "Maybe," she said eventually.

"OK," he said. "Well, that's how it was that day at Northeastern. I told David where to get off, but then he said this Bible passage and, you know, I'm just lost, Shannon. And then I realized what power those people have over me."

"Lost?"

"Blacked out. Just from a few words." He realized his voice was raised and Alice Mae was stirring.

"I don't get it," she said.

He went on, more quietly. "Catrine's dead, Shannon. She blew up a mall in Pensacola. Eighteen dead. It's been all over the news."

Her face and mouth went slack. "Shit. Why?"

"Simply put, I guess it was like me with David. They put her under, primed her and sent her off."

"Just by saying stuff?"

"Yeah, just by saying stuff. That's how it was with me, but I got lucky. A busybody came to my dorm room and scared David off."

"So what did you do next?"

"I ran. Been running ever since. Ed's not even my name anymore."

She shook her head. "Why did you bring this to me?"

"Because I had to. Because we're next. Because of Pensacola. Whatever it is they planned back then, it's started. They found me, and if they know about me, they know about you."

"To what purpose?"

"You think I haven't asked that question a million times? You know, I don't think the Lot was an isolated incident. I bet there's a cabin full of kids in every desert, in every forest, on every range in the United States. Brainwashed future terrorists. And not one of us can protect ourselves. There are no authorities to appeal to because half of them are in on it."

"No one can make you carry a bomb or a gun, Ed."

"You think? There's a lot about the Fromes' basement I don't recall too well. I bet it's the same with you. Complete blackouts. Could have been doing anything and no recollection of it. It was the same for me at Northeastern when David showed. Our minds are conditioned. One day very soon it's all going to go dark again and we'll do what Catrine did."

"My God." She looked over at her sleeping child.

"I came to warn you, Shannon. After Catrine there's only the two of us left."

"What are you going to do?" she asked.

He shook his head helplessly. "I ran once. I changed my identity. I have a wife. A pregnant wife. And a house and that job. I thought it was finally all coming together. I was free." He took a deep breath. "But it was an illusion. They found me somehow. I have to run. Maybe, after a year or two, I can reach out to Sarah, see the kid, but I don't know that even…"

She gestured around the apartment. "I don't have that choice. I have the kid, a habit, and no dough."

He put down the now empty cup and reached into his jacket and pulled out his wallet and took out all the money. There was some $120 in notes.

"Here," he said, "take this. Go to a motel or something."

"You sure?" she asked.

"I have enough," he said. "Just take it."

She reached forward and her fingers brushed his as she took the money. Their eyes met. He wondered if, the minute he was gone, she would buy more drugs with it.

"You need a lift?" he asked.

"I got my own car," she answered. "Besides, I can't just up and go. There's too much stuff and Nate will be back soon."

"Tomorrow then?"

"Maybe."

"It has to be tomorrow. I'm going tomorrow night. I'll come late afternoon with more money."

"OK, Nate's on the same shift tomorrow. And I won't forget this," she said and put a hand on his arm.

He felt uncomfortable and looked away into the dark recesses of the room. He noticed for the first time an object sitting on the kitchen counter. Given the absence of a TV or radio in the apartment, it was odd to see something high-tech. He recognized it immediately. The blocky white plastic brick of the Motorola DynaTAC. Exactly the same cell phone as he had in a dresser drawer back at Lenox. A $3,000 price tag. He should know: Benzema had certainly emphasized its value when she had given it to him at that employees' awards. "Only partners can expect this level of perk," she'd said. "And you, Ed," squeezing his arm as she handed him the box.

The cold fell on him. "You have a cell phone?" he asked, as neutrally as possible.

Shannon followed his gaze. "That? Things came to a head with Nate a week or so back. I broke and went to the Victims Assistance Center and complained about this." She pointed at her bruised face.

"The woman I met was super nice, but she said if I pressed charges Nate could go to jail. He's Alice Mae's father, after all, and the breadwinner. She said to try to patch things up and that she'd call me to see how things were going. I explained our phone was cut off. It was then she gave me this. Showed me how to use it and said she would call me on it soon."

"You know how much that thing's worth?"

Shannon shook her head.

"One-tenth of all I earn in a year. And I'm on a decent salary. Kind of expensive for an underfunded public unit, wouldn't you say?"

"I dunno, the lady seemed really concerned, you know?" Shannon said. "Anyway, I hid it in the cabinet under the sink, but Nate found it. He gave me the third degree and I told him where I got it. Thought he was going to give me a whipping, then go out and sell it, but he just laughed and said, 'You just wait for that little lady of yours to call.' And gives it a little pat, like he approved of it or something. It's been sitting on the counter ever since."

"Shannon," said Ed, "whatever the circumstances between now and tomorrow, don't use that thing, OK? Not to receive a call or to call out."

She didn't answer but glanced at the wall-mounted clock ticking over the stovetop. It now showed twenty-four minutes to midnight.

She looked from the clock to him.

"You better go, Ed."

They both stood. "I'll be back late afternoon," he said.

"Just come back, OK?" she said. "But if you see a black El Camino outside, that's Nate's truck and he's home. Don't come up. Leave a message with Mr. Zielinski. He'll get it to me. I trust him."

"OK," Ed answered.

They were very close. Ed put his hand on her shoulder, and there was the memory again: the yellow bus, the day bright with the sun through the pines and the dusty windows and the smell of hot buttoned upholstery. He found that her hand was on the front of his shirt, tugging him a little toward her.

"It'll be OK," he said without really meaning to say it.

Then they kissed.

After a few seconds she broke free.

"I want to ask you a favor—a big favor," she said a little breathlessly.

"What is it?" His voice was hoarse.

"I want Alice Mae to be safe, whatever happens to me. Can you promise me that, Ed?"

She didn't meet his eye.

"Yes," he said. She let go of the shirt.

There was a loud engine noise out on the road and both of them started.

"Tomorrow," he said.

Tomorrow Martin Cruz would cease to exist, just as Ed Constance had ceased to exist before him. But before that he would do something for her, even if it was just money.

He kissed her again, awkwardly, this time on top of her hair, then turned and quickly exited the apartment.

CHAPTER FORTY

There were no more birthday phone calls after the year of Ed's disappearance. Coughlin had been desperately ill when Vermeulen last spoke to him on October 25, 1979. He had died two days later. Since then Vermeulen had stood alone. Uncertainty gnawed him. The rotary phone did not ring anymore. His life's work was in abeyance. Only three agents remained. Hardly enough to send shockwaves through the country even if they did carry out their respective missions.

His sense of purpose only returned through a chance discovery. Some details of Ed's movements had emerged in the months after his disappearance. Stu's Volvo was found in the forestry clearing off the Golden Road. The kid had afterward somehow made it all the way to Eagle Lake. What's more, he had somehow acquired a gun. They'd found Carl weeks later: sniffer dogs had unearthed the grave by the abandoned engines. They left the corpse where they found it, though the agents did take away one memento, the copper engine plate, not knowing if it might be important. It wasn't, but Vermeulen put it on display on the front of his desk. He looked at it often. A reminder of failure.

After Carl's death there were only the three agents left: Shannon, Catrine, and Ed. And Ed had vanished from the world. It was difficult to imagine Typhon's great scheme as it had once been: America in flames, civil anarchy, military dictatorship. In fact, it was difficult to imagine the scheme at all. But, because of the compartmentalized way Typhon worked, he was only one of many tentacles. Even now other cells would be bringing forth agents—the mission would go on. Just not with him.

The fact that Ed might still have Stu's little red notebook had haunted Vermeulen ever since the cops reported it missing from the Winthrop wall safe. Its existence was dynamite. If he was smart, Ed would have hidden it someplace; maybe left it in a package with an attorney somewhere: "to be opened in the event of my death" etc… If they found him again he would have to be approached with extreme caution. No more bull-headedness until the red notebook was recovered.

Trivial things had a way of eventually shaking the earth—a butterfly's wing in Brazil causing a tornado in Texas and all that. David's suppressed memory of a solitary mark of a canoe keel on some lakeshore mud caused everything that followed. The old guy he had seen drive away from Seboomook that morning had had no canoe in the bed of his truck. The conclusion: he had given the canoe to Ed to escape. David's memory was like that of all the other kids: he instantly brought back to mind the number of the pickup's registration.

Vermeulen's contact at the DMV identified the owner of the pickup as James Dove. Address: Dove's Bait and Tackle, Tranquility, Maine. It seemed the guy had befriended Constance, maybe sometime during the four long summers at Stu's cabin. Stu had forgotten to mention the connection either to Pastor Bates or to Vermeulen himself.

Vermeulen did a little digging; Dove's service record was impressive. Maybe things went deeper. Maybe *he* had shot Carl. Carl had been one of the best, after all. A tap was put on Dove's phone. They waited for Ed to call. But the call never came. After nearly ten years of no contact they gave up on monitoring it.

It was two years after Ed had disappeared from the face of the earth that Vermeulen's informants in the intelligence services made another discovery. By then, Dumfries had fallen on hard times. A back injury from his service days had begun to plague him. He had tried to manage the issue with painkillers, but the loads had gotten ever stronger as his tolerance grew and soon he was forging prescriptions. He passed one too many of these and the trail ended with an FDA raid on his cabin outside Wheelerville.

When the scale of the counterfeiting operation became clear, the FBI were called in. Dumfries in all matters, apart from his forged prescriptions, had been meticulous—he had destroyed all evidence pointing to those he had helped. But one agent did find something of note on a sheet of paper in a Bible in the house. It had multiple practice signatures of a Martin J. Cruz.

The name produced several dozen hits at the SSA and DMV. It only took days to whittle the most likely candidate down to a prelaw student at Miami Dade.

CHAPTER FORTY-ONE

Black Monday. Ed went into the office as if it was just another day. Though it was still almost a month away, Christmas decorations had begun to appear. There were cards perched on filing cabinets, some silver and gold tinsel slung on a picture rail, reindeer bunting, and a little plastic tree with plastic baubles on one of the secretaries' desks.

The atmosphere in Merriweather's was anything but festive. People nursed holiday hangovers or were tired from long journeys. No one asked Ed how he was feeling, despite his long absence. Maybe they already knew the truth about his fake diagnosis.

The clatter of the typewriters was curiously muted, the conversation more so. There was an air of weary anticipation. The post-holiday firing, promotion, and bonus session was about to begin.

Ed was immune from any worry; he guessed he could have spent the entire year sipping piña coladas on the beach: Merriweather's would have picked up the check. Too bad he had worked himself to the bone billing so many pointless hours.

Benzema had requested that all staff be there in person. It was not so much a request as an order. Excuses for sickness would be considered malingering. Some of his colleagues had turned up dressed in their best suits, as if dressing for their own funerals. Others dressed down. Some snuck in bottles wrapped in brown paper bags. The only change to Ed's routine was the Magnum in his coat pocket. No one noticed the bulge. They were all too preoccupied. Hell, maybe some of his colleagues were packing too.

But even without the prospect of firing or promotion, Ed was nervous enough. He glanced at Raffaella, Benzema's secretary. Benzema had told Raffaella on her first day she should do everything possible to make "Mr. Cruz" happy. Raffaella smiled shyly and batted her false lashes at Ed, as if sure that the favoritism exhibited by Benzema to Mr. Cruz—the siting of his desk; the Employee of the Month Award; the frequent exotic trips to the Caribbean; Benzema's frequent pit stops, when she had a habit of sitting on a corner of Ed's desk revealing quite a bit of thigh as her pencil skirt split—was surely a sign of something a little more than regular office business. Raffaella was more than happy to oil the wheels of what was going on; if that was what it took for her to get on at Merriweather's, so be it. Ed's coffee had kept coming on the hour. Ed wondered if she personally ground the Desoxyn into it.

But no coffee was offered today. Raffaella rigidly maintained her seat, never stirring from her phone, which rang frequently. She answered in inaudible whispers. In the downtime, she tended to her nails and stared down at the harbor.

Benzema's door was shut. Through the frosted glass, Ed could see her and Mo Fallows pacing up and down. Fallows was a lean, grim-faced ex-SEAL who handled office security. They were joined occasionally by a senior partner who marched through the outer office and back again without looking left or right.

Ed could hear the voices in Benzema's office but not make out the words. Silhouettes moved in front of the glass, arms occasionally gesticulating. During the afternoon, two associates were summoned by Raffaella. They came, heads bowed, dragging their feet, and shortly afterward emerged with empty cardboard boxes in their hands, escorted by Fallows. Fallows took the condemned to their desks, allowed them to gather their personal possessions and escorted them to the elevator bank.

The two terminated associates had probably billed more hours than Ed that year. It was another clue to his special status: he was untouchable.

The clock slowly circled. His last day at Merriweather's was approaching its end, as was his life in Miami and his life with his wife and unborn child. He could not think about Sarah and the child for long. He had to believe he would somehow find them again after tonight.

Midafternoon, the phone rang on his desk. Ed started out of his reverie. It was Godin.

The surgeon was brusque. "Mr. Cruz, despite frequent reminders from my nurse I see that you have yet to schedule your procedure."

"It's been a busy time," Ed answered.

"Well, Mr. Cruz, there's no point being busy when your health is at risk. Delay is not an option."

"Yes, sir, I understand," Ed answered.

"With the holidays coming my schedule is nearly full. Please call my nurse at the earliest opportunity."

"You have my word," Ed answered.

He put the receiver down. If Godin was personally hustling him, things must be moving fast.

More partners and associates came and went. The empty boxes were produced again and Fallows' death march repeated. Others went in to Benzema like condemned men but left smiling, clutching envelopes undoubtedly informing them of promotions or bonus payments.

More time passed and still Ed was not summoned. Too bad. It was approaching the official knocking-off time. If Benzema was saving him for one of her after-hours schmoozes it was too late.

On the stroke of five he got up, grabbed his coat and briefcase and hustled out. Raffaella stared at him, her mouth slightly open, but if she said something Ed didn't hear it, because he was already at the elevator bank.

He exited the Merriweather building. First stop was an ATM to get cash for Shannon, then a cab to Allapattah. He was just about to cross the road to the bank opposite when his eyes fell on the headline displayed on a nearby newsstand: "POLICE KILLED IN HIGHWAY GUN BATTLE." The Dade County Wars were at their height, so the headline was not a surprise. But, despite this, it arrested him. It was November and mild in the Sunshine State, but he suddenly felt cold. He dug in his pocket for change and bought a copy of the paper.

The *Herald* didn't give every fatal shooting in the Miami Dade area in 1989 the front page—there were any number of those drug cartel incidents—but the death of Shannon Quincy had made it there, principally because she took two policemen with her.

According to the report, it began when a traffic cop pulled her over for running a red light in Hialeah Gardens that morning. She had been driving her partner's El Camino over the speed limit. Instead of producing a license as requested, Shannon brought out a pistol from the dash and shot Officer Logan Patrick through the right eye.

A high-speed pursuit followed until Shannon's vehicle was cornered beneath an underpass on the Don Shula Expressway. Despite being cautioned to surrender, Shannon continued to return fire. An unlucky shot caught another officer in the jugular and he bled out at the scene before paramedics could save him. The other cops, a dozen or more at the final count, reported that Shannon had not taken cover behind her vehicle but stood in front of it as she took down the second policeman. In return, she was hit by eight police bullets. The phrase "suicide by cop" was used by the reporter.

Ed stared at the newspaper without moving, as the bustling pedestrians on the sidewalk divided either side of him.

The blood of dead men. As with Catrine, so with Shannon. His body, every corpuscle, felt numb, was invaded by that deadly cold. There was a thin keening in his mind like a barely audible radio frequency.

He realized he was drawing attention to himself, standing stock-still in the middle of the busy sidewalk. There was a Cuban café across the street where he sometimes took breaks. He went in and ordered a coffee, then promptly forgot its existence. It took a few moments for his eyes to clear so he could continue reading. The report was nothing but thorough: the writer had covered some ground to get all this into the evening edition. Motives for the shooting were at best anecdotal. The sad sequence of foster homes; the minimum wage jobs; the bad relationships; the opioid addiction... They had discovered all this very quickly, it seemed to Ed. As if they had a privileged source who knew everything about Shannon.

The police had visited the Allapattah apartment. Here was a new twist: Nate and Alice Mae were missing. The police recovered what was described as Black Power literature inside, most notably the autobiography of the Panther Huey P. Newton, *Revolutionary Suicide*. A note next to the book written in Shannon's hand cast doubt on Newton's murder earlier that year by Tyrone Robinson, a member of the Black Guerrilla Family, and ascribed it to FBI-sponsored assassins. Ominously, Shannon's note ended with Newton's assertion about Malcolm X and black liberation: "Only with the gun were the black masses denied this victory. But they learned from Malcolm that with the gun, they can recapture their dreams and bring them into reality."

Neighbors on NW 15th Avenue reported violent arguments emanating from Apartment 2C over the course of several weeks. They expressed neither surprise at nor understanding of Shannon's actions—she was largely unknown to all of them. However, her downstairs neighbor, Jakub Zielinski, seventy-eight, was reported as being shocked by events and was quoted as saying that Shannon was incapable of doing what had been done that morning.

Ed rifled through the inner pages looking for any continuation. There was none. It seemed the moment the story had dropped it had taken the front page, fully formed.

He tried to get his breathing and heart rate under control. He somehow knew his visit last night had killed Shannon, and the two policemen as well. His first instinct was to call Sarah. He went to the diner pay phone, numbly picked up the receiver and loaded in a dime, then thought better of it. The house phone could be bugged. He hit the coin return and went back to his seat.

There was nothing in the report that made sense apart from Zielinski's statement. He agreed: the Shannon he had met last night was incapable of these actions. She was downtrodden, down on her luck, addicted, yes, but nevertheless hopeful of escaping her situation. He was confident she would have fled with the cash he was going to bring her. There had been none of those revolutionary books visible in 2C last night. In fact, there hadn't been any books at all apart from the baby ones. They must have been planted there after the event. The Black Power theory was beyond bogus. It was a Typhon play. The Panthers had been dissolved seven years before. Newton's murder had been widely reported as a narcotics-related killing.

The deaths of the two officers would cause a nationwide furor, an outcry against the defunct Panthers: even those now pursuing careers in mainstream politics would be derided as ex-terrorists, their reputations tainted by association with Shannon's actions.

There was a purpose here: a perpetuation of the race war, the threat level increased nationwide, public paranoia, cries for more law enforcement, more funds for the FBI, more liberal arms regimes… Who benefited? A right-wing, militaristic government intent on repressing the people. Maybe one day, when the fear levels were ratcheted to maximum and anarchy loomed, the people would accept a right-wing dictatorship.

Nate and Alice Mae had disappeared. Why? If Shannon had acted alone as suggested, why had Nate fled? Shannon's description of Nate's courtship came back to him. The guy falling over backward to make nice, interspersed by violent outbursts. The sudden move to Miami, the pressure to have a kid. At first, he had thought Nate was just some kind of manipulative asshole.

Now he began to wonder whether Shannon's partner had had an agenda all along. He had wanted a child, nothing more. He had used Shannon.

A suspicion dawned on him. Why were all the children on the Lot untraceable? After their rescue on Highway 11, surely someone would have come forward to claim at least one of them? Despite nationwide and international appeals, no one had. The conclusion had been that the abductors had killed every single one of their parents, a theory that statistically was vanishingly unlikely.

So where had the kids come from? What if they were the product of the same kind of honey trap as the one that had existed between Shannon and Nate? One partner lured in, rendered powerless, abused; a child produced, the excess partner gotten rid of in a Typhon-inspired act of violence, or, if not biddable, coldly assassinated, the child taken to whatever new compound had taken the place of the Lot. Kill the Vessel, abduct the child. Simple. A much more familiar story in the United States, where this narrative of partner homicide and child abduction happened virtually every day.

His head spun. Vessels. It had never occurred to him what the description on that recovered piece of paper from the Lot had meant. Now he knew: more robot agents were being produced for Typhon's war. Maybe right now there were Nates out there looking for the next vulnerable single woman. Or vice versa: women looking for a vulnerable male.

He presumed Alice Mae had now gone into the same kind of hell as the Lot. Not Maine, but somewhere else, like the wilds of Wyoming or the deserts of New Mexico, thirty minutes from the nearest road. Another house with lonely, desperate children who would never be heard of until the day they were released, unwitting, upon the world.

And then it came to him. As with Shannon, so with him. Was his relationship with Sarah a lie? Whatever could be said of men surely could be said of women. How well do we ever know our partner?

He reviewed his relationship years: the first meeting in the Over and Under, the first date, the Paris story, the disengaged relatives at the funeral and at the wedding, the unexpected job offer at Merriweather's, everything that had followed...

He knew the Miami life was a lie. Was his marriage one as well?

He paid up, left the diner and hailed a cab. Twenty minutes later, he was at NW 15th Avenue. By now it was after six and getting dark. There was not much going on outside the apartment considering the notoriety of the crime committed that morning. By now the police forensics van was gone, and any reporters had lost interest. Even the cops, who had no doubt posted an officer outside on the sidewalk for the hours after the shooting, were gone.

The police tape fluttered in the breeze. There were no gawkers. From when he had worked as a legal intern before Merriweather's, Ed knew the period of interest in an accident or crime was about the same time as the police presence at the scene. The minute the cops went, the story was over.

Nevertheless, he told the driver to go past Shannon's apartment. He saw that the parking lot hosted the same rusted, semi-derelict cars as the previous night, the leaves of the shade trees fallen dead and sere on their hoods. But as they cruised down the road he saw something else. Some five driveways down, a black Cadillac was parked at the curb. Tinted windows, the heat of its exhaust distorting the warm evening air as it idled. A black shark, out of place in this neighborhood.

The sidewalks and porches were curiously deserted, as if sensing the menace from the car. He told the driver to circle back on the parallel street. He paid the guy off and took a service back alley parallel to NW 15th, counting the blocks until he came to the fence of the Zielinski/Quincy block. He stood on a dumpster and took a peek over. There was a scrappy communal back lawn laid with buffalo grass. The upper apartments were dark, but there was a single light on in the lower apartment. It fell on the back stoop, where there was a canopied swing bench with a figure sitting on it. A shock of white hair glowed in the shadows: Zielinski.

Ed took hold of the top of the fence panel, got a foothold on a cross-strut and levered himself over. He landed quietly in the buffalo grass. The yard looked like it had been cultivated some time ago, maybe when Mrs. Zielinski was still alive, but now the lawn was shin high and the borders were overgrown with weeds and untrimmed bushes. He wondered how to approach Zielinski without giving the old guy a shock, but when he looked again Zielinski had stood up and was staring right at him. Zielinski jerked his head toward the apartment, as if telling Ed to follow him, and disappeared through the screen door into the kitchen. The light went out. Darkness fell on the garden.

Ed went at a crouch to the porch and, looking around the dim yard to check he wasn't observed, slipped through the screen door. A match snapped and there was Zielinski's underlit ghost face.

"Good thing these old eyes're still good," he said. "Here," he added curtly, and applied the match to the stub of a candle that stood in a wax-pooled saucer on the kitchen table. The space came into view. It was a mirror image of Shannon's combined kitchen/living room above.

"Sit," Zielinski said.

Ed pulled out a chair, his eyes fixed on that ghostly white face. He was about to speak, but Zielinski held up his hand. "I know why you've come. You want to find out the truth. Same as me."

It was muggy in the apartment, but Zielinski was wearing a ragged cable-knit sweater as if against a chill. The sleeve on his right arm had ridden up and there was a numerical tattoo as blue as his veins on his forearm. Zielinski saw the direction of Ed's stare. "The Warsaw Ghetto. I was one of the few of my unit to survive. I escaped through the canals, threw away my gun, but was rounded up anyway. I survived Treblinka." Before Ed could interject, he held up his hand.

"Spare your sympathy. Braver men committed suicide."

Ed looked up to the ceiling at Shannon's apartment, then back at the old man. "Can you tell me what happened?" he said.

Zielinski didn't respond directly. "These walls and ceilings are thin. You hear everything, even when you're old. Always the arguing. Then the blows. I should have called the cops, but she always said, 'Don't call them, Jakub. Nate's OK. I'll figure it out.' I shouldn't have listened. Now she's gone."

He was silent a beat. "It was late. I had the TV on, the sound was up, not because of my hearing, but mostly not wanting to hear them upstairs. Anyway. Cars arrived outside. The curtains are pretty thin—the lights shone through. I peeked. It was Nate's truck and another car, quite a fancy sedan, pulling up into the lot. I thought, hope Nate's sober and there's not another argument. The headlights went out and I saw two men crossing the lot and going up the steps to 2C. Nate and a stranger. This is unusual. Neither of them ever have people around. I turned the TV down. Maybe I heard there was, I dunno, like a note of surprise when the door opened upstairs, then I guess the stranger's voice. He says something quite short, a couple of sentences, then there's nothing more—that I heard, anyway. Least there was no screaming and shouting. I think that's good. Maybe they're all sitting down and having coffee. My show ends. Like most nights, there's not much to do after the show. But I don't sleep too well. Don't even need too much sleep. That comes later.

"Just then I hear the two guys coming down. Nate says to the other guy something like, 'She going to be OK until the morning?' The other guy answers. He sounds smooth, not like Nate at all. 'Relax, she'll be quiet as a mouse until the call comes.' Then they go out, leave Nate's pickup and take the guy's car, and I'm thinking maybe they went to a bar or something. Good riddance. At least it's all quiet upstairs. No baby crying, nothing.

"They didn't come back that night as far as I know. But the next morning, I'm up at first light. It's still all quiet upstairs, which is unusual. Normally the baby's crying. I'm just wondering if I should check on them when I hear this sound that I never heard before. Like a bird, you know, chirping but electronic."

"Like a cell phone ringtone?" Ed asked.

"Could be. Never heard one. Leastways, the sound cuts off, so I guess she answers it. A minute later I hear the door upstairs. I go out and there's Shannon coming down the steps. No baby. She has this handbag, which ain't like her, but she's not carrying it on her shoulder but in her arms, like it's Alice Mae, and there seems something heavy in it.

"'You OK?' I ask, but she just brushes past and heads down to the pickup in the lot. 'Hey!' I say, but she don't even look back, just unlocks it like one of them hypnotized people, fires it up and takes, off down 15th. Transmission's whining, rubber's burning. She don't even shift gears, it's like in first and she's going forty or more.

"First thought I have is she flipped and just run out on Alice Mae and no one's at home looking after the baby. So I grab my spare key and go up there. Crib's empty, but there's this strange noise. It's that cell phone the social worker gave her. It's on. There's this tinny voice coming out of it and I pick it up and have a listen. It's a recorded voice, you know, like a robot on a science fiction show. It's repeating this message over and over. Makes no sense, sounds like the Bible but something I don't know. Something about wheat and barley and oil and wine."

Ed felt the room spin.

"You OK, son?" Zielinski asked.

Ed held up a hand. "It's alright. Go on."

Zielinski said, "Midday, I turn the news on, same as always, and there it is. Not naming names, but two cops and a young black woman dead in a shootout. News helicopter over an underpass, and there's that old El Camino with its driver door open and a sheet covering something on the ground next to it. I dunno what I did. I guess I just stared at the screen.

"Not long after, the cops and reporters were here like a swarm of flies. Well, I guess you read the papers—it's all in there." He smiled grimly "'Cept it ain't. Nothing about that cell phone. Guess they took that as evidence. Then there's those commie books they said she'd been reading. I been up in that apartment dozens of times. Never a book in sight. And Shannon with a gun? That's a joke. Maybe you can tell me what's going on, mister?"

Ed shook his head. "It's a long story."

"All bad?"

"All bad. What do you think happened to Alice Mae?" Ed asked.

"Nate and that other fellow must've took her the night before. It's odd she didn't cry out."

"Did you get a look at the second guy?"

"They turned the headlights off before walking up. But I saw his face as he passed the window in the streetlight. It was weird, like he knew I was watching. He stopped and looked right at me through the crack in the curtain. His eyes were deep-set, a pale face, widow's peak, thin lips like Dracula, a lot of pockmarks."

David, Ed thought.

Zielinski fixed him with his pale eyes. "You were her friend. You gotta find that girl."

Ed stood up. "I'm going to do what I can. Listen, Mr. Zielinski, I'm sorry I came here. There's a car out the front. The apartment is being watched. I may have placed you in danger."

Zielinski held up his hand. "I saw it. It's OK, you were cautious."

Ed said, "Nevertheless, I think you need to leave for a while."

Zielinski nodded. "I thought the same. I have a nephew in Chicago. He'll take me in. So, it's shalom, Miami. Everything I need can fit into a suitcase."

"Do you need any money?" Ed asked.

Zielinski fixed him with a cold stare. "Young man, I've been looking after myself for a long time now. I don't need your charity."

Ed held up his hands. "OK, sorry. Just promise me you'll go as soon as possible."

"First, do something for me, will you?" Zielinski stood and went to the dresser, where there were used envelopes and a stub or two of pencil. He scrunched up his brow as if trying to remember something, then wrote on an envelope and handed it to Ed. "Here's my nephew's address. Just drop me a line if you find the girl. You don't even have to sign it. Just write something like, 'Alice Mae sends her regards.'"

"I promise," Ed answered.

They locked eyes. "OK," Zielinski said. "Go now, and God be with you."

Ten minutes later, Ed was heading back east on a Line 110 bus.

Zielinski was true to his word. Shortly after Ed left, he called a cab to the Amtrak station in Hialeah and boarded the Silver Meteor.

Jakub Zielinski's suitcase was still in the luggage rack when the Acela arrived in New York the next day. He never made the connecting train to Chicago at Washington Union.

What was left of him was found twenty-four hours later near Okeechobee. The Silver Meteor had made an unscheduled stop there after the emergency brake was pulled by persons unknown. CCTV footage had been installed at the station a year or two earlier and captured Zielinski's last moments. He had disembarked and taken off in a limping run down the platform. He had looked anxiously behind him as he had jumped down from the platform end and disappeared up the tracks to the north. It looked like he was being pursued, but no other figures appeared in the camera shot.

Zielinski had been trying to cross the express track a mile or so further up when the southbound Miami Amtrak hit him on a stretch of line where the Acela got up to about 80 mph. The coroner determined he had been killed instantly and his torso flung into some trackside bushes. The maintenance workers who found him initially thought they were looking at a few discarded hobo clothes until they noticed body parts littered by the side of the track. The Treblinka tattoo helped to identify him. His detached skull, when it was found, bore a rictus of terror. Whether it was caused by the Acela bearing down on him or by whoever he was running from was never established.

The news item appeared in the inside pages of the Miami papers. One old man's death was not big news that day.

Ed missed it altogether—by that time he had become what he had always feared he would become.

CHAPTER FORTY-TWO

The journey home was twenty-five minutes. Ed's racing pulse was at odds with the bus, which kept rigorously to the limit on the 195. He was barely conscious of the Julia Tuttle Causeway, the Welcome to Miami Beach sign, and the floodlit Romanesque campanile of St. Patrick's.

By the time he got to Lenox, the blood was coursing through him so fast he had reached a stage of mental blindness. So, as a blind man, he pulled out his key, went up the path and stepped up to the porch—only to find the door was already slightly ajar. It was the moment that all homeowners most feared. He pushed it fully open and stepped into the hall.

"Sarah?" he called. His briefcase fell from his hand onto the rug and burst open; papers scattered out of it. He tried the hall light, but it didn't work. The problem was just in the hall—the kitchen down the corridor was lit up. He could just make out muddy prints on the corridor carpet leading to and from it. It hadn't rained in Florida for two weeks. It seemed very cold in the house. Someone had turned the air-conditioning up to maximum. There was a distant roar from the system. Some of the fallen papers blew past him in the frigid blast from the vents.

He followed them, but on the threshold of the kitchen he tripped on something in the gloom. He pushed open the kitchen door to get more light on it.

He saw it was a copper plate. It had writing stamped on it:

"ENG NO.8 SHOP NUMBER 4553 ALLOWABLE PRESSURE 190LBS HYDROSTATIC PRES 239LBS."

The "3" of the shop number was printed the wrong way around.

He'd thrown this thing into Carl's grave a decade before: the backplate of one of the engines on the Eagle Lake and West Branch Railway. Clumps of mud and some rotten cloth still stuck to it.

He couldn't feel his hands or feet anymore. They were like blocks of ice. He backed against the frame of the door and inched around the plate.

It was bright, so very bright, in the kitchen after the corridor.

Sarah's paring knife was on the fake marble countertop.

So was a spreading pool of blood about a foot across. In the center of the blood was an object. A small, pink object.

He was still some twenty feet away, but even in the sudden glare of the lights he saw what it was.

A finger. A little finger. Even from here he could see the nail polish was a soft shell pink. Sarah's favorite.

He wondered then at the almost God-like prescience of Typhon. How, no matter how far he had run and whatever measures he had taken, they had predestined this evening, this homecoming: the pool of blood, the severed finger—just like in the movies shown to him long ago.

The icy tendrils in his veins were inching into his mind. A glacial breath soughed over his back. He turned slowly, his neck muscles frozen, expecting to see Carl standing there, covered in grave mud, his face and clothes hanging in rotten threads.

Nothing. Just the copper plate lying there in the corridor, surrounded by the muddy footprints. *Bloody* footprints, he corrected himself.

He staggered into the kitchen and grabbed the countertop to steady himself. His right hand smeared through the blood. He looked at his bloody palm and then to the house phone on its bracket on the wall. There was one last chance. He would call 911. The consequences didn't matter anymore.

Then he saw the phone cord was cut. The severed length lay in a spool on the tiled floor.

There was the pay phone he had used the week before in the corner store down the street. He would go there. He took a step back toward the front door. The room seesawed one way and then another. He braced himself against a wall, leaving a bloody handprint.

He zigzagged back down the corridor like a drunk, leaving more handprints. Through the cold fog he noticed the main bedroom door was open. Had it been open when he'd come down the corridor? Was there someone, some*thing* in there?

He pushed the door further open.

The bed sheets were in a twisted heap on the floor. There was a bloodstain in the center of the mattress. One of the pillows had burst and the feathers stirred in the blast of the air-conditioning. Every drawer but the one in the cabinet on his side of the bed had been pulled open and tossed.

From that unopened drawer came a *brrr-brrr* sound, like the stirring of a giant hornet.

He pulled it open with his bloody hand. It contained the detritus of bedroom life: loose change; a pair of cufflinks in a velveteen box; a half-used blister pack of painkillers; a scattering of condoms—and the unused office cell in its box.

The vibration was coming from that.

The cell had never been charged. It had never even been taken out of its box. But now, somehow, it was alive.

He lifted the lid and there it was, eight inches long, a black fascia with white buttons and white casing, a chunky black antenna.

A red LED display. Its message: "CALLER UNKNOWN."

There was a green Call Accept button.

Nothing would have made him answer that call, but they had taken Sarah. A polar choice: press the button and he would die, but there was a chance, at least, that Sarah and the child would live.

He pressed the button.

It was Mrs. Frome's voice on the end of the line.

She said, "A measure of wheat for a penny, and three measures of barley for a penny; and see thou hurt not the oil and wine."

And that was the last thing he knew.

PART THREE
TRANQUILITY
DECEMBER 1989

CHAPTER FORTY-THREE

When he found himself again, it was just a tiny piece. Like something lost down a couch back that reminds you of a long-forgotten day and the person you once were…

In that instant of coming back, he realized he had been seeing and hearing for some time, but there had been no connection between what he saw and heard and his mind.

But now there was.

He was in a warehouse. There was strip lighting overhead and metal tables stacked with cardboard boxes stamped with the name "Speedy Enterprises" on the ground. It was very cold. His breath plumed in the air.

He was sitting on a folding chair, his hands were on his knees and he was staring at two men dressed in bomber jackets standing in front of him. He found he resented their scrutiny, just as a drunk would resent someone staring at them when roused from a stupor.

He guessed the scrutiny had been going on for some time. The scene was just like in a movie, he thought… a movie? He tried to recall what a movie was. He could not associate words with things. His brain churned on the word for a beat before it engaged. Yes, he knew about movies. Bad movies. Hiroshima and split eyeballs and little pinkie fingers severed at the joint. Knew about the other kind: Bogie and Bacall, *Casablanca*. Black and white greats, the Golden Era of Hollywood. Golden, gold—colors came back…

The goons (another word) weren't really like the ones in the movies. They looked young, for a start, and didn't have that six o' clock shadow favored by movie bad guys of the Golden Era. The one thing they did have in common was that they were both holding pistols and the pistols were pointed at his chest. And their eyes were hard. One of them had a discoloration on his neck—the word for that came then: *tattoo; a* gang *tattoo*—and the other a scar that ran up his cheek from the corner of his mouth.

"Who are you?" he asked. His voice sounded slurry, drunk. The room spun when he spoke.

Scarface grinned. The overhead lighting was so harsh his teeth looked yellow. "We're the ones who ask the questions, bud. What's your name?"

His mouth opened and his jaw moved, but nothing came out except for a strange honking noise. He didn't know his own name. The two goons laughed. He felt a flash of anger, helplessness. Good. It was good to feel. Feeling would lead to remembering. He could remember Bogie and Bacall. He must have a name too, but his memory was a *tabula rasa*. He did remember the cell phone ringing, ringing, and a splitting pain in his head like an ice pick in his skull, and then nothing until he was in this warehouse, as if he had been beamed here like in... *Star Trek*. Kirk. Spock. Scotty. Uhura. More names.

"I dunno," he answered. "What're your names?"

"Quite the joker, ain't you?" Scarface laughed. Then he said to the gangbanger, "We gotta make sure it's the right guy."

Tattoo said, "He knew the numbers of the keypad. Hey, bud, what're the numbers?"

He answered without thinking, "Sixty-six. Sixteen. Sixteen. Fourteen."

Tattoo said to his companion, "See? Just as Vermeulen said: walked right in here and sat down, didn't he?"

Vermeulen—a name he knew.

"Yeah, he's a real zombie show," the other said. "Just stared through us when he came in."

"Well, he's woken up now. Check him for ID."

"Hey, bud," Gangbanger said. "You got a wallet in your coat?"

Wallet. Money. Credit cards. ID. The universe was filling in a little now. Like a vast paint-by-numbers. He was in a corner of it, working his way out.

Wallets were kept in pockets. There was something weighing down the inside of his coat. Quite a lightweight coat, given how cold it was. He wasn't sure it was a wallet, though. It felt heavy, solid, a little uncomfortable. Under that he had a jacket. In addition he felt a package under his shirt, next to his skin. He ignored that and the heavy item and slid his hand into the inside jacket pocket. Slick leather. A wallet. He took hold of it.

"OK, nice and slow," Scarface said. Ed drew the thing out. He saw it was leather: brown crocodile.

"Good, bud, now slide it over the floor," Scarface ordered. Ed leaned down and skated the wallet over the concrete floor. It hit one of the goon's feet and credit cards and a photo spilled out. A woman's face. Dark hair. Attractive. A jolt to the heart. Who was she?

Gangbanger leaned down and picked up the spilled cards and the photo. He showed the photo to Scarface. "Not bad, eh?" He had gotten Scarface's attention. The other guy leaned in to have a look.

He was surprised to find that his hand was back inside his coat, to where he'd felt the heavy object. His hand closed on a checkered grip. A revolver: what a revolver did arrived in the same instant as he withdrew the gun and stood up from the chair, his index finger engaged with the trigger as he did so.

The two men looked up from the photo at the same time. Because his gun was pointing at the gangbanger, he shot him first. In the solar plexus. The gun kicked like a mule. A heavy charge. The man doubled up. One of his legs pushed back as if he was fighting against a furious wind, then he sank to his knees, laid the photo and his pistol almost gently on the concrete floor in front of him and clamped his hands to his stomach. Blood spurted around them. His mouth opened stupidly as he saw it.

He thought it was strange that time should be like this: taking so goddam long to unspool as his gun tracked around to Scarface. He was seeing everything in a very detailed way, as if in slow motion, yet still Scarface hadn't lifted his own weapon until it was too late.

He fired again, his arm jerking back. He liked the kick of the gun, he decided. He also guessed he'd had some practice firing guns. When? This round hit Scarface higher up than Gangbanger. Under his left armpit, as the man tried to ward off the shot. Scarface took a few sideway steps, traveling in an oddly balletic way on his toes. His gun discharged once and the round zinged off the concrete floor. There was a bee-like hum past his ear and a sudden punching sound as the round went through a metal divider. But, again, he didn't really mind this feeling of being shot at. He found he was immune to fear. Scarface continued his strange ballet, tiptoed to one of the metal tables, fell onto a Speedy Enterprises box, then slid to a sitting position on the floor in a shower of Styrofoam peanuts, his back propped on one of the metal stanchions of the table. His eyes were directed at him, but they weren't seeing anymore. He guessed Scarface was dead, or at least he would be in a few seconds.

He was pleased he had time to register that detail too, just as in all the details of the shooting of Gangbanger, to whom he must now return his attention.

Like his pal, he was not moving. He was still kneeling in the same position. Blood was pumping from the stomach wound and he was panting heavily.

Something must have alerted him to the fact that the shooter had turned to him again, because he looked up. His face was sweaty, the whites of his eyes rolling.

"Please…" was all he said.

He was a little surprised when the gun jerked in his hand again. And he was surprised to see Gangbanger's right eye socket disappear and red and gray matter instantaneously shoot out the back of his head onto the concrete floor. He noticed that because it was so cold inside the warehouse, the scattered brain matter steamed a little where it lay.

Gangbanger was on his back now, one leg tucked awkwardly under him, his remaining eye staring at the ceiling.

He walked from the chair to the dead man and picked up the billfold and the picture of the woman. She looked back at him. Dark hair, dark eyes. Another little stab to the heart. There was writing on the back. *To Ed, always on my mind, xoxo*

He looked at one of the fallen credit cards. It had a different name to the one on the picture: Martin; Martin J. Cruz. He put the things back in the billfold. Martin, Ed? Why did he have two names?

He knew one thing. The two men had been sent here by Vermeulen. He remembered that name. It was in a little red book. And now he remembered: the little red book was one of those things in the package next to his skin.

He listened for police sirens. There was nothing. He went to a side door and found it unlocked. Outside there was an alleyway with a frosting of snow. A solitary sodium light shone on a car. A black Volvo estate. He knew it was his car. He looked through the window. The keys were still in the ignition. There was a lot of stuff in the back. Black trash bags, overspilling with clothes, and what appeared to be boxes of dry food.

He opened the driver's door and noticed something else: a black leatherbound Bible lay on the passenger seat.

CHAPTER FORTY-FOUR

He drove away from the warehouse with a squeal of tires, hunching forward as the wipers fought the ever-heavier snow. The alley gave onto a dockside presided over by massive cranes; moored ships and stacks of containers reared up into the night sky. No one was out. Beyond the container ships, a bay stretched away, and over the far shore aircraft landing lights could be seen on approach to a brightly lit airport. The word "Logan" popped into his head, then "Boston" followed. Memory was stirring in him like a green shoot. He'd lived here once, in this city.

He drove along the dockside and onto a bridge. More names were given to him by green overhead signs signaling an exit to South Boston Waterfront, then another to the Harbor Area. He took this: the run-down piers, storage units, and derricks gave way to brightly lit streets. A sign told him he was now in North End.

A mile and a half was as far as he could drive. His hands and feet were shaking. His steering was off. His mind was still spinning. He needed to park, regroup, remember more. Then he saw the waterfront hotel: the Marriott, North End. He pulled to the curb and studied the hotel front. Bellboys and guests were milling around the well-lit foyer. Too public. He drove around the side of the building into a side alley whose major features were overflowing dumpsters and a feral cat caught in his headlights.

He cut the engine, switched on the courtesy light and examined the contents of his coat and jacket. His billfold was nearly empty, just one five-dollar bill. He stared at the face of the man on the note and knew him first to be a president, then to be Lincoln. Little bubbles of recollection were popping in his head.

He pulled out the revolver. Best not to carry it in. He opened the glove compartment and made a new discovery: a padded envelope. Inside was a thick wad of cash: he riffled through the notes. Faces flickered past in the dim light: Lincoln again, Hamilton, Jackson, Grant... More names. He estimated there must be some $5,000 here. The money was all in used notes, a few fifties, but otherwise small denominations. In addition, there was a clasp knife and a flashlight. He took $100 from the bills and placed the bag and the gun in the glove compartment.

There was still that mysterious package he'd felt between his shirt and skin in the warehouse. He unbuttoned and pulled out a newspaper-wrapped package secured with tape. The red Woolworth's notebook with Vermeulen's name. There were also some charred, stapled A4 pages. He placed them next to the Bible.

He entered the hotel by unmanned revolving doors at the rear lobby, where a sign directed newly arriving guests to the front registration desk. He ignored that and took the sign to the bar instead. It was a dimly lit, quiet space. No one stared at him as he came in. Good.

He sat on a stool at the end of the bar. He wondered if he stank of gunshot residue. In fact, he wondered if he stank, period. Though he was dressed in a new lightweight gabardine suit and overcoat, he had the impression he had not changed out of them in a couple of days.

There was a mirror over the bar and he studied his surroundings in it. What he saw was, again, familiar yet unfamiliar: he knew it to be a hotel bar like any other hotel bar the world over. The waitresses were three college-age girls in black T-shirts and jeans. They stood together at the other end of the long stretch of dark wood, mostly chatting and gesticulating. It appeared to be a relatively slack night. Drinks trays laden with empty glasses piled up in the service area.

Despite the lack of traffic, it was difficult to get served. The manager was in his midthirties, button-down powder-blue shirt, conservative striped club tie, receding hairline. He was not getting the waitresses' attention either. He was pouring most of the drinks himself, pounding the register's buttons with unnecessary force as he made each sale. The clientele were largely middle-aged businessmen sipping beer and bourbon. The men's attention was half on the waitresses, half on the football game showing on the TV high in the corner over the bar. Wherever the night-time game was happening, it was far to the south, untouched by the snow falling here.

Suddenly the overworked manager was in his face, breaking in on his reverie. "What'll you have, mister?"

"Club soda," he answered, not looking him in the eye. The manager brought it. Little ice, no lemon, the liquid spilling onto the paper coaster and onto the edge of the five-spot that he had left on the bartop. A real drink would have been good, but a voice kept telling him that alcohol would make him forget again. And he was a man who desperately needed to remember.

The sodium lights glowed faintly orange-yellow through the net curtains mottled by the silhouettes of large, drifting flakes. Nothing else could be seen of the outside world, of the harbor or the distant airport across the water. It was as if the world had ceased to exist beyond the reach of the bar, the chattering girls and the flickering TV screen.

He was sitting quietly, listening for sirens from the dock area a mile and a half to the southeast and wondering what to do next, when the woman came up and asked if he would like a drink, just like that. She was, as far as he could tell, the only businesswoman in the bar. Auburn hair, center parting, hazel eyes. A light freckling over the nose, as if her pale, milky skin had seen a little sun even in this northeastern winter. A two-piece suit, understated gray, and white silk T-shirt underneath. The only jewelry she wore was two heavy scalloped gold earrings. He noticed she gripped the inside of her left suit sleeve, half concealing her wedding and engagement rings in the folds of material. Her perfume had a beguiling scent reminiscent of peonies and sandalwood.

Her smile was as winning as her scent: rather shy and sweet. He felt there was no danger from her: more, should the cops suddenly arrive, her presence might deflect suspicion from him. In fact, she could be the saving of him. She got up on the stool next to him.

"So, you drinking?" she asked.

"Well, I wasn't up till now."

"But you'll join me?" That smile again. It was difficult to resist. Besides, one drink couldn't hurt, could it?

"Sure," he said.

"It's on me, then," she said.

He exchanged the soda for a Manhattan, another name that had just popped into his head. He'd decided he'd call himself Martin. Martin will have a Manhattan, he thought to himself, and smiled, and the woman said, "What's so funny?"

And he said, "Oh, nothing. Just been a long day." And that seemed the right thing to say, he was glad to notice, because she gave another tentative smile. She ordered a martini for herself and told him she was called Nell Smith, but he wondered if that was her real name.

She had a quiet voice, only just above whispering, which he found hard to make out against the noise of the football game. Wherever she was from, there was a reserve about her. He found it confusing, but he decided he liked Nell's slightly contradictory mixture of assertiveness and reserve.

One drink followed another. The conversation, perforce, was mainly on her side. In fact, it was so one-sided maybe she thought he was already too drunk to talk. There were periods of silence, but she didn't seem to mind. It turned out she was a pharmaceutical rep. She told him of the meetings she had had that day in the city. The details of which eluded him the moment she had uttered them. The alcohol was having its effect. She leaned in as she repeated something. Almost imperceptibly the top of her foot came to rest on his calf and didn't leave. Her eyes didn't leave either. The drink seemed to give her Dutch courage. What would happen next?

Her hazel eyes, slightly glazed now, flickered from the martini on the bar to Ed and back again. It was her third since they had met sometime after nine. It was 10.35 now. She was heading on a tide of gin to whatever lay at the end of this road. Already her quiet words were a bit slurred. He was really only understanding about half of what she said, if that. Perhaps he was no better?

He wondered whether this was her first time with a stranger in a bar. Also, he wasn't sure what the protocol was. Was she waiting for him to initiate things? Or would it be more subtle than that: would she flash her key card and abruptly leave and see if he followed?

He hadn't thought it through. At first he'd decided she would be good camouflage while he gathered his thoughts. But now it occurred to him that spending the night with this woman might save him. He didn't know if he liked himself, whoever he was, for this idea. Should he just up and leave and take his chances on the road? By now, Scarface and Gangbanger's friends might be looking for him. And if they were looking for him, the police would certainly follow soon after.

He realized she, too, might be caught in indecision. The flirtation had, after all, been noncommittal. Now the moment had come. There was responsibility even when you were free: free and damned to do what you pleased all at once—such was the lot of the stranger. In his bones he knew he had once been like Nell, lonely and rootless in a strange place. Maybe she had no wish to do this thing other than to prove it could be done.

She was rummaging in her purse. A quick glance in a compact mirror, a tilt of the head, a model's moue transforming her; this, too, reminded him of a moment with someone else. The woman who had signed that picture?

Then Nell snapped the compact lid, bringing him back to himself.

She waved the manager over for the check.

"Let me," he said.

But she shook her head. "I said, it's on me." She leaned over the check and scrawled a signature that he didn't see. She shut the purse and slid from the stool. She didn't catch his eye, but looked instead at the purse clasp. He'd forgotten how petite she had been when he first saw her. Five six, he guessed, in her heels.

"Are you coming?" she whispered, her voice not quite controlled.

He slid off his own stool and reached out an arm, steadying her. As he did so, his eyes went to the mirror. He scrutinized the back of the bar in it. No one new, no one looking at them. He picked up his coat and helped her to the elevator bank in the foyer.

She was fumbling in her purse again; again, no eye contact. They got off at the sixth floor, walked a step or two down the corridor. She punched the room card down into the keyslot and there was a faint click and a green light shone on the display. They hadn't spoken a word since the bar.

"Listen…" he began, but she shushed him, holding up a finger to his lips. It trembled a little. That faint exotic scent again. Familiar but enchanting. A night in an exotic garden. She pushed open the door, slid the room card into the interior light array.

She must have left all the lights on standby when she went out because now every single one blazed into life. A small bathroom suite was on the left. Makeup scattered on the countertop, a wet towel untidily forced back on the rail, and a wet mat with her small, wet footprints still pressed into it. The room was small, the space between bathroom and window mostly taken up by a double bed. She walked toward it, then turned. The far wall was taken up by a window, a single standard light over an armchair, a minibar and a dressing table with a mirror. The curtains were open and fat flakes of snow were dancing in the blackness outside. One or two hit the window and slid slowly down the glass. The door's weight finally overcame the resistance of the latch and chunked shut behind him.

He shrugged off the overcoat. They stood close in the small space, without touching. He could feel her breath faintly on the front of his shirt. Her head hung, looking at the carpet. Her open purse in one hand, her other twisting the front of her suit jacket.

"Well, here we are," she whispered, then she looked up, for the first time since the bar. A small, wry smile as she bit her lower lip. In the hard overhead light she looked like a young girl. A sad young girl. She dropped the purse on the table. Its contents slid out. The compact again, lipstick, the room card, change… and a picture.

Her partner was good-looking. Blond, bronzed, fit… a sporting type. Could have modeled in *Men's Health*. There were two girls on either side of him. Blond like their father, but with their mother's face. Dad's arms were around them. The girls smiled shyly. The breeze was blowing strands of hair over their eyes and brace-covered teeth.

Then the people in the forefront of the picture rushed away and the background came sharply into focus. Behind the dad and kids was a lake. Ed distantly heard himself draw a sharp breath. A calm expanse of blue-black water framed by a tree limb fronded with green. A sailboat out in the middle distance, a haze of pine-covered forest beyond the water.

The Lake. A voice said: "You need to go to the Lake." But what lake? Some homing instinct in him, the scintilla of magnetite in his brain, told him it was north.

He realized both Nell and he were staring at the picture on the table.

"My family," she explained, needlessly. She reached forward and swept the photo and the rest back into the purse.

"Maybe I could use another drink," she said thickly. She knelt by the minbar. She pulled open the door. The inside light shone on her face, her foundation, the small imperfections of her skin, and a smear of mascara where she had wiped away a tear.

He sat on the bed as she pulled out two whiskey miniatures and poured them into plastic glasses. She held out one. He took it and knocked it back.

She sat next to him, thigh to thigh, and turned her face up to his.

They kissed for a few moments. Contradictory waves of lust and wrongness hit him simultaneously.

"Maybe this wasn't such a good idea," he said, standing abruptly.

She stood quickly as well, pulling down her rucked-up skirt. "It's fine. We don't have to do anything; just have a drink with me." She stared up at him. "I could use the company," she added.

He took a deep breath. "Listen, you're a beautiful woman, but"—he gestured—"I have to get somewhere."

"Why?" she asked. "It's late."

"There's a place I have to be. It's important." He reached down and picked up his overcoat from the bed.

She stood. "Stay, please."

He took a step back. "It's better I go, believe me."

Her brows knitted suddenly and the quiet woman was immediately gone.

"So, you're just one of those assholes, are you?" she said.

"I'm going, OK?" He held up his hands and backed to the door and unlatched it. He glanced quickly up and down the corridor. Empty. Then he looked back. She stood there, shoulders slumped, looking at the floor. He let the door go and hurried away.

It was just before twelve when the knock on the door came. By then Nell, whose real name was Gail McReedy, had had a couple of vodkas out of the minibar and the room was spinning slightly and out of focus at the edges. She had discarded the suit and her tights on the bed and was sitting in front of the vanity mirror in her underwear, staring mournfully at the small wrinkles around her eyes and mouth.

So he'd come back, she thought wearily. Maybe he had gone back to the bar for Dutch courage and had now conveniently forgotten about his wife or whatever else had been bothering him. Well, it was too late now. The rap came again, insistent. She would have to get rid of him before he made a scene. She pulled on the hotel bathrobe and opened the door, ready for sharp words.

But the words never came out because gloved hands grabbed her throat and mouth and bundled her back into the room. She realized there were two of them. Both wearing high-collared jackets and hats. Why hats indoors? she thought inconsequentially as the first man bore her backward onto the bed, where he straddled her, his hands like iron on her mouth and throat. The other shut the door softly behind him and advanced into the room. He paused, took off his hat and placed it neatly on the provided stand, like nothing so much as an office worker returning home after a busy day at work. He came to the bedside. There was a click and a switchblade gleamed in the soft light. He showed her it and then played it down her cheek. She felt its razor edge scraping the foundation and down away. He had a widow's peak and pockmarked cheeks. Her eyes were locked on his. She thought she had never seen such cold, blue eyes before. His teeth glinted with metal. Braces of some kind—a dental prosthesis? Why, in a grown man?

"Where's Ed?" he asked, taking his hand from her mouth.

"Ed?" she replied.

"He might have called himself Martin," the man said.

"He left. An hour or more ago."

"Too bad for you then," he said.

Then he clamped his gloved hand over her mouth again and it began.

CHAPTER FORTY-FIVE

Just after half past twelve there was a call from the Marriott house telephone about a disturbance in Room 611. No one ever discovered who made the call. When the night security went up to check on things, the man got no response from within. He used his pass key to enter. Gail McReedy was lying on the bed. Her tights were tied tight around her neck. Her eyes bulged in death as they never had in life and her blue tongue hung out of her mouth. Her panties had been torn away and her legs lay open. There were several distinctive bite marks on her breasts and inner thighs. Perfect dental sets.

It was not long before the place was swarming with cops. Guests trying to see what was going on were being held back in the corridor. The medical examiner made sure the SOE took careful photographs and measurements of the teeth marks. Dental forensics might be an incipient science but these perfect imprints were probably good enough to send someone down for life. Soon, the fact of the bite marks got out to the reporters; even before the early editions of the papers, the late-night radio shows started talking about the killer as the North End Cannibal.

There was a picture of the guy. The hotel's CCTV footage, which in those days only covered the lobby, showed McReedy with a dark-haired man who looked about thirty heading toward the elevators at just after 10.30. The man had reappeared in the footage some fifteen minutes later, walking rapidly toward the rear of the hotel. He looked flustered and jittery. Had he been gone long enough for rape and murder? Perhaps, the homicide detectives concluded.

The bar manager remembered the couple very well. He thought there was something off about the guy. Furtive, constantly checking his surroundings. He'd overheard the lady introduce herself as Nell something, but when she signed off the bill he saw her real name was Gail McReedy. He witnessed a lot of these bar hookups in his line of work and hadn't thought any more of it when the two had left together. But the lady—the dead lady—had seemed into the twitchy guy. Despite the fact that he had served him, he couldn't add much to the CCTV description.

The CCTV tape was bagged and taken to the station for further review. This time it was played right through from beginning to end. When the time marker reached a point just before midnight the tape went mysteriously blank for some minutes, as if it had been accidentally wiped. CCTV was a relatively new technology; these glitches sometimes happened. The police didn't mind the missing tape segment: they had already found their man. All they had to do was identify him.

CHAPTER FORTY-SIX

It was just after two in the morning. David was spending far longer than he wanted in the washroom of the Shell gas station on the I-95 near Reading. He was having problems unhooking the dental prosthetic that he had worn since he'd arrived at the Marriott a little after twelve.

In this matter of the prosthetic, as in the collection of all medical materials from Constance, Typhon had been, as always, very thorough. They had Ed's blood and urine through the regular medical checkups conducted by Merriweather's doctors, then, thanks to Godin, X-rays of every part of his body and even some tissue samples. Enough material to incriminate Constance at any self-respecting crime scene.

The records in their possession included the dental ones happily surrendered by his Merriweather-appointed orthodontist. There was, therefore, in David's opinion, no part of Edward Burns Constance they didn't possess—apart from, sadly, his mind, which had, it appeared, eluded them once again.

Typhon had owned it once and should have cashed in when it had a chance. Ten years ago, he should have completed his mission. "And the sixth angel poured out his vial upon the great river Euphrates; and the water thereof was dried up, that the way of the kings of the east might be prepared." What great truths lay in Revelation.

And what a great disappointment that twice now Ed had broken from Typhon's grip.

Ed would still come in, David was sure of that: the wife should see to that. Though David had begun to disagree with quite a few of Vermeulen's orders, he might just be right about this one thing. It was Ed's character flaw: noble Ed, always protecting the girls back at the Lot. He wouldn't have a choice but to obey, not if he wanted to save Sarah and his unborn child.

And yet, now the end had come for the Maine operation, David wondered if the risk of bringing Ed in was worth it. The incidents involving Catrine and Shannon had proved headline grabbers but their impact would likely be short-lived. Neither unrest nor riots had followed. Shock, certainly. But enough? America, though angry, had surprisingly exhibited patience, shown faith in the authorities to resolve the aftermaths of the incidents.

Yes, things were not as febrile as they had once been. Coughlin was gone: other shadowy figures now controlled Typhon, shadowy figures who apparently looked upon David with favor. He sensed their agenda was quite different from that of the Typhon founders in the thirties. There was the new project in the Gila Desert. Nate and Alice Mae should have reached it by now. Word had come that he might very well become the new director there. If so, he would not repeat Vermeulen's mistakes.

It would be easy to take Ed out. McReedy's murder was their guarantee of that. David agreed that "in a frenzy" was the right way to describe how she had been killed, as the helpful media put it. Thanks to him, Constance was now portrayed as a crazed, homicidal deviant. A federal agent or policeman would not take any risks when he was eventually cornered. No one would complain if the North End Cannibal went down in a hail of officers' bullets.

No one but Vermeulen: he was still convinced that Ed had hidden Stu's notebook somewhere. That in the event of Ed's death a bank vault somewhere would be opened and there would be all those names. Not David's, though. Should his old boss go down, he would go down without him.

There was still the irritating matter of ridding himself of the prosthetic. Murdo, the tame, addicted dental lab tech who had made it from Ed's dental records, had taken quite a few minutes to hook the device with rubber bands to David's back teeth.

That was before David went to the Marriott. Murdo wasn't around anymore to remove it—he was dead in his studio apartment in East Boston, a syringe of novocaine inserted apparently by accident into an artery. The coroner would determine that, as often happened, a junkie had tried a shot too many when they were too spaced to see what they were doing…

A voice came from outside the cubicle. "How ya doin' in there?" It was Fallows. He had been sent up from Merriweather's in Miami to join David's team. Perhaps to spy on him. He felt he was Vermeulen's man, not his own.

"'Ood, 'ive me a minute," David mumbled. He couldn't manage plosives with this contraption in his mouth. His jaw frankly ached and he hated the way he sounded dumb and backward, speaking through an extra set of teeth. He also regretted that his jaw wasn't double-jointed. He opened as wide as he could. Wiggling the prosthetic out from his teeth was like solving a Rubik's Cube.

"You nearly done?" Fallows asked.

David's patience boiled. "I told you to thay in the 'ar," he said thickly.

"Come again?" Fallows said.

"Fothet it. I'm thoming." Actually, the attempt to talk had joggled the prosthetic and suddenly it detached and was halfway out of his mouth. Thank Christ. He pulled it out. Ribbons of flesh and saliva clung to the intersection of fake incisor and molar. The woman's flesh. He had bit good and deep.

He rinsed his mouth and exited the cubicle.

"OK, let's get on the road," he said to Fallows. They exited the washroom into the bitter night. He tossed the prosthetic in a dumpster behind the neighboring McDonald's.

"You drive," he ordered as they reached the Suburban.

He got in the SUV and pulled a Motorola from his briefcase. It was similar to the ones once owned by Shannon and Ed.

"It's David," he said when his call went through.

"He's heading north on the interstate," the voice on the line from Mt. Lebanon said. David knew the owner of the voice only as the Operator.

"You got a tail on him?" David asked.

"Yeah, Bailey. He picked him up on the 95."

"OK, I'll call him." David hung up, then dialed a new number. It rang a few times before the call was picked up. There were the sounds of windscreen wipers churning at high speed, the whine of a transmission, fumbling, and a curse. The Motorolas were awkward, particularly if you were driving at the same time.

"Bailey?" David asked.

"Yeah, it's me, boss," the reply came eventually.

"You still got eyes on Constance?"

"Yeah, he's up ahead, gonna reach the New Hampshire toll in about a half-hour."

So they were about two hours ahead. It didn't matter to David. His destination was the private area of Bangor airport, where a helicopter was waiting. Once he was in that, however fast Constance moved, he would be in front of him.

David had discretion to call the shots on the ground. It was the dark of the night; there were few potential witnesses about. There were other Eds in the making right now in Gila. They would not be so mentally obdurate as Constance. New Vessels, new Vials, end-lessly renewed, until the Euphrates ran dry and they were kings of the east... Carl had had the right idea all those years ago: cap Ed and move on. History was full of subordinates turning a blind eye to their superior's orders and gaining victory. Tonight would be the night David came into his own.

"There're new orders," he said to Bailey. "If you have an opportunity, end him." He hung up.

Fallows had taken his eyes off the road and was looking at him.

"Just drive," he said. He inserted a finger and picked at his mouth. Goddam it if there wasn't something stuck in his real teeth now. "Got any gum?" he asked the ex-SEAL.

CHAPTER FORTY-SEVEN

It took Ed a half-hour to navigate through the harborside streets and tangle of flyovers and ramps. Then the Northeast Expressway bore him over the dark roofs of the Boston suburbs. The city fell below as if he was a bird flying over the dark skyline. Five miles, ten… each mile without any sign of pursuing stutter lights. The road plunged into rural Massachusetts. The interstate was virtually empty of other cars; the sky was black, the snow still dancing and slapping on the windscreen as the wipers churned.

The Lake. He needed to know more than that. In the dim cabin light, his eyes fell on the Bible sitting on the passenger seat.

He passed the turnoff to Salem. There was another trace memory there. A witch hunt in a witch's night. Broomsticks and high-peaked hats and long black gowns and a cat…

His eyes snapped open. He had been sleeping at the wheel. He yanked the nose of the car back from the central reservation. The Manhattans in the Marriott had dulled him, the adrenaline from the warehouse shooting had long worn off. When had he last slept? He needed adrenaline or coffee, or both.

Twice he passed massive truck trailer rigs lit up from cab to rear, like ocean liners thrumming through the sea of darkness. The Volvo eased past them, touching seventy, never more.

The state line at New Hampshire. Tollbooths ahead. Cameras operated in these places. There would be a record of his passing.

No matter. He would be off the toll soon. There were coins in the console. He would have to delay more seconds and count the right amount. He looked in the rearview. Nothing in the lane immediately behind him. A truck and a couple of cars idling at other barriers. He wound down the window. The cold air was like a slap in the face. He threw cash into the bucket and the barrier lifted.

New Hampshire. A short transit of sixteen miles. He crested a rise and looked in the rearview again. Now he could see a mile or two back into the great bowl of land through which the interstate ran. There were perhaps a half-dozen headlights behind, like a string of pearls. He knew he had made this journey before; a long time ago…

His eyelids weighed like stones and he knew he couldn't go any further. The intersection with Route 1 appeared and he took the down ramp. No tolls, less scrutiny. Blinking to keep awake, he turned the radio on and looked for a station. A buzz of static, then a late-night news show.

The headlines: the horrific rape and murder of a businesswoman, Gail McReedy, in the Boston North End Marriott earlier in the evening. The police were seeking a suspect they'd found on CCTV footage. There followed a description of himself, even down to the tan gabardine suit.

The newscaster said other media sources were already dubbing the killer "the North End Cannibal." She didn't divulge why the killer had been given this moniker; leaving that, perhaps, to the imagination of her listeners. The report ended, unnecessarily, with a warning that the perpetrator was dangerous and should not be approached.

His blood felt like ice and his hands gripped the wheel until the knuckles showed white. Nell had been Gail, then. No matter her name—because of him she was never going to see the blond-haired man and kids in the picture again.

The newscaster was not finished. There were two more homicides, reportedly drug-related, in City Point.

He shut the radio off. Three murders to be pinned on him. He stared almost blindly ahead. By now it had stopped snowing. The headlights showed a causeway through frozen water meadows south of Freeport. A sudden memory flashed: the meadows scattered with wildflowers in summer. The sun beating through cracked windows. Two adults in the front seat. Unknown silhouettes without voices.

Now he was in Freeport itself. The lights of the outlet factories, L.L. Bean, Lacoste, and the dozens of others, scrolled past. Mannequins posed in the windows, as if frozen in time, staring emptily upon this intruder into their night-time world. He slowed as the lights turned amber. The sidewalks were deserted. A sign warned pedestrians of icicles falling: they hung from the eaves of the clapboard houses like spears.

He left the lights of Freeport behind and went on into the bitter night, through Brunswick to Bath, looking for a place to stop. The nineteenth-century cantilever bridge over the Kennebec River loomed ahead. There was memory here: names forming like wraiths. He had spent time here on those journeys north.

He looked in the rearview. Far behind there was a single set of lights, but surely too far to be a pursuer. He crossed the bridge. There was a ramp down to the waterfront. He made a split-second decision and took it, rolled 100 yards down the ramp and switched off his headlights, then waited with the engine running.

The lights behind didn't reappear. The driver must have turned off. He took a breath, engaged first, drove on and reached the waterfront. There were banks of snow and pools of slush all around. By the dock there were fishing boats, crates, nets, drying sheds, and small cranes. On the other bank were the Bath Iron Works and the gray hull and upper works of a guided missile destroyer under construction on a great floating dock on the riverbank; there were arc lights on the jetties and high up on the cranes, lit up like Christmas. Further along the bank, looming out of the gloom, were the twin masts and massive booms and bowsprit of an old ship. The name came: the Grand Banks schooner *Sherman Zwicker*.

He went along the slip road to where the fishing boats lay slowly bobbing by the piers and found a dark spot by a shed, away from the sodium lights. There he did a U-turn back to the ramp. He turned off the engine and immediately felt the cold begin to settle around the car.

He breathed deep and his breath condensed in a great cloud as he exhaled.

He took the flashlight from the glove compartment, switched it on and shone it on the passenger seat. The papers he had found hidden under his shirt lay there.

The Bible sat next to them. It was a Morocco calf bound King James Bible, printed on wafer-thin India paper, gold rubbing on the outside of the paper, set in double columns inside.

Inside, on the first page, were two inked names. The first, a young life briefly noted. *Lieutenant Anthony R. Constance, April 16th, 1916– December 7th, 1941.* "Lieutenant" and the death date had been added in another, wavery hand. The words "Pearl Harbor" came into his mind. A great battle in which this young man had perished.

Written underneath Anthony's name, in a third hand: *Edward J. Constance, July 4th, 1961–.*

Edward, Ed. As written on the photograph of the dark-haired woman. His real name then?

Little gifts of remembrance came as his fingers splayed over the little undulations of the calfskin cover. Stu and Bettie had given him the Bible. The two people in the car driving along this road. They were his parents, but not his blood parents: his adoptive parents. He heard his mother say, "The child needs a Bible for Sunday." It had been on one of the crowded bookshelves, cobwebbed and faintly dusty.

Other memories of that place, of nooks and crannies filled with stuff: frayed fishing nets; old rods; old gauge-shot cartridges, their red casing faintly yellowed by many suns; rusty tins with old feather flies, others containing nothing but dried earth and the dust of long-expired worms; vests with hooks and more feathered baits. A taxidermy mallard and an otter caught on its haunches, its two teeth giving it a gimpy look, peered down from the shadows.

A scrap of paper hidden in the first pages of the Bible fell onto his lap as he riffled through it. There was a series of handwritten numbers on the paper:

1.16.2.18.4,5
1.351.1.28.1,2,3
2.93.2.10.2
1.1088.1.34.4
1.1.24.49.23,24,25,26
1.28.13.13. 23,24,25,26
1.23.44.14.27

He was sure that the writing was his. What did the numbers mean? His eyes went back to the page from which the paper had fallen. It was from the beginning of the Bible, an index, the heading of which read: "The Names and Order of All the Books of the Old and New Testament, with the Number of their Chapters."

He stared at the word "number," then at the slip of paper. The answer to the puzzle suddenly came into his mind. It was a code. The first number indicated Old or New Testament; the second, page number; the third, column number; the fourth, line number; the fifth, the number of the word in the line.

He quickly went back and forth through the Bible seven times, the thin paper crackling under his fingers:

Genesis 11.4: "And they said, *go to*, let us build us a city."

Judges 12.1: "We will burn *thine house upon* thee with fire."

Luke 8.22: "Let us go unto the other side of the *lake*."

Daniel 4.27: "A lengthening of thy *Tranquility.*"

Genesis 24.49: "… that I may *turn to the right*."

Hosea 13.13: *"in the place of."*

Isaiah 1.23.44.14.27: "he planteth an *ash*."

The message: "Go to thine house upon Lake Tranquility. Turn to the right in the place of ash."

And then it came fully back: the ash stand by the dirt road, and, down the track, the cabin by the lake, Nakuset rising behind, Katahdin under cloud, the green forest cladding the mountains, the gray-blue lake and the blue sky above: Brantwood.

Underneath the first set of numbers were two more:

1.4.26.22

22.2.14.3

Then a list of some of the books of the Bible:

Job

Judges

Exodus

Ruth

Ruth

II Timothy

II Kings

He repeated the process:

Genesis 4.26: *"call* upon the name of the Lord."

The Song of Solomon 2.14: "O my *dove*, thou art in the clefts of the rock."

The meaning of the list of books revealed themselves then. They were the numbers of the 66 books of the Bible:

Job 20

Judges 7

Exodus 2

Ruth (twice) 8

II Timothy 55

II Kings 12

A phone number. And a name flashed: Jim Dove's phone number, 207-288-5512. He'd called it recently—very recently.

There was a road map of the northeast in the side pocket of the car. His fingers seemed to find Lake Tranquility without thought. Almost due north. After a short, necessary sleep, he would be there by first light.

He closed his eyes. A kaleidoscope of images came: palm trees in a mild breeze; an open front door, a dim corridor, a brightly lit kitchen, a pool of blood on the counter, a dismembered finger...

He wasn't sure if he moaned in his sleep or in waking. He opened his eyes, disoriented. There was a sudden white light coming through the windshield. It came from the headlights of a car on the ramp leading down to the dock.

A silhouetted figure, a long shadow reaching ahead, was walking down the ramp, skirting to Ed's left. The light glinted off the barrel of a shotgun aimed at his window.

Ed simultaneously grabbed for the key in the ignition and pulled out the manual choke. The Volvo engine coughed and caught, and he slammed the car into first and ducked down. The driver's window exploded in a cloud of glass and he felt a fierce nick on his left ear as the car lurched forward. He hauled the wheel over, the rear end of the Volvo fishtailing, sliding on the slush, without any traction. The front wheels bit. Then he was racing toward the man, the raised shotgun aimed directly at him. It flashed again, but the shot was wide, only starring the left side of the windshield.

Ed slammed into second, floored the gas, and the station wagon was on the man. He had broken the shotgun and was trying to eject and reinsert new cartridges. He looked up at the last second. For an instant Ed saw him. Conservatively dressed, gray suit, white shirt, black tie, in his late twenties. His mouth opened in an "o" of surprise, then terror when he saw Ed was intent not on escape but on running him over. The hood of the Volvo seemed to swallow him. The car's clearance was only some six inches, but the snow added a couple more. The man was pulled under the one-ton car and there was a series of momentary dull thuds as the bumper caught him, and then he was worked feet first underneath the exhaust and suspension system. The Volvo braked with the drag and then there was one last thud and it was released, racing toward the on ramp and the blazing lights.

Ed rammed on the brakes and the Volvo skidded in the slush. He looked in the rearview. There was a wide path in the snow behind him that ended in the tangled, motionless form of the man he'd run over. One of his arms and his head seemed to have been put on the wrong way around. The snow was absorbing a pool of blood.

Ed's breathing was out of control, his breath almost a squeak. His hands trembled on the wheel. He realized his foot was clamped down on the brake. His senses began to return. He looked up at the car on the on ramp. Was the shooter alone, or was there someone else waiting? He hit his own brights, floored the gas again and reached the ramp at forty, scraping the side of the parked saloon car in a shower of sparks. Ed caught a brief glimpse of it as it flew past. A navy-blue Ford, empty.

Then he was fishtailing onto the feeder road to Route 1 and the interstate. Bitter wind howled in through the shattered window. It felt like a scalpel was slicing his ear where the shot had grazed him.

He drove for ten miles. By then the cold wind was freezing his hands and face. He needed to stop.

The red star came up out of the night on his right-hand side, floating in a sea of light in the otherwise pitch-black. It was red, with the letter T indented into the bottom of the star. A truck stop. More memory came cascading back.

He turned onto the off ramp. The gas station lay bathed in sodium light. There was an all-night diner next to it. He pulled in where the big rigs were parked.

He stared at the sign. Texaco. His mind was breaking from its cocoon. The last day at the Lot. Suddenly he was no longer in the freezing gas station. He felt the hot buttoned cushions of the yellow school bus and Shannon's braids on his shoulder. Shannon—he remembered her. Dead because of him. The names in the papers he'd found taped next to his body began making sense: David, Carl, Kevin, Hope, Catrine, Shannon, and him. Vessels and Vials—God's sacrifices, *Typhon's* sacrifices. The Seven Apostles. All dead apart from him and David.

Yes, Shannon was gone. The thought hit him hard. How could she be dead when she had been so alive, asleep on his shoulder in the yellow bus, lit by the slant of the sun as they turned into that crazy, abandoned gas station lot and the red Texaco sign rose up into the June evening and the song of the white-throated sparrow came from the trees: *Ah, te,e,e,te,e...*?

His memory, so slow up until now, unraveled quickly: Winthrop Road, vacations on Tranquility, Jim, the day it all changed at Northeastern, Eagle Lake—

Miami. That was where he had come from. Miami was why he had two names. There had been a life before and a life after. He had become another person in Florida. He'd had a life, a job—and a wife. A pregnant wife.

Sarah. He stared blindly ahead. Sarah: they'd taken her. Why? Because she was collateral; a tool to bend him to their will should their mental coercion not work.

He remembered the cell phone. The choice. Accept the call or refuse. Accept and Sarah and the child would live. Refuse, they would die.

His life was over either way. He was alone: a wanted man pitted against an organization that spanned every police, secret service, and judicial organization in the country.

He looked at his head in the mirror. The entire left side of his throat was soaked with blood. Some of the shot had shredded his left earlobe. The freezing night air had at least stanched the bleeding, but, with his haunted face, dark rings under his eyes and the blood that had turned his white collar red, he looked like an extra from *Dawn of the Dead*. "When there's no more room in hell, the dead will walk the earth."

He got out of the car stiffly. A shoal of broken glass fell from his lap onto the asphalt. He looked around. No one was to be seen. He reached in and removed more handfuls of shattered glass. There was a dumpster near the truck stop and next to it a pile of cardboard facings. He went to the passenger door, opened the glove compartment and pulled out the clasp knife he had seen there, then went around to the rear door of the station wagon and took out a roll of duct tape. He quickly cut two layers of thick cardboard and taped them over the broken window.

He hurried back to the tail door, threw in the tape and some extra cardboard and slammed it shut. Only then did he notice a length of fabric, he guessed from the gunman's coat, trailing in the slushy gravel from the suspension of the Volvo. That and the broken window would be enough to excite the suspicions of a highway patrolman. He reached underneath and grabbed the fabric. It seemed to be caught on the lower control arm. He used the knife to cut it away. The fabric was thick with blood. He threw it into the dumpster, then wiped his hands in a bank of snow.

There was a pay phone at the side of the diner and some coins in the console. He scooped them up and went to it. He was reluctant to pull Jim into this again, but needs must. He dialed the number. Half wanting to hear Jim's voice, half hoping he wouldn't be there. The phone rang and rang. No answer. He hung up. He realized that, despite his qualms, he had been desperate for a friendly voice.

He was staring at the coin return when the side door of the diner opened, casting a shaft of light on him. A busboy came out with a bag of trash. He stared at Ed, taking in the bloodstained collar, before going to the dumpster and throwing in the bag.

Ed quickly got back in the station wagon. A few starry glass crystals nipped his ass as he sat down. The engine stalled when he turned the ignition. He cursed. He'd left the choke pulled out all the way from the Kennebec and now the carburetor was swamped with gas. He smashed the choke back in, knowing the damage was probably done and he would have to wait for a half-hour or so before the engine fired again.

The busboy had disappeared. Ed wondered if he was already on the phone to the police. He turned the ignition again. By a miracle, it suddenly roared into life. He didn't look back as he peeled out of the lot.

★

The Operator in Mt. Lebanon had been busy coordinating things between David, the two other Suburbans, Bailey, and the team already in place in the backwoods. Sometime in the depths of the night, perhaps about half past two, Bailey went silent on him.

An hour or so later, as he stretched and looked around, he noticed a light on a switchboard he barely looked at anymore indicating an incoming call to Dove's Bait and Tackle. His heart began to beat a little faster as he flipped a switch. He waited for the call to be picked up, but it was not.

He rang Bailey's cell again, but there was no response. He kept at it until about four o'clock, when, on maybe his twentieth attempt, the phone was abruptly answered.

"Yes?" a strange voice said. There was a burst of static as from a transceiver in the background and the Operator immediately thought, "Cop," and hung up.

He picked up the dedicated phone to Vermeulen's rooms.

CHAPTER FORTY-EIGHT

Ed reached Hadsville at 7.15. The early-morning gray revealed the socioeconomic slide of central Maine: boarded-up and paint-peeled clapboard houses lined the county road; apple orchards had been abandoned, their trees gnarled and black like twisted human limbs; a psychedelically painted trailer was an occult healing center; the hoarding outside the next church warned him that "Christ Died for *Your* Sins."

Over a rise and the trees closed in and the mountains rose up gray and ghostlike in the cold dawn. A brown sign indicated the road to Tranquility.

For everything he now remembered, he knew there was still plenty missing: the unknown lay ahead. He had last been there ten years before. What would he find? Fear was for specific, known threats; dread was for everything else, for the great unknown. And for Ed that was all that was left.

He drove fast, the cold whipping in through the cardboard-covered driver's-side window. Yellow moose warning signs whipped past. After ten miles the road crested another ridge. There hadn't been another car since Hadsville. The first bars of gray light sat in the east, but the sun wasn't hurrying, still in irons to the gray clouds that had closed over Maine after yesterday's snowstorm. The slate-gray surface of the lake was emerging from the gloom of the surrounding forest below, stretching into the distance to the northwest, toward cloud-covered

Nakuset. In front, the road ran down an incline for the last three miles, going straight as a die through the wilderness to the lake. He now recalled that the road was simply known as the Three Mile Road.

Suddenly the asphalt came to an abrupt end and the Volvo was crunching over unpaved gravel, fishtailing slightly as the tires slid over the loose surface. He slowed, wrestling with the wheel as the car slid toward one of the deep drainage ditches that edged the side of the road. He remembered then: the "Pavement Ends" sign had toppled over into the ditch many years before and had never been replaced.

The road-surface transition triggered more memories. Ahead was a junction. The right branched toward the bait store, the eastern log cabins, and the Sun Mountain Hotel. The left branch went to Brantwood and the sparsely populated west side of the lake, then arced around the northwestern edge, following it to its northern tip, to Dickson Camp and the logging tracks that Jim and he had taken ten years before.

Ed caught a glint in his driving mirror and instantly his eyes flicked to it. Car lights had appeared in the notch of pines at the crest of a ridge five miles back toward Hadsville. The lights flared as they came level with the mirror and then dimmed slightly as the car began its descent toward Tranquility. Close behind there was a second set of lights. One other car on a lonely winter's morning heading toward a virtual dead end might have been coincidence, but two? Deer season was over. Two cars could only mean pursuers.

Ed boosted the gas and the engine surged, sending gravel spitting out behind: thirty, forty... The telegraph poles by the side of the road flicked past faster and faster. The road incline was easing, the forest giving way to a grassy, marshy, snow-covered waste on either side. The junction was just ahead. He looked in the mirror again just as the vehicles behind crested another ridge. It was difficult to gauge at such a great distance, but it looked like they were going fast, the headlights swinging slightly, even on the straight stretch of road, as if the drivers were struggling for control. Ed goosed the engine again.

He was now going over fifty, recklessly fast on the unpaved road. The cardboard ripped off the driver's-side window and the cold air slapped him in the face.

Ed rammed his foot down: the speedometer leapt toward the red. The Volvo was hitting sixty now. A line of trees crossed his path 100 yards ahead, marking the junction.

He braked fast and the station wagon slid onto the snow-covered verge, sending up a spume of mud, before he got it back on the gravel and onto the intersection.

He pulled the wheel to the left, toward Brantwood, pressed down on the gas again, and the Volvo took off. From here there was no sign of the lights behind. He guessed that they would be at the junction in about fifteen minutes.

On his right, he began to see tracks leading off to cabins by the lake. Two or three flashed past and then he saw what he had been looking for. Stark against the sea of evergreen conifers, the white trunks of ash trees, the last ghostly, sere leaves hanging from the black latticework of their thin branches. "Turn to the right in the place of ash." Beyond them was the driveway to Brantwood.

He turned right and switched off the headlights, cursing the Volvo's safety features; the side and rear lights remained on whenever the engine was running. He hoped these lesser lights would be hidden by the trees that now closed around on either side. He squinted ahead in the gloom. After 100 yards there was a turning point in the gravel. Two driveways barred by low metal gates led toward the lake. Even in the gloom he could read the names on the sides of the mailboxes by the gates. The left leaned drunkenly to one side, spotted with rust, and read "Constance;" the right, painted a pristine white, read "Sproule." Both gates were padlocked and chained.

He remembered he had once had keys to this place. He had a memory of throwing them out of the window of the Greyhound bus into a water-filled ditch as he had crossed the Florida state line ten years earlier.

Ed pulled open the glove compartment, took out the gun and got out of the car. The heater had made a little difference, despite the broken window, but the air outside was frigid and his breath immediately condensed as he exhaled. He shivered.

He looked at the padlock. Heavy brass. He wasn't sure whether a shot would take it out. Or, for that matter, whether a ricochet might strike him. He cocked the gun and took an oblique angle about a foot away, turned his head away and pulled the trigger. Instantaneously the gun bucked, there was a metallic *chang* and he heard the bullet whine off into the forest. He opened his eyes again to find the padlock blown off its hasp, the metal lock hoop slightly bent in its docking slot. He pulled it free with a screech of metal and opened the gate. He quickly got back in the car and drove it through, then got out and pulled the gate to behind him.

Seconds later he was rolling down a slight slope toward the lakeshore. There were no other marks in the fresh snow on the drive apart from a set of chipmunk paws. Ahead, the lake glimmered gray in the dawn light, its surface living up to its name, barely marked by a ripple. Patches of mist drifted over it. It stretched away far to the north, to the whaleback forest-covered mountains of the Appalachians. On his left, as he came around a corner, he saw the beechwood cabin. There was an air of desertion to the place. Weeds grew up through the gravel drive, dead leaves lay mounded at one end of the porch, a rocking chair lay on its side. One of the front windowpanes appeared cracked and the shingles were covered in green moss, but otherwise the roof seemed in a fair condition. A wooden sign was tacked over the screen door. Carved in it in imitation of an old-world copperplate hand was the word "Brantwood."

The drive continued around the front, between the cabin and the boathouse. There was an empty carport on the flank of the house. He pulled into it, cut the engine and got out of the car.

He remembered the key to the rear door was hidden under the oil tank in the port. He crouched by it and reached into the gap between the cylinder and the concrete platform. As he touched sere leaves blown under the tank, something scuttled away under his fingers, then he felt metal and pulled out a Yale key. Despite it being stainless steel, the damp had corroded it in places.

He straightened and went to the back door. The interior of the cabin was veiled by a lace curtain. He wasn't exactly certain what he would find inside.

He slid the Yale into the lock. The door swung open onto his past.

CHAPTER FORTY-NINE

The two black Chevy Suburbans were the type typically used by federal agencies. The vehicles had been equipped with enhanced six-liter V8 engines, and with the added torque and horsepower, and laden as they were with only two passengers, each with minimal equipment, they had effortlessly cruised down the Maine Turnpike, eating up the miles and Ed's head start.

The SUVs' windows were tinted, concealing the occupants. The first of the two drivers appeared quarried from unmoving stone: he looked to be ex-special forces. His head was about the same width as his bulging neck muscles. His Typhon codename was Hulk.

The passenger next to him was occupied with some syringes and vials laid out on the lid of the metal attaché case on his lap. He was known within the organization simply as Doc. He was to have administered the final checks on Constance before he was sent off to Colorado, but after the deaths at the City Point warehouse it turned out that the victim was not only conscious but a killer. Hence the extra backup in the Suburbans. Doc was still proceeding with Vermeulen's original orders: bring in the subject, if biddable. It seemed that some chemical intervention might be required should Constance prove resistant, hence the syringes. Whether they would be used to tranquilize or euthanize remained to be seen.

Doc didn't look like a person used to even moderate activity, let alone a dangerous pursuit. He was in his early sixties, quite slight, with a narrow face and gray hair; round, steel-framed reading glasses were balanced on his pinched nose. He had once been dubbed Doctor Death by the press, having worked as a lethal-injection expert in several states after the Supreme Court had readmitted the death penalty in 1976.

Doc had been kept busy by Typhon over the years. His drugs had deprogrammed David Krige. He had saved the boy only to find he was now that boy's employee.

Doc sensed a tension between Krige and Vermeulen over this matter of Edward Constance. The former indubitably regarded Constance as a loose cannon, a threat to the whole organization, but Vermeulen didn't seem to be able to let go of the idea that Constance could still fulfill his mission. With Coughlin dead and others pulling the strings in the government, military, and secret services, Doc knew which way the narrative was going—and it was all against Vermeulen. David was the coming guy: a dyed-in-the-wool fascist who would one day replace Vermeulen. Vermeulen was, after all, in his seventies and from another, lost, age. The objectives of the American Nazis had changed in the fifty years since the events of the late thirties. Doc was not one to be impressed for no reason, not with the things he had done for Typhon, but there was something raw and merciless in Krige that even he admired.

If they could not bring Constance in, the staging of his death would be Doc's responsibility. The attaché case contained more syringes and enough sedatives, hypnotics, lethal barbiturates, and chemicals to put down a small town.

So now Ed was the last Apostle. There had been more success-ful Typhon operations, such as the Weather Underground and the Unabomber. But their involvement with the Weather Underground had ended two decades earlier when their agent had been killed in an explosion in a Greenwich townhouse. Others, unrelated to Typhon, had carried on the Underground's work in later years.

Ted Kaczynski, the Unabomber, had been attracting front pages with his attacks across the country since '78. He had been a sixteen-year-old math prodigy at Harvard before falling under the spell of the Harvard psychologist Henry A. Murray, one of the leading lights in the CIA's Project MKUltra and one of Doc's scientific heroes. Murray's dream was to create the perfect truth drug and explore the power of mind control. In Kaczynski they had found an ideal subject, and an ideal agent. But Kaczynski had now been inactive for two years. Even Typhon did not know where he was. A big statement was needed, bigger even than Pensacola and the Hialeah shooting.

There was a chance that Constance could become a legend bigger than the Unabomber. His fake backstory was already written. As with the papers and books in Shannon's apartment, extremist literature had been planted in the Tranquility cabin. After the dam, the media would revel in the story of the kid who had had everything but turned terrorist.

In the second Suburban, the driver was sandy-haired, had a permanent goofy smile, and was slightly goggle-eyed, until you looked properly into those eyes and saw they were dead as ice. His colleagues called him Woody. But Doc knew that Woody wasn't his real name and that Woody was neither intellectually limited nor, for that matter, habitually cheerful.

The passenger next to Woody was new to the team: wiry and spare, sunburned to a leathery mahogany, with dark, piercing eyes and a habit of silence. He didn't really give himself to a nickname, so by nominative determinism they just called him "the Sniper." They had picked him up on an up ramp on the 93 in South Boston in the early hours. He had been standing there with his gun case tucked under his arm, as cool as a businessman about to ride the Green Line.

A fifth operative had been lost along the way. It seemed Bailey had contradicted the standing orders and approached Constance on his own. He had paid the penalty. That was three Typhon operatives killed by Ed in one night. Maybe the Sniper was going to be more a necessity than mere insurance. The Doc would have been happier if Vermeulen's orders were to shoot on sight.

When they hit the 201 just before dawn, both vehicles hit the gas. They were soon speeding through Hadsville and along the small country road leading to Tranquility. The ride now became wild as the road twisted and turned around hairpins of unpredictable cambers. It took all of Doc's willpower to control his stomach as the Suburban lurched from side to side like a flying brick. He swallowed bile and a vein began to tic on his forehead. Perhaps he was getting too old for field missions.

The final stretch of road before the lake straightened. The Suburban stabilized and Doc gave a sigh of relief and craned forward, trying to get sight of Constance's black Volvo ahead in the early-morning light.

His respite was short-lived. On the straight stretch both drivers floored the gas, the transmissions whined and Doc was pinned back in his seat.

The second SUV was right behind the first when the accident happened.

Woody was concentrating on the back of the other car and was surprised by the sudden transition of the road surface to gravel. The Suburban skidded, its rear end sliding into the marshland to the right in a geyser of ice, grass, and mud, before it slammed into a half-submerged tree bole. Woody and the Sniper disentangled themselves from their seat belts and pushed open the doors.

Doc's SUV backed up next to the crash. He and Hulk got out and inspected the damage to the other car. The rear passenger-side wheel arch was crumpled, the metal crushed into the tire, now deflated, the axle bent backward, the heavy vehicle sunk at the rear into the bog.

It looked like Woody had been slammed against the window despite his seat belt. He had a bloody nose and his left cheek was red as beet. He certainly didn't look good-humored anymore. The Sniper had fared a little better, but the Doc noticed that he was wringing his trigger hand as if it had been jarred.

"You OK, son?" he asked him.

"Guess so, no thanks to him," he replied, jerking his head at Woody. Woody rewarded him with a dead-eyed stare.

"Move the equipment. We'll use the other truck," Doc ordered.

"What about the wreck?" Woody asked.

"We're not going to get a tow out here," Doc answered.

Chastened, Woody wiped his bloody nose and helped the others transfer equipment from the trunk of the wrecked vehicle to the other SUV, then clambered in the back with the Sniper.

The surviving Suburban went forward more circumspectly than before. They reached the junction in the gravel road a mile south of the lake. Hulk cocked an eye inquisitively at Doc, who was leaning forward, getting his bearings.

"Left," he grunted.

The SUV turned and started to inch along the road, Doc staring ahead, checking the drives snaking off into the trees.

He saw fresh tire marks in the snow by a stand of ash trees and said, "There." The SUV slowed even further and then almost silently turned off the road.

It was just over a half-hour since Ed had made the same turn.

CHAPTER FIFTY

Days earlier. Thanksgiving on the lake was really no season at all; there was no one around, but Jim had long ago decided he didn't mind the solitude.

In the ten years since Ed had gone, Laramie had sickened and died. Jim had waited a year, then replaced him with another dog, Max. At this time of year, apart from weekly supply trips to Hadsville, it was just Jim and the dog.

Evenings, there was the TV, with its couple of fuzzy channels, and the bottle. No more White Widow—not since Eagle Lake. The telephone rang on average once or twice a week. Summer people, suppliers. No relatives. No girlfriends. That was how it had come to be.

The day before Thanksgiving, he watched the WMTW coverage of the bombing in Pensacola. The images bled across his vison. The smoke and flames triggered the smell of Nam: napalm, burning trees, rubber, and human flesh… The name of the perpetrator flashed up under a mugshot. A chill passed through him. He didn't know why.

Until the call came that evening he hadn't known if Ed was alive or dead. There was no contact between Jim and Dumfries: for Jim's sake and the kid's.

But over the years, he'd kept an eye on the local news, and every week during his resupply trips he flipped through the *Boston Herald* in the Hadsville Public Library. Nothing about Ed, missing or dead, in Maine or Massachusetts. Jim felt in his bones that the kid was still alive.

Tired of the endless looping of the bombing news, he changed channels.

He had just started on *Cheers*. He was not a fan of comedies, but something about the bar where everybody knows your name sparked something in him; a memory perhaps of the camaraderie of the Corps. Those days had been the best of days, and the worst—

That was when the phone rang. No one called in the evening at that time of year. He had a premonition of something bad. Nevertheless, he found his hand straying to the receiver on the twelfth ring. And when he snatched it up he heard Ed's voice for the first time in ten years.

He refused to do what Ed was asking him to do at first. It was likely the end of the kid: all that he had survived and achieved in the decade since Eagle Lake gone in an instant. And the kid married and soon to be a father. It would be down to Jim to end all that?

It wouldn't be the first time he'd been called upon to kill a friend. When he'd given Ed that Colt on his eighteenth birthday, he hadn't told him its true history or why, perhaps, he was glad to part with it. Sergeant Lenny Piazzola had not died instantly in that Cong ambush in '71. He had been leading the patrol when he'd stepped on a hidden mine. The blast had thrown his body over the raised path into a paddy field. When Jim had jumped down to help him he discovered that everything below Piazzola's waist had been taken off by the blast, and the muddy waters of the paddy were turning red, but Piazzola was, somehow, alive. And he was looking at Jim. The look told Jim one thing: his friend knew he was dying.

The sergeant nodded to the sidearm in his holster just above his shattered hip.

"Please, Jim," he'd whispered. And though Lenny was his best friend in the Corps, Jim had stared for a moment without ruth, with pitiless calculation, thinking that Piazzola had only minutes to live and no tourniquet could save him because there were no legs left to apply tourniquets to, so maybe he could just let him bleed out. But Piazzola's pleading eyes could not be avoided. There was human left in Jim deep down—somewhere very deep—despite this hell of explosions and bullets, despite the blood and body parts and the cries of the dying...

"Please, Jim," Piazzola had repeated, and Jim had reached forward and unfastened the gun from its blood-soaked holster. He was conscious of the platoon returning fire and the crack and whistle of bullets as he thumbed the safety and leaned into Piazzola. The sergeant nodded and closed his eyes. Then Jim placed the pistol to his friend's head, shut his own eyes and fired.

He guessed that gun had been cursed. First Lenny, then Stu...

And now this request. Not so different from Piazzola's in that, given the right circumstances, it would guarantee Ed's death. By his, Jim's, hand.

Twice in a lifetime. It was too much for any man. Yet, as he had pointed out, what Jim was about to do might kill Ed, but, if so, it would save thousands.

Of all the Thanksgivings Jim had lived through in his forty-three years, that one in 1989 was the loneliest. For most of it he didn't even have his dog with him. He was up at dawn, fed Max, then locked him in the store and flipped the Closed sign.

The heavy snowstorms blanketing New York and Massachusetts that day hadn't reached this far north but it was colder than a witch's tit. The cab heater was on full, but his breath still came in clouds. The drive was as solitary a drive as any man ever took, and the nearer to his target he got, the presentiment that came out of the blue, the same one he'd had in Nam a couple of times that something dreadful was on the cusp of happening, just grew and grew.

The roads and forestry checkpoints of northern Maine were deserted for the holiday. He drove on, unchallenged and alone. He found the place Ed had described: it was as desolate and strange a place as any he'd seen. As Ed had promised, after he'd used the code and gotten in, he found everything he needed. He did his work quickly.

It was dark when he returned to Tranquility. He hadn't the heart to cook a meal, so just opened a can of Spam and fed half to himself and half to Max.

As the days passed, the presentiment and misgivings did not relent. He guessed Ed was in deep trouble. He checked on Brantwood every day, but there was no sign of the kid. That Tuesday, during his weekly supply trip to Hadsville, he scoured the newspapers in the library with even greater attention than before.

That night he drank a skinful of Four Roses at the bar and stayed in the one flea-bitten motel, sleeping off the bourbon.

It was about eight the next morning when he took the Three Mile Road back to the lake. He had WMEF on. A rape-homicide had been reported in a Boston hotel. The police were looking for a man the media had dubbed the North End Cannibal. There followed a description of a Hispanic person caught on the hotel's CCTV. The description on the radio was necessarily vague but had just enough detail to make Jim wonder if they might be describing an older version of the Ed he had known. The certainty that Ed and this Cannibal were one and the same settled on Jim like a lead cloak.

As he had this thought, he saw the first sign of trouble ahead. A black SUV was half on, half off the track, its rear end up against a tree bole sticking out of the muskeg. Jim slowed and pulled up alongside the wreck. Tinted windows. Massachusetts plates. A cold hand went down his spine. An outsider's car. But why were they here? It came to him then: it must be because Ed was here. He stared down the road toward the lake. Nothing moving.

Jim switched his engine off, stepped down from his truck and peered through the Suburban's tinted windows. Empty. He tried the doors: locked. He felt the hood: still warm. The crash had been quite recent, less than an hour before; the cylinder block would cool quickly in the sub-zero temperature. There were other tracks in the snow around the crash. Looked like two cars had been here.

Jim had a bolt-action Winchester 70 in the bed of his truck. It was a replacement for the 94 he had thrown into Eagle Lake. These days, nearly everyone favored semiautomatics with scopes, but Jim had kept to the old ways; bolt-action, open sights were just fine by him. He drew the gun out of its case, checked the three-way safety was engaged and pulled back the bolt to see that a round was chambered. Good to go. He slung it over his shoulder.

By now, Max was practically jumping up level to Jim's chest, sensing a hunting trip. Jim curtly ordered the dog to sit. Max promptly obeyed with a little whine. Jim had made a decision. If Ed was here, his life was at risk. Two carloads had arrived. Jim didn't like those odds, either for Ed or for him. MacDonald had moved on from Hadsville and was now the sheriff at Madison. He could trust him—and the rest of the local police. He got the transceiver from his truck, a handheld Motorola model some ten years old.

He got on the frequency to the local deputy's office in Hadsville. The police transceiver was barely used in the winter months and a call would come as some surprise to the one local cop. Stan Pollitt was the only officialdom for miles around. Pollitt was a gregarious, red faced, overweight individual, kind and efficient, and popular both with the sheriff in his distant office and with the small communities in this part of rural Maine for his ability to get along with people and not to poke his nose too far into anyone else's business, particularly when it involved out-of-season hunting or illegal stills.

There was a delay, a crackle of static and then Pollitt's voice. "Hadsville sheriff's office. Please state your business. Over."

Jim keyed the mic. "Stan, it's Jim. Over."

"Hey, Jim, how're things? Over."

"Not bad. Want your help with somethin', though. I'm out here on the Three Mile Road and guess what? There's a wreck. A Suburban. Massachusetts plates. Over."

"A Suburban from away? Don't see many of them this time of year. Over."

Jim keyed the mic again. "Airbags deployed. No sign of the occupants."

"They got a walk then."

"Maybe not. There's another set of tracks. Looks like they were picked up."

"Two cars? That's kinda unusual."

"You bet. I know everyone with a cabin around this lake and not one of them is here right now."

"So, what's your guess?"

"Dunno, Stan. I hope it ain't trouble."

"Well, the wreck is enough trouble. Looks like I better come out there. Be about twenty minutes. Over and out."

Jim sighed. He didn't want to drag Pollitt into this, but nor did he want to face whatever was in front of him alone. Ed's call the week before had been warning enough.

Maybe he better tell Stan everything when he got here. He stared over to Brantwood, listening for shots.

CHAPTER FIFTY-ONE

Ed stood in the rear hall. Brantwood was in twilight, a mausoleum. Dust motes rose in the disturbed air. It's been over ten years since he'd returned that September day in '79. The shades and curtains were drawn and the furniture covered with dust sheets, just as he had left them when called back to Bettie's deathbed. His memory was not yet perfect, but he remembered he had hidden something important here, something only he could find. Memory was coming slowly back to the surface, like a long-sunken secret from the bottom of a pond.

Something was not right in the picture as far as he remembered it. He bent down and inspected the pine floor. The dust covering the boards had been disturbed where one of the rugs had been pulled to one side. Ed pulled it further back. There was a loose floorboard underneath where Stu had stored cash and valuables during their vacations. He remembered the planted evidence in Shannon's apartment. He knelt, got his fingers in the crack between the boards and levered it up.

He had been expecting explosives and weapons, but there was only books, magazines, and papers. Using his shirttail, he leafed through the material, careful not to leave fingerprints. There were a number of well-thumbed, roneoed pamphlets from left-wing terror groups: the Weather Underground, the Symbionese Liberation Army, and May 19th. In addition, works of satanism and pornographic magazines involving S&M, minors, and even creatures. Inevitably, there was a copy of *The Anarchist Cookbook*, with its handy bomb-making instructions. And, of course, there was a detailed map of the Hoover Dam area and a schematic of the dam itself.

Typhon had outthought him again. He wondered if there was any detail, however trivial, that his enemies might neglect. He guessed he would make it perfect for them if he left fingerprints on their planted stash. It had been foolish to think they would have forgotten about his connection to this place. As evidenced by the two cars behind him, Brantwood was no refuge: it was a trap. But maybe he had known this the last time he'd been here. At any rate, this was where he'd make his last stand.

One thing was sure: if Typhon had already been here, they had also made the connection with Jim. Wherever he was this December morning, Jim was in just as much danger as Ed.

He let the floorboard fall back into place. There were only minutes left, but the edges of his consciousness were still blurred, still suffering under the pall cast by that cell-phone call back in Lenox. The adrenaline that had gotten him here now flatlined. A sudden fatalism, a passivity, replaced it. He was trapped and alone, facing any number of pursuers. He had to rid himself of that feeling, and quickly.

To his left, through an open door, was the large living room. It was decked out in plain frontiersman style. Stripped pine, comfortable settles and rocking chairs. Audubon pictures of birds of the North American wilderness, some landscapes from the Naive school, woven rugs on the floor. A good library, some of the volumes bearing the handsome spines of Loeb Classics—Bettie's books. There was a Yamaha acoustic guitar in a corner.

Further into the hall was a side table on which stood two things. First, a yellowing, once-white wristband with "1979 N Welcome Week" printed on it. He was certain the police had come here after Stu's death, but they had apparently shown no interest in it, though it surely would have been a significant clue in his disappearance. He picked it up and slipped it into his pocket.

Apparently, the police had not been interested in the second item either: a battered clothbound volume. He stepped forward and looked at it through the brain fog. *The Collected Shorter Poems of W.H. Auden.* The old Ed had left these cues ten years earlier and they may just have eluded the scrutiny of the Typhon operatives who had been through the cabin. He guessed reading wouldn't be high on their priorities: books would be just books to them. When they weren't burning them, that was.

There was a bookmark in the Auden. He opened it at the place. The first verse had been highlighted in yellow crayon: "Funeral Blues," or "Stop all the clocks." Another clue, like those in the Bible?

To his right stood a longcase clock; a bit of an anomaly in this wilderness cabin. He suddenly recalled it was quite the antique: an eighteenth-century piece by Richard Rayment, Bury St. Edmunds, Suffolk, England. He had no idea why it had been taken out of Winthrop Road and brought all the way here. All he remembered was Bettie had always impressed on him its rarity and value and some distant family connection.

He examined the clock. The long case was walnut veneer, the white dial face finely crazed, the four corner spandrels an elaborately wrought brass pattern. The mechanism was behind a small walnut door with a bronze keyhole. The key was missing. There was a small barometer underneath. The dial was still indicating low pressure. The clock hands were still and the mechanism, judging by the small cobwebs within, had not been operational in all the time since he had left. The clock hands pointed to eight minutes to eight. A beam of sunlight in the east stabbed through the gray cloud bank and struck the lake, sending a glittering path across its surface to the lakeshore, dazzling his eyes. The placement of the hands meant something: another clue the old Ed had left behind. He had been fond of these puzzles, he remembered now.

On a whim, he turned to his left and took eight paces. The corridor gave onto the cabin's principal bedroom. He opened the door: a pine double bed, pine headboard, patchwork quilt, yellow and orange gingham curtains, drawn but letting in quite a lot of that eastern light—as he now recalled, they often did so, and during the long summer nights it seemed there was barely any darkness at all before the early sun at five began to glow like a fire through the curtains.

A chest of drawers faced the bed on the left-hand wall and, sure enough, eight more paces took him to it. A pewter mug sat at the center of it. There was nothing inside, but as he picked it up something slid in its base. He looked again. Still nothing but dust at the bottom. Then memory came again and he grasped the handle with one hand and the bottom with the other and twisted. The bottom compartment screwed off and a small brass key fell on to the chest of drawers. It was the key for the clock.

He went back to it, inserted and turned the key and opened the door. The reason for the clock's inaction was immediately obvious. A letter was wedged between the two pendulums inside the case, preventing the rise and fall of the weights. He took it out. The weights fell and the clock gave two small ticks before expiring again into its long silence.

He ripped open the envelope and scanned what he had written that September day ten years before, one of the last days of Edward Burns Constance. After Northeastern, young Ed had clearly been terrified of having his memory robbed. For the first page, the scrawl merely related who he was and where he had come from: his story from the Lot onward, his adoptive parents, the name of Jim Dove, his life by the lake and Boston, ending with the day he met David at Northeastern and Stu had committed suicide. What Ed had known about Typhon was all here, as were the names of Fitzgerald and Vermeulen. Here was Gloria's name, written only a few hours before her murder. The letter ended with a wild plan that might just save his life. But of course, it wasn't just his life anymore. There was Sarah.

Finally the brain fog lifted completely.

His pulse thudded in his head. Words came from nowhere: "Death is kind. It is only Life, and the things of Life that hurt. Yet we love Life, and we hate Death. It is very strange."

He went down the hall to the mudroom and pushed open the pine door. Like the rest of the cabin, it had a stripped pine floor and cabinets. A large window overlooked the drive and the boathouse. Mounted on the wall on his right was a gun cabinet with housing for three shotguns and a handgun drawer underneath, but the housing and drawer were empty. He tried to remember if there had ever been guns here. Maybe not. Stu had been, as far as he could recall, the antithesis of a countryman. Ed's only weapon was the Magnum steadfastly weighing down his coat pocket. He pulled it out and checked the chamber. Two rounds left.

Next to the gun cabinet was a key rack. Unevenly arranged Letraset stickers indicated which key belonged to which bit of the property. He lifted a Chubb from a hook under the sticker that read "Boathouse." He picked a Bic disposable lighter from a shelf near the gas hob. He clicked it and, at once, an inch-long finger of flame shot out. Finally, he picked up a Sabatier carving knife from the block and went out the back again, into the small, enclosed extension that contained the cabin's only toilet and the compressed natural gas cylinder.

After checking the room's one glass window was firmly latched, he opened the cylinder's regulator. There came a faint hissing as the compressed methane exited the cylinder and came up to metered pressure. Ed sawed through the rubber feeder hose that led through a small hole into the kitchen and immediately smelled the unmistakable odor of escaped gas. He exited quickly, shutting the door firmly behind him, and shoved some empty charcoal sacks under the door to guarantee it was sealed. Then he squeezed past the Volvo and ran around the corner to the boathouse.

*

Doc ordered everyone out of the remaining Suburban at the turning place in front of the gates to the Constance and Sproule properties. He immediately saw that the Constances' gate had been forced; the padlock was nowhere to be seen and paint was scraped from the metal of the locking mechanism. Though he estimated from his map that there was at least another 200 yards to go to the cabin, he wasn't going to drive any closer, just in case.

At his command, the men pulled on hooded parkas and boots. Then Doc fetched four clear plastic bags. They contained lightweight Tyvek coveralls, as used by law enforcement forensic teams. Instead of being white, as normal, they were black. The men quickly pulled them on over their boots and parkas. Then Doc distributed face masks. Possibly overkill, but there was to be no contamination. Vermeulen had made that clear. They strapped on comms units with black plastic earpieces and mics. Hulk wordlessly fixed up a unit for Doc. Doc's attire was less pragmatic than the other three's: his footwear was a pair of tasseled loafers. The thin polyethylene of the forensic outfit did nothing to keep out the chill. He hadn't really been prepared for a wilderness expedition when the call had woken him. But the three men with him should be able to carry out the job. He was not a soldier, but the commander, and, of course, the one with that attaché case full of drugs.

"OK," he said. "You know the drill. I want no trace of us beyond this point: no skin exfoliation, blood, spit, hair follicles—masks on."

The men duly obliged. Doc picked up his medical case as the Sniper slid the rifle out of its bag. It was a brand-new Barrett M90, made of lightweight stamped steel and fitted with tripod, scope, and a five-round box magazine. The Sniper screwed on a bulbous suppressor, checked his scope and slid several extra magazines into his parka pockets. Hulk and Woody armed themselves with H&K MP5s, snapped magazines into the magazine wells and screwed suppressors on the barrels, then slid laser sights onto the receivers. They tested the sights by zeroing in on the Sproule mailbox, the small red dots dancing like sinister red insects about the black lettering on its side.

When they were ready, the Doc gestured them over to the hood of the truck, where he now spread his map. He indicated a small hillock some 150 yards to the northeast that stood between the Constance place and the Sproule one.

"We'll set up on this hill," he told the Sniper. "Should have a good view of the cabin." He turned to Woody and Hulk. "We'll cover you from up there. Squawk once on the radio when you're going in, twice when you've secured the target. Remember, capture is the objective."

"And if that ain't possible?" Woody asked.

Doc gave him a look. He wondered if Woody had heard about the two dead agents back in Boston. He had surely been listening to the emergency service bands when Bailey's death was reported. "I'd imagine one civilian won't prove too much of a problem for you. Vermeulen wants him alive, but if things go belly-up..." He glanced at the Sniper. Enough said.

"Give us ten minutes," he said, then nodded to the Sniper and plunged into the snowy undergrowth. The Sniper hefted the Barrett and followed him. They went through the forest at an angle to the Constance drive, their steps partially cushioned by the pine needles that matted the ground. The Sniper moved soundlessly, Doc less so. Soon they were climbing a slight incline and the forest thinned. He could see the bald, rock-strewn summit of the hill above. He indicated to the Sniper to get his head down and they crouch-walked the last few feet to the summit line. Doc peeked over a granite boulder. They were on a bald hilltop covered with rocks, heather, ice patches, and stunted pine saplings, some fifty feet above the lake surface. There was a slight but bitter wind streaming in from the north, pushing back the clouds. The view was magnificent, stretching eight miles or so up the lake between mist-wreathed, snow-covered mountains. Below, some 100 yards away, were the cabin and the boathouse; both were apparently deserted, no car in view. The boathouse doors were ajar.

By now the Sniper had set up between two boulders to his right. He'd deployed the small tripod under the Barrett and was peering down the scope, his left eye screwed shut, accentuating the deep lines on the part of his tanned face not covered by his mask.

A few minutes passed. Doc was wondering what had happened to Hulk and Woody when he saw movement to the side of the driveway below and they came into view, hugging the tree-fringed margins of the gravel and moving cautiously, HKs at the ready, the red dots of the laser sights darting ahead of them like red fireflies. They reached the edge of the gravel turnaround by the cabin.

The Sniper had been absolutely motionless up to now, but as there came a faint click on Doc's earpiece the Sniper tensed, his finger suddenly curling on the trigger of the rifle, applying a little pressure but not too much, the concentration lines on his face deepening.

The two men were practically indistinguishable in their forensic suits and masks, but Doc fancied he could pick out the Hulk's squat posture. He was the first to dash across the space between the forest and the south flank of the cabin. He reached it without incident and gave the thumbs-up to Woody, who joined him at a loping run. They inched along the wall toward the back of the property, ducking under the side windows, the HKs in two-handed grips in front of them. Then they disappeared around the southwest corner.

Silence. Then a faint, distant tinkle and the sound of breaking glass.

And then the rear of the cabin exploded in a bursting cloud of orange flame and flying wooden fragments that rose some fifty feet into the air at a level with Doc's vantage point, casting fiery meteorites of material into the forest, onto the driveway and over the lake. A split second later came the sound of the detonation, like a rolling thunder.

A burning man staggered around the rear end of the cabin. One of the two ex-soldiers, but it was difficult to tell which, as he was completely engulfed in flames, the polyethylene suit burning like a match. It burned off quickly, surrounding him in a halo of fire and smoke. He was clawing at his face and chest where the synthetic material was burning into his skin. There was a high-pitched screaming like a stuck pig's death note. The man made it a few yards up the driveway before some trigger in his brain switched off, his legs buckled and he fell face first in a smoldering heap.

There was no sign of the other Typhon operative. Doc got to his feet. As he did so, he heard the Sniper shout a warning. A figure had emerged from the smoke at the far end of the cabin and was running around the northern flank of the burning building. No hazmat suit. Constance. There was only a narrow angle between the cabin and the boathouse, where the guy was obviously headed. The Doc turned toward the Sniper to tell him capture be damned, take the shot, but before he could say anything he saw the man's trigger finger squeeze, unhurriedly, to avoid a snapshot, and the rifle jerked against his shoulder.

CHAPTER FIFTY-TWO

Ten minutes earlier. Time: some days the same span seems to stretch to infinity and other days it passes in the blink of an eye. Ed now existed in that second state where time seemed to be traveling at the speed of light. His whole being once more buzzed with adrenaline. And yet, some part of him was calm, just as at City Point, just as at the Kennebec.

Light spilled into the boathouse from the open door and the two large windows overlooking the driveway and the lake. There were two boats stored here. The one nearest the big double doors and slipway onto the lake was a rubber dinghy with a Yamaha 9.9 horsepower outboard. It was sitting on a low trolley ready for launching, just as he had left it ten years before. The other was a clinker-built, fifteen-foot sailing dinghy up on trestles, its mast and rigging stored under a side window. It had been donated by the previous owners of the cabin but Stu had never used it.

Ed unbarred the big double doors overlooking the slipway and hauled them open. In front of the green, algae-slicked concrete slip the water stretched north to the distant mist-shrouded mountains. A chain and pulley fed to a twelve-volt generator set on the floor that allowed for the safe hauling in of the dinghy for the winter. Now he released the tension on the chain and pushed the dinghy on its cradle down the concrete ramp until it was in the water. There was a long length of rope coiled by the door and he tied one end to the dinghy's transom and the other to a stanchion. Then he dropped the outboard into the water and, using another, smaller bit of rope, tied it off to the gunwale so it was set to steer directly away from the shore. Finally, he took some duct tape and left it near the throttle so he could tie that off when the time came.

He threw a sail sack into the bottom of the dinghy at the stern, just to give the appearance, if seen at a distance, that the dinghy was manned by someone crouched low behind the outboard. The dinghy bobbed restlessly in the cold December wind. It looked good enough. He turned back inside. Only moments left. Perhaps none at all.

Both windows, the shelves of tools, paints, turpentine, rags, gas cans, and kerosene lamps were covered by a patina of gray dust and festooned with cobwebs. Ten years ago he had placed an empty brandy bottle next to a plastic funnel. He admired the younger Ed's foresight. No need for Typhon to plant *The Anarchist Cookbook* under the boards: apparently, younger Ed had already owned it.

He picked up one of the gas cans and, using the funnel, filled the bottle nearly to the shoulder. Then he tore some lint, soaked it in petrol and pushed the material into the mouth of the bottle so it acted as a wick, dipping into the liquid. He used several turns of duct tape to secure the soaked rag to the top of the bottle. Then he had it: the twentieth century's cheapest and easiest home-made weapon, the Molotov cocktail.

He picked up the bottle and went to the half-open garage doors. He peered out, quickly scanning the cabin, the drive, and lakeshore. All was still outside: no bird sang, not even a gull screeched over the lake. A sinister quiet. He steeled himself, then ran across the gravel and into the line of trees between the lakeshore and the side of the cabin.

As he inched his way around back toward the cabin, he was careful not to step on the dry branches and cones on the rocky ground. His eyes strained in the gloom. The gray shingles on the side of the cabin came into view. Twenty feet to the west of the outhouse there was an old woodpile, some five feet high, possibly dating from before the carport extension had been built decades earlier. The logs were black with damp and covered with clumps of white mushrooms. The ground was partially covered with dead bracken. He slid himself behind the woodpile in a prone position, the Molotov in one hand, the lighter ready in the other.

He didn't know how many men would come or from which direction. He needed to be lucky: *very* lucky. There was no sound apart from the patter of snowmelt falling from the boughs and the thin soughing of the wind.

He looked at his watch: 8.18. He'd gotten to the cabin almost an hour ago. It seemed a lot longer. Were they coming? Could he have been mistaken? Maybe the car lights he'd seen behind him had been perfectly innocent vehicles heading toward Tranquility?

There was a faint snap of a twig from the southern flank of the house and instantly he was alert, pulling his body back into the woodpile, staring at the corner from where the noise had come. A strange red pinprick of light flickered on a tree bough to his right. A gun barrel appeared around the corner of the cabin with a light shining under it. The red bead moved from the tree, passed over the woodpile and along the side of the cabin. A man emerged slowly behind it. His whole body was covered by a Tyvek suit, but instead of the familiar white color this one was jet black. A mask obscured the wearer's face.

The figure inched along the side of the cabin, machine gun extended, then crouched down beside the Volvo and gestured behind. Now another figure, similarly clad and armed, came out of the shadows and followed the same route as the first.

The second man advanced in an awkward loping run and joined the first gunman at the side door. Looks were exchanged and now they both uncrouched and the first slowly pulled open the screen door. The second wedged something underneath it to prevent it swinging back, while the first man tried the handle on the inside door. It opened without a whisper.

It was the moment of reckoning. By now the cabin must have reeked of gas fumes, but perhaps the men's masks retarded the smell. They slunk into the shadowed hallway without hesitation.

For a moment, Ed was lost, but then his breath and consciousness came back in a rush and he rose and clicked the lighter. The flames licked around the rag protruding from the bottle and it instantly caught, starkly lighting the woodpile and the side of the cabin.

He threw the bottle at the open doorway. Twenty feet: an easy throw. The bottle flew like a meteor into the black mouth of the hallway beyond. One of the men was momentarily visible in it, turning, attracted by the sudden flame of light behind him. The bottle shattered on the pine boards of the hallway and instantly boiling fire was eating the figure's feet. The flames whooshed up, engulfing his suit.

Time stood still for a millisecond as the burning man stood motionless, frozen, it appeared, by the caul of flame now entirely surrounding him and running up the hall walls to the ceiling. The machine gun emerged from the flames, pointing in Ed's direction. The hood of the suit suddenly melted. A shriek pierced the roar of the flames. Ed felt a displacement of air and a thwack, like an axe into wood, as a round thudded into a fir behind him. The figure pirouetted, staggered and fell to its knees. There was now a strange blue glow from inside the gas-filled room that rapidly expanded outward toward the gas-tank housing, turning orange as it came.

Then the world exploded. A shingle came spinning toward Ed out of the light, slowly but very quickly at the same time. It caught him a glancing, stunning blow and he fell behind the woodpile just as a split second later a hundred other missiles from the explosion speared the place where he had been standing and flew into the trees behind. A thousand fires blossomed, contending with the snow and ice, steam and smoke intermingling.

A second or two later, Ed came to in this strange burning yet freezing world. The woodpile had been blown back over him and he had been saved from the worst of the firestorm by the damp logs covering him from head to foot. He was half in and half out of a layer of snow, but he felt his hands and face scorching, his eyebrows singeing, and an instant later smelled the acrid odor of burning hair. Then the fireball was gone.

The explosion had sucked the hearing from him. All there was was a distant ringing.

He shrugged off the rotten logs and struggled to his feet. The woodpile lay all around him, smoking from the heat. There were gobbets of fire burning in the woods; the dry bracken had caught light in odd places. There was now just a raging orange and red inferno where the rear of the cabin had been. He was driven back by the savagery of the fire, his face burning, raw.

Miraculously, one of the two men emerged and staggered back the way he had come, the Tyvek suit hanging in black strings around his blackened body. White and red flesh sizzled. The man's eyeballs looked like they had fused, showing as white orbs in his black, blistered face. He appeared to proceed silently, despite the fact that his mouth gaped open and he was being burned alive, but perhaps his screams were inaudible to Ed, deafened as he was by the explosion. Then he was gone.

Beyond the front of the cabin the air warped and bent in the nova-like heat between him and the boathouse. He crouched and fumbled around in the disintegrated woodpile until his hand closed on the checkered grip of the revolver.

The flames were higher than the trees. In front, the carport was blazing, an unearthly orange glow surrounding the Volvo. Its tires were already alight and Ed realized it would be only moments before its gas tank blew to add to the hellish conflagration. He backed away shakily.

Two cars had been following him. There could be several more men out there. For a few yards he was safe, but then there was that strip of gravel and lakefront some thirty feet wide. Unless the inferno of the cabin distracted any shooters, he would, briefly, be a sitting duck.

He flung himself into the gap.

The shot came a second later.

CHAPTER FIFTY-THREE

Jim had put Max back in his cab and was pacing up and down beside the abandoned SUV when he saw Deputy Pollitt's truck, a white GM Sierra, with the yellow flashes and star of Somerset County's Sheriff's Department, approaching from the direction of Hadsville. Pollitt pulled up next to Jim's truck and climbed down. He clamped his slightly undersized brown Stetson onto his head. The portly deputy's gut protruded from his parka, straining somewhat at his brown uniform shirt underneath.

"How ya doing?" he asked, giving Jim's scrawny right hand a good pumping with his own beefy mitt. But the beady eyes set into his puffed face were not looking at Jim, instead assessing first the SUV, then the Winchester slung over Jim's shoulder.

"You expecting trouble?" he asked.

"Just being cautious," Jim answered, chewing his gum reflectively. He jerked his head at the Suburban. "Like I said, don't know why people from away would be here this time of year."

Pollitt grunted and squatted to inspect the skid mark of the SUV and its mashed rear end. From the plates, the truck was only a year old.

"Looks like government issue," he decided. "I'll get the plates checked. One thing's for sure, the driver didn't know the roads hereabouts." He stood up and looked toward Tranquility. With the recession and the economy in free fall, things were hard and burglary was on the up. The summer houses around the lake would be easy prey with only Dove living up here out of season. But hard-up burglars didn't drive nearly brand-new SUVs.

He was still staring over toward the lake when a black and orange mushroom cloud erupted over the treeline to the northwest. The sound of the explosion reached the two men a couple of seconds later; it was like a protracted roar of thunder. Max barked frenziedly in Jim's cab.

"Jesus, what the hell was that?" Pollitt asked as in the distance small blazing meteorites began to rain down from the burning cloud onto the forest.

"Gas tank has blown," Jim said calmly. "Could be the Constance place."

"That place has been deserted for years," Pollitt said.

"Well, those tanks don't blow themselves," Jim answered.

Pollitt stepped back to his cab and pulled out the mic from the stand on the dash.

"Hello, Madison, do you read, over?" he asked, flicking the mic to receive.

A few seconds later came the crackling response from the dispatcher.

"This is Madison receiving you, over."

"Hey, Agnes, this is Stan Pollitt. I have an incident up here at Tranquility. An explosion at a cabin, possibly suspicious persons involved. Am requesting additional units and a fire truck stat, over."

"Roger that, Deputy. What's your 10-20? Over."

"On the Three Mile Road. I'm here with Jim Dove. We have a suspicious vehicle wreck that might be related to the fire. The license is Massachusetts Feb 89 316 BG4. Please run it through the database. In the meantime I'm going on to that fire. It's two miles to the northwest. Jim reckons it's the Constance place. Over."

"Roger on the license and on the backup. We'll get the Rockwood engine on its way, but be advised there are currently no additional units near your position."

"Can you advise when the backup might arrive, over?" Pollitt asked.

There was a pause as if the dispatcher had referred the question to someone newly arrived at their end, then a fresh voice came on the line.

"Stan, this is MacDonald. I hear you have an incident?"

Just then there came another belch of flame into the winter sky at the source of the initial explosion, then another roar, slightly more muted than the first.

"You bet, Sheriff: it looks like we have a major gas explosion, make that explosions, on a cabin by the lake and we also have a 10-37 in the road into Tranquility. Something strange is going on."

"I'll mobilize the backup."

"I'm going over there to see what's happening."

"Be careful. Observe only and keep this frequency open."

"Roger that." Pollitt replaced the mic on the dash and looked at Dove. The bait store owner had always been a hard man to read. It was always the way with these vets—teak-hard and undemonstrative—but even so he was surprised that Jim was not showing a little more animation at the way the day was proceeding. If he'd had the time to think, he might even have said Dove had been expecting the turn of events. But there was no time for questions.

"I'm going to have a closer look," he said. "You comin'?"

Jim shifted the wad of gum to the other side of his mouth and spat. "Sure. The Constance place is my responsibility."

"OK, but we'll go in my truck. Official business."

"Fine, but the dog's coming too."

"Alright. He can ride in the cage in the back."

Jim fetched a battered maroon fishing hat from the back seat of his truck and a backpack with some spare ammo, clippers, wire, and other odds and ends, then, on reflection, locked the vehicle. He'd never bothered locking his truck this time of year at Tranquility, but he was suddenly not sure when he would be coming back to it.

Pollitt swung open the tailgate and opened the animal cage where the county placed impounded strays. Max jumped up and allowed himself to be latched in as Jim got into the passenger seat.

The cruiser took off toward the pillar of smoke. Jim pointed out the turnoff to the Constance place. There were tire marks in the slush. Pollitt stopped the cruiser and rested for a moment.

Jim turned to him. "Place is still burning, Stan."

"I know. I'm just wondering about the stutter lights and siren."

"Don't. If these are bad guys, we don't want to give them warning."

"I guess you're right," Pollitt answered. He took a deep breath and put the cruiser back in drive and they inched up the gravel track under the trees. As they approached the gate, they saw a second SUV, identical to the first, parked there. Pollitt drew up behind it and got out, unholstering his service sidearm. Jim got down too, hushing Max's yapping from the cage. Both men peered through the SUV's tinted glass. The vehicle was empty and locked.

"Looks like they've gone on," Pollitt said unnecessarily.

They both looked north. The smoke column was very close now and in the utter silence both of them thought they could hear the distant crackle of flames. The smell of burning was strong.

Pollitt reached into the truck, got the mic and keyed it.

"Madison, do you copy, over."

"Hi, Stan. Please confirm your 10-20, over."

"We're at the driveway to the cabin that's afire. There's another suspicious vehicle parked here. Another Massachusetts plate. Could be something to do with the fire. Please advise on backup, over."

"Sheriff won't be there for an hour, and about the same with the fire truck. Sorry, Stan."

Pollitt muted the receiver. Jim was checking the slide on his Winchester. "You wanna go on?" Pollitt asked.

"I guess," said Jim.

"OK." He keyed the mic again. "Agnes, please tell MacDonald that Jim and I are going in on foot. I'm taking a handset with me."

"Roger, Stan, and good luck. I'll keep the frequency open and advise the sheriff."

Pollitt rehoused the car mic, reached in and took a handset and a yellow slicker from the back seat, then circled around to open the tailgate. Jim got Max out of the cage and put the dog to heel.

Pollitt keyed numbers into the combination of the gun safe welded to the floor pan next to the dog cage. The mechanism clicked open, revealing a shotgun on a Styrofoam inlay and a half-dozen boxes of shells. He took out the gun and two magazines, one of which he slotted into the underside of the gun. He slammed the lid of the safe and whirled the rollers again.

"Locked and loaded," he said. "You?"

Jim nodded his head at the Winchester. "Same," he answered.

He told the dog to heel again and set off after Pollitt down the gravel drive. The jetting column of smoke dominated the sky. His blood buzzed like wasps, his fingertips with electricity. The feeling of déjà vu was almost overwhelming. He snapped "Heel" again at Max.

CHAPTER FIFTY-FOUR

Ed was halfway across the ten-yard gap between the blazing house and the boathouse when the Volvo's gas tank exploded. Up to that millisecond, his head had been in the middle of the sniper's crosshairs like a fat, overripe melon.

The force of the blast made him take an extra, stumbling step forward. The Sniper's first round passed about an inch from the rear of his skull. The shockwave of the bullet was like a giant fly swat smacking just past his ear. There was no sound of the gunshot itself, just the hornet passing of the round. He took another stumbling step. Another violent movement in the air. Something plucked the rear of his flapping suit jacket. He rolled as the round slammed into the gravel and whined away into the forest.

The side window of the boatshed was in front of him. Its ledge was only some three and a half feet high. It was an old-fashioned sash that had seen better days, the grille work rotten, the panes loose. He took the momentum from his roll, regained his feet and threw himself forward, raising his arms to protect his face as he hit the window. There was another supersonic disturbance and at the same instant an almighty tug on his left upper arm just as he hit the glass. He crashed through the pane, twisted off balance by the hit, feeling suit material and skin rip as his thighs scraped the broken glass at the sill.

He landed hard on his uninjured right shoulder. The fall was slightly padded by the sail and rigging lying under the window. The Magnum spun out of his hand and slid across the floor into the shadows on the lakeside of the boathouse. Sudden daylight appeared in the clapboard there, followed by an eruption of splinters from the counter opposite, then more glass shattered as another round missed him by inches and smacked into the old sailing dinghy, rocking it on its trestles and sending a cud of dust into the air. He crawled under the dinghy.

Then the shooting stopped. A magazine change? He glanced down at his arm wound. It was just a graze. The suit sleeve, already burned from the explosion, was scored open in a long diagonal; underneath, there was a gouge and a spreading patch of blood. Only when he saw the wound did the pain begin, as if it had been waiting for him to look and make it real.

The boathouse was filled with the orange glow of the burning cabin. Smoke drifted in through the shattered window. The concrete floor was covered with broken glass, smashed grille work, and smears of his blood. Ed saw the Magnum lying next to a pile of wood shavings under the workbench by the lakeside window. His eyes flicked to the broken window and the open double doors to the shed. He was sure the shots had come from the small hill near the Sproule property. He could barely make out the shape of the hill through the window, so the reverse must be true: the smoke would make the interior of the boathouse dim. But the building was in the sniper's arc of fire. And the high-caliber bullets could pass through the walls easily. Without the gun he was pinned down and defenseless. It was just a matter of time before whoever was up there came down and finished him off. And it was unlikely that the shooter would miss at close quarters.

He had to move again. If it was to be an execution, best to die with a fighting chance. He crawled from under the dinghy over to the gun, felt its checkered grip, snatched it up and with a freestyle lunge threw himself under the cover of the workbench. No shot. He listened. There was just the roar of flames. Maybe the shooter was coming already. He raised the Magnum toward the boathouse doors. No, too easy. The shooter would likely come to the shattered window, glance in, maybe even see Ed's legs sticking out from under the bench. Ed twisted onto his back and whipped the gun to the window. Nothing. Glass was piercing his suit back. He rolled under the bench again.

The world spun. He checked his wounds. His burns were smarting. Blood was dripping onto the floor from his arm. Both legs of his pants were ripped at the thighs from the broken glass, and some of it was still embedded there like evil little teeth. He laid the Magnum on the floor and plucked the glass shards out one by one as blood welled over the wool.

He needed first aid. There was a red plastic case with a white cross on a housing over the workbench. He slowly got to his haunches and tentatively reached out to it.

The box exploded. Plastic fragments whistled past his face. Bandages, Band-Aids, Tylenol, tubes of Neosporin, scissors, and other first-aid material flew in all directions. He threw himself back down.

The gunman hadn't moved from the hill. Maybe he'd sent someone else down here to finish Ed off. There was only one direction of escape: the lake. He had planned for this contingency ten years ago. Putting the plan into action was another thing altogether. The chances of success now seemed vanishingly unlikely.

A roll of bandage had fallen on to the floor beside him. As he tried to figure out what to do, he began, clumsily and laboriously, with teeth and one hand, to tie a rudimentary dressing around his wounded arm.

CHAPTER FIFTY-FIVE

Up on the hill, the Sniper cursed softly. Never in his long career, which had spanned conflicts in Southeast Asia and the Middle East, had such a simple and easy killing shot been snatched away by such a stroke of bad luck. A man with his head in the Sniper's scope was, by definition, a dead man.

He had lived a life without remorse, but he felt a judgment coming. Maybe the missed shot was something to do with that. His dreams had begun to trouble him. In them he couldn't rid himself of the faces of the dead. There had once been a woman in Yemen, a young mother according to the agency report, and a terrorist to boot. He'd almost felt bad about that mission in Sana'a. The Sniper hadn't been able to figure a word of the Arabic writing on the front pages of the papers next day, but there she was, lying on the sidewalk in her hijab, surrounded by a gawking crowd held back by a couple of policemen, the headscarf thrown over her face, a pool of blood three feet wide, or more, around her shattered head. A woman, probably her mother, was kneeling in the blood, her hands raised to the skies, her face creased in horror.

When he got back Stateside and was passing through Miami airport, he saw the same image had made it to the front pages of the liberal press: the *Washington Post*, the *New York Times*, the *Herald*—the mourning woman reproached him from half the world away.

The dead woman visited him in his dreams more and more often as the years passed. Perhaps God was in these fragmentary stabs of conscience. If so, he was an avenging God and the Sniper's time had come.

Maybe Constance had some kind of deal with the Almighty. For sure, he'd had all the luck the previous dozen victims of the Sniper's art had not. It was always more difficult hitting a moving target, of course, but that was why the Sniper got paid what he did. He could shoot a jumping squirrel out of the trees at a thousand yards, so Constance shouldn't have been a problem.

But the car explosion had saved him. Then a smooth and efficient stream of bullets had been sent down on him, yet had only winged him at best.

The smoke and heat haze were still making a clear sight of the boathouse difficult, but he had been quite pleased with the shot that had nearly taken Constance's hand off when he reached for the first-aid kit. It was also good to know he was wounded, albeit apparently not gravely.

He was annoyed Doc had seen the whole shit show up to now. He didn't want a bad report to mar his chances of future employment. Anyway, the Sniper was confident of getting his man eventually. It was best to be patient, hold position, take your time for the shot to come to you. Constance couldn't have set himself up better than coming to this deserted cabin, by this deserted lake, in the middle of the winter. Now he was holed up in that shed with nowhere to go. Doc and he could lay siege as long as no one spotted the pillar of smoke and called the cops.

His eyes flicked to the blackened figure on the drive. Wisps of smoke still came off his smoldering clothing. He thought he detected a faint stirring of one of the man's arms. Judging from the build, or what was left of it, it was Woody and not the Hulk lying there. He'd seen a few instances like this in his time. Blackened figures crawling out of burning armored vehicles when they had no right to, taking their time to die. He might have to deal with Woody. Wouldn't want him alive and able to talk if the cops did come.

His eyes went back to the scope and the reticulated image of the boathouse window. Nothing since the hand. Then something caught his eye in the periphery of his vision. He looked up. Two figures were heading down the driveway from the turnaround, keeping to the side of the road away from the knoll, practically in the shallow ditch that separated the drive from the forest. He glanced at Doc. He had seen them too.

One of the new arrivals bore the distinctive Stetson and hi-vis rain slicker of a deputy. He had a shotgun at port arms. Behind him came an older man in camo carrying what looked to be a Winchester. Perhaps he was the guy from the bait store he had been told about. He, too, had made the mistake of wearing some conspicuous clothing: in his case a maroon fishing hat with a bright yellow badge. A black and white collie tracked the second man's heels obediently, ears pinned back, adopting the low herding position ingrained into sheepdogs through the centuries.

It was inconceivable that these two hadn't radioed in. Backup would be coming sooner than expected. Time had run out.

The two men had reached the curve of the road where the cabin finally came into view and here they stopped, taking in the blazing wreck of the house and Woody's body. The deputy lifted up his poncho and pulled a handheld radio from his uniform jacket.

The Barrett tracked around to him without a conscious thought and there was the man's white face right in the reticle of the sights.

"What are you doing?" the Doc asked.

But the Sniper's finger had already closed on the trigger.

CHAPTER FIFTY-SIX

The dread that Jim had lived with ever since he had seen the abandoned Suburban and then the explosion was intense now. It was sixteen years since Vietnam, but he'd not forgotten. Lights flashed behind his eyes and high-volt electricity was running in his veins; his skin felt as if it was on fire.

He was not sure whether Pollitt was alive to the danger. He regretted involving him. The deputy looked dogged, stolid, as he crunched down the gravel drive to the Constance place, but he also looked out of place in that yellow poncho, as if about to direct traffic rather than enter a combat zone. Jim was tempted to rein the guy in, tell him to exercise some caution, but since Pollitt had gotten the shotgun out of the trunk he'd looked like a man on a mission, not to be held back.

Jim was not entirely sure that Stan or any of the other deputies hereabouts had ever fired a gun in anger. He knew that there was a big difference between firing on the range and intent to use.

As he wondered about his own chance of blending in, he cursed his choice of headgear. The maroon fishing hat from the West Indies, threaded through with a dozen brightly feathered lures, had a loud yellow badge in a claret shield, showing palm trees and a desert island in a blue sea.

They had reached the curvature of the track. To the right were the granite boulders and fern- and heather-covered side of the hill that separated the Constance place from the Sproules'. Stan signaled for them to slow and they both crept forward, Max following at heel. Now the source of the heavy plume of smoke came into view down the gravel slope. The beechwood cabin was burning pretty much all over, the shingles and creosote making a blaze that raged with an orange flame at its core, the column of smoke soaring up into the frigid gray sky over the lake. A burning station wagon lay on its side next to the house and, beyond it, the side window of the boathouse was smashed. There was a fire-blackened figure lying a few feet away from the fringes of the cabin fire.

"Sweet Jesus," Stan whispered. He let go of his two-handed grip on the carbine and with one hand reached under the slicker for the radio.

There was a wet thwacking noise, a sudden red mist hazed the air and Jim's face was stabbed violently in a couple of places by flying debris. He had the vaguest sense of Pollitt's yellow rain slicker falling to one side. There were still legs and arms sticking out of it, but no head. The Stetson was rolling up the ditch, a few yards away.

There was a part of Jim that had stayed in the jungle. Suddenly he was back there. There were two types of men in these situations: those who stood and gawked and died and those whose bodies did something and saved themselves.

He dived left, head first over the little drainage ditch into the conifers, and rolled on the wet bed of needles. He felt the tree next to him vibrate like a tuning fork as another round slammed home, leaving a fist-sized white pulpy wound in the bark and sending a shower of water from the sodden branches. He threw himself behind the cover.

No sound of a shot either time. Was he deaf? Sometimes in combat it was like this—the adrenaline blocking off sound, everything happening in a soundless bubble. But he wasn't deaf—he could hear the undergrowth crash under his feet as he rose and stumbled further into the trees and the furious burr as another invisible round passed near his head. A suppressor, then. And a suppressor meant someone intent on killing silently and efficiently.

There was a wide trunk ahead and he flung himself behind it. He yanked off the maroon hat and stuffed it into a pocket, then quickly doubled around to the other side of the tree and glanced back. The hill from which he judged the killing shot had come was now invisible. He could just make out the yellow glow of Stan's slicker twenty yards away on the gravel drive.

Max had disappeared. Panicked, no doubt. He sure as hell wasn't going to call to the dog. The Winchester, of course, was still in his hand. The drill instructor had made that clear: if you didn't have your gun in the jungle, why weren't you dead already?

He worked the bolt and clicked off the safety. There were few choices and no good ones available to him. The undergrowth was unlogged virgin forest and it would take some time to fight his way through it, an hour or more to get back to the cruiser and warn MacDonald and the others. The shooter might anticipate that move and could be heading back to the cars now to lie up and wait for Jim to break cover. He assumed the guy had telescopic sights, unlike the Winchester, and there would not be much of a contest when shooting at range. The one advantage was his army surplus camo: now he had gotten rid of the maroon hat, this deep in the woods he deemed himself invisible. Furthermore, he was used to stalking and moving silently in pursuit of prey.

His heart was quietening down, his breathing catching up. However much this guy had fought, Jim had fought too. Two tours and the worst that humanity could serve up in explosions and screams and blood. He had survived it all, as he would now.

He would take range out of the duel. He was going to go back to the driveway and surprise the sumbitch. Now that was a move the shooter wouldn't anticipate.

He wiped at his face. It was sticky with blood. His cheek stung like hell and he pulled something white out of it. A skull fragment, he realized. There was another in his forehead.

He stooped down to a muddy pool between some exposed tree roots and smeared the foul-smelling liquid on his face and hands. Then he began working to his left, toward the cabin.

CHAPTER FIFTY-SEVEN

"You just killed a deputy," Doc said to the Sniper as he stared at Pollitt's body.

"I done worse," the Sniper answered. "The mission is compromised. Best we can do is shoot Constance and get the hell out."

"Did you at least get the second guy?" Doc asked.

The Sniper's patience, which was usually very long, was now getting short.

"Goddam reactions like a snake," he said. "He was in the trees in a second."

Doc looked at him coldly.

The Sniper gave him a similar look back. "So what now?"

Doc said, "If he has any sense, the second guy'll be heading back to the road."

"So, we follow?"

"Correction, you follow. I'm going down to fix Constance. He's a busted flush."

The Sniper jerked his head at the carnage below. "That deputy is bound to have called for backup before he came down here."

"You just worry about the other guy. I'll do the rest."

"Vermeulen is going to be pissed."

Doc's stare was glacial. "On the contrary. Constance is wanted for rape and murder. Woody and Hulk are former servicemen. They, the deputy and the bait store owner all died trying to bring him in. What a tragedy. The press will love it. After we shoot him, we can throw Constance in the fire. He'll be crisped. It'll look like he died in there, shooting the others. At least, that's what our tame forensics guy will conclude. And we'll be nowhere in sight. Case closed."

"One thing—I'm not sure Woody's dead," the Sniper said.

The Doc peered through the heat shimmer. His face set. "Let's not tempt fate, shall we?" he said.

The Sniper didn't like it. He'd never shot one of his own before. He zeroed in on the fallen man. Luckily Woody was looking away and he could only see the side of his ruined face. The skin oozed. Red, yellow, and black.

He squeezed the trigger. The body jerked and a shower of black and red splattered over the gravel behind Woody like some obscene diarrhea.

"You got him at least," Doc said dispassionately.

The Sniper had been promised $50,000 for the trip, but he was tempted to swing the Barrett around and shoot Doc in the gut and see him die slowly. But if he did that, as the Sniper well knew, getting out of here would be next to impossible, and should he escape, Vermeulen would want an explanation as to why he alone of this bunch of highly experienced killers had escaped Tranquility.

Doc unlatched the attaché case, revealing the rows of small serum bottles and hypodermics packed in foam, a walkie-talkie, and a Glock handgun. Doc pulled out the radio, switched the set on, extended the antenna, and keyed the mic. "Deep Harbor, do you read me, over?"

There came a crackling voice, "Deep Harbor, please identify, over."

"Salt Cracker here."

"Copy, Salt Cracker. Please confirm status."

"We require pickup at…" Doc checked his Rolex "…zero nine thirty hours at the north depot."

"Copy that. What is your load?"

Doc eyed the Sniper. "Just two cases."

"Two cases? Do you have the premium product?"

"Negative. We are about to destroy it. It passed its sell-by date, over."

There was a pause on the other end. "Understood, Salt Cracker. Please tidy up the warehouse before you get to the depot. Over and out."

Doc grimaced, replaced the set and removed the handgun. He racked the slide to put a round in the chamber. Despite his words to the Sniper, he wasn't sure about Vermeulen's reaction to the day's events. But at least Krige sounded pleased that Constance was about to die.

"OK," he said. "See you at the boathouse for the clear-up."

The Sniper slid back from the shooting position. He rose to a crouch, keeping his head low so it wasn't silhouetted by the skyline, and moved off to his left.

CHAPTER FIFTY-EIGHT

Ten yards from the forest margin, Jim had gotten down on his knees and elbows and started crawling, the Winchester cradled between his forearms. Brutal on the elbows, good for having a weapon ready in a second if he needed it. The orange glow of the burning cabin came through the latticed branches of the pines to his left.

Directly ahead, he could see the body on the drive that he'd noticed on the approach. It looked like he was coming out directly opposite it. He stopped and studied it. Just then, the thing raised its head. It was a horror of red and black peeling skin without a blade of hair remaining; a white, poached eye stared out of the ruin. The burned man seemed to look directly at him for a moment. Then there came a thwap in the air and the head disappeared in a shambles of white, red, and gray. A splattered arc of matter showered the gravel in front of Jim.

His heart, which had calmed for the few minutes of his crawl, now fought to burst his chest again. He rolled and aimed the Winchester at the hill. There was no further incoming.

On the skyline he briefly saw something bob into sight, a head, he realized, but it was obscured by a mask and what looked like the hood of a forensic suit except it was not white but black. He also glimpsed the tip of a scoped rifle. The sniper. He braced the gun. The man's head was briefly aligned with the open sights, then vanished under the brow. Jim cursed.

The sniper looked to be making his way down the hill to the right, back toward the turnaround. He must think Jim was heading back to the vehicles. As he had this thought, another head bobbed briefly into view on the hillcrest, and then it, too, was gone. Same weird hood. This one was heading sideways down the hill toward the Constance cabin. Jim was in the middle of the two assailants, about to be outflanked. On a whim, he took the maroon fishing hat from his pocket, shrugged off his combat jacket, hooked the hat over a low-lying branch and the jacket on a branch next to it, then cut off to the left toward the blaze.

There were fewer trees on the hillside and after the Sniper had looped around the slope he advanced in short bursts, taking cover behind scrub and boulders. There was no logical reason why the other guy with his old-fashioned rifle would have stuck around; anyone in their right mind would have hightailed it back to their vehicle. It was likely that he'd circle around, get to the drive out of sight of the cabin and head to the turnaround as fast as his legs could carry him.

Part of the Sniper's DNA told him that this was right, he should abandon his cautious skirmishing and just hurry up the drive and catch the guy in plain sight as he fled. But the other part told him that the remarkable reflexes of the man spoke of an opponent to be wary of.

He was perhaps only fifty feet from the curve of the drive, the dead deputy with his yellow poncho in front, the blaze off to his right, and the upward slope to the turnaround on his left, when he saw not the old man on the drive but a white and black blob: the bait store man's dog. He took cover as it approached in the crouched herding position common to all collies, its belly close to the ground. It paused briefly at the corpse and snuffled around. The Sniper expected it to follow its owner's trail into the trees, but instead it scented the air and then, in a sway-shaped advance, its haunches down on the ground and its tail working furiously, as if in fear of being chastised by its master, it advanced down the drive toward Woody's corpse.

"What the…?" the Sniper whispered. The tail-wagging increased in frenzy and it let out a half-joyous, half-nervous bark, not over Woody's corpse but at something hidden within the treeline.

The Sniper lifted the scope. The trees zoomed into focus. It was dark as sin in there, but he found what he was looking for. That old Bahamian fishing hat with its feathered lures pinned through its crown, and beneath it, harder to see, a camouflage jacket. He braced the rifle on a rock, pushed the select button to auto and squeezed the trigger. All five bullets in the chamber released silently in under two seconds, the tree and branches around the jacket exploded, and the hat went whirling.

The dog appeared confused by the riot of splintered wood and needles caused by the rounds and went scampering down the drive toward the fire.

Nothing else moved. He must have hit. Time to check his work. He slammed another magazine home, broke cover and went running across the gravel.

Jim hadn't forgotten Max, but he hoped the dog, confused by the sudden turn of events on the drive, had hightailed it back to the turn-around and would stay there. Max was well trained. But he was also loyal. This last troubled him. He had just taken up position a few yards to the left of where he had left the decoy by the burned man's corpse and was glancing from right to left and back again, trying to get a bead on the flanking parties, when Max appeared in the curve of the road and came slinking down the drive. Jim let out a soft curse. Max was sure to pick up his scent even with the blood stink and smoke in this particular corner of hell. Sure enough, the dog paused, sniffing at the blood and brain splatter on the ground by the corpse, then let out one nervous bark, as if fearful of reprimand, and stepped toward where Jim had hung his hat and jacket.

There was a sudden commotion of cracking branches and the dull thud of rounds impacting wood. Max turned on his heels and went scampering down the drive, past Jim's position.

At that moment, a figure appeared from cover at the edge of the drive and began to cross it in a crouching run. It was a man in a black forensic-style suit, holding the scoped rifle in one hand. Jim brought the Winchester up in one motion: eighty yards, no windage, a level shot and the guy not crossing his sights laterally but actually running almost directly toward his position. He aimed just a little ahead of the mass for deflection…

CHAPTER FIFTY-NINE

The Sniper was in mid-stride when the bullet came out of the woods. It was as if a baseball bat hit his chest as the .308 round smashed his right fifth rib, sectioned his right lung and nicked the right pulmonary artery. The shot turned him around, the gun falling from his suddenly nerveless hands. He rolled twice, staring up at the gray sky. He tasted blood in his mouth.

Christ, he thought. Everything was slipping away... But it was OK, the gradual blackening of his vision somehow numbed the pain, like a kindly nurse drawing the curtains against the harsh light of the sky. Yes, it was getting darker, but there was a white dot growing bigger and bigger in the darkness, filling his vision. Something was emerging from the coming night, taking shape, displacing the darkness.

It was the newspaper picture—that long ago picture of the old woman screaming over her headless daughter... and then even that was gone...

One shot. One goddam fine shot, Jim thought. The guy was lying on his back, both arms splayed out to his sides, the rifle by his feet. He had come to rest only a few feet from the burned corpse. Jim was sure the guy was dead. He had seen his chest heave a few times, but now it was still.

Jim remained motionless, staring at the distant hilltop through the trees. No movement. The second man had vanished in the direction of the cabin. Had he heard the shot?

Now Max reappeared from that direction, tail going sideways.

"Still, boy," Jim ordered and the dog went prone, cocking his head to one side inquisitively.

Jim didn't know how the other guy was armed. Another sniper? The smoke and heat haze made the hillside near the boathouse difficult to discern. He wasn't going to make the same mistake as the sniper and cross the driveway. He was going to have to work his way through the dense undergrowth. He removed his belt and looped it through Max's collar.

"Still, now, very still," he whispered to him. The dog whined, then hunkered down. Jim's camo pants were slipping slightly down his narrow hips and even the heat of the fire could not keep off the December chill. He went into the trees and unhooked his camouflage jacket from the branch. Four ragged holes had pierced it, but it would have to do. He left the maroon fishing hat where it had spun away after being hit by the first shot. He took a deep breath. One more guy, then find Ed.

Ed had found a blister pack of Tylenol lying on the ground and dry-swallowed a couple. Despite the chill, he was thirsty. His tongue felt like a dead snake.

He glanced to his left—boat doors and the concrete slipway and the dinghy bobbing there. One last chance. He wondered if the outboard would work, despite the years of disuse. Why hadn't he checked the spark? He imagined the contact: corroded, inert...

There was a new sound: the report of a rifle. He knew that sound. Had heard it a thousand times in his youth. A Winchester. Jim was here.

His arrival might distract the guy who had him pinned down. He got to his knees, praying that the sniper no longer had the boathouse under his scope, and scuttle-ran to the slipway and the dinghy and pulled on the outboard's start cord. He cursed himself for not checking the outboard earlier; the cord felt slack, but halfway through this pull he felt the telltale resistance, a sudden roar, blue-gray fumes erupting from the exhaust. He clamped the throttle grip, quickly wound the duct tape he had left hanging next to it around it three times, pushed the inflatable further out into the lake and dropped the outboard into the water. It set off in an almost straight line as Ed ducked back inside the double doors.

Doc started gingerly down the steep slope, cursing his choice of footwear. His loafers were office use, with slick soles. He was careful to place them so he didn't trip over the rocks and fir saplings, but he was finding it hard to balance with the case in one hand and the gun in the other.

It took about five minutes to climb down the hill. Ahead, the fire had reached the front porch of the cabin. The wood was being eaten in a frenzy of orange and red flames that cast a hellish glow over the surrounding area. As he approached the boathouse, the trees began to thin. He took a deep breath and ran forward from tree trunk to tree trunk, then squatted behind a thick pine on the edge of the drive and risked a peek around it. The air at this lower level was thick with smoke. The boathouse doors were now masked by the corner of the cabin. The only visible point of egress was the shattered side window overlooking the parking lot. No movement there.

Had one of the Sniper's rounds actually done for Constance? There was the sudden sound of a dog barking and then a shot off to his left. He immediately crouched lower. It must be the older guy engaging with the Sniper. Because of the suppressor on the Barrett, Doc had no idea whether the Sniper had returned fire. The single audible shot could be a good thing, or a very bad thing…

Another sound. The roar of an outboard from the lakeside of the boathouse. So Ed had had an escape plan all along. Doc broke cover and ran across the gravel drive and along the side of the boathouse.

Ahead, the lake lapped against the gravel shore and slipway. There was a dinghy gamely nosing its way through the short, choppy waves, heading to the mist-hazed northern shore. There was something in the stern by the outboard. He lifted the Glock. But something was wrong about the picture. The lump looked more like a sail bag than a person and there was a painter lifting up from the water at the rear of the dinghy. It snaked back to the boathouse.

He turned in that direction and there, standing in the boathouse entrance behind him, was Ed Constance, looking like a grime- and blood-covered ghost. He was wearing town clothes, a burned and torn tan suit, cut to shreds and bloody at the thighs. There was a bullet score in the top left of his suit arm. His eyes and teeth were white in the bloodied, fire-sooted face. These observations were all incidental to the one that otherwise totally occupied his vision: the black hole of a Magnum barrel pointing at him.

Doc squeezed the trigger of the Glock just as the revolver kicked back in Ed's hand.

CHAPTER SIXTY

Their eyes locked for a millisecond, then the Magnum kicked in Ed's hand. The shot struck the point of the other man's elbow, shattering it. The man's gun fired high and wide before falling on the gravel six feet away. The deflected bullet lodged just above his hip and he was in the process of staggering from the twin impact when Ed fired again. The next bullet hit his center mass just below the ribcage on the right side. It ripped through stomach lining, liver, and spleen. The man fell backward, the attaché case falling from his left hand. It landed on its edge and the latches sprang open, spilling some small glass vials, hypodermics, and a stethoscope from their yellow Styrofoam housing.

A vaunting, ugly triumph mainlined in Ed's racing heart. He'd gotten the bastard good. Now to finish him. But then he remembered: he was out of ammo. He better get the guy's pistol. He moved out quickly toward the fallen gun. The wounded man was trying to raise himself on his one good elbow. Blood pooled under his arced back. Bone showed through the elbow of the Tyvek suit where Ed's first round had struck. He looked behind, trying to stretch the obscenely shattered arm in the direction of the fallen pistol, but his forearm and hand flopped limply like a broken puppet's. The mask was drawn in sharply as he inhaled, outlining the contours of the man's face. He sank onto his back, panting for breath, staring at the sky.

Ed approached, the empty Magnum aimed at the man's chest, but it looked like his attempts to pick up the fallen weapon were over. Ed glanced up. They were hidden from the ridgeline by the end of the boathouse. Maybe the sniper was waiting for a signal before coming down. Or maybe he was still locked in the shootout back down the drive.

Ed leaned down and picked up the pistol, discarding the Magnum. The man's face mask was pulsing with his labored breath: blood was seeping through it from his mouth.

Ed looked upon him as dispassionately as he would at a wounded fly. Then stood on the man's right arm just below where the bone showed through. A high-pitched scream issued from behind the mask. Ed leaned down and ripped the covering off the man's face.

"OK, motherfucker," he said. "You better tell me where my wife is or I'm gonna put another round in you."

"Shoot then." The man's breath was asthmatic and rasping.

"Maybe you prefer this?" Ed spat. He applied more weight on the shattered arm.

The man gasped. "Fuck. No. I'll talk."

Ed took his foot off the arm, keeping the pistol steady on the man's face.

"Where is Sarah?"

But now the agony in his arm was gone, the guy's eyes drifted. "Where did you learn to kill, kid?"

"I had good teachers. Typhon, for starters. Now tell me about my wife, asshole."

But the man's mind was clearly wandering. "It had to be you. David warned me." The guy was semi-coherent now. "There's nothing— *nothing...*" he said with futile emphasis. He sucked air again, taking in the gray sky. He faded, then rallied a bit. "Nothing you can do about her. She's... insurance. Make you do your stuff... even if the psych shit didn't work."

Psych shit. Yes, that was what all this was. Just psych shit. The face of Typhon. The severed finger in Lenox. It was as far as he allowed himself to go. He could not go back into that silent darkness. His sanity could be gone with one word, one image. Did this man know the triggers? Cold sweat beaded his forehead.

Enough. He savagely reapplied his foot and twisted. The bones worked back and forth through the rent at the elbow.

"Stop!" the guy screamed. "Fuck, stop!"

"Tell me where she is."

"OK! She's at the old gas station near the Lot."

And there was that memory, any small missing details filled in. The Fromes, the yellow bus, the kids chanting… It was all back.

"The Texaco station? Why?" Ed asked.

"Krige and the rest thought you were more likely to go along with them if you saw she was alive."

"That station's two hundred miles away. How were you going to get me there?"

"A chopper. It's already inbound."

Ed looked around at the tree-fringed shoreline and the dense wood behind. "There's nowhere to land here."

"Up at the hotel." The guy's eyes rolled and he lost consciousness for a moment. Ed thought he was gone until they flickered back open. "I need something for the pain," he whispered.

"Where do you think you'll get that?"

"In my medical case," the guy said, grimacing toward the open silver attaché case and its scattered contents.

Ed reached out a foot and kicked the case over to Doc's side. "Knock yourself out," he said.

The wounded man's teeth were chattering together. He reached out his only working hand and pulled the case closer to him. Amongst the other stuff, there were three preloaded syringes in the Styrofoam, all labelled: Sodium Thiopental, Pancurium Bromide, Potassium Chloride.

With trembling fingers the guy took the last syringe and pressed the plunger. A little liquid squirted out the end. Another shudder of pain passed through him. He looked up at the sky as if steeling himself, then plunged the needle into his thigh, pressing down on the plunger. Then he lay back. He smiled strangely at Ed. His stentorian breathing eased, the smile fixed, and he was still. His eyes were suddenly sightless, reflecting the passing gray clouds.

"What the fuck?" said Ed. He kicked the wounded arm again. No reaction. He leaned down and touched the guy's neck. There was no pulse.

He stood, cursing. Then he sensed movement coming from his left, through the smoke. He whipped around in that direction. He'd forgotten all about the sniper.

Then he saw it was Jim Dove coming through the murk, face blacked with mud, wearing the same old camos as always. His friend looked older than he remembered. Shrunken physically, peering almost timidly forward through the smoke, as if his eyesight wasn't as good as it used to be. But he held his Winchester steady. A collie came at his heel, but it wasn't Laramie. No black patch over the right eye. The dog carried its tail low to the ground, spooked by the roaring flames and the scent of blood.

As he came nearer, Ed saw Jim's camo jacket had several bullet holes in it. But there was no blood. Ed was still puzzling over this when Dove came to a stop a few feet away and squinted at him.

"Ed?"

"Yeah, it's me, Jim."

"Well, ain't you a sight?"

"I guess I could say the same about you."

Ed jerked his head back down the drive. "What about the other guy?"

"Dead. Got him good. Bastard shot my friend Pollitt," Jim said. He looked down at Doc. "What happened here?"

"Killed himself with that needle. Claimed it was a painkiller. I guess he didn't want to be around when the cops arrived."

"I guess not."

"Anyone else out there?"

"No. But Pollitt called for backup."

"Listen, Jim, I can't be here when the cops arrive."

"Understood. I heard about that woman in Boston. That something to do with you?"

"They framed me."

"I hear you, kid. But I don't see any way out of this mess but giving yourself up. Too many dead."

"If it was just me, Jim, I'd do that. But they took my wife."

"Jesus."

"Yeah, she's collateral. But our friend here told me where she was before he killed himself: the old gas station."

"The place I went last week? Why?"

"I told you: I have to go there. She's insurance that I'll turn up." He looked his old friend in the eye. Jim stared back. "Did you do as I asked?" Ed asked.

"I did, God forgive me."

"I can't risk being put under again, Jim. They can take my mind, any minute of any day. I bet this fella's needles have some drugs in them that would make you forget your own name. Just like that. Lights out. I barely escaped this time. And after? They've got a hold over me every way you look: drugs, terrorism, murder. If I carry off their job the stories will be bad—really bad."

"We beat them here."

"There'll be more. But first I have to get Sarah."

"How do you figure on doing that?"

He nodded at the dead man at his feet. "A chopper's going to land at the hotel to take me and him out. We'll take the dinghy and surprise them."

Before Jim could answer, they were interrupted by a noise, at first distant, then stronger; a sinister, throbbing beat over the hills to the east. A dark shape loomed out of the cloud. A helicopter painted in drab gray camouflage labored through the sky like a flying dinosaur out of the Jurassic. It seemed for a moment to be heading directly for them, and they both ducked into the shadow of the boathouse, but then it banked, its rotor blades churning the clouds, and veered north toward the lakehead and the old hotel.

"What the hell—a Huey," Jim muttered. Just then, the radio in the Styrofoam pocket in the attaché case burst into life with a buzz of static, startling them both.

A distorted voice. "Salt Cracker, this is Deep Harbor. Do you read me? Over."

Jim looked down at the radio. "What should we do?" he asked Ed.

"Don't touch it," Ed warned.

Jim looked like he would sooner pick up a snake.

"Deep Harbor here," came the voice again, "approaching depot. Salt Cracker, please advise ETA, over."

As the noise of the rotors faded, they heard another sound on the still winter air: the far-off sound of a siren approaching from the Three Mile Road.

They both looked at the dinghy. "I guess we better get going," Jim said.

He slung the Winchester over his shoulder and began hauling the vessel back with the painter, fighting the outboard, which was still gamely trying to drive the dinghy northward. It was soon churning and bobbing in the small waves by the slip. He killed the engine and turned to Max. He was lying on the gravel drive, half an eye on the raging fire, half on Doc's corpse.

"We can't take him with us," Jim said. "He already nearly gave me away." He put two fingers in the side of his mouth and emitted a high-pitched whistle. Max's ears pinned back.

"Come here, boy," Jim said. Max got up and came forward, his tail wagging low, his tongue hanging.

Jim patted him, then said, "OK, home, boy, git. Git." Max whined. "Now!" he said more firmly. Reluctantly, the dog turned and loped back down the drive through the smoke. He stopped and turned, looking back at Jim through the heat haze. Jim shouted "Home!" once more and Max took off again, and ran around the bend in the drive.

CHAPTER SIXTY-ONE

MacDonald had picked up another patrol car and they now approached the Three Mile Road in convoy, sirens blaring. Pollitt was not answering his radio and MacDonald hoped it was because of the notoriously bad backwoods reception, nothing worse; nevertheless, he sensed something bad in his bones.

MacDonald's wingman was Deputy Archie Lime. Lime was two years from retirement and now entirely devoted to manning the front desk at the Madison station house. As far as he was aware, Lime hadn't been out on patrol or on active duty for five years or more. But as he was the only available deputy, so be it. Behind him came another county patrol car that had been near Greenville when the call had come in. MacDonald had been assured that no fewer than two fire trucks and three more patrol cars were somewhere in his wake, but he had no idea how far behind they were.

He braked at the crash site only long enough to ascertain that the abandoned Suburban and Dove's truck were empty. He knew where they had to go. Even an hour after the explosions at the Constance house, a thick column of smoke could be seen rising into the frigid December air.

As he and Lime drove on, he witnessed one of the curious things of the many curious and, in the end, downright terrible things he was to witness that day. It was the sight of a black and white collie dog slinking along the side of the road toward them as they approached the Constance turnoff. It seemed spooked by the sirens and lights and ducked into the treeline. To MacDonald it looked very like Jim Dove's Max. If it was, where was Jim?

The next day, as the police and National Guard searched the woods and lakeside, they found the dog lying on the porch of the bait and tackle store, waiting for Dove's return. He was impounded.

Meanwhile, the search went on for Ed Constance, the kid who had gone missing after his father's suspicious suicide some ten years before, and who now had an APB out on him for a rape-murder in Boston and the deaths of five people at the cabin. He was now the most wanted fugitive in America.

CHAPTER SIXTY-TWO

After Max had gone, Jim pulled in the rubber dinghy while Ed ran into the boathouse. There were some outdoor clothes hanging on a peg: parka, work pants, and a pair of work boots. Ed grabbed these. He took out the letter he'd retrieved from the antique clock, then bundled up his suit jacket and, fighting against the heat of the flames that had reduced the cabin to its concrete foundations, threw both into the blaze. He expected the trail of evidence from Boston onward would be enough to get him several life sentences, but at least everything in the Volvo, the trash bags, the Bible, and the planted evidence against him in the cabin were now just ashes.

The sirens were closer and he knew he had scant minutes. He looked through the heat haze at the dead men lying on the drive. He didn't know what was waiting further up that lake with the helicopter, whether the crew, having failed to raise them, would spook and fly off before he and Jim could get there. But if they didn't spook, if he was going to have an advantage over them, that sniper rifle would sure come in handy. He hobbled back to where the shooter had fallen near the burned man, picked up the rifle with its bulbous suppressor and studied the mechanism. He ejected the magazine and then unzipped the dead man's suit and found two blood-caked spare ammo clips. He limped back to the boathouse. Jim was topping up the outboard with fuel from a can.

"Set?" he asked.

"Sure," Ed answered. He put the sniper's gun onto the bottom boards of the dinghy, then held the painter steady as Jim got in. He yanked the starter cord on the Yamaha. It roared to life again. He gestured for Jim to take the tiller and went forward to sit on the middle strut of the dinghy, cradling the sniper's gun. The outboard increased in pitch as Jim opened the throttle and they described a wide arc away from the slip and into the far reaches of the lake, the arms of the pine-crowded shores falling away.

Ed looked behind. The cabin blaze got smaller and smaller until it became a tiny, angry orange eye. He didn't see any stutter lights yet. The boat hit some little waves as Jim opened the throttle even more.

They reached the north end of the lake in twenty minutes. In front of the hotel entrance where the steamer used to put in, there was an old landing pier, now sagging, its piles sunk into the lake floor, but Jim had no intention of taking her up there. There was a little cove, a beauty spot hidden from the hotel by a rocky outcrop, a mile down the west coast of the lake. He aimed for that, hoping they would not be seen by any watchers.

He cut the engine and the inflatable drifted into the cove. Ed jumped down as it grounded on the shale bottom and tied the painter to a cedar root exposed by the wash of the lake. A path zigzagged up through an outcropping of the mountain into the forest.

Ed hefted the sniper's rifle as Jim picked up his Winchester and took the lead. Though there was deadfall and cones and a thick mat of needles, Jim moved up the unused path like a ghost. They reached a viewpoint with fallen safety railings and a bench. An information board had been placed here in some distant past, the frame carved with the words "Arrowhead Path," but the glass panel covering the legend had long ago broken and the information sheet had vanished.

They went on for a half-hour, the gray lake flitting in and out of view to their right through the pines and boulders. The rhyolite that had brought the Native Americans here lay fractured in shards that had fallen from the outcropping above the path. Jim suddenly stopped, crouched down. Ed wondered if he had seen or heard something, but instead Jim picked up a particularly vicious-looking blade-like arrow-head and slid it into his camo vest.

Sunlight began to assert itself through the overhead foliage and the path began to dip down. Ed could see a large expanse of overgrown lawn ahead. It was separated from the forest by a dry-stone wall, pierced by a wooden gate that hung lopsidedly from one hinge. Behind was the white stucco gleam of the hotel itself and, like an alien insect dropped from the heavens, the helicopter.

CHAPTER SIXTY-THREE

David Krige was seething. His near-thirty years on earth had taught him that in life forward progress was only made about five percent of the time. The other ninety-five percent was wasted holding on to what little had already been achieved. This applied as much to mundane enterprises as it did to maintaining the place of Typhon in the world order.

The organization that had brainwashed him and ordained his early death had reprieved him, brought him out of the darkness to be a leader. The leader of the future when the old men, Vermeulen and Fitzgerald and the others, were gone. Coughlin was already in the grave. It was his time. The world was bad, taken over by the faithless, the left-leaning, minorities, people of deficient will. He had never speculated about his birth parents. Only one thing was he sure of: unlike the other kids from the Lot, his blood was pure Aryan. There were Vessels, Vials, and Angels, as ordained by the Book. He was the last: God's avenging angel on the corruption of the world and its peoples.

Only this final bringing to account had thwarted him. It was ten long years since Northeastern and Seboomook. Today the long wait was about to end. Might already have ended if Doc's radio message was anything to go by. And yet, looking at the distant pall of smoke over Brantwood, something told him Ed Constance was still alive. Their final reckoning was going to be face-to-face.

There had been no further word from Doc. But as long as Krige had Sarah, he was sure Ed would come to *him*.

He kicked a stone on the driveway into the overgrown lawn that separated it from the steamer pier. He turned and there was the gray mountain looming over its back. Nakuset. Sun Mountain. Certainly no sun today. Its 2,000-foot peak was hidden in wreathing mist and low-lying clouds, and he worried for a moment that the cloud ceiling might fall further and the helicopter would be stuck here just as the police turned up.

David looked anxiously at the hotel road. Though it hadn't seen regular use in nearly twenty-five years, it was still passable. For the last mile of its course, the single-lane track came around a bend in the lakeshore and traversed a rocky, treeless heath before passing over a little humpbacked bridge that led into the hotel grounds.

He had been checking it ever since they had landed a half-hour before, but it was as empty of life now as it had been when they had touched down. His only other companion was Fallows. Having led the team down in Miami, the Merriweather's security chief had arrived on a private jet into Logan with Sarah the day before. As well as serving in the SEALs, Fallows had transitioned to become a Seawolf, a Navy combat helicopter pilot. He'd been unfazed by the low cloud cover and looming terrain as they'd flown in from Bangor, comfortable enough when blinded by the cloud to fly on instruments. Fallows sat huddled in the cockpit, monitoring the radio. Despite the overcast he was wearing sunglasses. He opened the side hatch as David approached.

"Nothing?" David asked.

"Nothing," Fallows said. "Can't raise them."

David looked at the empty stretch of road skirting the eastern lakeside and cursed.

"We gonna abort?" Fallows asked.

David looked at his Rolex: 9.41. "We'll give it to ten."

Fallows craned his head up at the sky beyond the Perspex. David had no idea with what clarity the man could see things through the sunglasses and the dusty plastic. "Winds shifting to the east. The weather will keep off for now."

Well, that was a relief. A blizzard from Canada was all they needed.

"OK," David answered. "I'm gonna try and get more of a view from up there." He pointed at the fourth-floor balcony of the hotel, then reached into the open hatch at the back of the chopper where he had left his equipment and retrieved an Uzi submachine gun and two spare clips of ammo. He dropped the extra magazines into a pocket in his camos and strode across the cracked, weed-strewn drive to the porte cochere. Someone had decided to relieve the hotel of its front doors in the last couple of decades. No doubt some expensive hardwood was now serving as a dining-room table or shop counter somewhere in the county.

The management company had since boarded up the doorway and all the ground-floor windows with plywood. But in the case of the entranceway, the panels had been kicked in and no one had returned to fix them. In fact, it looked like they had not been back in years.

He entered the hall. A double staircase arched up from either side of the lobby to a second-floor gallery serving the floors above. Gray light filtered down from the glass light dome high above in the atrium, showing the faded red carpet, now a ghostly pale pink.

The reception and concierge desks, no doubt also made of hardwood, had been removed, making the big space seem even emptier than it was. The metal fittings had also been ripped out, as had the wall paneling, leaving ugly distressed plasterwork underneath with dangling wires and empty electrical sockets. An elevator cage stood across the lobby, denuded of brass fittings. Even the lift grille had been removed.

The only decorations left by the plunderers were two massive and flimsily clad caryatids that held up a small entablature flanking the ballroom doors at the far end of the lobby. David guessed it would have taken a crane to remove the sculptures, so there they had remained.

He took the stairs up three levels. Ahead lay a long corridor with the most prestigious rooms facing the lake. He turned right and went to the furthest of the suites. The doors were gone. Beyond what must have been a large reception room was a wide interior with no fewer than two French doors leading to an expansive balcony. This was the presidential suite, by the looks of it. What appeared to be a bedroom and bathroom suite were on the left. The suite was empty of furniture and fittings. The French doors had not weathered the storms of the last winters well and only a couple of the panes remained. Leaves and broken glass lay scattered on the faded patterned carpet.

He pulled open one of the doors and stepped out. The whole vista of Tranquility lay before his eyes. A ten-mile stretch that grayed into nothing in the misty distance. But above the mist, like a biblical sign, there was the column of smoke marking the Constance cabin.

He was about to turn and inspect the stretch of road again when movement caught his eye a mile or two out. A small dot with a V-shaped wake behind it. It was the only thing moving on the lake. He pulled out a set of small field glasses from a top pocket of his camo jacket, lifted them to his eyes and adjusted the focus. An inflatable with two figures in it. They were not heading directly for the hotel but off to one side, to the western shore. The dinghy disappeared behind an outcropping of rock. David saw that an old path led up over the greensward surrounding the hotel in that direction. Whoever was coming was trying to do so inconspicuously.

It was Constance, he was sure. Maybe with the guy from the bait store. How had they beaten one of the best teams Typhon had ever put in the field? The little wimp who would cry himself to sleep every night at Mrs. Frome's had turned out to be a world-class killer, but not in the way Typhon had anticipated.

Well, now the irritation of watching others fuck things up was over. It was down to him, David: kill or capture.

He called down to the helicopter. "Fallows! We got company."

Despite knowing the Constance saga must now end, one way or another, David had misgivings. Fallows only had a Glock handgun.

And the Uzi was hardly the weapon of choice for range. On the other hand, he was aware that the sniper had had a Barrett and, hard though it was to believe, if Ed and this other guy really had overcome Doc's team, they might now have it.

CHAPTER SIXTY-FOUR

The Huey sat on the overgrown parking lot, its blades drooping like a crane fly's legs. Its hatches were shut and there was no sign of the occupants.

"Think they're waiting for us, kid," Jim said. "Must have seen us comin'."

"We can't hang around for the cops."

"No cover out there," Jim said.

"I have an idea," Ed said. "Take this." He offered Jim the Barrett.

Jim laid down the Winchester and took the sniper's gun. He inspected it properly for the first time, then lifted it. The hotel facade zoomed at him through the scope. He carefully traversed the windows and balconies with it.

"Eureka." There was the top of a head and hint of a blue parka peeking up from the nearest of the top-floor balconies, the snub nose of a submachine gun braced on the parapet. Had they been seen? At about 200 yards, Jim guessed they were pretty much at the maximum range of the other guy's gun. Not the Barrett, though. He thumbed off the safety and gradually brought the reticles down on the target so that the head was right in the center of the cross-pieces. "There's a guy up there looking this way. I got him bang to rights."

"Don't shoot," Ed hissed. "It could be the pilot. We gotta get north, remember?"

Jim cussed. "So what do you want me to do?"

Ed pulled out the Glock and checked the magazine. It was full, bar the wayward shot Doc had gotten off before Ed had hit him. "Lay down some covering fire. I'll go in the back."

"You nuts, kid? There could be a half-dozen of them in there."

"I'm guessing this is just an extraction team. They'd need room in the chopper for the four at Brantwood plus me. I'm thinking there'll be two at most."

"Sure as shit hope so."

Ed looked over to his left. The stone wall surrounded what might have been lawn but was now an overgrown meadow with rhododendrons crowding in on the northern end in the lee of the mountain. Broken gazebos and a crumpled pavilion stood around a croquet lawn surrounded by overgrown beds. Steps led up to a wide terrace and side entrance. Around the back were service buildings and, Ed assumed, the rear doors of the hotel.

"I'm goin' around that way," he said. "When I get into the bushes, lay down fire on that guy's position and keep him pinned. I'll make a dash for the back."

Jim shook his head. "It's a dumbass plan."

"It's the only one I got."

"Just watch yourself."

Ed patted Jim on the shoulder, took a deep breath, then slipped away, using the dry-stone wall as cover as Jim reapplied the scope to his eye. The guy was still there, peering over toward the Arrowhead Path. The easiest shot of his shooting career. But one he couldn't take. He tracked Ed's progress for a couple of minutes as he crouch-ran to the end of the wall. Jim guessed that Ed could barely see him in the foliage but nevertheless gave a little nod as Ed raised a hand with a thumbs-up. Jim returned his attention to the scope, aimed a foot or so above the balcony's guy's head and squeezed the trigger.

★

The woods to the west were very dark. David was staring at the path and the little gateway in the wall leading into them. The air was suddenly displaced as a supersonic hornet whirred past at 900 yards a second just above his head. The stucco wall behind him on the balcony exploded, hailing his back and neck with cement powder fragments. He dropped instantly below the level of the parapet.

No sound of a shot. It was the sniper's M90 for sure. The rotten brickwork in front of him suddenly bulged inwards with the force of another impact. Flaking paint and more cement powder blew into his face, half blinding him. He crawled desperately through the open French doors to the reception room just as Fallows came running into the suite. Another round blew a huge white hole in the plaster in the back wall.

"Get the fuck down," David shouted, but Fallows was already flat on his face.

"It's just covering fire. Go to the rear," he said. But then he heard the splintering of glass downstairs and realized it was too late. Someone was in the hotel and the hunt was on.

Ed found a loose panel in the service area at the back of the hotel. He hadn't heard any shots, but there had been a succession of dull thuds that he recognized as the noise of the Barrett's suppressed rounds striking home. That had been his cue for the final dash.

The glass behind the loose board was intact and he had to smash it with the butt of the Glock. He reached in and unlatched the window. The corridor behind must once have served the main hall and the conservatory area at the other end. There was a servants' call-bell system mounted on the wall. A double doorway led into a black-and-white-tiled ballroom, which in turn must lead forward to the reception area. He stalked through the vast ballroom, his feet in the newly acquired work boots clumping on the tiles. Dim green light came down through a dome-shaped atrium above him like the light under the sea. Ahead, heavy drapes covered the glass doors leading to the lobby.

Gun or no, now he was actually in the hotel his plan seemed impossible. Jim had been right. To get the pilot to surrender and fly them out seemed an absurd fantasy. For all he knew, the guy might be another of Typhon's mind-controlled zombies and as likely to fight to the death as acquiesce.

He got to the doorway into the reception area and gingerly pulled the heavy, dusty drapes aside. Flanking the entrance facing the hall were two marble caryatids. There were the massive double doors gaping open to the lake and the rotors of the helicopter poking up above the outside steps. The large space was empty. No cover, and whoever was upstairs would have heard his entry. He took a breath and stepped out.

The guy in Jim's scope had disappeared. There was a fist-sized hole in the plaster of the hotel wall just above where he'd been crouching and another one in the stone balcony. No more targets visible. Whoever was in the hotel would have retreated and would be waiting—waiting no doubt for the exact move that Ed had planned.

It wasn't a conscious decision. Jim got to his feet slowly, tensing for a shot from the Sun Mountain, but none came. He crouch-ran to the gate in the wall, then across the overgrown lawn. It was fifty yards to the entrance.

CHAPTER SIXTY-FIVE

David and Fallows had crept down two flights and were now at the gallery overlooking the reception hall. Inching out of the shadows of the ballroom came Ed, looking a little different to when David had last seen him back at Northeastern ten years earlier. The child had become a man. The sleeper who had woken and was now about to die, Vermeulen be damned. He aimed and pressed the Uzi's trigger.

Ed saved himself in a split second. He glanced up instinctively and saw David and someone else silhouetted on the gallery. Before his brain knew it, he had thrown himself behind one of the statues, just as the world exploded. The three-second burst from the 32-shot magazine caused a hurricane of flying splinters of wood, glass, and stone. The Carrara marble at the neck of the caryatid must have had a flaw ever since it had been quarried in Italy, for as several rounds impacted its head, it sheered off the torso and fell on the side of Ed's head and shoulder. He slumped to the ground just as the last bullets from the magazine bisected the air he had been standing in a moment before.

David slammed another magazine home. He peered through the cloud of cartridge smoke at Ed's prone body. It looked like it was finally over. No mission for that particular Vial, but no more bother either. There were plenty more brain-dead kids in New Mexico to step into Ed's shoes. The Hoover Dam would still be there in a month, or a year.

"Watch out for the other guy," he ordered Fallows. He stalked down the stairs, the Uzi tracking between Ed's body and the front doors of the hotel. He expected to find Ed in a pool of blood, but in the dim light he saw there was none and he was still breathing. The broken head of the caryatid lay next to him. Not one shot had struck him directly, just the stupid head; there was a lump on the side of Ed's temple where the stone had hit him a glancing blow. The Devil had spared him. He cursed: the rendition part of the mission was still possible and Fallows was a witness to that fact.

Ed groaned and stirred. It was tempting to unload the Uzi into him at point-blank range, and damn the consequences, but when David glanced up he saw Fallows was watching him from the balcony.

If the Devil and fate were against him, so be it. The wife was collateral. Ed had already shown his blind loyalty in trying to protect Shannon. What extremes would he go to save his own wife and unborn child?

David kicked Ed over, picked up the Glock and stuck it in his belt. He rolled him over quickly again, pulled his hands behind his back, took some plastic ties from his camo jacket and tied them around Ed's wrists.

Just as he finished, he heard the shuffle of boots behind him from the front entrance. A beam of light danced in the periphery of his vision. It wavered on the arm of the broken statue, on the dusty velvet ballroom curtain behind it, then flashed into the corner of his eye and rested there. David turned slowly. Sunlight flashed from the sniper scope of a rifle that was pointed at his head. He recognized the guy. It was the owner of the bait store, Jim Dove. He had last seen him ten years ago driving away from Seboomook the morning they had lost Carl.

"Drop that weapon slowly," Dove ordered, and David put down the Uzi, then shielded his eyes against the reflected light from the scope.

"If you got a partner, tell him to show himself," Dove said.

"I'm alone," David answered. Where the fuck was Fallows? He had disappeared from the balcony.

Dove didn't take him at his word—he entered cautiously, the rifle tracking around the lobby and up at the gallery. What he couldn't see was that Fallows had now reappeared immediately above and behind him on the balcony. He had his handgun leveled at Dove's back.

Dove suddenly noticed the direction of David's gaze. He took a quick step forward, swiveled and pointed the gun up just as the whip-crack of Fallows' pistol sounded twice in quick succession. A round ricocheted off the tiled floor of the lobby and whined past David's head, but the second shot hit Dove's left thigh. The blow-through sent a shower of blood, tissue and shredded cargo fabric over David's feet. Dove cried out and crumpled, the rifle skittering away from his hand.

There was a sudden silence, broken only by the wounded man's keening. He was trying to stanch the bleeding thigh with both his hands, but it looked like a bad one. Blood had begun to pool under him.

"Shit," he intoned.

David picked up the Uzi and came up out of his crouch as Fallows descended the stairs. Fallows was still coolly chewing gum.

David stood over the fallen man. "You're the guy from the bait store, ain't you?" he asked.

"What's it to you?" Dove spat back.

"Saw you driving away from Seboomook all those years ago. Wish I'd put it together then. Would have saved ourselves a lot of bother chasing down old Ed here. I'm guessing that it was you who shot Carl?"

Jim was silent.

"Thought so," David went on. "Lucky we caught up with your friend Dumfries and finally made the connection. Same fire team in Nam. Marine combat engineers. You two had quite a record blowing up gook villages. Respect for that. You guys really understood the power of terror."

Jim said, "Fuck you. You're not going to get away with this. Every state trooper and National Guardsman within a hundred miles is heading this way."

David laughed. "Mister, as far as anyone's concerned, we *are* the National Guard."

Jim didn't answer. His face was frozen in pain. He was trying to stanch the bleeding from his thigh with both hands. David thought he saw the gleam of white bone through the fatigues. He wasn't going to be any more trouble. He might even quietly bleed out. But he didn't really want to leave him here for the cops to find.

He motioned Fallows to drag Jim to the chopper. Fallows got him under the armpits and dragged him through the lobby and down the steps. Jim's useless leg bumped along the ground and he cried out. They left quite a slick of blood. The police forensic teams might have fun with that. But at least it wasn't his or Fallows' blood.

He turned to Ed. Now Fallows was momentarily out of the picture, the temptation to end the whole mission returned, just as when he'd ordered Bailey to terminate Ed. Ed had a way of escaping every situation Typhon put him in. The same could be true now, Sarah or no Sarah. He pressed the barrel of the Uzi against the unconscious man's head. The safety was off. Just a little pressure on the trigger and Ed's head would be splattered all over the lobby—end of. He and Fallows could fly away. And too bad if the little red notebook came to bite Vermeulen's ass. David would be in New Mexico by then.

And yet it would be sweet to switch on the news, see the Colorado gushing through a great breach in the dam, see Ed's mugshot up there just as Shannon's and Catrine's photos had been up there on the TV screens. He pulled the barrel away and waited for Fallows.

Ed opened his eyes to find David staring down at him. Once more it felt like there was an ice pick in his skull. The only good thing about the pain was that it told him he wasn't dead or under the Typhon spell. His hands were tied behind him. As his eyes focused, he was somehow not surprised to see Mo Fallows standing behind David. The last time he'd seen him had been in the Merriweather offices, what felt like a lifetime ago but was barely a week. Fallows gave no hint of recognition behind his aviator glasses.

David grinned. His teeth looked yellow. Just like the goon Ed had shot back in Boston. Maybe none of them believed in fluoride.

"Wakey, wakey, kid," David said.

Ed finally got control of his tongue. "Where's Sarah?" he asked.

"The noble husband, eh?" David answered. "She's up the road at the old Texaco station. Remember it? Don't worry, your beautiful wife is right as rain, 'cept her finger. Boy, did she squeal when that thing came off."

"You bastard!" Ed spat.

"Shhh," David said. "Mrs. Frome taught us better than that."

"What do you want from me?"

"Why, Ed, what we've always wanted: cooperation. Seeing how we can't tell you to do things anymore, we thought we'd get ourselves some insurance. Your nine-fingered wife and your unborn child. Carry through with the mission and they live. Fuck us around again and they die. *Capisce?*"

"How do I know you won't harm them when I'm gone?" Ed asked.

David shrugged. "You know, we prefer live people to dead people. Live people can do things for us. Dead people? Not so much. Perhaps we'll take them to our place in New Mexico. Your wife looks like a good breeder. May even have a go with her myself."

"Fuck you," said Ed.

"Warned you," David said, slapping him hard. Ed's head rocked back. He tried to raise himself, but it was impossible with his hands tied behind his back. David pushed him back to the floor. "So, we got a deal, Ed? All you have to do is get in the chopper nice and easy and we'll take you to her."

"Then what?" Ed asked through his split lip.

"We have our bag of tricks up there and a car. We'll pack the explosives in it and then you drive out to Colorado. I'm sure you can't miss the Hoover Dam. Remember, you detonate only when you're on top of it. Then it's lights out for you and half the western US."

"Sounds peachy."

"Don't be sore, Ed. We've booked you into some nice motels along the way. A bit of comfort before you go to glory, you know what I mean?"

"So everyone'll think I am another of your commie insurgents, like Shannon—dying for the cause?"

"That's right—got your legend nice and tight. Too bad you burned the cabin. We put lots of good stuff in there. The Feds would've thought Che Guevara had been staying. But don't worry—when they get to it, your place in Miami Beach looks like a revolutionary shrine, just like Shannon's did."

"What happened to her kid?"

"Boy, you two were really tight, weren't you? I'd worry about your marriage if Shannon wasn't dead. Anyway, Alice Mae is doing well. She'll be in the desert by now. Sure as hell hope she turns out better than her ma."

Ed turned his face away.

"OK, let's go," David said. Fallows leaned down, grabbed the top of Ed's parka and hauled him to his feet. They walked him out to the Huey. David bundled him onto a bench seat in the rear next to Jim. Jim's face was white and he was struggling for breath, but he was still conscious. David took up position in the open hatchway.

Fallows went around to the cockpit, climbed in and put on a headset. He started pre-flight, punching buttons and adjusting levers. The engine roared to life and the rotor blades began to slowly circle as he brought the bird up to power.

David picked up a headset from a bracket and keyed the mic. "Get us over the mountain," he shouted over the increasing rotor noise. "We'll dump the old guy, then get up to Armageddon."

"What shall I tell the team?" Fallows asked.

"Tell them we have Constance. Plan's back on. Have his wife ready. He'll want to check she's OK before we set him on his way. We'll be an hour, maybe a little more."

Fallows opened the throttle, engaged the collective, and the helicopter soared up from the hotel lot and climbed above the mist-wreathed firs and the snowcapped summit of Nakuset. The vast swathe of the state forest opened up northward all the way to Canada. To the south, the column of smoke from Brantwood was visible, but nothing else.

"Head northwest," David said over the headset, eyeing the compass over Fallows' shoulder. Fallows banked. Three thousand feet below, the forest canopy spooled under the open hatch.

CHAPTER SIXTY-SIX

The bitter wind was blowing strong in Ed's face. It felt as if a sledge-hammer had cracked the side of his head. Spots of light circulated in his vision.

David stood braced against the hatchway entrance, half in, half out, looking down at whatever was below. He was speaking into a headset. The noise of the rotors drowned his voice.

Jim was lying on the bench seat right next to Ed. His face was drained, and he was holding the ragged wound in his left leg with one hand. The leg of his combat trousers was soaked red and Ed could see he was almost spent from pain and blood loss. But Ed also saw that Jim had worked something out of his pocket with his free hand: a bit of sharp slate; the arrowhead from the trail near the hotel. Then, without looking at him, Jim reached out to Ed's back and found the notch between Ed's hands, and there was a desperate sawing motion on the plastic tie. Ed's heart leapt in his throat. For a second there was resistance, then the ties gave with a snap, the sound inaudible under the rotor blades.

David spoke on the headset again, making a chopping motion, and Fallows pulled back on the cyclic. The cabin reared slightly. Blustery clouds hurtled past the open hatch and the helicopter came to an uneasy hover.

David turned. His eyes were stone-cold blue. Then, in one fluid movement, he stretched forward and grabbed the lapels of Jim's hunting coat. As easily as if he was lifting a small child as opposed to a 200-pound adult, he hauled the older man to his feet. Jim's wounded leg buckled, but David paid it no heed, twisting Jim around so that now his back was to the open hatch and the whirling cloud outside.

The two men stared into each other's eyes for a beat. Jim's lips twisted into a snarl as David pushed him in stutter steps toward the open door. One of Jim's hands was bunched into the front of David's parka, but, unseen by David, the other still clutched the arrowhead. Four inches of razor-sharp shale. Jim drew his hand back and rammed the arrowhead savagely upward under David's sternum. It disappeared into the material of the parka.

David barely flinched, but looked down, distracted, and released his grip on Jim with one hand to touch the place where the arrowhead was lodged. His hand came away smeared with blood. He looked at Jim. The older man lifted his free hand up. It, too, was covered in blood, cut to the bone across the palm where the arrowhead had cut deep as he had pushed it in.

David's face contorted. He shouted something Ed could not hear. Ed tried to get to his feet. The yo-yo effect of the helicopter in hover in the turbulent sky and the blow to his head made everything spin. He reached out to grab a stanchion for balance, missed it and nearly fell.

David's free hand closed on Jim's neck. Jim's hand gouged at David's eyes. David's strength seemed unaffected by the stabbing. Jim was being pushed back until his right boot caught in the metal threshold of the hatch and he tipped backward, his hands ripped free of David's face and parka front, and he was gone, falling away, out of sight.

David went to the hatch and looked down, one hand bracing on the hatch frame, the other clutching the arrowhead in the ragged hole in the front of his parka. Bloody down spilled out of it, red on blue. The end of the arrowhead rose and fell with each jerky breath.

Ed held his position for a moment, swayed, then staggered forward. David must have felt movement behind him because he had just enough time to turn and meet Ed's eyes as Ed's shoulder crashed into him.

And now it was David's boot that caught on the threshold of the hatch and, for a second, he stood suspended there, his hands windmilling in the air, but the center of his balance was too far gone and he began—slowly, so slowly, it seemed—to fall back into the whirling gray cloud.

One of his hands ceased its windmilling and shot out toward Ed's jacket, grabbing the collar. Ed stumbled forward from the force of the tug and grabbed the hatch frame. David fell backward, his grip broken. The headset detached and was left dangling out of the hatch. David's free hand grabbed at the helicopter skid and for a second it looked like he might take a grip on it, but then his blood-slicked fingers slipped off it one by one and he fell.

David's eyes never left Ed's as he plummeted to the gray-green canopy of the woods. And though by now he was some thousand feet down, it seemed that David's lips cracked into a smile as he looked back up. Ten seconds later, his body was abruptly swallowed by the forest.

The helicopter yawed again. Ed was nearly pitched out of the open hatch. He twisted around. Fallows was staring at him from behind his aviator glasses, then he yanked the cyclic again. The deck tilted and Ed's boots skidded over the metal rivets on the deck. He grabbed the seat back and hauled himself up the steeply sloping cabin. Fallows gave up trying to pitch Ed out. His free hand grabbed at the Glock in the holster on his belt. The restraint popped and he pulled the gun out, but before he could do anything else, Ed's hand clamped on his wrist. They wrestled for a moment. The struggle threw Fallows to one side and the cyclic with it, so the chopper now yawed in the opposite direction. Fallows' head impacted heavily with the Perspex canopy. Warning lights began flashing on the instrument panel and the chopper suddenly dropped. The gun fell clear as Fallows desperately grabbed the cyclic with both hands and tried to bring the chopper's nose up. Ed fell back onto the bench seat behind, the Glock skittering to a halt against one of his boots. He picked it up and racked the slide. The spinning descent eased.

Fallows seemed to have regained control. Ed stood and pressed the barrel of the gun to Fallows' right ear. The noise of the rotor and the wind on the open hatch was still too loud for conversation. The headset was swinging in the hatch door and he grabbed it as it came toward him, clamping it over his ears with his free hand. He keyed the mic.

"OK, listen, Fallows. If you do exactly what I say, you may come out of this alive," he said.

Fallows dry-swallowed and nodded.

"You know where my wife is?"

Fallows nodded again.

"Take me there."

"What then?" Fallows asked.

"You're free to go."

"You think I'm going to believe that?"

"Remember, I'm not one of you fuckers, Fallows. I broke free."

"I've been in this game for decades, Constance. No one gets free."

"Spare me your philosophy. This is the deal. When we get to the landing site, you hover a few feet off the ground. I'll jump out and you can fly off to Area 51 or wherever the fuck you came from."

"OK, if that's what you want, you got it," Fallows said.

Fallows turned the nose of the chopper to the northwest again. Below, Ed saw the twenty-mile-long outline of Chesuncook Lake, where he had camped out with Jim ten years ago.

On they flew, now over Eagle Lake. The engines in the deserted clearing were invisible. But Ed knew they were there. Rust-red Cyclopes waiting out the end of time.

The Huey flew over the course of the Allagash down which he had fled all those years before, and then swooped over the giant blackened pit where Eriksson's Lot had once stood. Memories cascaded.

The Huey began losing altitude as they approached the Texaco station.

Fallows pointed to a straight stretch of Realty Road ahead. A forest fire had cleared the trees to blackened stumps on either side.

"That's the landing site," he said over the headphones. "Too many trees around the gas station." He eased back, and the chopper came to a hover and gradually started to descend toward the gravel road surface.

"Take me down to ten feet," Ed said, then took off the headset. Still pointing the Glock at Fallows' head, he backed his way to the hatch and glanced down. The road surface was getting close. Thirty feet, twenty... He slid out and put two feet on the skid, still pointing the gun at the pilot.

Perhaps Fallows knew there was no returning to Typhon after what had happened. Just as Ed was about to jump, he ducked and yanked back on the stick and the Huey reared back up. The Glock kicked in Ed's hand. It was close range and only the top of Fallows' head was visible over the pilot's seat, but the Perspex canopy behind him splattered red and gray.

Then Ed was falling backward, the Glock flying out of his hand. He waited for the shattering impact of the road surface. Instead, there was a cold shock and his mouth filled with freezing water. He bucked back to the surface, choking. He had been pitched into a drainage ditch by the roadside. The freezing water came to his waist. Five feet either side and he would have had hit the road surface hard.

The Huey was still rising about a quarter of a mile away, but in a westward arc, the banking becoming more and more pronounced until it reached the apex of its upward curve and began to fall first on its side, then upside down. It disappeared into the treeline beyond the burned area of forest and then there was a massive fireball of orange and black flames.

Ed climbed out of the ditch and got to his feet. He checked himself. Nothing broken, but there were plenty of bruises to come. His teeth began to chatter in the cold. There was one benefit of the numbness; the injuries to his shoulder and head were aching a little less. Something glinted in the middle of Realty Road and he saw it was the fallen Glock. He picked it up and struck out east, toward the station, to Armageddon.

CHAPTER SIXTY-SEVEN

It was now a little after noon, but the sun as it neared its zenith was only just over the fir and spruce trees lining Realty Road. It would be getting dark at four. He walked in the shadows.

After twenty minutes, he could see the tip of the Texaco star jutting up above the treetops ahead. He slowed his pace and hunkered down. Whoever was waiting could hardly have failed to hear the chopper crash in the winter silence of the north, far less fail to notice the column of smoke rising from the crash site.

The camber of the road would provide cover. He crept along to the place where the unpaved section gave way to the blacktop. The asphalt ahead was cracked and warped and clumps of sere ragweed grew from the cracks; cones and small branches lay in a thin covering on the road surface.

It was eerily quiet, unlike his last two visits in '70 and '79, when the cicadas and white-throated sparrows had been deafening. In the ten years since he was last here, nature had asserted herself a little more. The canopy over the four pumps had sagged and grayed with time, and the pumps, once a fire-truck red, had now faded to a light pink. The office behind, as it had been then, was weatherboarded, but was now spray-painted with graffiti. There were still no panels over the front doors; it was just an open, black mouth.

But there were two additions to the scene. A dusty Corolla with Canadian plates sat in the back lot in the same place the yellow bus had parked all those years before. Presumably it was the car David had mentioned; the one Ed was meant to drive to Colorado.

The second was two tailors' dummies that stood either side of the office entrance. One mannequin was dressed in a flowing white bridal gown, the other in a bridegroom's tuxedo. Both outfits were familiar: he'd last seen them lying on the beach outside the Fontainebleau on the night of his wedding two years before. The sight took his breath away: even in this, Typhon had had complete foresight; had anticipated this day, this scene. It was just another nail in the mental torture, but it nearly brought Ed to his knees.

He forced himself forward. Inside the office he could see the metal display stands lying in a jumble on the floor and the dim outline of the cashier's desk toward the back.

The silence and stillness were puzzling. He had expected a big reception committee, but there was no one in sight. And Sarah was meant to be here somewhere. That was, if the helicopter crash hadn't spooked whoever was holding her and they had gone. He couldn't admit to that possibility... yet.

He stopped by the broken office doors. Curiously for a gas station that had not pumped gas for more than three decades, there was a strong smell of it in the air. Briefly, he felt high. Old gas. Ethanol separation. Alcohol entering his lungs. His shoes splashed something. A puddle of liquid pooled in the doorway. In the winter sun he saw its oily rainbow sheen: spilt gas. A lake of it disappearing into the dark office. The place had been primed.

Perhaps there was a hint of movement back there in the darkness. He moved forward, over the threshold, splashing through the inch-high gas lake. His leg made contact with what felt like fishing line at mid-shin. There was a brief resistance. Then nothing. Trip wire.

He froze, heart in mouth. Why the trip wire? A warning device, to let whoever was out there know he was here?

He listened. There was now a faintly discernible dripping.

Then there was a moan from the darkness.

He instinctively knew it was her. "Sarah," he called. His voice was loud. Too loud; he hadn't spoken since the chopper. His ears still rung with the rotor noise. "It's me, Ed."

She answered. "Ed? Is that really you?" Her speech was thick; perhaps she had been beaten or drugged.

"Yes, it's me." His own voice sounded stronger than he felt inside.

"Ed, don't come in. Go!" she hissed.

"It's OK," he said.

"No! It's a trap," she answered.

He splashed forward a few more steps. His eyes were adjusting to the darkness. There on the cinder-block wall at the back of the office was splayed a pale form, like a ghost, face framed by dark hair, scared, roving eyes, white in the dark.

She was in an X-form crucifixion: wrists and ankles pinned to the back wall between two rusty steel supports. There was a bloodied rag around her left hand where they had taken her finger. She wore just a soiled bra and underwear. Her pregnant belly was showing a bit, straining at the filthy elastic of her underwear. Her skin was blue with the cold. There were white wires looped around her body and packs of what looked like gray modeling clay attached to the inner surface of the support columns.

She was looking straight at him. "I didn't want you to see me like this, Ed."

"It's OK," he said.

She shook her head. "Just go, Ed."

Before he could answer, another voice came. Tinny and artificial. He started and looked up. There was a PA speaker in the shadows of the corner eaves over the cashier's desk, the sort that once might have piped music and staff messages when the station was open.

Apart from the mechanical distortion, he knew the voice. He had heard it every day of his childhood.

It was Mrs. Frome.

CHAPTER SIXTY-EIGHT

"Hello, Edward. So, you've finally come. I'm a little surprised that David isn't with you."

Where was she? Could she see him, and, if he spoke, could she hear him? He turned from the speaker and looked around. There were no cameras, just the speaker, but on the desk there was an old-fashioned mic on a stand, pointing in his direction. It might be live.

"David's dead," he said, "Fallows too, along with your other four goons. And your helicopter crashed. I guess you're trapped. The cops will be here soon."

There was a touch of amusement in Mrs. Frome's reply. "Oh, the cops are always coming, Edward. The thing is, they never seem to quite catch up, do they? I think you know why."

"Enough games," Ed answered. "I have a gun here. I'm going to take Sarah and I'll shoot anyone who tries to stop me."

"All very admirable, Edward," Mrs. Frome answered. "I'd expect nothing less. Always the spunky one, protecting the girls. Shannon, now Sarah… Thing is, you're not in a bargaining position. You'll have noticed your darling wife is a bit… strung up, shall we say. There's a trigger strapped to her. If you try to help her, she'll blow. Mr. Frome tells me there's enough Semtex there to bring down the Empire State, let alone a tiny little gas station in the middle of nowhere. In addition, he's had fun pumping out that old gas. Bit of overkill, you might say, but you know how he is. He likes an explosion *and* a cremation."

Ed looked from the speaker to Sarah. "Can she see us?" he whispered.

She shook her head. "I—I don't know. Maybe. Just get out, Ed. Go."

He ignored her and addressed the mic again. "OK, what do you want me to do?"

Mrs. Frome answered, "What you were meant to do ten years ago. Just follow the instructions. Go up to Armageddon with Mr. Frome and collect the package waiting for you. Then on with the mission."

"Just like that, eh?" Ed answered.

"Just like that. Really, we should have put you down, Edward, years ago. Any day in Miami we could have taken you. Even on the beach after your wedding. We didn't expect you to go skinny-dipping, I have to say. But it gave us a chance to collect mementos of the day, as it were. I hope you liked the personal touch outside? Anyway, despite the obvious irritations, I persuaded Vermeulen to give you one last chance. If you knew him, you'd know how surprising it was that he agreed: he's quite ruthless. Now, when you do what you have to do, you'll be conscious, unlike Catrine and Shannon. That's going to make your end particularly bitter, Edward. That was the reason for all that Beast and One business, you know. Anesthetizes the brain. Makes things easier for you. I'm sure Catrine and Shannon felt the benefit. You won't have that. It'll be eyes open for you. And I guess you already know what your legacy will be. Identity thief, commie, drug addict, terrorist, rapist, mass murderer. The North End Cannibal—who would have thought it? Such a pity about that nice girl in the hotel. I'm sorry to say it in front of your wife, but the bite marks on that woman's body were like a wild animal's. The police think you're some kind of monster, Edward. I'm sure they'd take great pleasure in shooting you on sight. But you're not going to let that happen, are you? You have to get to the Hoover Dam, no interruptions. You have to think of your wife and the baby."

"Fuck you," said Ed.

"Tskk. I taught you better than that, Edward. But, enough chitchat. First things first: throw the gun out of the door."

Ed looked at the Glock, then at Sarah. It hadn't worked out as he'd hoped. He had broken free of Typhon, for what? It'd been an illusion. Everything since City Point had been improvised. One desperate decision after another. Even his planning before the blackout had been pointless. Even if Jim had done as he'd asked, he was sure they'd anticipated that as well.

He reversed the gun, took hold of its barrel and tossed it over the fallen shelving into the pool of gas at the entrance. It skidded through the liquid and came to rest on the threshold.

A large figure appeared in the doorway, almost filling it. Six foot four, 280 pounds, a giant red and black mackinaw jacket, and a peaked cap. Frome's beard was now salt and pepper and filled almost all his face. Red lips broke the beard in the parody of a smile. The shrike-like eyes were dead. That hadn't changed.

Frome had a pump-action shotgun aimed at Ed.

"Hey, buddy," he said, that yellow grin splitting his beard just as it had always done. He took his left hand off the barrel of the shotgun, bent and picked up the Glock, checked the safety, then rammed it into the belt ringing his capacious gut. He returned the hand to the barrel and jerked it from Ed to Sarah.

"We got to get going," he said. "But fair's fair, why don't you check out your lovely wife? See she's OK. I ain't fooled around with her... Well, you know, not too much." He gave Ed that shit-eating grin again. "There's a canteen and a bucket of water. Give her a drink, hose her down a bit, if you like. She's a bit high."

Ed went quickly to Sarah. There was a canteen on the floor and he picked it up, unscrewed the top and held it to her lips.

She pulled her head away. "You don't have to do this, Ed," she said.

He kept his voice quiet, hoping Frome couldn't hear him. "I'll get you out of here, I promise," he whispered.

"How?" she said.

He glanced behind at Frome, then back at her. "I'll think of something."

417

He hated the final desperation in his voice.

There was a toilet roll next to the waste bucket. He ripped off a length, upended the bottle onto it and wiped her face. Then he shucked off his camo jacket. It was still damp from his fall into the drainage ditch, but it was better than nothing. He carefully wrapped it around her shoulders, keeping his hands well away from the wires.

"I'll be back soon, OK?" he said.

He turned. There were now two people at the door. Mrs. Frome had arrived. She had aged too. Gray hair, beady blue eyes behind her glasses, full makeup even for the Maine backwoods; the only gesture to utilitarianism was her light blue parka, slacks, and flat shoes. She was pointing a gun at him with her right hand. A Beretta. It looked tiny compared to Frome's shotgun but was no doubt equally deadly at such close range. She was holding something else in her left hand.

"OK, Edward, come here," she said.

Ed glanced once at Sarah, then went forward.

She held the object up so he could see it. "This is a state-of-the-art wireless detonator, courtesy of the US Army. They tell me it has a range of a couple of miles. It's kind of untested, so be very careful when you take it. To be honest, it may just detonate anyway. It's set up to trigger that Semtex around your lovely wife."

Ed inspected it. The thing looked like a grenade wrapped in duct tape. Wires hung from it like sinister antennae and, just like on a grenade, there was a lever trigger that Mrs. Frome was pressing into the side of the device.

Mrs. Frome gestured. "OK, Edward. Take it, very delicately. Once you have it, keep squeezing the handle, and, if you try anything on the way to the dump, rest assured Mr. Frome will shoot you and you will let go of the handle and that will be end of your wife, *capisce?*"

Ed came forward. His hands twitched as he reached out for the detonator. If it hadn't been for Sarah, he would have quite deliberately released the trigger and blown them all to kingdom come. Instead, he stared at Mrs. Frome's slim, blue-veined throat, desperate to crush it. The blood pounded in his ears, but he got control of himself and reached out so that his hand closed on hers. It was cold. Like a corpse's. She smiled at the touch, but the smile didn't reach her periwinkle eyes.

"My, your hands are warm. I expect your wife appreciates them on a cold night. Now, take hold and don't let go." She pulled her hand suddenly from his grip. In a split second his was clutching the lever. Sweat dripped into his eyes despite the cold.

"Good, I think you've got the gist of this," she said. "Are you ready, Mr. Frome?"

"Sure," the giant man answered.

"Then I'll leave you to it." She looked Ed up and down, as if inspecting him at muster. He guessed he didn't look much with his swollen head and filthy clothes. Blood was beginning to seep out from his arm wound. "Goodbye, Edward," she said. Her voice was a bit strangled. Why? She turned abruptly and walked out of the station.

Ed stared after her. Frome jerked his head. "OK, jackass, we're going to take a little walk together, through that gate. You remember? Armageddon?"

They exited. He saw Mrs. Frome was walking up the road toward Ashland. He could now see another car parked up there, some sort of red sedan, near a bend in the road a couple of hundred yards away. He looked behind, but Sarah was invisible in the gloom of the office.

"I'll be back," he called. There was no answer.

CHAPTER SIXTY-NINE

Frome pointed the shotgun toward the back lot. Ed remembered the way well enough from '70. He went ahead, both hands on the detonator lever, Frome's heavy breath and steps behind. There was no sound: just the dead, leaden absence of winter. The grass of the spoil mound at the back of the station was brown and covered in patches of snow. Behind was the forest. There was the faintest suspicion of a track between two birch trees and, prompted by the shotgun barrel, Ed took it.

Images popped in his head like camera flashes. The moments before the OJ. The crucifix swinging. The children chanting.

Here was the gate in the rusted chain-link fence. The padlock hung from the latch.

He felt the pressure of the shotgun barrel on his back. "OK, do the numbers," Frome ordered.

Ed turned. "Gonna be difficult with this thing." He held up the detonator.

"You don't have to hold it with both hands. One will do."

They stared at each other, then Ed released his right hand from the lever, keeping the left clamped in a dead man's grip. He carefully lifted up the padlock. There were eight numbered tumblers. The brass rotators should have been stiff, having been left to the elements for twenty years, but the tumblers ran easily enough.

He thumbed the numbers: 66161614.

The great bronze jaw of the padlock fell open. Frome pushed Ed away with the barrel of the gun, unhinged it and pulled the gate open with a rusty squeal. He indicated the way with the gun.

Ed clamped his right hand back on the lever and went forward. The dripping forest closed around them and everything became twilight. It was below thirty and dressed in only a shirt he was cold enough that his hands were turning numb. He feared the detonator might slip from his frozen fingers.

The faint trail was obstructed by branches and deadfalls, the fallen wood mossy and spongy. The path soon began to go up a hillside; rocks and muddy declivities filled with ice made the footing treacherous. He looked closely at the path for evidence that Jim had come this way the week before, but he saw no signs.

He and Frome exchanged no more words, concentrating on their footing. Ed slipped once, but kept his death grip on the detonator. By the sound of his heavy breathing behind him, Frome was struggling with the climb. Wherever he'd been these last twenty years, it had not been a gym.

After a half-hour, they reached a ridgeline and emerged from the trees, panting, into daylight.

It was a place of flat, gray rocks. Below them was a panorama of land stretching some twenty-five miles to the distant Appalachians. The waves of the trees swept away westward, as close-packed as the stalks in a rye field, undulating over ridges and mountains. Below them was the blue eye of a lake in the green immensity. Far in the distance, a bald eagle circled lazily.

There was no obvious way forward; the ground fell away perpendicularly in all directions. "Where now?" Ed asked.

Frome gestured to the right. Now Ed saw it: there was a narrow rock ledge, only some two yards wide, slanting down the cliff face. The treetops swayed in the breeze 200 feet below.

"Go on," Frome ordered, waving the gun. Ed stepped down. Frome came behind. He nudged him with the shotgun barrel again and Ed nearly stumbled.

"Easy," Ed said through gritted teeth. He set off downward, careful on the ice and slush-rimmed ledge. The sheer fall to his left was an almost physical presence. He tried to counter the vertigo by pressing against the sloping face of lichen-covered granite on the right. Some twenty yards further on, there was a recess in the cliff face.

Of all the man-made anomalies in the wilderness, here was one that outstripped all of the others. Set into the cliff was an iron door with a steel wheel fixed into its middle. The door was held in a metal frame some four feet square.

It was the sort of hatch you might find on a nuclear bunker, its face riveted and reinforced with steel bands, with hinges on the left. Evidently, when opened fully, the door would lie flush with the cliff face. Under the wheel was a brass inlay a couple of inches high and six inches wide. There were eight numerical tumblers and an unlocking switch set into the plate.

Beyond the steel door the ledge vanished after a few steps into empty air.

"Welcome to Armageddon, kid," Frome said.

"What now?" Ed asked.

"You do the numbers again."

Ed took a deep breath. Now everything relied on Jim's work. He repeated his movements at the gate, releasing one hand and slowly manipulating the tumblers on the door face. His eyes were tearing with cold; his hand was by now numb and the numbers in the inlay difficult to align with the bar. All the time he was conscious of the steepling drop just two feet behind him. Eventually he had all eight lined up: 66161614. He pushed the Enter button and there came a *kerchunk* as the locking mechanism disengaged.

"OK, now get the wheel," Frome said.

"What about this?" Ed asked, holding up the detonator. "Need two hands."

"Think you're smart, don't ya?" Frome answered. He pointed the shotgun down the ledge to where it ended in the sheer drop. "OK, get down the path a ways, right to the end."

Ed shuffled along to the very limit of the cliff. He looked down. The snow-covered pine and spruce tops below waved languidly in the winter air. He thought this was likely the last thing he would ever see.

"Now, hands up against the face and keep 'em there," Frome commanded. Ed did so, flattening himself against the cold, gray rock, right hand firm on the detonator lever.

"Hey, kid, you don't have to ball the rock, you know." Frome laughed. He leaned the shotgun against the cliff face, never taking his eyes off Ed, ready to pick it up if he made a move. He grabbed hold of the wheel and turned it counterclockwise until there was an audible click from the latch.

He smiled, hauled back on the wheel, and the door hinged open. In a nanosecond, Frome's smile disappeared. In Ed's last glimpse of him there was an O of surprise in that bird's nest of a beard.

Ed closed his eyes and there was white light and a detonation like a thunderclap. The cliff face bulged and shook from the explosion, rocks fell on him, and a fist-shaped one glanced off his shoulder, nearly unbalancing him.

He embraced the rock for a few seconds after the cascade had passed. He had saved his sight from the flash, but he was, once more, utterly deaf from the explosion. Both his eardrums felt as if they'd burst. The hatchway door had been blown flat against the cliff face, missing him by inches. It now hung drunkenly from one hinge. Smoke eddied out of the interior. There was no sign of Frome or the shotgun.

Ed carefully levered himself off the cliff face, wobbled toward the void, nearly overbalanced and then thrust himself back onto the face. With his ears gone, his balance had gone too. He took hold of the open hatchway.

A severed cord hung from the inner locking mechanism of the hatch; its other half was on the floor and ran into the darkness of the interior. The eye-prickling stench of cordite billowed out from the smoke-choked interior. There was a small cave beyond. Through the smoke he saw stacked boxes in drab military olive-gray with stenciled serial numbers. One or two of the boxes had been opened, revealing pale packages of plastic explosives. There was a case of semiautomatic rifles, another case of gleaming bronze cartridges. Pieces of bullet-proof armor lay scattered over the floor like dismembered body parts.

There was one empty box. Jim had chosen well when he'd come up the week before. Stenciled on its side was "Claymore M18A1." Blown back into the interior and mangled against some boxes were the bent scissor stands of the device. The twin double feet stuck into the air like the limbs of a dead insect.

Ed had told Jim where to go and what to do. And, that Thanksgiving morning, his dead friend had done what he'd asked.

Seven hundred steel balls had been blasted into Frome at 4,000 feet a second.

Ed stumbled into the smoke-filled interior. Positioned in the back of the cave was an open packing case with semiautomatic rifles. A smaller metal ammunition box had been breached next to it and one of the carbines already had a banana-shaped magazine fitted. Jim's work, perhaps. Ed lifted it clumsily with one hand and hung the strap over his shoulder.

If all else had miraculously gone his way in the last few moments, the detonator now threatened to end everything. Mrs. Frome would have heard the Claymore explosion down below. As far as he could tell, it had just been her and Mr. Frome. What would she do now? He struggled back to the ledge. He looked down. Far below there was a scattering of red and black on the tops of the pines. Frome's mackinaw and parts of his body. His head swam. He clenched his eyes, then his teeth.

He went up the ledge, reached the summit of the ridge and plunged back into the trees again. He hurried down the rocky, slippery path, fearful of a tumble and of dropping the detonator in his hand. Each time the borrowed boots skidded, it sent a cold thrill to his heart.

CHAPTER SEVENTY

It seemed hours before the path's gradient eased and he saw the brick and concrete of the gas station and the red of its star sign through the forest ahead. He carefully unslung the rifle with one hand and laid it on a waist-high granite rock, one of the many that broke the leaf- and stick-strewn hillside, and disengaged the safety before rehanging it, Rambo style, under his right arm. The detonator remained gripped in his left hand.

He knew that, whatever you saw in the movies, the chances of being able to control let alone aim this weapon in a one-handed stance were next to nothing. But it was all he had.

The gate in the chain-link fence was still open. He used the cover of the mound to peer over the back lot of the station. Empty of life. If the explosion had brought the cavalry, they were well hidden.

His hearing was coming back a little now; he could hear his boots on the gravel as he skirted the mound and crouched behind the parked Corolla, the rifle clumsily raised in front of him. From here he could see the office entrance beyond the pump island with the mannequins flanking it. They were the only figures in sight.

But 200 yards up the road, the red car toward which Mrs. Frome had been heading when he'd last seen her was idling in a cloud of exhaust. He could make out the light blue of Mrs. Frome's parka in the driver's seat. But was there another figure behind her, on the back seat, craning forward? Whoever was in the car had a perfect eyeline on the gas station. There was no way of getting into the office without being seen.

He called out. "Sarah!"

He thought he heard a faint answer through the ringing in his ears. He made up his mind to make the dash.

"I'm coming!" he yelled. Again, maybe there was another barely audible sound from the interior. There was something odd about it: something he didn't really understand until a long time afterward.

He broke cover and ran.

CHAPTER SEVENTY-ONE

The FBI investigators told him afterward it was the trip that saved his life. He had taken only half a dozen steps forward and had reached the point where the yellow school bus had turned into the station twenty years before when he fell. The nylon jacket with the yellow Snoopy badge that Shannon had been wearing that day had never been recovered from the gas station lot. Ed had found it those ten years ago and hung it on the rusted air pump. The first storm had blown it down into the weeds. There, like the patient eye of Bear and all the haunted things of the kids' childhood, it had waited. It had not decomposed, but had blown back and forth across the lot for another ten years, spending some time hooked on the chain-link fence before another gale blew it back onto the gravel. Snoopy had faded and peeled away, and the nylon had frayed and degraded, but was resilient enough to still be intact. Ed's left foot stood on what remained of its body and then his right hooked into what had once been its hood and he fell face first toward the gravel.

His right arm shot forward in an attempt to brace himself. His right finger was on the trigger of the semiautomatic and as he impacted the ground it discharged, a three-shot burst that tanged around the cast-iron pumps and pinged off the asphalt. His left arm also attempted to brace. His knuckles slammed hard into the gravel, scraping them back to the bone and jarring the detonator out of his fingers.

Again, it might have been false memory after the explosion, but there was something slightly off about what happened in the next two seconds. The detonator spun away, the released lever springing from the body of the device. He may have screamed her name as he watched it open.

There was no explosion. Not in the two seconds. The bomb had not gone off. Sarah was alive.

He had those two seconds of this possibility.

Then the possibility ended.

The gas station suddenly rose into the air, as if pushed up by a giant hand from below. It paused, suspended, a few feet up, still the blocky shape of all gas stations worldwide, red brick and white outer finishing, for a millisecond intact and composite. Then a white cloud with a red core blossomed out of the place where the gas station had once stood, just as the building fell back into it.

Time, which had stopped, now went very fast and the heat displaced by the falling masonry flew outward. The heat flashed over his flesh and cooked it, his hair burned. The sound wave hit a second later. Objects were in the cloud of fire, fragments of rock and metal and cloth; the tailor's dummy with the bridal gown streamed over him.

His senses gave up. There wasn't much more they could endure. Certainly not this maelstrom. The lights went off. Blackness.

The blackness was filled with pain, and there was more pain when he woke in the emergency room in Portland where he had been medevacked. Now the pain became mental as well as physical. Sarah was dead.

When the FBI investigators were allowed to speak to him after a week of recovery they found him closed, unforthcoming. They had arrived at the scene an hour after the explosion as the short winter's day closed in. Ed's unconscious body was the only recognizable human in the vicinity. He had third-degree burns to his face and hands. Afterward, they found Mr. Frome's shredded flesh in the trees beneath Armageddon and a crisped mummy that might have been Fallows in the wrecked Huey.

Even less identifiable were the human remains found in the cratered ruin of the station. The bones discovered there were denatured by the intense heat and unidentifiable: the underground tanks had exploded and a raging petroleum fire had lasted some five hours, reducing everything within the forecourt precincts to ash. It had to be assumed the bones, no more than crematorium relics, once belonged to Sarah Constance.

The device he had been told was a detonator was a hoax. The gas station explosion had been set off by a wired rig.

The bunker had been examined, the stolen US Army reserve armaments and explosives recovered. As much as he had been lucky to survive the gas station explosion, the FBI informed Ed he had been doubly lucky to escape the booby trap, laid by an explosives expert, that had killed Frome. They assumed this had been put in place by Typhon to protect their cache and Frome had accidentally triggered it.

They assured him they would find the people who murdered his wife.

But first there was the small matter of questioning him about the last ten years.

What was behind the identity theft? Had he abducted his wife? Where had he been in the missing two days after he was last seen at the Miami offices? Why were his blood and teeth marks at the murder scene of Gail McReedy? What did he know about the arms cache? He didn't need to pretend: he honestly couldn't remember much. What he did remember was that he had acted in self-defense. After medical offices in Miami and Boston were raided, it was determined that Ed's blood and dental records had been stolen and evidence planted at the McReedy murder scene. In retrospect, the CCTV footage confirmed that he couldn't have been in her room long enough to commit the crime. The lead detective who had suggested this in the first place was taken off the case.

Ed's interrogators never questioned any of the other deaths: Carl, the two goons at City Point, Bailey by the Kennebec, Doc's team,

Fallows, David Krige, and Jim Dove… He was never publicly linked with the deaths of Catrine and Shannon. The two women were deemed lone wolves: unhinged by their childhood experiences, extremists turned against society, Catrine's action inspiring Shannon's. Cases closed.

He told them about the names in the little red book. They said they would look into them, but the information led to no arrests. The book and the pages recovered from the Lot had burned at Brantwood.

Ed realized the lack of progress was part of the bargain. The Feds knew there were dirty agents in their organization. They would clear the problem up discreetly. The less probing, the better for Ed and for them. It was a cover-up. There were retirements, but no arrests.

A house in Mt. Lebanon was raided in the New Year. The agents found it long abandoned and stripped, without a scrap of incriminating evidence. There was one oddity: the agents found an upstairs window had been smashed. In the garden below, they discovered stained-glass fragments. When pieced together, part of an image emerged. A human monster with snakes spurting from its skull head, hands, and feet. One of their number, classically educated, pronounced it to be Typhon.

The ill-named Merriweather's foundered. The Feds hadn't even needed Ed's testimony to sink that ship. Its assets had been seized; its principals had either disappeared or been incarcerated in federal prisons, indicted for a series of felonies, but not murder.

In the end, Ed was exonerated of any wrongdoing in the events of December '89. The state's attorney's office gave him a quiet intro-duction to a Boston law firm, Berenson and McCatter, that han-dled a large amount of government tax work. Given the amount of mutual back-scratching between the state's attorney and Berenson and McCatter, the latter were happy to allow Ed to continue his career as an associate with them.

The authorities then washed their hands of him. He wondered if collectively they had achieved some sort of closure. If so, it was a closure not available to him.

No one was ever arrested for Sarah Constance's murder.

The forensics people explained that the body he was going to bury was, necessarily, only a token. A tiny, ashy fragment of bone. The coffin he helped carry into Our Lady of Perpetual Help weighed nothing. There had been no family: he had never had one; she had lost all hers. There were only professional mourners and agents on the lookout for any criminals tempted to witness the last act of the saga. Ed guessed they particularly hoped that Mrs. Frome might show. If so, they were disappointed.

There was no funeral for Jim Dove. His remains were never found. He had become part of the woods, as he had foreseen back in Chesuncook, that last evening of peace before the killing began.

Ed had taken Max out of the Madison pound and given him a home.

Alice Mae and the other children awaited the next wave of terror against America in the Gila Wilderness in New Mexico.

In the fall two years later, near Chesuncook, a hunter followed a wounded buck through a thick stand of trees, lost the blood trail of his quarry and was making his way back down a game trail toward the lake lodge when he saw something strange: the remains of a blue parka hanging above him in a lattice of tree branches. He got closer and saw that the parka contained a yellow rib cage. The hunter's boot crunched and he looked down on a human skull. There were other yellowed human bones lying in the leaf mold.

The medical examiner was flown out. He discovered a four-inch arrowhead lodged under the lowest of the ribs of the skeleton. The degeneration of the corpse being absolute, he could not tell whether the arrowhead had caused death or, as the many shattered bones suggested, a fall from a great height had done it. He was about to appeal for information about the dead man when the FBI intervened. He was told that the corpse without doubt belonged to a DEA operative gone missing two years before. It now appeared he had been murdered and dumped from a helicopter in the backwoods by the drug cartel. There was to be no publicity: the dead agent's operation was still ongoing.

The remains of David Krige were buried in a corner of Potter's Field in Blue Plains, Washington D.C., close to the last resting place of six Nazi saboteurs executed in the Second World War.

EPILOGUE

ENDGAME

December 1999

The people at Berenson and McCatter were true to their word. The leaving party was over in a half-hour. The speech was brief, the toast made. Then came the incident with the gift and, after that, all was a blur. He believed he had thanked them quickly before hurrying back to his office.

Now he was alone. Beyond the large plate-glass windows was the night: Boston in December. The end of the millennium. In two weeks the harbor would be lit up like it had never been before. A sprinkling of snow fell, dusting the sidewalks, fretting the black sky and the bright windows of the financial district. Christmas lights twinkled in the streets.

He looked for a long time toward North End. Gail McReedy had died over there because he had walked into that Marriott bar. One of his too many regrets. Jim and Sarah had followed. Dead because of him. He stared at his reflection. A reflex made him touch his brow. His forehead was ridged and red from the burns from the gas station explosion, his hands too. The scar from the graze on his shoulder pulled in the cold weather.

He had spent the day packing up. All that was left was to take the box of possessions and be gone. Ten years in a box. Terminus. The taxi waited outside. Berenson and McCatter had given him a good life: now it was over. The house was sold, its contents auctioned. Max had died the year before. He was going to get in his car and disappear.

He had had ten years of waiting, knowing it was not over. Many of those in the little red book were still free. Mrs. Frome and Vermeulen had simply disappeared, Fitzgerald had retired without an indictment or the slightest smudge on his name.

The state's attorney had found him this job, sure, but in the end he'd found it as bogus as the one at Merriweather's.

He was the last Apostle. Ed had no idea how it was he had survived. Some dark angel had preserved him—for what? Future acts unknown. He was, despite the years of counseling, a ticking time bomb waiting for a trigger. The world did not believe that Manchurian candidates existed in real life. How wrong they were. In 1973, as Watergate blew up and the intelligence services fell under suspicion, the director of the CIA, Richard Helms, had ordered all papers relating to MKUltra destroyed. For want of any evidence to the contrary, the official line was that the secret services had never created any robot agents. Yet every year it seemed there were more incidents: actions not by foreign powers or Arab jihadists but by citizens. Ted Kaczynski's reign of terror had ended in April 1996, but there were, it seemed, many others out there.

Ed was in no doubt that no one ever left Typhon: however far you ran, those serpent tentacles would one day catch and seize you. He had tried to live life as others lived it, but, short of holding down this job, had only fleetingly succeeded. There had been casualties along the way. A marriage to a fellow attorney had foundered. Thankfully, there had been no children. Friendships died on the vine, killed by his distant demeanor. He marched to a different drum from other people.

One of his imperatives was his promise to Shannon. His vacations were spent searching for Alice Mae: combing official records for New Mexico, driving the dusty roads, asking questions in lonely towns and trailer parks out in the desert where strangers weren't welcome. There were no clues. She, like all of the lost children, had vanished into thin air.

Maybe he would go to New Mexico now and live like a hermit in a ring of rocks in the desert, on an old iron bed with rusty springs, waiting for the rain to come or Alice Mae to appear.

Every time he read about a child abducted by a parent after killing their partner he wondered: was a new story, just like his, starting? Vessels and Vials and Angels, all over again… His flesh and blood had given him up into captivity. A mother or father he had never known, would perhaps never have wanted to know.

No one, even to this day, knew his true age. But by the measure of his invented age, he was far too young to retire. There had been many physicians, counselors, and a good many therapeutic drugs since '90. None of the interventions had worked for long. The medics, young and old, naive or cynical, all knew: it was the whole life that needed curing, not an isolated day, week, month, or even year. His childhood had been stolen. Afterward, there had been too many dead people: gone in bullets, explosions, dropped from a helicopter, or, simply, disappeared as if they had never been.

The office was all packed up, not a knick-knack remaining on the desk: the steel balance, the model of the sailing dinghy, the Empire State snow globe, framed pictures, awards, diplomas with their waxed seals—all now in the box. There was one other memento: an old, yellowing white wristband with "1979 N Welcome Week" printed on it. No one had ever thought to ask him about it. He slipped it onto his wrist.

He'd made partner a couple of years after the incidents in Maine. Partner at just over thirty. Practically unheard of. Berenson and McCatter had been a new firm going places fast, with many government contracts. He had gone with them. It had surprised Ed, and maybe the partners at Berenson and McCatter, to learn that, after his past and being foisted upon them by the state's attorney's office, he was not so bad a tax attorney after all.

Rivals muttered at his fortune or, worse, the undue influence his past had brought. He was a man who knew too many secrets, and those who know secrets end up two ways: privileged, or dead.

The cabin he had built on Tranquility over the burned-out wreck of the old one had never held any attraction for him. He had done it remembering better times, but better times were gone. No one had bought Jim Dove's old bait store and it was boarded up, another relic of Tranquility's past, like the steamer pier next to it and the ruins of the old hotel at the end of the lake.

On the couple of occasions he had gone up to the new place, it was difficult to forget the man in the black Tyvek suit who had been cremated in the inferno of the old one.

He dreamed of his enemy's fire-blackened ghost. In his dreams it sat at the new breakfast counter in singed clothes with a peeling face, pupil-less eyes cooked like egg whites and a lipless smile, and stared wistfully at Ed's mug of coffee. The ghost would say: "You know, Ed, I'll never see my family again. Never see *anyone* again. And it's all down to you." Then Ed would wake up in a cold sweat, his heart racing.

The last time he had gone to the cabin it had been only one night before the sightless ghost drove him back to Boston again.

You can run, but you can't run forever. His life had been running, even when he had sat still at this desk. Nowhere was safe. One day the words would be spoken again. The Beast and One. Even if he lived to be 100, they would come. They would come as they had come before, when he was not watching. "Ye know not the hour." Mrs. Frome had taught him that. That, above all other things.

A snow flurry slapped against the black glass and slithered down the picture window, obscuring the reflection of his face.

Yes, it was December: killing weather.

One item remained on the desk. The gift. Earlier it had been wrapped in silver paper and presented to him by the managing partner. He hadn't really thought what token the office might have deemed worthy for him. A pen, perhaps.

But when he had unwrapped it there was a blue and white box with the legend "NOKIA 3210" in blocky letters, a picture of the cell phone and the slogan: "We call this *human* technology." There had been a ripple of laughter from his colleagues when they saw Ed's face. It had been said many times that Ed Constance was the only attorney in Boston without a cell phone. Over the years there had been a few frantic searches for him during emergencies when he couldn't be contacted.

There was an ironic note with the gift: "Hey, Ed, we guessed you might have time to learn how to use one of these now. Enjoy! Maria McCatter."

After the laughter there had been applause. Perhaps the applause set off his tinnitus. The eardrums perforated by the Claymore and Semtex had never healed. But maybe this distant ringing was caused not by those injuries, but by something else: it was the phone. No one at Berenson and McCatter knew what had happened at Lenox Avenue.

Or did they? Had Typhon been here with him these ten years?

The ringing grew loud, deafening. Suddenly his vision closed to a pinprick. Gone was the boardroom. Instead he was back at Lenox in the white light and cold of the air-conditioning. There, as actual as the night he had seen them, were the muddy backplate and the severed finger and the pool of blood.

After he had thanked them, Maria asked him if he was OK, and he had answered that he just needed some air and, taking up the box, had felt his way out of the room and back to his office. He'd laid the box on his desk. For a minute he breathed deeply, fighting to restore his vision.

The panic attack had finally passed. Some of his colleagues had stuck their heads through the door to check on him and wish him good luck. Now they were all gone.

It was 9.09 p.m. The central heating pipes began to knock, signaling that the system had been turned off. Standard office practice—keeping the energy bills down. It would slowly start feeling cold as the night air began pressing through the plate-glass windows.

So why tonight, looking over to the Marriott where Gail McReedy had died, did it feel like the temperature had suddenly dropped some twenty degrees? The thermostat still read 73, but the cold played on his spine. Beyond the hotel, further out there in the dark of the winter's night, in the woods, were all the bones: Carl, Jim, David, Fallows... Sarah...

He shivered. He had to shake this thing off. He was alone, the way he wanted it. Nothing could touch him here. He turned and picked up the gift. He'd give it to the first street person he saw outside. No doubt it would bring them a few dollars at a second-hand electronics shop.

The box suddenly vibrated and his hands jerked and he dropped it back onto the desk.

The lid flew off.

The phone was revealed.

The screen was lit up.

And there were the words: "CALLER UNKNOWN."

His vision closed in again. All he could see was the phone, nothing else.

He took a deep breath. This prank, if that was what it was, had to stop now. He was not one for practical jokes. Whichever colleague was calling him was going to get a piece of his mind.

He lifted the thing out of the box, pressed the green button and lifted the phone to his ear.

There was a hiss of static, then a voice said, "Hello, Ed." There was a brief pause. "I guess you never expected to hear from me again."

It was Sarah.

ACKNOWLEDGMENTS

Any editor of forty years' standing, of which I am one, knows you don't write alone, and you certainly don't get published alone. So, there are a legion of people to thank, but most particularly: Dave Morris, writing friend and inspiration for more years than I can remember; Mark Booth, a visionary publisher and author; Anne Perry, a treasured colleague, now destined for bestsellerdom; the rock who is my agent, Jim Gill; Wayne Brookes, my editor and publishing's greatest empath; and finally, the dedicatee of this book, my wife, Caroline—a true and constant mainstay.

© Mark Rusher

Oliver Johnson was born in Paris and pursued a career in academia before going into bookselling and then publishing. He has been a commissioning editor for many years, working principally at Penguin Random House and now Hachette and has edited many bestselling and prize-winning authors. He is the author of various gamebook and roleplaying series and a fantasy trilogy. He splits his time between London and a small hamlet in the Sussex countryside with his wife and two cats.